Profit and Sheen

JAMES COLBERT

Profit and Sheen

Houghton Mifflin Company   Boston   1986

For Charles

This is a work of fiction, and all of the characters in this book are fictional.

Library of Congress Cataloging-in-Publication Data

Colbert, James.
  Profit and Sheen.

  I. Title.
PS3553.04385P76   1986   813'.54   86-7319
ISBN 0-395-39411-2

Printed in the United States of America

S 10 9 8 7 6 5 4 3 2 1

1

THE STREETCAR rolled with a pleasant sway on its uneven tracks, but it was Friday afternoon, the end of the work week, and the car was filled to capacity. For those standing, the jostling crowd made the agreeable motion into an uncomfortable test of balance. Some of the passengers held the small brass handles on the backs of the wooden seats, but a three-fingered, waist-high grip was an inadequate anchor in the crowd's surging currents. The streetcar conductor seemed to enjoy the passengers' difficulties. At every stop he looked in the rearview mirror as he applied the brakes in abrupt bursts. The lurching halts bounced one passenger against another like billiard balls after a sharp break.

Sheen Vicedomini stood in the aisle. Balanced on the balls of his feet he faced the windows and rocked easily, effortlessly compensating for the streetcar's lurches. Beside him an old woman clutched shopping bags, trying without success to anticipate the irregular halts. She stumbled often, and the blue veins on the back of her hand pulsed with the effort of holding the small brass handle. Sheen fixed his greenish eyes on the scene outside the car. There was nothing he could do for her.

A solid mass pressed suddenly against him. Reflexly he rolled his shoulder down and bunched the thick muscles in his back to absorb the shock. The mass bounced away then pressed against him again. Sheen bumped the old woman before he saw her hand next to his own on the seat back. He looked up, out the window, his face drawn and set. He tried not to think about the contempt he felt for himself, but a sour taste rose in his throat. He hated the wage-earning routine. The crowded streetcar ride was but one more symptom of what he saw as a sickness, the work-cycle sickness.

"How else can you explain it, *except* as a sickness?" he had asked Andrea. "How can anyone justify arranging your life around an arbitrary, external structure?"

When Sheen was serious the muscles corded in his jaw and the skin pulled tight over his high cheekbones to create an expression so intense Andrea was able to feel the strain. She ran her hand through his thick black hair.

"You have to eat," she had answered simply.

"I have to eat," Sheen agreed. "If I don't eat, how else will I get to be one of those fat, sloppy people who ride the streetcar with me?" Sheen admitted his greatest fear, then covered it. "But I guess everything has its place, even complacency."

"Why does that bother you so much?" Andrea asked. She was naked. Still damp from the shower, she stepped past him to look at her face in the mirror over the sink. The angle of her lean pushed the moist globes of her hips back toward him. "You couldn't be complacent if you tried, and there are times when you *should* be satisfied with yourself. You need to learn to relax." She turned back to him. Her hands gripped the edge of the sink. Her closely trimmed pubic hair looked like a week-old beard.

"Doesn't that itch?"

"No," she replied, and looked at him seriously, but Sheen knew she did not have on her contact lenses; at more than three feet, he was nothing but a soft blur.

"Maybe complacency bothers me because I fear it in myself — maybe I'm afraid that if I relax, I'll never get up again."

"You'll never know until you try." Andrea turned again

2

to the mirror. "You watch what you eat. I'll watch what you wear. You won't ever be either fat or sloppy."

Andrea expertly smoothed an eyebrow, the corners of her mouth drawn down critically, and just then Sheen felt a warm intimacy as she allowed him to see her frank appraisal of her own face. He moved behind her and ran his hand along the curve of her hip and thigh.

That night his doubts had been forgotten, but in the morning as he had shaved for work, he had thought of the day before him. And rising in his own eyes he had seen a fog as thick as the heavy smoke in an opium den.

The streetcar stopped. The seat in front of him was vacant. Sheen turned and leaned back against the mass pushing toward the empty seat. The old woman sat down with a sigh and put her packages in her lap. Sheen again turned sideways and faced the windows. When the streetcar lurched forward, a heavy work boot stomped down on his foot. A pain shot past his knee.

"Excuse me," a surly voice said slowly.

Sheen looked up into the sneering face before he turned away, straightening his shoulders. His foot throbbed, but he refused to bend down to rub it. He unclenched his hands, and again he set his eyes in a rigid stare. The muscles stood out on his jaw.

Spurred by anger, the image came quickly, not unexpectedly, a memory so vivid it still brought fear — and another, deeper anger.

The expanse of the Mississippi River was a broad band of shiny blackness where small lights' reflections defined the water's boundaries by their absence. A tugboat's diesel pulsed close out on the water. He waited on the batture, the area between the levee and the river. Before he got out of the car he pulled up the right leg of his trousers, rolling the cuff and bending his knee to pull the material tight so he could use both hands on his leg. The fiber glass tape made a ripping sound as it pulled from the shaved skin on his calf. The small .22 derringer fell into his hand, and he quickly slipped it into his hip pocket. Sheen hoped the man would not give him trouble, but the meeting was a risk and he had to be prepared. He rolled down the leg of his trousers before he got out of the car in one quick motion, leaving the door open.

He leaned back against the blue and white automobile, his right arm loose at his side, his left hand on his hip. The two-way radio squawked softly. The single dome light in the car made a pocket of dim yellow light.

The man came out of the shadows at the water's edge.

"What did you put in your pocket?" the man asked, a looming shape in the darkness. "I saw you in the car, bending down."

"Your money, pal." Sheen made his voice easy. "No one but a fool carries cash in his pocket. I didn't think you'd take a check."

The man made a harsh, snorting sound before he spoke. "I didn't think *you'd* bring the police car."

"I had to," Sheen replied. "I'm on the job. My shift doesn't end until midnight."

"No shit, huh?" The voice was derisive, the speech slowed by contempt. "You on patrol?"

There was a movement near the river. They both saw it at the same time.

"Pig," the man hissed.

The sound of the small-caliber shot was muffled by the levee and by the pulsing of the tugboat's diesel. The man crumpled, his face contorted grotesquely, then rolled down into the gray mud at the water's edge.

Sheen looked with stunned amazement at the man who came out of the shadows to push the body into the water. He became aware that he held his service revolver. As he put it back into its holster, his hand trembled. Anger rose with the fear.

Out on the water the tugboat diesel had throbbed with the

same rhythm as his stomped foot. Sheen limped to the back of the streetcar. Two more stops and he had to get off.

In his apartment, the air conditioner kicked on with a loud hum and a shudder before it settled into a dull vibration that rattled the windowpanes. Sheen made a pot of coffee then sat on the couch to take off his shoe. The walk from the streetcar had loosened up his ankle; it seemed unlikely there would be any swelling. He raised the leg of his trousers. The fiber glass tape made a ripping sound as it pulled from the shaved skin on his calf; he slid the small .22 derringer into a holster attached to the underside of the couch. Absently he rubbed his foot and ankle with a gentle, circular motion.

On the low table in front of the couch, lifted by the faintly musty air from the air conditioner but held down on one corner by a heavy brass medallion, a pile of clippings fanned open. The thin newsprint fluttered, drawing attention to itself, and as the pages lifted up and down, Sheen read the title of each article. He smiled, amused by Andrea's selection of recipes and household hints, and moved the heavy medallion to the middle of the pile before rolling onto one shoulder and stretching out on the couch. Soon he was not quite asleep, not quite awake, drifting, swinging on a lazy, soft pendulum. At some level he heard Andrea's steps in the apartment and interpreted the sounds as posing no threat, but he was undisturbed.

Andrea knew Sheen's naps never lasted more than ten minutes, and she also knew never to try to wake him before the ten minutes had passed. Once she had shaken him during a nap, and he had almost choked her before he had waked up enough to realize what he was doing. Her neck had been bruised for a week. That had been almost a year before, and Andrea had decided to pack her bags; but Sheen had been so profusely apologetic she had changed her mind. As she watched him nap, she knew she was glad she had stayed. For all his eccentricities — and there were many — he was always gentle and thoughtful. He also made her nervous. It was an exciting combination, an emotional speedball, simultaneously up and down, secure and apprehensive. And when she wasn't with him she felt his absence, a dark feeling that made her somehow less alive.

By the time Andrea heard Sheen moan — she recognized the end of the nap — she had changed to shorts and a T-shirt. She walked back into the living room. Sheen stretched on the couch, his legs pushing out, his arms extending over his head.

"Hey," Andrea said, seeing him move. She waited for his eyes to open before she sat next to him. "How was your day? Did you miss me?"

"I survived," Sheen replied, and reached up to her lazily. "And yes, I missed you."

Andrea kissed him perfunctorily. "I don't understand how a ten-minute nap does you any good, especially since you're so groggy after."

Sheen thought of the fast *whoosh-thump* of heavy, long helicopter blades beating the air and of the short hops between landing zones under hostile fire when he had first learned the value of a ten-minute nap.

"I've tried to explain it," he said.

"I understand the nap part — it's the grogginess that seems so difficult." Her hand traced a line down Sheen's chest. "You want a little eye-opener? Profit left some for us to have this weekend."

Sheen did not reply. His eyes fixed on a framed certificate on the wall, as if he were for the first time seeing the bright blue letters and the official gold seal of the city.

Andrea continued uneasily, responding to his detachment. "If Profit wants to give away coke, I'll take it. He has plenty, and the little bit he left doesn't mean anything to him. Anyway, I like it. You do too."

Sheen looked away from the award and shrugged. He didn't really like cocaine, but when it was offered, he always took it. It was difficult to understand, an undesired treat.

"An oxymoron," he said out loud.

"What's that?" Andrea asked. She stood up to reach behind the bookshelf for the neat packet of folded tin foil.

"A paradox, like me," Sheen said. He sat up to watch as Andrea poured cocaine onto the glass-topped table. Moving her hand from the wrist with a short up-and-down motion that reminded Sheen of a sewing machine, she began to chop the cocaine with a single-edged razor. "What happened to Profit's face? The marking looks like a powder burn."

"I think it looks like eye shadow," Andrea replied without looking up, her attention focused on the table. "Profit told me that a firecracker exploded near his face, but Debbie told me — "

"Debbie is the woman he was with?"

Andrea nodded, and with her free hand pushed a stray flake of cocaine back into the pile.

"They've been together longer than we have. I don't know how she puts up with him. Anyway, Debbie told me that somebody owed him money, and that, when he went to collect it, to scare him off the guy shot him in the face with a blank pistol. You know he's lucky: on him it looks sort of sexy; anyone else would just have lost an eye."

"Did he get the money?"

Andrea licked the sides of the razor blade, and Sheen flinched. "Don't do that," he said.

Her cheeks drew in momentarily from the bitter taste of the cocaine, and she wiped the razor on her shorts before she replied.

"I doubt it. If he did, he didn't collect it himself. That's not his *style.*" Andrea's eyebrows arched slightly, emphasizing the scorn in her voice, before she stood up and walked into the kitchen, effectively communicating the fact that she did not want to continue.

Sheen sat forward, about to follow her, but she reappeared quickly, a red-and-white plastic straw and a pair of scissors in her hand. She knelt by the table, cut the straw in half, and snorted a line of cocaine, half in one nostril, half in the other.

"But he *does* get good coke," she said, and rubbed her nose with one finger. She sat back on her heels and handed the short straw to Sheen.

Sheen rolled the straw back and forth between thumb and first finger. The red stripes spiraled, reversed direction, spiraled again. He leaned forward and snorted a whole line in one nostril.

"I have something for you," Andrea said, "if I can find it." As she stood up, the long muscles in her thigh flexed. She saw Sheen watching and exaggerated the movement, turning her feet to make her knees flare out before coming together. Then she bent at the waist, hands on her hips, and playfully stuck out her tongue before she went into the bedroom.

Sheen smiled in return, but he was tired, glad the weekend finally had come. The fatigue, coupled with relief, magnified by the cocaine, created in him a shifting mood ambivalence he controlled only with effort. He turned the radio on, changed stations, turned it back off. He poured himself a cup of coffee then discarded it in favor of Scotch. When Andrea returned, he was standing over the table looking at the seemingly undiminished pile of cocaine.

"How did you meet Profit?" he asked.

Andrea pursed her lips. "You don't like Profit, do you?"

"He's a little too smooth for me," Sheen replied, "a little too slick."

"You're just not up to his level of deviousness."

"What's that supposed to mean?" He shook the glass in his hand, and the ice clinked.

Andrea's eyes were uneasy. The compressor in the air conditioner came on, and she put her hand against the window to stop the glass from rattling.

"We should fix that," she said, and moved her hand. The rattle began again. "For a few months Profit had a girlfriend named Star — that was her real name, sort of her character, too. After a while they drifted apart. Star started dating someone else, someone she liked a lot. After they had been together a few months, Star's parents invited her to go with them to

8

Europe. It was only for a few weeks, but guess who showed up to visit her while she was in Europe?"

Andrea paused, but Sheen did not understand what the pause was meant to convey.

"So?" he asked.

Andrea's brow furrowed, and in her expression there was a tolerant patience, as if she were explaining a moderately complex toy to a bright child.

"Profit didn't go to Europe to look at cathedrals, Sheen: he went to see Star, so he could come back and wink at her new boyfriend and say what a good time Star had shown him in Europe. He knew their relationship was new enough to be vulnerable, and he wanted to create doubt."

"If that *is* why he went, that's not devious, it's vicious."

"No, Profit isn't strong enough to be vicious. He didn't want Star back, he wanted a place in her new relationship. He wanted something of what she and her boyfriend had because he knows he'll never have anything of his own. It's sad, really. He's like one of those buildings you see downtown that are painted and decorated like a stage set. Profit's clever and amusing, but there's nothing there, no substance. He has to live through other people."

Sheen looked again at the cocaine on the table. He pressed a single flake against his finger and rubbed it on his gums.

"What happened to Star and her new boyfriend after the trip?"

"Star didn't think anything of Profit's visit. She had been glad for the company, and she knew what had happened — or what hadn't happened, whichever. She never really realized the pain the *not* knowing had given her boyfriend. Profit loved it, of course, because he had counted on just that. He knew Star was just naive enough, just young enough not to recognize the depth of the hurt and to gloss over it rather than to resolve it. The longer any uncertainty remained, the longer Profit held a place in their lives." Andrea bent down and neatly aligned the table with the couch. "But they got past it. It wasn't that big a thing — it just shows what Profit is like."

9

Sheen took a cube of ice out of the glass he held and cracked it with his teeth.

"How long were you in Europe with your parents?" he asked.

"Three weeks," Andrea replied. Her voice was brusque, but her eyes were soft. She turned away, adjusted the height of a lamp, reached in her pocket. When she turned back, she removed her hand from her pocket and extended it toward Sheen, palm up and flat. "This is for you," she said, looking at the key on her palm with some relief, knowing it would change the direction of the conversation and prevent Sheen from asking why she had allowed Profit to visit *them*. "It's a key to my apartment."

Sheen looked at the key for a long moment before he picked up his blue blazer from the arm of the couch and, holding it by the collar, shook it roughly back and forth. When he heard a jingle, he searched the pockets for his key ring, found it, and dropped the blazer back on the couch.

"Has Becky been after you again?" he asked as he took the key. He began to push it into the tight wire loop.

"She does have a point, Sheen. I'm never at the apartment, and she doesn't want to live by herself — it's frightening for a woman. I'll have to spend more time there. I don't understand why we pay for two places anyway."

The key ring closed with a click.

"I don't want you to feel trapped here."

"Wrong," Andrea said, the vowel drawn out for emphasis. "*You* don't want to feel trapped here with *me.*"

Sheen looked at the rounded rectangle of aluminum that was on his key ring; with his thumb he rubbed the letters stamped into the metal.

"That's not true," he said softly. He put his little finger through the wire loop and pressed the keys into his palm, but the aluminum dog tag was wider than the keys and he felt its sharp edge more than the keys' rough ridges. "Give Becky enough time to find a new roommate. When

10

we've been together a year, we'll find a place of our own."

"You promise? That's only two months away."

Sheen's eyelids drooped as he chewed the inside of his lip. He looked at Andrea with a steady, even gaze.

"Only two months, eh? Better make it a year and a half," he said, but he could hold the pose only a moment before he smiled.

Andrea knew Sheen was covering his uncertainty with humor, but she also knew he never spoke with haste, not when it was important. She stepped close and hugged him tightly.

"We've known each other for ten months," she said, more to herself than to him, her voice low. "It's been six months since you quit the police." She turned her face to look up at him. "Do you still miss it?"

Sheen was slow to reply. "I'm not even sure why I *was* a policeman," he said.

"Well, you look cute in a uniform. You can always go back to it."

"No," Sheen replied quickly, his voice surprisingly harsh. "I can't."

Andrea chose a new direction.

"So what's up for tonight?"

Sheen slipped his hands inside the elastic waistband of her shorts.

"You mean you can't feel it?"

"It's Friday night," she protested, and pushed against his chest. "I want to do something."

"Do what?"

"I don't know — do *something.*"

Sheen laughed and let her go.

"Do *something,*" he said, mimicking her.

The phone rang as he turned on the stereo. Andrea was back before he had found a record.

"Who was that?" he asked.

"Debbie. She was looking for Profit." Andrea absently rubbed her nose. "I wonder why she thought he would be here?"

11

Sheen raised one shoulder then dropped it, dismissing the question.

"Let's get in the bed."

"Maybe," Andrea replied coyly, a warm light in her eyes. "Then will you take me out to dinner?"

"First we check out the hors d'oeuvres," he said.

2

PROFIT WAS burned out. His movements were jerky. His speech was fragmented and distorted. As the taxi let him out on the steps to the parish court building, he checked the small digital stopwatch he kept in his pocket. It had been seventy-eight hours since he'd slept.

"Seventy-eight hours," he said out loud, reassuring himself that it was only the lack of sleep, in combination with the huge amount of cocaine he had ingested, that made him feel he was rapidly losing control. He put the stopwatch back in his pocket and looked uneasily at the large stone building. He tried to remember whether he wanted Division B or Division D, but his memory was barren. Aggravated, he took the steps two at a time.

The parish court building was dirty and hot. The halls smelled of people under pressure, the rank smell of fear that even strong disinfectant couldn't mask. Profit followed a stripe of peeling green paint on the floor, hoping it would lead to the courtrooms, but after a turn in the hall he saw that the stripe ended at a heavy wooden door with an inset frosted glass panel.

In the men's room, his attaché case clamped firmly between his legs, he slapped cold water over his face and neck again and again before he looked in the mirror to survey the damage. The circles under his eyes were so dark they blended into

13

the green-black speckling of gunpowder and gave the appearance of bruises, bruises that sharply contrasted the chalky whiteness of his complexion. His blond hair had the same sagging limpness as his expensive white linen sports coat. His brown eyes were glazed, lit by a strange light that seemed somehow wild. Profit knew he was on the edge. He shook his head from side to side, disapprovingly, before he dried his face and left the men's room. He found the stripe that led to Division B, and luck was with him: Judge Ronnie Fraiche sat the bench in Orleans Parish Court, Division B.

The courtroom was packed, and activity was just below the level of frenzy. Lawyers in sharp suits, policemen in wilted uniforms, victims and suspects in dress that ranged from elegant to sleazy, swarmed in the large room like bees in a disturbed hive. The uninterrupted hum of conversation, amplified by poor acoustics, made a resonant buzz. All movement seemed random, without direction. Profit paused momentarily, one hand on the low railing, a blank expression on his face, and let his confidence build. When he was certain no one would notice his twitching in the chaos, he approached the bench.

Judge Ronnie Fraiche was young for a judge, and he was determined to overcome the conservative image usually associated with judicial functionaries. His black hair curled down past his shoulders, and his open black robe exposed a pink turtleneck sweater. In spite of the trappings, however, Judge Fraiche's bearing was stern and serious, a mien that reflected the hard confidence of a man strong enough to be purposely frivolous. He was the vortex of court activity, literally surrounded by concentric layers of humanity, pressing, pushing, all talking at once.

Profit waited patiently, shifting his weight from one foot to the other. A woman in a low-cut dress explained how she had simply been out for a walk when she had been arrested. Simultaneously, a man with no front teeth explained that he had not started the fight but that his baseball bat had ended it. An attorney broke in to argue a point of procedure. The judge's head seemed to swivel rather than turn as he scanned the faces and responded to the explanations. His large beak nose gave him the profile of a predator. Profit saw the hesitation, the brief shadow of recognition, when the head finally swiveled toward him. The court took a recess, and the judge adjourned to his chambers.

Profit was already in the richly paneled office by the time Ronnie Fraiche made his way out of the courtroom. With the office door closed and locked, the silence came in a rush, as tangible as the courtroom's pulsing hum.

The judge took three steps, stopped, rotated his elbow to adjust his open robe, went behind his desk. Profit tried to speak first, but a jerky nod and a "Hey" were all he could manage.

"You could have picked a better time," Fraiche said irritably. He unlocked his desk and opened the upper drawer across his thighs. He looked up as one hand searched among the papers. "You look terrible. You should know better."

Profit put his brown leather attaché case on the judge's desk and with his thumb spun the numbers on the combination lock. The clasps opened with a distinctive *click-click,* and he took out a sealed one-ounce Baggie of cocaine.

Ronnie Fraiche handed Profit a heavy brown envelope before he sliced the Baggie with a letter opener. The judge reached inside his sweater and took out a small gold spoon attached to a long gold chain around his neck. He dipped the spoon deep into the bag and delicately lifted the cocaine to his nose. He snorted cocaine into both nostrils before he looked up at Profit again.

"Good shit," he said. "How *do* you get it? No, don't tell me — I don't even want to know."

Profit jerked his chin down and up and closed the attaché case.

"I haven't got much time," the judge said, his tone dismissing any possibility of cordiality. Carefully he began to pour the cocaine into an antique silver snuffbox.

Profit sat down and put his attaché case on his lap. He drummed his fingers on the hard leather surface as he tried to remember what it was he had wanted to ask. Fraiche locked the snuffbox into his desk.

"Can you check on something for me?" Profit asked, suddenly remembering.

The judge pocketed the key before he said, "Depends." His voice was as noncommittal as his expression. "I've told you, I won't do anything for you I wouldn't do for anyone else."

"I understand that," Profit replied seriously, but the corners of his mouth turned up in a curious grin. "I know a guy who says he used to be with the New Orleans police. Can you make sure he's not still with them?"

"Easy," the judge replied quickly, relieved that the request was small. He stood up. "Give me his name. I'll call you later."

Profit used a pen from the desk set to write Sheen Vicedomini's name on a memo pad. The writing was barely legible, scratched at a speed the pen wasn't meant to accommodate.

"I'm going to the Hilton to get some sleep," Profit said. "You can leave a message."

The judge took the small yellow piece of paper, folded it neatly into quarters, and put it in his pocket, behind the key to his desk.

"Thanks," Profit said.

The judge moved with exaggerated haste to the door, unlocked it, and held it open; Profit responded with a deliberately languid pace across the office.

"I look forward to your call," he said formally.

The judge shut the door and twisted the key before he looked at Profit, his heavy black eyebrows pulled together in a solid line low across his forehead.

"Next time, phone first," he said. "Don't just arrive."

Profit started to reply harshly to the order, but he knew he was tired, prone to overreact. He allowed the judge to walk away without comment, the open black robe flaring behind him like a cape.

"Later," he said to himself, and turned to find an exit.

* * *

16

At five A.M. he awoke in darkness and lay unmoving. Under one arm he felt the edge of the mattress, and he knew from his angle across it that the bed was huge. The linen was fresh and luxuriously crisp. He blinked once, rolled onto his elbow, groped for a light, found one by touching the sharp ridges of a lampshade, turned it on. The dim bulb cast a soft glow on thick gray carpet. When he sat up, he realized that much of the psychochemical shock had passed, and he didn't feel too bad.

He turned on all of the lights before he began his customary search. On his hands and knees he looked under the furniture, and he kneaded the carpet as he moved, his fingers probing, digging into the rich pile. When he stood up, he stripped the sheets off the bed and patted the mattress before he turned it and checked the box spring. He took the curtains by the hem and shook the heavy material until it billowed. In the bathroom, he stripped the wrappers off the glasses and the soap. He put his hand down the toilet and his fingers down the drains in the sink and tub. He checked the light fixtures, the dresser drawers, the closet. He found nothing. He had expected to find nothing, but, like going in good health to a doctor, somehow it made him feel better to have his own prognosis confirmed, to know the room was clean.

He pulled a chair next to the bare mattress, and, hunched forward intently, his forearms on his knees, he opened the attaché case and began to count the rewards of his three-day stint. He separated the bills by denomination, stacked them neatly, counted them twice, wrapped them tightly with a rubber band. He recorded the number of bills in each stack in a small account ledger. His breathing was regular and even; his lips moved and made a small smacking sound as he added up the totals.

Other than the seven thousand dollars he had on front, less expenses he had netted sixteen thousand three hundred dollars.

"And change," he said out loud and sat back in the chair.

He looked at the stacks of money with grim satisfaction.

17

Once again he felt he had won, but he knew deep down that it was a false victory. There was no winning against the past, not *his* past.

Before he had become Profit he had been Daniel, the eldest of three children, the only son of a petroleum engineer and his ferociously ambitious wife. They had lived in a modest house, one of seven models the builder had offered, in the kind of neighborhood where there were always well-kept lawns, children's toys on the sidewalks, and dreams of more elaborate houses, better cars, more exclusive streets; the kind of neighborhood where at dusk men in Bermuda shorts and T-shirts, each in his own space of lawn, leaned across low fences to talk about the problems they were having with their plumbing, their pool, or their dishwasher as their wives went to bridge clubs and worked for charities and washed down their Valium with gin. Some of the neighbors were surprised — others claimed they were not — when Daniel's father left, taking with him only the clothes on his back and exactly one-half the family's savings. But all of the neighbors were shocked when Daniel's mother decided to cut her losses rather than her ambitions and to begin again, without the children.

It was summer — he remembered that because an oily, rolling sweat had soaked his shirt and stung his eyes as he had run home from school along the sidewalk that was new and smooth, pale gray, made for speed. He was released, free, out of school early for some mysterious grown-up reason, some reason that meant whispers and sad looks and doors closing gently, some reason that meant he should run.

He forgot to close the outside door and came up quietly, his tennis shoes padding softly on the linoleum floor. He stopped when he heard the voices, stopped before he pushed open the swinging door between the kitchen and the dining room. He remembered his mother's voice clearly because he had recognized the tone, the same one she had used to explain to him that his dog had been hit by a car — soft at first; then he had cried too long, too self-indulgently, and there was that same brittle edge glinting on each word like sunlight

18

flashing on a long blade. And Daniel felt a dread that held him motionless, listening.

"No, I don't think it; I don't even hope for it, because I know it's not going to happen. I know my husband that well, believe me, and to hope that he'll return is only to deceive myself. I won't see him again. He's gone, *gone,* and self-deceit won't help me. Neither will self-pity. I need all my strength and what good sense I can muster. There's no money. There's no money for schools or doctors or clothes or food. There's not even enough money to keep the house. What else *can* I do? No, don't tell me they need a mother's love — what they need now is *money.*"

Daniel clearly remembered the worn, discolored paint below the clear plastic rectangle on the door, the fingerprints and smudges made by his little sisters, who weren't tall enough to reach up to the rectangle to push. He could see, through the crack between the door and the door frame, a thin slice of his mother in profile, calmly sitting at the dining room table, a plume of smoke rising straight up from the cigarette in her hand to the chandelier that seemed to have too few pieces of crystal, like a Christmas tree without enough ornaments.

"Sometimes I think money *is* love, love in a real sense, distilled. I'm still young enough, attractive enough to make a life for myself, but there is no way I can afford the children. I can't give them the love they need. Putting them up for adoption is the reasonable thing, the best thing. What they need now is money."

Daniel remembered the thick arm that pushed open the kitchen door and the voice of the neighbor saying, "Your son is home. Explain it to him, not to me."

And Daniel saw his mother's icy stare and heard the hard edge on her words as she spoke to the neighbor's challenge more than to him. But the message already had been passed: he was being sent away because there was no money, and money was love.

As he grew older, Daniel began to realize that his memories

of childhood were really memories *from* childhood, memories that had been altered by time, distance, and emotional content to form an amalgam of the real and the imagined. He knew his mother's message had been reinforced by the separation from his parents and sisters, and that, altered by time, he had allowed it to become a creed, a constant in his churning memory: "Money," he repeated over and over, "is *everything.*" But not surprisingly, as he acquired the money he wanted so badly, as he became Profit instead of Daniel, he learned that money was a means, not an end — he learned that money was *not* everything — and his belief in it waned, leaving behind only a residue of expensive tastes and a void that needed to be filled. He knew he needed to move on to something else, but he didn't know what that something else was. Only one thing was certain: whatever he did, it would cost. He needed a retirement account.

Profit sat forward and carelessly threw the sheaves of bills into his attaché case. With the heel of his hand he rubbed the speckling of gunpowder around his eye as he stood up; the embedded powder felt mildly electric, prickly, and his eye twitched. He took his hand away from his face and looked at it as if it were the source of the shock.

Before he used the telephone to call room service, he sat on the corner of the bed and unscrewed the mouthpiece and the earpiece and checked the speakers and the wires. He ordered a huge breakfast — waffles, sausage, eggs, biscuits, raw oysters, and a quart of milk — then retrieved his single message: "Call Ronnie."

The phone rang only once. Ronnie Fraiche was flying. He had been tooting all night and had hit the cocaine meridian. "Judge," he answered, his voice low and somber, "lest you be judged."

Profit laughed into the phone. "Come on, this is Profit. I don't understand legal talk."

"Profit, I'm glad you called." The rhythm of the judge's speech changed immediately: he began to speak very quickly, the words firing out in staccato bursts. "I checked on that guy, Vicedomini. I have his folder right here. Strange name, huh? And that's not all that's strange. There's some stuff you should know."

"Like what?" Profit asked, stretching out on the bed. He crossed his ankles and shifted his weight onto one elbow. With his free hand he reached into the attaché case and fingered a sheaf of bills, fanning it like a deck of playing cards.

"Like this: if Vicedomini is after you, you got a big problem." There was the sound of rustling papers followed by the slap of a stack of file folders dropped on wood. "I had his folder pulled. I said I thought he had a case coming up in my court, and I wanted to see if it was worth subpoenaing him. Once I saw the folder, I called his former watch commander. I told him I was considering what kind of witness Vicedomini would make — I mean, I can do that. You know, in parish court, I can sort of be prosecutor as well as judge; I can be defense, too. That's why I like it. I use my discretion, and we cut all the bullshit."

"So what about Vicedomini?" Profit interrupted. He knew too well how cocaine could send a train of thought on a tangential course to the moon.

"Well, here's the thing: his folder is good, and I mean *very* good. He got two awards for valor under fire. They don't hand those out like lollipops."

Ronnie Fraiche's rapid speech stopped abruptly, and Profit heard a short sniff. The corners of his mouth turned up in a grin as he resisted the urge to say, "You should know better."

"He worked the housing projects, uniformed patrol," Fraiche continued. "Right there you know he's sort of crazy. Jesus, those places are battlefields. He was in Vietnam for a year, too — Silver Star, among other things. The man just collects medals."

"What about the shootings, Ronnie?"

"Oh, yeah. He was in two different shoot-outs. In the first, he got a call that came out as a one-oh-three unknown — that's a disturbance call. When he arrived at the scene, some

21

kids told him they had been playing basketball and a man had come out on his balcony and told them to stop because they were making too much noise and he was trying to sleep. They didn't stop, of course, and the man comes back out on the balcony with a .45 and starts popping caps. One kid got hit in the foot, so they know he's serious and they call the police. Whenever they call the police in the projects, it's serious: a lot of those people have been in jail themselves, and they've got no love for cops. Anyway, your boy Vicedomini locks down the button on his radio so he's got an open mike hanging on his shoulder. The whole thing is on tape, and you ought to hear it, it's eerie. His voice sounds like it's coming from a machine or from an airline pilot giving you your cruising altitude. I mean, he is *cool.* First he calls an ambulance for the kid who's been shot in the foot, then he takes the basketball and goes out on the playground. Those police portables are great radios, and you hear *everything.* You hear his footsteps and you hear the kids in the background and then you hear this *thump, thump, thump,* real slow. At first I thought it was his heart pounding, but there's this hollow, ringing sound to it, and it's too loud, anyway, and then you realize he's out there on the playground dribbling the freaking basketball. I tell you, he's crazy."

There was a knock at the door, and a man's voice said, "Room service." Profit said into the phone, "Hold on a minute." He found some loose bills, gave the waiter an extravagant tip, and pushed the cart beside the bed before he picked up the phone. He cradled the receiver between shoulder and cheek, said, "Okay, go ahead," and began to mix ketchup and horseradish for the oysters.

"In a way, bouncing the basketball was a smart move. He hadn't *seen* the crime, so he couldn't kick in the door without a warrant, and it got the guy to come out of his apartment. But the guy himself must not have been wrapped too tight, because he came out blazing, three quick shots from the balcony. Then one close up, *boom:* your boy caught him between the eyes with a .357. One shot. I got that from the coroner's report." There was an odd, embarrassed quality to the pause Ronnie Fraiche made, and the pace of his words slowed as he added, "The last thing you hear on the tape is Vicedomini starting to cry."

Profit made a slurping sound as he sucked the first oyster from the half-shell.

"What was the other shoot-out? You said there were two."

"A psycho," Fraiche replied, the enthusiasm gone from his voice. "Some guy started shooting out of his window with a rifle. He wasn't hitting anybody, but that's a very bad situation. You ever wonder where those people hide so long before they come up crazy?"

"Not really. What happened?"

"Vicedomini just about walks up to the window, and when the guy pops up for another shot, he nails him. Forty yards away, and he caught him in the throat, with a pistol. Don't *ever* let that guy pull a gun on you."

Profit smiled and lifted the small silver dome covering his toast.

"He can shoot, huh?"

"Can he shoot?" Fraiche said, the pace of his words accelerating. "Listen, that's where the rub begins. He used to go to the police range every day. His watch commander said in a year and a half he never missed a day. He never shot the bull's-eye; he'd only shoot the practical combat."

"What's that?"

"Hey, I did it myself. Did you know I wear a gun in court? Ever since that judge in California got shot most of the judges do — that's one of the reasons I leave my robe open, so I can get to my gun if I have to. Anyway, the practical combat, it's great, but it's tough: quick draw up close, then you back up and shoot left-handed and right-handed, then you back up some more and shoot from all sorts of positions, and all the time the targets are moving on you. This guy Vicedomini, he got so good he shot a better score than the southeast regional champion. He has about every range record there is."

"So what's the rub?"

"You know how the police are, Profit. They have a sort of chummy in-house fraternity. About the only way different departments compete is in shooting matches. So here was a guy who could just about hand them trophies, and he refused to compete. He never did give a reason — he must have taken some real shit, too, but he never did compete."

"It couldn't have made him very popular."

"That's only part of it. He also refused to ride with a partner."

"Is that unusual?"

"Yes, it is, *really* unusual. Don't you ever watch TV? And especially in the projects. Most of the Urban Squad police I know would pack eight guys in a car to roll the projects."

"So he didn't want a buddy. There's no law against that."

"Yeah, well, while he was riding around out there all by himself, there started to be these unexplained killings, always in his beat. Three times neighborhood bad-asses just turned up dead, and it was always the same: a .22 in the left ear and a different gun each time. A couple more just disappeared."

"Who were these guys?"

"They were punks, definitely not the sort you want on your block. All of them had records and were out on something pending or dismissed."

Profit left an oyster in the sauce.

"Vigilante city," he said.

"Right. And that's dangerous. There never was any evidence against him, or they'd have yanked his string fast. It was just a suspicion."

"Maybe it was coincidence."

"Stand by, there's more. They told him he'd have to have a partner on patrol. There wasn't much he could say because they came out with a policy that all project cars had to have two men, which makes sense. It's a battlefield in there."

"That's what you said. What happened then?"

"He quit."

"Just like that?"

"Just like that."

"And he's definitely not with N.O.P.D. anymore?"

"Definite. They wouldn't have him back on a bet." Ronnie Fraiche paused as he closed the folder on Sheen Vicedomini. "See, since he left, they haven't had any more .22 killings."

Profit sat back, away from his breakfast. He was smiling, but he made his voice serious. "Thanks for the information, Ronnie. I owe you one."

"Yes, you do. Be careful of that guy. A lot about him doesn't add up." Ronnie Fraiche's voice took on the tone of one accustomed to giving orders and having them obeyed. "And Profit, like I said, next time call first; don't just arrive in my court."

Profit's smile faded, and his lips pressed together in a tight line. "You bet. Thanks again," he said, and hung up the phone.

Absently, Profit removed the cover from the waffle and poured syrup over it, watching as the thick liquid filled one square after another. He thought of Fraiche's voice, of the tone he had used to issue the order, and he stopped pouring the syrup and dropped the small pitcher onto the waffle. The pitcher landed with a thick splat and rolled slowly until it lay on its side. Profit knew he needed retirement — needed it before he began to make mistakes — and he knew he would soon go again to see Sheen Vicedomini.

3

USHED TO its limit, the engine made a frenzied sound, and a pulse settled in the seats of the small car, making Sheen think of a saxophone in the middle of a clear note. Off in the distance, the airport grew perceptibly larger. The pitch of the engine changed suddenly as Profit geared down for the exit from the expressway. On the ramp, in the low, early light, the guardrails cast long shadows, and as they drove through the black lines, the light flickered, freezing expressions and movements in quick frames. Profit's hand arced to his face, pressed against his eye, arced away to the gearshift. Sheen felt a curious detachment, as if he were watching a movie on a fitful projector.

The access road to the terminal building ran parallel to the north–south runway, and a huge jet touched down gently as they drove. Profit parked in the short-term lot, shut off the engine, and turned to Sheen, his right arm draped over the seat back. The Porsche creaked and popped with small hot-metal noises.

"We have about thirty minutes. Stay close but not with me."

"I'll have to check my bag," Sheen replied. Neither the .45 nor the .22 would make it through the airport's metal detector.

"There shouldn't be any problems on this end. All I'm doing

is loading the mule." Profit raised himself off the seat to reach into his hip pocket. He took out a black leather wallet, opened it, handed Sheen a driver's license. "I'm going to meet her in the coffee shop. Get a good look at her, then forget about me and stay with her. If something *does* happen, see what you can do." Profit flicked the license in Sheen's hand. His fingernail made a sharp, snapping sound on the plastic. "The address is good," Profit added. "There shouldn't be any problems. Easy money."

"Easy money," Sheen repeated softly, his lips hardly moving.

They got out of the car at the same time. Profit took a small blue suitcase out of the trunk and turned to walk into the terminal building as Sheen shouldered his heavy flight bag. Sheen shook his head as if to clear it; again he wondered how events had moved so quickly, why he had allowed himself to become involved. He gave Profit a twenty-yard lead before he followed him into the airport.

There were few passengers in the main terminal. Sheen checked his bag, sauntered across the waiting area to the coffee shop, and moved along the serving line. He sat down two tables away from Profit and sipped his coffee, both hands wrapped around the large mug. Profit did not look up from his newspaper, not even when the woman the license identified as Susan Richardson sat down next to him.

Susan Richardson was not as young as she tried to appear. Her brown hair was frizzed, framing her face girlishly, but her facial skin sagged slightly, and there were creases near the corners of her eyes. Her loose-fitting blue dress was embroidered with bright colors on the hem, and on her shoulder was a small, faded tattoo of a rose. She sat quietly, slowly stirring her coffee with a white plastic spoon.

Profit laid the newspaper flat on the table. "There's a rental car on the other end reserved in your name," he said without looking up. "A Chevrolet. The rental counter is behind the baggage claim. Use your California driver's license."

"I'm familiar with the San Francisco airport, Profit, and I *have* to use my California license because you have my Louisiana license." Susan took a bite from her breakfast roll and before she started to chew looked closely at the crescent her bite had made. Apparently satisfied, she chewed and said, "I pick up the car from the agency lot and bring it back to the terminal. You'll meet me there. We've been through this before, you know?"

Profit made no attempt to disguise his irritation. "The suitcase goes in the trunk *before* you get back to the terminal," he said.

"I know," Susan replied dully, a sour note of indulgence in her voice.

Profit pushed back his chair, stood up, put change on the table. He winked at Susan, the speckles of gunpowder around his eye folding into a dark slash.

As he walked away Susan sipped her coffee, watching him over the rim of the cup. Profit had left the small blue suitcase near her feet, and with her free hand she checked the clasps to be sure they were closed securely and locked.

Susan did not notice Sheen, and he trailed her through check-in and onto the concourse. In the waiting area he took a seat directly behind hers, two rows back; when the flight was called, he followed her onto the plane. Profit boarded late and sat behind both Susan and Sheen. They all relaxed slightly when the plane was sealed and the engines started with a soft electric whine.

At cruising altitude Sheen unfastened his seat belt, and as he leaned one shoulder against the wall of the plane, he rested his chin on a tight fist. He felt a peculiar tension, a restlessness he had almost forgotten. The first time he had noticed the heavy buzz in his ears he had been in Vietnam. The buzz was like the hum in an overloaded bass speaker, and it made him nervous and tense. His senses seemed painfully acute: he heard his own heartbeat as clearly as if he were connected to a monitor; his eyes seemed literally to swell. His throat was dry, and his skin was pale and clammy. Yet despite the discomfort, the tension was oddly reassuring, a measure of alertness, and he welcomed the edge. Even as he had agreed to the trip, he had known it was wrong, a mistake, but now that it had begun, he didn't want to make other mistakes. He closed his eyes and tried to think of the money.

The landing gear locked into place with a jarring thump, but the landing itself was so smooth it was hard to discern when the wheels first touched the runway. It seemed to Sheen that they were drawn to the gate rather than propelled there, as if the long bellows extension ramp were a great vacuum hose first pulling the plane, then pulling the passengers out of the plane.

Sheen followed Susan down the concourse. She walked confidently, the small blue suitcase swinging lightly in one hand. Sheen found a spot equidistant from the baggage claim and the rental car counter and waited for his bag while he watched Susan as she went through the formalities of renting a car. His head pivoted slowly back and forth like a scanning device.

The paperwork complete, Susan Richardson walked through the electric double doors and stood on the curb to await the courtesy bus that would take her to the parking lot. When the doors opened for him, Sheen noticed simultaneously the crisp, cool San Francisco air and Profit parked near the curb. Profit was hunched down low, and as Sheen approached he moved across the seat with an awkward crablike motion.

"I don't want Susan to see me," Profit explained as Sheen got in behind the wheel. "The bus will take her to the agency lot. She'll put the bag in the trunk, then drive back here. Follow the bus, then follow her. She'll probably drive fast." Profit twisted his wrist to look at his watch. "She only has forty minutes before her flight leaves."

"That's a quick trip."

"She's not a tourist," Profit said and smiled, but his smile was tight. "She'll leave the rental car down from the terminal. As soon as she's back in the airport I'll take her car, and you follow me."

The courtesy bus pulled up to the curb. Susan was the only passenger to get on. Sheen put the Oldsmobile in gear and followed at a distance as Profit sat up in the seat.

"If for some reason you lose me," Profit said, "wait in the bar in the Holiday Inn on Van Ness. I'll page Mr. Ware, as in where the fuck are you?"

The brightly painted courtesy bus moved with surprising speed through the labyrinth of ramps to a service road that was straight and flat, bordered on one side by a high chain link fence. When the bus turned into an open gate, Sheen drove past, made a U-turn, and stopped. They watched as Susan picked up a pale blue Chevrolet and started to leave the lot.

"That stupid whore," Profit said suddenly. His teeth were set together, and the words hissed furiously through them. "That stupid fucking whore. She didn't put the bag in the trunk."

Sheen didn't take his eyes off the Chevrolet. He knew Profit was right: to be even reasonably secure, the bag had to be in the trunk — the laws of search and seizure said so. He moved the gearshift to lock the transmission in low and started back down the service road.

As if in response to Profit's anger, the Chevrolet pulled abruptly to the curb, and Susan got out carrying the small blue suitcase. With one hand Sheen opened his flight bag. He wedged the .45 under his right leg before he braked to a stop. The Chevrolet was seventy-five yards in front of them.

"Move in closer," Profit said.

Sheen put his right hand flat on the seat beside his leg. "I want the distance," he replied. His eyes moved rapidly back and forth. He checked the rearview mirror. The road behind them was clear.

Susan opened the trunk, dropped in the bag, closed the trunk, and began to drive again toward the terminal. Sheen pulled in close behind her.

"Do you think she was marking us?" he asked. He kept

the transmission in first gear, and the engine whined, revving high.

"Who knows what the hell she was doing," Profit replied. He was again slouched low in the seat, twisted slightly, one arm straight out against the dashboard. "She's made five trips for me — six, including this one. Maybe she just forgot." He shook his head. "But she's hungry, or she wouldn't make the trips at all. Shit, we're *all* hungry."

"Is she connected?"

Profit turned his head and looked at Sheen with eyes that were both assessing and earnest. "There are *always* connections where there's coke, Sheen."

In front of them, the blue Chevrolet heeled in a steep turn. Sheen leaned forward until his forearms wrapped around the steering wheel, and he drove with movements of his whole upper torso.

"I'll drive her car," he said, changing Profit's plan. "You pull out in front, and I'll follow. Make sure I'm behind you, and check often. If there *is* a problem, stay clear, and I'll page *you* in the Holiday Inn."

Profit hesitated a moment, his eyes questioning, before he said, "Okay. You got it."

Sheen put the .45 back into his flight bag, and as soon as Susan stopped in front of the main terminal, he was out of Profit's car and walking toward the Chevrolet. He moved with less urgency than he felt. He adjusted the seat, checked the mirrors, buckled his seat belt. He drove cautiously away from the terminal and was on the exit ramp before Profit passed to lead the way.

Profit turned north on Highway 101, toward San Francisco. He drove exactly at the speed limit, and he was smiling. He tapped his hand on the wheel in time to some tune only he could hear. In the rearview mirror he could see the blue Chevrolet in good position behind him, five car lengths back, and he could see Sheen leaning forward, his arms draped over the steering wheel, his body rolling with each small turn in the road. Profit was somewhat irritated that he had left the blue suitcase empty, but he was glad he had instructed Susan to wait to transfer the bag to the trunk. Sheen had reacted immediately and well, taking the risk himself, protecting the bag, and Profit was reassured — the reassurance was worth a few dollars, worth a suitcase without a load. Properly handled, Sheen could add a whole new dimension to his business.

Profit had always used for security his own ability to avoid — erratic schedules, an inherent ability to manipulate a given circumstance into any of several situations, and a predisposition not to trust anyone but himself, all had made him as elusive as an oiled wrestler — but he knew he needed security in the ability to confront. The two modes were opposite, yet complementary; used in appropriate combinations, they covered all bets. When Sheen had reacted well, Profit had seen in his movements a cold confidence, a certainty in confrontation that allowed him a glimpse of retirement. Profit had plans for Sheen Vicedomini.

As always when he felt he had pulled something off, Profit was happy. A pleasant smile fixed itself on his face. He turned on the radio and began to enjoy the trip to San Francisco.

Through industrial South San Francisco, they continued north on Highway 101. Sheen was tense. Concentrating on his driving and at the same time trying to pick out cars that might be following, he noticed little more than the steepness of the hills before they came to the Golden Gate Bridge and he saw the panorama of the ocean coming inland to form the bay. Across the bridge the road went up, then through a tunnel; past the tunnel, far below the water seemed too blue to be real. As they coasted down the long decline, Sheen lost sight of the bay, and he was sure the color had been an illusion. It was his first sense of illusion.

Past Sausalito they left the freeway and veered west on Highway 1. The two-lane road coiled unpredictably up and around the hills. Sheen rolled down the driver's window; his perceptions heightened by tension, he caught the faint smell of salt in the air. Then the road turned down, a ledge broken from

32

the face of the hills, and the great expanse of the ocean literally burst into view. Profit had pulled onto the shoulder just past the turn, and Sheen had to brake sharply to pull in beside him.

A cloud of tan dust enveloped both cars, but the sea breeze quickly whisked it away. Profit got out of his car and walked around it to stand next to the rental car. Through the open window Sheen noticed two things: that Profit's expression and posture were relaxed, and that his gold Omega wristwatch was twisted on his arm, face down, unreadable.

"I think we're all right," Profit said. "Susan is kind of dizzy — she probably did just forget." Profit smiled easily and shifted his stance to look out at the ocean.

Instinctively Sheen knew something was wrong.

A cloud's shadow raced across the blue ocean surface like some immense, half-submerged sea creature.

"So what do you think?" Profit asked, gesturing toward the ocean as if giving it as a gift.

Sheen pushed open the car door, got out, closed the door, and leaned back against it. His nostrils went in and out with his breathing; his lips pursed thoughtfully. Two hundred feet below them, waves foamed white, crashing on wet black rock.

When Sheen walked to the rear of the Chevrolet, his shoes made a grating sound on the packed, sandy dirt. He opened the trunk, took out the small blue suitcase, brought it to the front of the car, and set it on the hood. He turned to Profit and said softly, barely audible above the wind, "You hired me to help you get this bag out here. I don't care what's in it, but I *do* care if you've set me up to do something stupid."

"Open it," Profit said, his voice tinged with humor.

"I don't care what's in it," Sheen repeated.

Profit reached into his pocket and took out a key ring. "How do you know there's no coke?"

"I don't *know*. I just have a feeling you wouldn't play tour guide while you're working."

Profit was genuinely pleased. He pulled the suitcase across the hood, unlocked it, and opened it. Inside, padded by crumpled wads of women's clothing, was a bottle of Pisco and a salt shaker.

Sheen raised one shoulder and dropped it. "You still owe me five thousand dollars," he said.

Profit twisted the white plastic cap on the bottle and smelled the yellow-brown liquid before he took a long swallow. His mouth puckered from the biting taste, and he ran his tongue over his teeth before he said, "Nope. I owe you five thousand dollars after we make delivery."

Sheen felt a chill run up his spine and, oddly, a hot flush in his cheeks and ears. "My bag?" he asked, but he already knew. He remembered Profit offering to carry the bag out to the car. He turned around and put both hands on the hood.

Profit said to his back, "I wanted to let you know who has what before we get where we're going. Susan was for your benefit, my friend. You get an A." Profit put the cap back on the bottle, reversed his grip to hold it by the neck, and threw it out over the cliff. "But I wouldn't have you do anything I wouldn't do myself. Only half the load is in your bag; half is in my briefcase." When Sheen didn't respond, he added, "Of course your money goes up. It's not that much farther to the house. Let's go to work."

Profit watched Sheen carefully as he turned away from the hood. He noted the frightening directness of his expression and the obvious control of his anger. At that moment Profit had no difficulty believing that Sheen had killed before. His shoulders were drawn down, bunched like those of a sprinter ready to explode from the starting blocks, and there was a coldness about him that seemed to proceed from a practiced self-control of strong emotion. His greenish eyes flashed, but his expression was set, frozen. Profit pivoted on the balls of his feet, walked to his car, got in on the driver's side.

When Sheen opened the passenger door, Profit flinched; he started the car to cover the spasm.

Sheen dropped his flight bag on the middle of the seat before he got into the car and dumped its contents. He slid the .45 into a belt clip holster and taped the .22 to his calf. He looked into the plastic case and saw the thick, padded cocaine bulge beneath the bag's cardboard bottom. As if in exchange, Profit opened his attaché case and tore the lining just enough to show the cocaine in the bottom of it.

"Accidents happen every day," Profit said, looking at the seat rather than at Sheen. "There's no use risking the whole load by using only one carrier." Profit got out of the car to put both bags in the trunk. When he was back in the driver's seat, he said, "We'll go in this car and pick the other one up on the way back."

Sheen had a way of assuming isolation that was instantly communicable; Profit recognized the message and did not break the uncomfortable silence. He drove too fast on the winding coast road.

Profit had assumed that Sheen would not be happy with the switch, but he had worked it anyway. "It'll keep him on his toes," he had said to himself. But at a deeper level he knew the ploy had not been merely an effort to keep Sheen alert: he was establishing his ground rules, making sure that Sheen understood who was in charge. Profit knew he had pushed hard, and he knew he was playing a dangerous game.

"We're going to see two guys," he said finally. "They're not connected, so it's a low-risk run. They're stockbrokers — traders, they call themselves. They don't even deal with the stocks, just the options — some abstract game. They're assholes, but they're rich assholes."

"A flea can't afford to hate the dog," Sheen said evenly.

"I guess I deserve that," Profit replied, "but you better get it sorted out before we get there. Like it or not, it's done."

"I won't screw you up, Profit," Sheen said, his mouth hard around the words it formed. "Which is more than you can say to me."

"Hey, it worked, and now I know."

"Know what?" Sheen snapped. "Know that you can sneak cocaine into my bag? Know that I won't steal your suitcase? When you fool with years from my life, I'd *better* have some say. You wanted security, and that's what I agreed to give you. But I don't make deals, I don't mule, and I don't work blind."

"You're up on a pretty high horse, Sheen. I took the same risks."

"No, you didn't," Sheen said, his lips pulled tight against his teeth, his mouth a thin, brutal gash. "The difference is that you knew what you were doing, and I was in the blind. The risks weren't the same. You want somebody to work blind, put an ad in the paper."

"You're looking for a short career, my friend."

"I'm not looking for a career at all, *friend*. You have a job you want done and I agreed to do it, but don't be looking to jack me around because you have two toots of cocaine you think my nose can't resist. Play your silly games with someone else."

Profit suddenly pulled the car off the road and slid onto a dirt parking area. The dust blew by the windshield like a quickly passing storm. Profit looked out at the ocean.

"You're right," he said, and turned his head to look at Sheen. "Look, I've been doing this so long I've gotten some strange ideas. I feel everything is a hustle — even when I know it's not." He put the car out of gear and twisted on the seat, pulling his right ankle beneath his left knee.

Sheen had the sense that a scene was being played according to some script he had never read.

"I play games," Profit continued, his voice low. "Sometimes it's caution; sometimes it's just fucking around. Sometimes I need somebody to yank my string, but you know that isn't easy. It's something I have to deal with, something maybe you can help me with. You know the laws, the way they work, the way *they* make them work. Most of the time, I'm the one working blind." He gazed at Sheen, careful to look him directly in the eye. "I'm sorry," he said.

Sheen looked at his watch and saw the numbers changing, the seconds passing in black pulsing dashes, and he pressed the button that froze the display. He knew the moment was complete, and he knew the fault was not all Profit's; he should have been quicker to anticipate and to cut off the hustle. He was being paid far too much simply to handle a pistol. If he viewed it impersonally, the switch made good security sense. He wished it had been worked on somebody else.

"Forget it," he said tersely, glad he had agreed only to the one trip.

"No more hustles," Profit added.

"Right," Sheen said to himself, momentarily wondering if the hustle was the reason he had made the trip, wondering what he would have felt if the whole excursion had been un-eventful. He thought of his normal workday, of the routine events proceeding as predictably as a boat crossing a broad expanse of calm water, and he knew that uncertainty was itself an attraction, a relief from boredom, a relief from the sameness of one day following another and the days blurring together without distinction. He remembered too well the time he had spent in combat, the excruciating lulls between engagements, the lulls when he had learned for a certain fact that grace under pressure was no more difficult to achieve than grace *between* pressures. Sheen pinched his lower lip between his teeth and bit down on it. The ocean shimmered, golden in the bright sunlight.

Profit drove the swaying Oldsmobile hard, and in less than fifteen minutes, they were in the small oceanfront town of Stinson Beach. Sheen sat with his hands on his knees, looking straight in front of him as if he didn't want to see the beach houses and the miscellaneous stores. Profit stopped at a hot dog stand to use the pay phone. The beach was hidden from view by the white painted plywood shack, but there was evidence of its proximity in the wind-rolled litter and the roasted sunbathers who walked a path that led through low, mean-looking shrubs. Profit put three coins in the phone, consulted a thick address book, punched seven numbers as dexterously as an accountant using a calculator.

Sheen could not hear what he was saying, and it bothered him.

By design, Profit was never punctual. As he leaned against

the phone waiting for the connecting *click,* he looked at his watch, and the corners of his mouth turned up. He was a day and two hours late making delivery. He could as easily have been on time, but he knew he had a seller's market, and he also knew that the more difficult it was to buy cocaine, the more willing the dilettante buyers were to pay the exorbitant prices they had come to expect. In many ways, cocaine was a half-and-half mix of chemical and mystique, and Profit was a master of matching the blend to the buyer.

When his call was answered, he did not identify himself; he said only, "I'll be there in twenty minutes," and hung up. He turned away from the phone and rubbed his hands together as if he were warming them over a fire before he cupped them to his mouth and yelled to Sheen, "You want a hot dog?"

Sheen shook his head no, but got out of the car and leaned against the warm front fender.

Profit ordered, took the chili dog in one hand, squirted mustard over it, looked at the diced onions and decided against them. When he took a bite, sauce trickled down his chin, and he grabbed a wad of paper napkins before he moved near to Sheen. He swallowed and said, "I might have overprimed this pump just a little. I'm late — that is, *we're* late. They're stretched, and I suspect they're pissed."

"Enough to get stupid?"

"I don't think so. They're pansies. But the shit is all fluffed to hell. You could probably sell it across the counter — I'm the one they want in the schoolyards." Profit grinned, looked at Sheen, looked at the hot dog speculatively. "Don't get me wrong, though. I'm going to tell them it's shit. I brought you with me because you'll buy it no matter what. You're also giving me a ride to the airport, so they have to make up their minds. If they don't want it, you'll take it, no harm done. I'll get them another load, but it's a very unpredictable market, you know — it might be next year."

Sheen crossed his arms on his chest and rubbed one elbow tentatively.

"It sounds pretty thin."

"It's not *that* bad a line — I've gotten by on worse. Anyway, it's what we've got. Don't push it. Just make it clear you've made an offer."

Sheen seemed about to say something else, then to change his mind.

Profit crumpled the wax paper around the hot dog, put it in the trash, and got into the car. He turned back in the direction from which they had come. Sheen settled down into the seat, determined not to let small things annoy him.

Just past a hairpin switchback, Profit made a sudden turn, a sliding skid that took them off the road, and Sheen thought they were going over the cliff. Both arms started up to protect his face, then he saw the concealed entrance to a steep, unpaved driveway. Beside him Profit chuckled.

The driveway plunged down fifty abrupt yards to a parking area level with the roof of a house. Built on the face of the cliff, the house was cantilevered out over the ocean, the flat roof a clearly defined black plane floating over the open expanse of deep blue water that stretched shimmering to the horizon. White concrete steps with low risers and long treads dropped to a short sidewalk mottled with egg-sized brown stones. The house's exterior redwood was rough sawn and weathered to a light gray color that made Sheen think of a pallid complexion, the chalky gray pallor of long-term prisoners in maximum security. And suddenly he had an odd sense of paramnesia: even before the door opened, he knew what the house would look like on the inside. There would be leather couches, chrome and glass tables, a shag rug; there would be a bar and high stools and an expensive stereo prominently displayed; there would be heavy glass ashtrays and an adjustable bookshelf filled with how-to books. It occurred to Sheen that the house was a form of prison, as inescapable as a creed. Then the door opened and he shifted back to the immediate.

A short, prematurely balding man hesitated on the threshold before he extended his right hand to Profit. The man's eyes were as soft and brown as a cocker spaniel's. His face was a deep, rich tan. He was dressed in starched designer jeans, a sweater-shirt, and a heavy gold necklace. He seemed as much a part of the house as the shag rug.

"Hello, Profit," the man said, his voice so gravely sincere that Sheen was sure he was joking. "I'm so very glad you could make it. Welcome." His large brown eyes moved warmly to Sheen. "I don't believe we've met. My name is Stuart. Please, come in."

As they walked past Stuart into the short foyer, he dropped his chin in a curt bow to each of them, then stepped behind them and closed the door firmly.

"I'm glad to see the house is still here," Profit said as he looked around, one hand in his pocket, one hand carelessly swinging his leather attaché case.

"The last earthquake?" Stuart asked. "The best engineers have assured us we've nothing to worry about. We've spared no expense."

"Of course you haven't," Profit said mockingly. "Where's John?"

"Please," Stuart said to Sheen, "make yourself comfortable."

Sheen sat on one of the leather couches that ran perpendicular to the plate glass windows that overlooked the ocean.

"When you called, John was in the sauna," Stuart said to Profit. "He's showering now. Would you like something to drink while we wait? He won't be long. I have some excellent Chablis."

"Fine," Profit said dryly, a shade of annoyance in his voice.

"So," Stuart began as he moved behind the bar, "how is New Orleans?"

Profit sat on the couch opposite Sheen and looked out of the window. "Who said I was in New Orleans?" he replied without looking away from the view.

"No one, of course," Stuart said soothingly, his solemn sincerity unruffled. "Then, how are you?"

Profit put his elbow on the arm of the couch, ran his hand through his hair, leaned his cheek against his knuckles.

"I have a plane to catch," he said wearily.

"I wonder *why* you have a plane to catch?" a detached voice asked from the hallway.

There was a brief pause before a tall, casually disheveled man appeared in the doorway. The tall man wore a burgundy silk robe over faded jeans. He was barefoot. He kept both hands in the pockets of the robe, and as he walked slowly across the room, his shoulders rolled forward, giving the impression that he was ambling. But the slowness was too purposeful, too restrained to be genuine. His brows were thick, separated by a deep vertical crease over his sharp nose. His lips were thin, pressed into a tight line.

"Trying to make a living," Profit replied to the question, and stood up. "What you been up to, John?" he asked, then he introduced Sheen as John sat next to him on the couch.

Before they could continue, Stuart brought the wine and four glasses. He filled the glasses from a green bottle wrapped in a white towel, then distributed them to the four corners of the low table. Satisfied that his duty was done, he sat on the floor at John's feet, his legs crossed in front of him Indian style.

Profit tasted the wine, held it up to the light, put the glass on the arm of the couch.

"How is the options business?" he opened casually.

"John's trading is *always* the best," Stuart replied from the floor.

John silenced him with a glance, leaned forward on the couch, and said in a voice that gained emphasis from its deliberateness, "A better question might be, How is *our* business? You're two days late." His gaze left Profit, and he looked at Sheen with blue eyes that were bright but veiled by a watery film that gave them the slow, sleepy look a frog's eyes assume when a fly is near. "And what is he doing here?"

"He's with me," Profit said.

"So I had assumed. A little small for a bodyguard, isn't he?"

Sheen looked at Stuart and then back at John. "A little large for a lap dog, isn't he?"

The crease over John's nose deepened. He tapped his forefinger on the table.

"Let's see the coke," he said.

Profit put his attaché case on the table and with his thumb spun the numbers on the combination lock. The clasps opened with their distinctive *click-click,* and he took out two clear plastic bags the size of grapefruits.

"One thousand grams exactly," he said.

While Profit still had the bags in his hands, before he could drop them onto the table, John said, "I want to know why he's here." He used his glass to point at Sheen.

Profit was hunched forward, his elbows on his knees. He hefted the bags up and down like a balance scale seeking a balance. "He wants to buy the coke," he said, and put the bags on the table next to the attaché case.

"We're not going to bid on it," Stuart protested, his voice thin and high-pitched. "The price is set."

John shook his head. When his head stopped moving, he looked up. The film was gone from his eyes, and they were clear and hot.

"No, Stuart," he said slowly, "the price is still set. Profit wouldn't hold an auction, would you, Profit? He's worried we won't buy it — which means it must be real shit. Am I right, Profit?" With one hand John slid the two bags of cocaine down the table until they were in front of him. "How bad is it?"

Profit sighed and sat back on the couch.

"See for yourself, John. I'm not a chemist."

"What's happening here, Stuart," John said as he reached in his pocket for a small gold folding knife, "is a not too classic squeeze play. Sheen there may or may not be a buyer, but as long as he's presented as a buyer, we're in a non-negotiating position." John opened the knife and held it loosely in one hand, waving it in small circles as he spoke. "But Profit likes us. We pay cash. He'll even offer to get us another kilo —

of course, it may be some time before he's back out this way. What's your price?" John asked suddenly, the blade of the knife thrusting through the air, pointing at Sheen.

Sheen looked at the knife intently, not replying until the blade was lowered. "None of your business," he said evenly.

Profit saw the knife waver in John's hand. He picked up his wine glass and, holding it just slightly above the arm of the couch, rolled the stem between thumb and first finger.

"You have the first option, John — you're supposed to know about options."

John tapped the knife blade on the glass and looked at it thoughtfully. He knew no number of words would change what was on the table. He leaned back on the couch, stared momentarily at the ceiling, then sat upright quickly.

"Regular price?" he asked.

"It's not an auction," Profit replied.

"Then I'll hope for the best."

"It's not *that* bad." Profit looked at Sheen and winked. "Money, please."

Stuart stood up from his position on the floor as John used the knife to slice into one of the bags. John stirred the cocaine curiously, as if he were writing a message in the coarse white powder.

Stretching on his toes, Stuart reached to the top of the adjustable bookcase and took down a neatly wrapped brown paper package, which he handed to Profit. Profit closed his attaché case, put the package of money on top of it, reached into his pants pocket. He threw a folded sheaf of bills on the table and said, "Cut me out a thousand dollars' worth and let me go. I have a plane to catch."

Stuart obediently went to the kitchen and came back with a Baggie, a tablespoon, and a triple-beam balance scale. His soft brown eyes moved from Profit to John before he knelt by the table and carefully set the scale to fifteen and one-half grams: fourteen for the half ounce of cocaine and one and a half to compensate for the Baggie.

John stopped stirring the cocaine. Extending his arm slowly, with the very tip of the powder-covered knife blade he moved the weight slide down to nine grams.

"Give him the gram price, not the ounce price, Stuart," John said in a mocking tone. He put the knife beside the scale. "And let him buy the Baggie."

"You bastard," Profit said, but his voice was as amused as his expression.

John put the tip of one finger into the cocaine, took it out, shook his hand as if it were wet, sat back on the couch, and rubbed the finger on the gums over his front teeth. His face pulled taut in an ugly grin.

Profit stood up and moved around the table to watch Stuart make the short measure. When the scale balanced and began its fluid up-and-down motion, he said, "Always a pleasure" and reached for the Baggie as Stuart reached to hand it to him. Their hands collided, and the Baggie fell onto the table, spilling slightly. Stuart made a smug, you-should-have-expected-it face as Profit, irritated, grabbed the bag, pivoted on his heel, and started for the door.

Stuart pushed the spilled powder into a pile and rolled his finger across it.

"Goodbye," Sheen said quietly, keeping himself between Profit and John first by sidestepping around the table, then by backing a few steps before he too turned to the door.

Outside, they moved quickly, almost furtively down the mottled sidewalk and up the low steps. Profit put the attaché case and the brown paper package in the trunk before he backed straight up the steep driveway.

"We lucked out," Profit said as they turned onto the highway. "One more stop and we're on vacation, but we have to hurry."

Sheen didn't ask where they were going. Suddenly he felt very tired. He realized he was hungry. He cracked the window and took deep breaths of the clean, cool ocean air.

Profit stopped when they reached the rental car.

"Do you want me to follow you?" Sheen asked.

"No." Profit shook his head. "I want you in the car with me." He opened the car door, got out, reached in his pocket. Sheen saw him open John's small gold knife before he knelt by each corner of the rental car and slashed all four tires. He was back in the Oldsmobile, adjusting himself in the seat, before the Chevrolet had settled on its rims.

"Remind me to call," he said. "Somebody must have vandalized the car while Susan was out taking pictures. The rental people will come and get it." Profit saw the corners of Sheen's mouth draw down critically, and he added, "Hey, that's what insurance is all about." He rolled down his window, looked at the knife in his hand, leaned back in his seat, and with a vicious slashing motion threw it out the window. Sheen heard a dull thud as the knife hit the rental car. "We have to hurry," Profit said again, and rolled up the window. "The bank closes at three."

They drove back the way they had come, but the sun was past its zenith and the shadows stretched long across the road, giving the sense that it was a different route, a different, fading day. The evening chill was already in the air.

Profit drove fast, with the concentration the winding road required, but occasionally, out of the corner of his eye, he looked at Sheen slouched low in the seat, hands in the pockets of his light jacket, his head turned to look out of the side window. Profit was having difficulty adjusting to Sheen's long silences — he preferred an exchange of words, even a pointless one, to an extended lull in conversation — but he had already tried twice to get Sheen to talk and he didn't know which was worse, the silence or the sound of his own voice unanswered. He put a tape in the deck and tapped his hand on the wheel in time to the music.

The twisting road suddenly became straight, and they crossed under the freeway to the small town of Sausalito. Profit stopped in front of a bank on the main street.

"Wait for me, will you?" he said.

He got out of the car, opened and closed the trunk, went

into the bank; shortly he jumped back in the car and made a quick U-turn. Less than a block away he stopped in front of a post office and handed Sheen two manila envelopes.

"Payday," he said in a flat tone that hid his excitement, his anticipation of Sheen's response. "Mail one off; put the other in your pocket."

Profit watched closely as Sheen examined the envelopes, watched as he shook his head slightly and his eyes became bright. In one envelope there was a cashier's check for five thousand dollars; in the other there was twenty-five hundred dollars in one-hundred-dollar bills.

Sheen sealed the envelope that contained the check, then folded the cash and put it in his pocket. For a moment he did not move. He started to say something but thought better of it. He knew Profit was overpaying him, but he felt a lightness and an exhilaration and he didn't care why. Momentarily, the game was worthwhile. It was as if someone had given him something for nothing — and yet he had earned it — and there was in the whole transaction a feeling of freedom, a feeling of having beaten the work-cycle sickness. He thought of the crowded streetcar rides he would not have to take and of the time Andrea could spend studying rather than working. He thought of the time they could spend together.

"Here," Profit said, interrupting his thoughts, "mail this one for me, would you?"

Profit handed him a third envelope and again watched carefully as Sheen slowly opened the car door and walked numbly into the post office.

"Gotcha!" Profit said out loud, and slapped his hand on the dashboard. He turned on the seat, sat back against the door, closed his eyes, and allowed himself a glimpse of retirement, a glimpse of life without the pressure of dealing, a reverie of scenes and images that pleased him. "Have I got plans for you," he said softly.

"What plans?" Sheen asked.

Profit opened his eyes, startled to see Sheen squatting beside the open door, his forearm across his knee.

46

"You're going to buy me lunch," he replied, recovering quickly. "So how does this compare with being a policeman?"

Sheen pushed himself up and got into the car. "Same game," he said, "different side of the board."

"This is the *paying* side." Profit straightened the arm that was draped over the seat back and pointed through the rear window at the bank down the street. "There it all is: pieces of paper, magnetic codes on a computer tape, and you've got the world by the balls."

Sheen smiled, amused by the thought.

"Where to now?" he asked.

"There's a good restaurant not far from here," Profit replied, then the tone of his voice changed and became so emphatic it was almost bitter. "Money is *everything*. It doesn't matter how you get it, as long as you *do* get it. Poverty is a disease."

Sheen nodded, and he was still smiling, but inexplicably some of the exhilaration passed out of him, like air hissing from a slashed tire.

4

CROSS THE street, a waist-high ground fog covered the playground and hid from view the bases of the jungle gyms, the slides, the rope climbs, and the swings. Seen out of relation to the ground, the structures were bizarre, eerily like a scale model of a derelict urban area. As the taxi pulled away Sheen paused long enough to picture the playground in use, to hear the children's high-pitched voices and to see their tireless play, before he picked up his heavy flight bag from the curb and turned to go inside. He was glad to be home.

In the early morning quiet, small sounds were distinct. The lock turned with a heavy, solid thump that contrasted with the light jingle of the keys. His rubber-soled shoes squeaked on the bare wood floor. The light switch clicked sharply. The fluorescent desk lamp hummed.

Andrea was asleep, one arm thrown back over her head, the other arm by her side. Her breath whistled softly through slightly parted lips. Sheen sat on the edge of the bed, pulled down the covers gently, kissed her between her breasts.

She awoke with a start, her brown eyes huge in the soft light, then she saw it was Sheen and she hugged him to her tightly. His face pressed into the hollow of her shoulder. He smelled her warmth as much as he felt it, and he pressed his face deeper before he pulled back and sat up straight on the side of the bed.

"What time is it?" Andrea asked sleepily, and rubbed her eyes with her fists. "What are you doing here?"

Sheen put his palm against her cheek. "About six," he said. "The sun is coming up."

Andrea extended both arms straight out from her sides and rolled her head back, arching her back and pushing against the pillow in a stretch that made Sheen think of a cat. "What are you doing here?" she asked again.

"I *live* here," Sheen replied. His right hand moved beneath the covers, cupped one breast, moved to the other, kneading gently. "I caught a late flight."

"Is Profit with you?"

Sheen shook his head and withdrew his hand. "He stayed in San Francisco."

"Are you okay? You must be tired."

"I slept on the plane." Sheen put both hands on his knees and pressed down against them as he stood up. "I'm going to put on a pot of coffee. You can stay in bed, you know."

"I'm up now," Andrea said, and stretched again. "Are you hungry?"

Sheen jerked his head to one side in a gesture of uncertainty.

Andrea flung back the covers to get up.

In the kitchen Sheen rinsed the coffeepot, filled the white paper filter, turned the coffeemaker on, and listened as the water gurgled before it began to drip. Andrea turned the oven to broil and stood in front of the open door.

"It's cold," she said, and wrapped her arms around herself. "Everything is all right?"

Sheen rubbed her arms elbow to shoulder with a fast warming motion. "Everything is fine," he said. "It went well, I guess."

"At least it was a quick trip."

"As quick as I could make it," he replied too sharply. "It wasn't much fun."

49

A door slammed somewhere on the street, and he went to look out the window. An early-morning delivery truck rumbled around the corner. The fast-coming light was strong enough to dim the streetlights and the porchlights. There were colors in the sky.

"What did you expect?" Andrea asked.

"I don't know what I expected. *Something.*"

Sheen poured himself a cup of coffee, opened the door, went out into the yard. The coffee was warm in his hand. He squatted on his heels and leaned back against a small tree, settling into the quiet. The grass was wet. He saw his footprints in the dew.

"What's the matter?" Andrea asked.

Sheen hadn't heard her come up beside him; startled, he flinched and spilled coffee over his hand. He shifted the cup, wiped his hand on the grass, and said, "Nothing is the matter — nothing to worry about, anyway. I'm just a little confused. I'll get it sorted out."

Andrea looked at him closely, and in her expression he saw her concern.

"Can I help you with it?" she asked.

"You already have," he replied, and he pulled her to him and rested his cheek against her hip before he motioned with his head toward the playground. "Do you want to go play?"

"Will you push me on the swing?"

"Oh, I guess so."

Andrea trotted across the street and Sheen followed, walking slowly, holding the cup of coffee away from his body. By the time he had put down the cup and moved behind her to push, Andrea had already begun to swing. It took him a moment to catch the rhythm, and his first push was uneven. The swing veered at an angle it took three pushes to correct.

"I should be celebrating," Sheen said when the swing was back on course. "I just made more money in one day than I bring home from work in six months."

"So why aren't you?" Andrea asked.

Sheen gave one final push, moved to the next swing, sat

50

down, and watched as Andrea's arcs became shorter and shorter.

"How am I supposed to make sense of it?" he asked, his voice suddenly brittle. "How am I supposed to get on another trolley to go downtown to make sixty dollars for the whole day? Something is seriously out of whack, Andrea." Sheen shook his head. He felt strangely uncertain. The muscle pulsed in his jaw. "It's not the money; it's what the need for money does to our lives. Sometimes when you tell me about your day at work, how some jerk dropped a bottle of ketchup and you had to clean it up or how some old lady bitched because her coffee was cold, I feel ashamed. I let you literally wait on people and for what? For money?"

Andrea dragged her feet, came to a stop, turned to face Sheen. The chains crossed over her head as she twisted the swing.

"No, it's not for the money," she said, her voice low but emphatic. "It's so I can afford to go to school. There *is* a difference." She put her legs out straight and looked at her knees, the corners of her mouth drawn down. "Waitressing is temporary — you know that. It shouldn't make you feel bad." She gave a resigned shrug before she looked back at Sheen. "You give one service to get another."

Sheen leaned to one side and rested his cheek against the taut chain. He closed his eyes and thought of the house on the cliff and of a kilo of cocaine for recreational use. The chain was cold and damp against his skin.

"What would you do," Andrea asked, her voice softer, "if you had enough money to do *anything?*"

Sheen didn't reply, but Andrea saw his brow furrow and the muscle jump in his jaw. She got off the swing, stood in front of him, ran her hand through his thick hair.

What would *I* do? he asked himself honestly.

He thought of the years he had spent in school and of how he had left reluctantly, feeling there was so much more to learn. But school had begun badly, he remembered. At first there had been the antiwar demonstrations and the ridicule of returning veterans, then the war had ended and there had been nothing at all, nothing but a quiet so deep it was a tangible thing, as tangible as fear and resentment. For four years of college he had hardly gone out of his single room in the dorm, except to go to class or to the library. "I can't afford to go out," he had told himself, but he knew even then that there was more, that both money and resentment were excuses, the symptoms, not the sickness: he was too recently back from an experience in which he had learned that friendships too often ended prematurely. He had turned to school because new understanding was the only thing he knew of that could not be taken from him, and he had pursued his studies with the obsessive passion of a miser accumulating gold. When his GI Bill had expired and he had been forced to go to work, he had left school without one new acquaintance he would call a friend, but with an odd pride in the fact that he had the highest cumulative grade point average ever achieved in the classics department.

I don't know if I could be that alone again, he admitted to himself. Sheen opened his eyes to look at Andrea. Her face was open and questioning. *But now I have you.*

"It's not the money," he repeated out loud. "It's this feeling that there's more, that nothing is ever really *accomplished.*"

"That's because you don't like what you do for work," Andrea said. "Maybe you should look for something else."

Sheen nodded as if he agreed with her, and said, "Maybe," but he knew there were no simple answers — and he knew that the distractions had been forthcoming because the answers had not. The Marines, the years of intense study, the police, all had been poor attempts to find distraction, to look outward, away from the emptiness he felt inside.

"I wish I could want more simply," he said.

Andrea tucked her lower lip between her teeth, dropped her chin, and looked at him through her eyebrows.

"Then would you still want me?"

Sheen saw the start of a playful smile and the warm, teasing look in her eyes, and his doubts momentarily dissolved.

"You're pretty simple," he said seriously. "Maybe I would want you more."

Andrea stuck out her tongue. "Ha-ha," she said, and without warning shook the swing chains back and forth, causing the swing to bounce erratically. Caught off balance Sheen slid forward, and the seat went out from under him. He grabbed for the chains and missed. Suddenly he was sitting on the ground.

Andrea backed up three steps, her eyes wide, one hand over her mouth, both feigning surprise and hiding her smile.

Exaggerating each movement, Sheen slowly stood up, dusted off his pants, shook out his coat. As if he felt something out of place, he patted the side pocket, reached into it, and brought out a long, thin package wrapped in shiny silver paper.

"I brought you something," he said, examining the wrapping closely before he held the package straight out to her, "but you have to come here to get it." He held his other hand up in a fist and shook it at her farcically.

Andrea's playfulness vanished. Her hand dropped away from her mouth, and her smile faded. "No, thank you," she said. Her voice was soft but firm. "You got away with it this time, but I don't want to be any part of a next time."

"You'll like it," Sheen said.

Andrea looked down and did not reply.

Sheen bent his arm and tapped the end of the package against his chin.

"I'm not going to work for Profit again," he said. "It was a mistake even to try it. It made me feel cheap and dirty. Work that's legal is bad enough."

Andrea looked at him directly with eyes that were suddenly hard and challenging.

"Promise me," she said. "Give me your word."

"I promise."

"Really?"

"Really. It's just not worth it to me."

Andrea ran forward and hugged him, her body flat against his from shoulder to knee.

"I'm so glad," she said. She buried her face in his shoulder as she squeezed him tightly. "I'll hold you to it." She turned her face to look up at him. His expression was both amused and somber, his dark eyes unreadable. She knew he would keep his word; he always did. The corners of her mouth pushed up in a grin. She said, "*Now* I'll take my present."

"Ha-ha," Sheen said, mimicking her. He arched one eyebrow in mock seriousness. "You can have it, but you can't open it until after breakfast."

"Why not?"

"Anticipation — it *may* be the best part."

"It better not be," Andrea said, and laughed. She pushed away from him and started toward the apartment at a trot.

Sheen started after her, remembered his coffee cup, and turned to retrieve it. As he put the thin silver package back in his pocket, he thought of the small gold watch inside it. He wondered how long it would be before Profit called.

Profit had taken the top off the car, and the sun was hot on his shoulders and arms as he drove the uneven highway. A single drop of perspiration began at his hairline and worked its way haltingly down his forehead. Before it reached his sunglasses he took his hand from the shift lever, wiped his brow with his fingers, pressed the heel of his hand against the speckles of gunpowder around his eye. The eye twitched as he saw the red dirt road. He hoped the clay dirt was dry enough not to be slippery — the Porsche was exactly the wrong vehicle to take down a pitted, muddy road that was little better than a cattle trail.

The bottom of the car scraped the top of a low embankment, then the front bumper scraped the upside of a shallow dip. When the trail leveled, he looked in the rearview mirror to watch the heavy foliage close behind him; he enjoyed the sense of being swallowed by the pine woods, hidden by the thick undergrowth. Branches scraped the side of the car. The engine labored in first gear. It took half an hour to travel the two miles to his house. He parked in the converted chicken coop just as the white needle on the temperature gauge swung into the red.

In the dark garage Profit took off his sunglasses and pushed both arms straight out against the wheel, stretching, rolling his head and yawning luxuriously. He heard a low hum of wasps hovering about a nest, and momentarily he had a feeling of security, of safety. Although he kept two apartments in the city, Profit had bought the small house two years before, and for two years he had put money into it continuously. It amused him to see the money's power, to see the crumbling shell of a trapper's cabin transformed into a contemporary two-bedroom house. The house was the first place he had ever called home. He was sorry he would have to sell it.

He got out of the car and shut the door quietly. He reminded himself to spray the garage with insecticide. At the far end of the yard, he saw, Debbie was intently driving the tractor among the few remaining trees in the open clearing. The trailing gangmower made swirling patterns in the ankle-deep grass. She hadn't seen him pull into the garage, and he ducked into the house before she caught sight of him. He didn't want the lawn left half finished.

Inside, he took a quick tour of the house to see what had been accomplished since his last trip out. He was pleased by the huge crystal chandelier that had been hung from the living room ceiling, but he was annoyed by the new pastel blue in his bedroom. There were two new kitchen appliances, a dishwasher and a trash compactor. He took a bottle of beer from the refrigerator, dropped it in the compactor drawer, pressed the yellow start button, and waited to hear the glass crunch. Behind him the kitchen door slammed shut.

Debbie was three steps into the kitchen before she saw Profit; startled, she stopped in midstride and stood motionless, one hand to her throat. Her blue eyes flashed angrily.

"Damn," she said sharply, "at least you could've told me you were here."

Debbie was tall and slender, and her tense posture emphasized the bony angularity of her body.

"I didn't want to interrupt your yard work," Profit said, and turned away from the trash compactor. He smiled. In the compactor drawer, the beer bottle crunched with a sickening sound.

"You can be such a jerk," Debbie said, her voice matter-of-fact. With one hand she pulled up the collar of her T-shirt and wiped her face. "When did you get back?"

"Just now." Profit moved forward and gave her a brief, obligatory hug. "You're soaking wet," he said, and moved past her to the refrigerator.

"I'm sweating like a pig — that's what happens when you work, you know." Debbie took the beer Profit offered and rubbed the cold bottle on her face and neck. "I don't suppose it would do any good to ask where you've been?"

"Working," Profit replied automatically.

Debbie put the bottle of beer on the counter and in one quick motion pulled her T-shirt over her head. Her pendulous breasts seemed too large for her thin chest to support.

"Sheen got back a week ago." She unzipped her jeans. "I'm going to take a shower."

Profit started to say something, then thought better of it.

Debbie kicked off her jeans, left them in a heap on the floor, walked naked to the kitchen door, pushed through it. Profit stared after her until the door stopped swinging. He gave an exaggerated shrug, a self-reassuring gesture of nonchalance, then took a long swallow of his beer and turned to look out the window at the freshly cut grass. The yard seemed somehow fragile, a temporary island assaulted on all sides by a sea of thick, wild underbrush.

Profit would be glad to be rid of Debbie. She had always been too close to his business, too close from the very beginning; in a way, she had been the beginning. Debbie had introduced him to her previous boyfriend, Moses, and Moses had become his key connection in Miami, a connection that led to a seemingly endless supply of high-grade coke provided at a fair market price. Profit knew that Debbie and Moses were still close and that he had to keep Debbie happy because a word spoken in anger could sever the connection — and he needed that connection a little while longer. Profit thought then of Moses and tried to picture the Cuban's face, but all he could remember was the house with the red leather furniture and the red shag rug.

Then Profit suddenly thought of Sheen, of the frightening directness of his expression and of the coldness he could aim like a weapon. Profit smiled with his lips but not at all with his eyes.

He finished his beer, turned away from the window, dropped the empty bottle into the compactor drawer. Again he pressed the yellow start button. As he left the kitchen the empty beer bottle exploded with a sound so loud it was startling.

The door to the bathroom was open, and the newly installed floor-to-ceiling mirrors were covered with steam from the shower. On the mirror nearest the towel rack Profit wrote with a bar of soap a large dollar sign followed by a small question mark before he went into the bedroom and sprawled face down on the king-size bed. He heard the water stop and the shower door open. When Debbie walked into the bedroom, he rolled onto one side and propped his head on his arm.

"The receipt for the mirrors is in that drawer," Debbie said, pointing at the small table by the bed. "They cost twenty-seven hundred dollars."

Profit turned his head and looked at the drawer as if he could see into it. "Don't put any more money into the house," he said.

Debbie stopped toweling her hair. "Why?"

"I'm going to need money for a while," Profit replied, and kicked off his shoes. One shoe dropped to the floor; the other stayed on the bed by his foot.

Debbie looked at him for a long moment, a puzzled expression on her face. She knew better than to ask why twice. Questions directed to Profit invariably had an inverse result: one knew less after a question than before. Even the hint of query caused him to become vague or to change the subject. She shrugged, brushed the shoe off the bed, and started again to towel her hair.

"Okay," she said. "How did Sheen work out?"

Profit rolled onto his back and threw both arms over his head.

"I think I'll get you a push mower for Christmas," he said, smiling, "so you can cut the grass in closer to the house."

In spite of herself, Debbie returned the smile.

"You shit."

"How do you know so much about Sheen?"

"How do you think? Andrea called — several times, in fact. She wasn't very happy about Sheen working with you."

"She doesn't have to be. What did she say?"

"Sheen hadn't told her anything specific, only that he had agreed to help you. I didn't know what to tell her since that was the first *I* had heard about it. Andrea isn't very fond of you."

Profit thought suddenly of the hotel room that had overlooked the huge white cathedral. He remembered the garish blue wallpaper with the black stripes and the wide feather bed that was so unlike a real mattress; and he remembered lying full length, ear to the floor, trying to hear Andrea and her mother plan the day so he could suggest what they had already agreed on. And he knew that by having shared the time in Europe, by having shared the isolation imposed by the foreign language and the strange city, by having gone to the museums, the galleries, and the cathedrals, he had formed a bond as real, as recallable as the bond formed between survivors of the same shipwreck. Profit turned back onto his side, and his shrewd eyes were bright and pleased, as if he had just read a favorable balance sheet.

"Andrea likes me well enough," he said.

"You're wrong about that. She still blames you for what happened to Hal."

"I just sell the stuff. What they do with it is their business."

"Moses wouldn't agree," Debbie said.

Profit started to reply harshly, thought better of it, shrugged, and said, "Moses can afford not to agree. Have you heard from him?"

Debbie gave a quick, curt nod.

"He called three days ago to wish me a happy birthday."

"Oh, Jesus," Profit said, and slapped his forehead. "I forgot all about your birthday." He reached out, grabbed Debbie by the wrist, and pulled her onto the bed. "I'm sorry," he said, careful to look her directly in the eye. "Put on something dressy, and pack a bag. We'll get a suite at the Royal Orleans for tonight. We'll have a nice dinner. Tomorrow we'll shop for your present."

He kissed her lightly on the breast and trailed his hand over her stomach.

"Would you like to invite Andrea and Sheen to come along?"

Debbie drew back her head to look at him. Her eyes were questioning.

"I'd like that," she said, "but by the time we get into town it will be late, and I doubt they'll come. Andrea has early classes, and Sheen has work."

Profit's head jerked up. "Sheen kept his job?"

"Of course he did. What did you expect?"

Profit shook his head in disbelief. Usually the first taste of easy money made people stick to him like humming insects to a no-pest strip.

"When did he go back?" he asked.

"Andrea said he got in early in the morning and went to work that same day. She was pleased, to say the least."

Profit pushed himself away from Debbie and sat up.

"That bitch," he said, his voice low, the words hissing through his teeth. His hands clenched into fists. He needed Sheen, needed him unencumbered and ready to work, *willing* to work. And he realized then that the lever he needed would not be something as simple as money.

5

FROM HIS bedroom Sheen heard the irritating noise of the air conditioner, and he reminded himself to caulk the windows. Almost immediately he wondered what it was that was making him so lethargic and apathetic. In his hand the nearly empty glue bottle made an obscene splattering sound as he squeezed it. A thin stream of white glue formed a small droplet, which he spread with a straight pin.

For a week after his return from San Francisco, Sheen had continued to feel as anxious as he had felt the first morning back. The meaninglessness of his daily routine seemed magnified by the easy money he had made. At night he dreamed of the cashier's check he knew was in the mail, fleeting images that were so disturbing they interrupted his sleep and made him realize that the check's symbolic content was far more important to him than its cash value. For a week he had driven to work rather than take the streetcar so he could go home for lunch to listen to the children at play on the playground — and to await the mail.

The check had arrived sandwiched between the utility bill and a sweepstakes entry, and strangely, he had both read the rules of the sweepstakes and verified the amount of the bill before he had turned his attention to the check. Confronted by the check itself rather than by his dream of it, he had felt an almost overwhelming indifference as he had held the light blue paper stamped and machine-signed with dark blue ink.

That afternoon he had opened a savings account. The next evening he had paid his rent and taken Andrea to the ballet. While the dream did not recur, the feeling of indifference remained, and Sheen was astute enough to know that there was more to the letdown than a failed expectation. He suspected that his apathy was a mental pose, a way of hiding from himself a genuine problem he did not know how to solve. In the past, working with his hands had provided a distraction, and for want of something to do, and simply to keep himself moving, he had begun a project of his own design.

At the public library he had sorted through books and magazines, looking for pictures of the northern California coast, and he had found six that he judged to be neither too romantic nor too severe. He made photocopies of the pictures and then went to an art supply shop to buy heavy posterboard and foam-core board, new X-acto knives, and white glue. From a restaurant supply house he purchased a large white maple cutting board.

In his bedroom he had taped the pictures to the wall over his desk, and with a casual precision had laid out tools and materials. Early the next morning he began to model a house. He worked without renderings or plans, and the model took shape quickly. By the time Andrea got up for school he had a site, an approximation of a cliff made with stepped-back contours of foam-core board.

Sheen wasn't sure what he was trying to accomplish; he knew only that he took great pleasure in working with his hands. At times he fell into spells when it seemed his hands worked on their own, independent of his control. In those moments he looked at them with wonder, entranced by the innumerable functions and uses that hands could accommodate. Independent of the need for assurances, his hands worked simply because that was what they were made to do. The sinews and tissues and bones coordinated in movements and feelings for reasons that required no explanation.

Even though he could work on it only before and after his job, the model was nearly complete six days after he started it. The design was a disappointment — it showed no real improvement over the coast house he had visited — but the workmanship was flawless. On Saturday Andrea ran errands, and except for the rattling windowpanes, the apartment was quiet as Sheen applied the glue that would hold the house to its base. When the phone began to ring, he wiped away the glue he had just spread rather than rush the final placement.

Hearing Profit's voice, Sheen felt the same sense of deep familiarity he had experienced when the check had arrived.

"So, what have you been up to?" Profit asked, his voice cool but tinged with suppressed emotion.

"Not too much," Sheen said. "How about you?"

"I'm in jail," Profit replied, "and I could use some help."

The chill began in the base of Sheen's spine, worked its way up his back, settled into his neck. "You're where?" he asked.

In the background he heard a gruff voice say, "Two minutes"; the voice reverberated, and he pictured the holding cell at central lockup, the cage with the gray steel floors and walls.

"I think you heard me," Profit replied.

"But how?"

"I don't know, and it's not important at the moment. There must've been some mistake — like talking on the phone." Profit tapped his fingernail against the phone to make a clicking sound. "I haven't been able to reach my attorney. I thought you might know the procedure."

"I guess I know it, but I know it only from the other side." Sheen hesitated as if he were trying to thread a needle while looking at it in a mirror. "Has your bail been set?"

"I'm going to the magistrate now. One of the detectives told me to expect about a hundred thousand, a hundred fifty thousand at the outside."

Sheen whistled into the phone. When he had seen bail figures posted before, they had just been numbers.

"Yeah, that's what I thought too," Profit continued. "I don't have that kind of money, but maybe you could get together ten percent for the bail bondsman."

"I could get maybe half, but the rest — "

"I'm kind of in the *closet* here," Profit interrupted, emphasizing his words carefully, "but I'm *safe.*"

"Good," Sheen replied, covering himself as he looked for a pencil.

"Somebody vomited on the floor, but other than that, it's just boring. I've been here, who knows, forty-seven, nineteen, twenty-six, thirty-three hours?"

Sheen wrote the numbers on the base of the model, assuming that they were the combination to a closet safe.

"You can find my attorney at his house in the country. Andrea will give you directions."

"I'll give it a try."

"Do better than that, Sheen," Profit said, and the line went dead — whether cut off at the two-minute limit or hung up abruptly, it was impossible to tell.

The car veered, thumping on the plastic lane dividers, and Sheen chided himself for allowing his thoughts to drift.

Sheen knew that Profit had been dealing long before he had met him, but he could not shake the feeling that he was somehow at fault, somehow to blame for the arrest. What was worse, he knew that Profit would share the same thought. The timing of the arrest was so coincidental, suspicion had to fall on Sheen.

"He can think what he wants," Sheen said out loud. He knew he was no part of the arrest. No resolution, no justification was necessary. He felt lucky to have missed the bust — ex-cops did not fare well in prison.

The two-lane highway was so uneven, at cruising speed it tossed the car side to side like a small boat on a choppy sea. With relief Sheen saw the red dirt road, turned off, and began the arduous route to Profit's house. Just as he became convinced that he had taken the wrong road — Andrea's directions, reluctantly given, had been sketchy — the house came into view. Sheen saw Debbie on the front porch, rocking in the porch swing, and he waved as he got out of his car.

Debbie returned the wave, put her feet down to stop the swing, stood up, and shoved her hands into the hip pockets of her jeans.

"Sheen? What are you doing out here? I thought you were the carpenter — I've been waiting for the son of a gun for two hours. Where's Profit?"

Sheen stopped halfway up the steps to the porch. "I'd rather not say," he said, looking up at Debbie. "He gave me the combination to his safe. Which closet is it in?"

Debbie's blue eyes hardened as she took her hands out of her pockets and crossed her arms over her chest.

"Why?" she asked. Her mouth did not recover from the question but remained stretched in a thin line.

"I'm going to take some money."

"Oh, if that's the case — " she said, her voice sarcastic, a verbal sneer she checked only when she saw Sheen's deep-set green eyes flash a warning. "Would you mind telling me what this is all about?"

Sheen raised his hand from his knee, palm up and fingers spread in a gesture of helplessness. "I can't, Debbie, but Profit will explain, I'm sure."

"I'm not so sure of that." Debbie rubbed her arm from elbow to shoulder, and her face became concerned. "Is he in trouble?"

Sheen was deliberately slow to respond.

Debbie saw she would get no answers from him, and her concern changed back to anger. "Oh, take the damn money. The safe is in the bedroom." She turned, pulled open the door, and held it so Sheen could go through it first. "He's never trusted *me* with the combination," she said as he passed, "but he trusts his *friends.*"

The door slammed shut.

"Go to your left."

Sheen moved quickly, anxious to complete the task. Behind the mirrored closet doors, the stainless steel floor safe was concealed under a shoe rack and a thick layer of carpet. Sheen moved the shoes out of the way, folded back the carpet, knelt, and spun the dial. It took him two tries to dial the combination correctly. Beside him, Debbie was quiet, but she watched closely: she wanted to see how much money he took.

The deep steel cylinder was jammed full. Sheen removed as much as he could hold in both hands and put it on the floor beside the safe. There were eleven thick sheaves of bills, each one wrapped tightly with a rubber band. The thickness of the sheaves varied, but each packet totaled five thousand dollars; fifties and hundreds seemed to be the denominations of choice. Sheen put five of the packets in his shirt, then returned the others to the safe and reset it. He backed out of the closet and closed it, gave Debbie a curt nod of thanks, started out of the house.

Before he had crossed the porch Debbie was on the phone to Miami, reporting to Moses.

The drive back from Profit's house seemed protracted, and as Sheen neared New Orleans's suburbs, he felt both a sense of relief and a greater sense of haste. He tightened his seat belt, adjusted the rearview mirror, gripped the steering wheel firmly, and waited for the last few miles to pass: he was anxious to find a pay phone and call a bail bondsman.

Sheen took the first exit past the airport and promptly got lost. Confronted by row after row of identical houses in a new suburb, he could neither find his way back to the highway nor find a phone. He turned down one street after another until, aggravated, he stopped to ask directions; but when he got out of his car and approached a house, he realized the house was recently finished and unoccupied. Then he realized that the street was new and *all* the houses were unoccupied, still in various stages of completion. There were no automobiles in the driveways, no grass, no open windows — no signs of life. Sheen was the only person on the street, inside or outside, and his sense of waking in the middle of a dream was so strong it was disconcerting. He returned to his car and went back in the direction from which he had come, certain that there was a simple way out and a phone nearby.

Although he had never had business with them, Sheen had met bail bondsmen before. When he finally found a pay phone, he thumbed through the Yellow Pages looking for a familiar name, but he found none and simply called a number at random. He knew exactly what tone to assume, a tone that would match his mood perfectly.

A gruff voice answered, "Barrish."

"Yeah," Sheen said, his voice harsh. "You got the bail schedule for this afternoon?"

"You want the schedule, you go to the magistrate. You got legs."

"I also got fifteen grand in my pocket says I don't leave this phone."

"Hold on," Barrish said. His breath made a regular whistling sound, in and out. "All right, I got it. Which one?"

"Possession with intent," Sheen said. "Cocaine."

"Hah!" The bail bondsman snorted with evident satisfaction. "You're going to need more than fifteen thousand, son: bail for your buddy is two hundred thousand. In case you forgot your calculator somewhere, ten percent of that comes to *twenty* thousand dollars."

Sheen pulled the armored phone cord tight, and the serrated metal pressed into the heel of his hand.

"I got it. Type it up. I'll meet you at Parish Prison. You got fifteen minutes."

"Who're you kidding, son?"

"My name is Mr. Vicedomini to you, asshole. You got fifteen minutes. Sixteen minutes and I start dropping coins. They got plenty numbers left in this book."

The whistling sound, in and out, repeated itself twice before Barrish said, "All right, Mr. Asshole, I'll be there. If you don't have the cash, I'll knock your dick into your watch pocket, got it? And leave your smart mouth at home, or I might do it anyway."

"Don't show up, don't get the chance. Fifteen minutes," Sheen said, and hung up the phone.

As he left the phone booth Sheen saw the elevated expressway nearby, and he wondered how he had gotten so turned around so easily. He shook his head slowly, and his lips moved as if he were speaking. Just then he realized that the gruff conversation had actually improved his humor, but he didn't take time to consider why. He had to hustle to beat the bail bondsman to the prison.

The midafternoon traffic was light, and fourteen minutes after he had hung up the phone Sheen parked in the "police only" zone in front of the prison. He had been waiting less than a minute when he saw Barrish come around the corner. He knew it had to be Barrish: only money could make such an obese man waddle so fast.

Although he was less than five and a half feet tall, Barrish weighed over three hundred pounds. His massive bulk stretched a powder-blue leisure suit to bursting. As he walked, tilting his body back and forth so as not to bend his knees, his bulbous cheeks and triple chins jounced, the chins oddly out of sync with the cheeks, as if there were no connection between them. His dark, shrewd eyes were made small by fat puffs of flesh. His hair was greased straight back from his forehead and flecked with dandruff.

"You Vicedomini?" Barrish asked.

"Mr. Asshole to you, fat man," Sheen replied.

Barrish smiled, his small mouth puckering and exposing small yellow teeth.

"You got the money?"

"You got the contract?"

Barrish reached one thick arm into an inside pocket and took out an unsealed white envelope; by way of response, Sheen reached into his shirt and pulled out four packets of bills.

Barrish smiled again, and said, "Step into my office." He rang the prison bell, and added, "If you're carrying a piece, put it in your car. They got a metal detector at the gate."

67

Sheen shrugged noncommittally as the gate opened, moving slowly on its well-greased track. In the prison yard there was the smell of disinfectant and confined men, an acrid, piercing smell that permeated the receiving area, the guard shack, and the bleak, windowless room where Barrish sat behind a metal desk to count the money. Overhead a single fluorescent tube hummed, changing pitch, high and low. Barrish leaned back in the metal chair, rested his hands on his belly, licked one fat forefinger, counted twenty bills, licked again. His lips moved as he counted, and his breath made a soft wheezing sound, in and out. Finally he put the four sheaves of bills deep into an inside pocket and took out the bail contract, laying it flat on the desk and smoothing it with his fat fist.

"Your boy jumps and I'm sending out the dogs," he said.

Sheen looked past him at the peeling green paint on the wall. "Sounds like a personal problem," he replied.

Barrish leaned forward until his belly pushed against the desk. "It is, but you tell him anyway." He put both hands flat on the desk and pushed himself to his feet. He looked at Sheen directly, curiously.

"You're either an ex-con or an ex-cop, I can't figure which." Barrish moved awkwardly around the desk, taking small steps sideways and pushing his hands heavily against the desk top. "You gave yourself away at the gate. You *knew* there was no metal detector — everybody else looks to see where it is." The bail bondsman smiled, amused by his own observation, not expecting a reply. "I'll catch your buddy upstairs. He'll be down in a minute. You wait outside."

Sheen opened the door to leave, and said, "Thanks, Barrish."

"It's been a pleasure," Barrish replied, and patted his shirt over the money. "Be sure to tell your friends about me."

Sheen walked quickly to the guard shack, trying not to notice the prison smell. Outside, he leaned against the warm front of his car, crossed his arms over his chest, and watched two work-release prisoners wash a police car. There was an overt violence in the way they slapped the soapy chamois against the car and rubbed with a vengeance. In the guard tower a silhouette moved behind the windows. When the prisoners had finished one car, they moved to another.

It was half an hour before Profit came out across the prison yard. He was unshaven, and there were deep circles below his eyes, circles so dark that they blended into the green-black speckling of embedded gunpowder. His hair was matted and dirty. He moved with a slow deliberateness, a purposeful trudge that indicated a tight rein on strong emotion. Profit had never before been arrested, and the experience had left him exhausted, frightened, and angry. When he got close, it took an effort for Sheen not to turn away from the prison smell he exuded.

Profit nodded curtly to Sheen, jerking his chin down and up in more of a twitch than a greeting, then ran his hand indecisively through his hair and got into the car. Sheen got in on the driver's side and started the motor before he reached into his shirt, took out the remaining packet of money, handed it to Profit.

"I brought extra," he explained.

Profit looked at the thick sheaf of bills, allowing it to rest momentarily on his open palm.

"Good thing," he said, and lifted himself off the seat to put the money in his pocket. "Was Debbie at the house?"

"She was waiting for the carpenter," Sheen said. "I didn't tell her anything, but I think she knew there had been some trouble."

"She knew, all right," Profit said, more to himself than to Sheen. "The bitch. I told her not to put any more money into the house, and she calls a carpenter." Profit placed his little finger between his teeth and chewed the nail. "Go to my apartment — it's uptown, Short Street at St. Charles Avenue. I want to get my car."

Sheen moved the shift lever to reverse, and the transmission clanged hollowly.

"So what happened?" he asked.

Profit put his foot against the dashboard and his elbow on his knee; with the heel of his hand he rubbed his eye.

"How the fuck do I know? I woke up with a shotgun in

my face. I thought I was dead. I was actually relieved when somebody finally showed a badge." Profit again chewed the nail on his little finger; blood seeped from the cuticle. "The motherfuckers. I didn't even hear them kick the door. I wake up, and this big guy is kneeling on my chest jamming the barrel of a shotgun into my mouth. I hear other guys moving behind him tearing up the apartment, but I can't see anything but this big guy, just looking at me, *wanting* me to move. They know they scare the piss out of you, and they don't say a word." Profit tore off a piece of nail. "They got two kilos. I had just picked it up yesterday. I didn't even have time to cut it." He shook his head slowly side to side. "Man, they took all that, too: the cut, the scales, the strainers, even the goddamn bag sealer — I told them I took sandwiches to work."

Profit pounded his fist on the raised knee. There was the solid thud of flesh against flesh and a sharp crack as the plastic glovebox door split beneath his foot.

"Son of a bitch, Sheen, all I needed was some help, and I would have been out delivering the stuff, not sleeping with it. All I needed was somebody to cover my back."

Profit jerked his head to one side and looked out the window. After a moment he unclenched his fist and rubbed his knee. Sheen saw blood dripping from the gnawed nail, but he didn't say anything. They were near the apartment before Profit looked away from the window and said, "Hey, I'm sorry. It's been a long night."

Sheen turned his head toward Profit but did not look at him. "Don't worry about it," he said. He saw Profit's blue Porsche, pulled in behind it, put his car in neutral. "Where are you going now?"

Profit shrugged uncertainly. "I don't know — out to the country, I guess. I don't even want to *see* the inside of this place." He jerked his thumb at the small apartment building. "But if Debbie is impossible, I'll come back anyway." He sat forward and pushed on both ends of the glovebox door until the fresh crack was invisible. "I'll get you some glue," he said. He sat back, opened the car door, turned to Sheen. "I won't be able to work for a while, and there's a lot out. If you're available, I'd like to get you to tie up some loose ends."

Before Sheen could reply, Profit got out of the car, shut the door, bent from the waist, and looked back in through the open window.

"And say, Sheen, thanks."

Sheen looked at the jagged crack in the glovebox, the bloody cuticle on the hand that gripped the door, the chalky whiteness of Profit's complexion.

"Did you get a look at the warrant?" he asked.

Profit shook his head. "No. Why?"

"The warrant has to give a reason, the probable cause for the search. You can't do anything until you know what went wrong."

"Oh," Profit said, and ran one hand over his stubbly cheeks. "The detectives told me that: they had an informant."

Profit slapped the door in a gesture of finality. He stood up straight, walked to his car, got in.

Sheen saw a puff of blue smoke when the Porsche started. The engine made a strange noise, a resonant, clattering drone that sounded somehow angry. Sheen suddenly remembered a phone booth nearby, and he pulled away from the curb. He wanted to know more about Profit's arrest.

In an empty corner of a shopping center parking lot, Tony Avila sat in a dark blue Ford. The motor was running, and heat rose in waves from the hood of the car; the Ford was in gear.

Tony Avila was not a tall man, but he was broad in the shoulders and thick through the chest. In proportion to his long, powerful torso, his arms and legs were short, and when the seat was adjusted so that his feet reached the pedals comfortably, his chest was so close to the wheel that he had to bend his thick arms at an acute angle to drive. To Tony, however, the awkward posture often was an advantage. On surveillance, when he used binoculars he could slouch low in the seat, rest the lenses on top of the wheel, and hold the image very steady for hours, unaffected by the headaches that frequently plagued others.

Through his high-resolution German-made field glasses, a stop sign seemed to float in the thick, shimmering air, and behind it a woman awaiting a bus seemed weightless as she paced back and forth. Normally Tony Avila found the view through the field glasses soothing — people and objects were "out there," intimately close yet nonthreatening — but just now he could not seem to get the binoculars to focus. Irritated, he returned them to their case, pushed back the seat, and stretched out his legs. As he took a cigarette from the pack in his pocket, Tony idly wondered how many hours he had sat in a car, waiting to meet someone; more immediately, he wondered what Sheen wanted. It had been eight months since he had heard from him; then, out of nowhere, Sheen had called to set up a quick meet. Tony nervously drummed the steering wheel with his fingers. He turned on the radio, changed stations, turned it back off — the English annoyed him, and there were no stations that broadcast in Spanish. He opened a window and put the cigarette in the ashtray before he leaned forward and took the small .22 derringer from the holster on his ankle; twisting to his right, he slid it between the headrest and the seat back on the passenger side. Tony Avila was afraid, afraid of Sheen and the history he represented, afraid of the power Sheen had over him. When he stretched his arm along the top of the seat, the derringer was less than six inches from his hand.

Just as he finished his cigarette and flicked it out of the window, he saw Sheen pull into the parking lot. Tony honked his horn and waved cheerfully. Sheen parked two spaces away and walked over to the passenger side of the unmarked police car.

"Hey, amigo," Tony said as Sheen got into the car. "Long time no see."

Sheen closed the door, sat sideways on the seat, draped his left arm over the seat back.

"It hasn't been that long, Tony." Sheen looked at him directly with eyes that were wary and hard. "How have you been?"

"Good. Real good. I'm up for sergeant." Tony Avila laughed and pinched his own dark cheek. "Affirmative action, amigo. Cuban is now beautiful."

"I hear you got married again."

"Yeah? How'd you hear that?"

"You sent me an invitation."

"That's right," Tony said, and laughed again. "I did. If you sent a present, thanks."

"I didn't send a present for the same reason I haven't called, or visited, or written," Sheen said, the evenness of his tone not concealing his anger. "It was too soon, too close."

Tony Avila twisted to his right to face Sheen and moved his hand along the seat back until it bumped Sheen's forearm, but Sheen didn't change position, didn't move the arm that was over the seat, so Tony put his hand in his lap and twisted one finger until the knuckle popped. His deep brown eyes were uneasy.

"It hasn't gotten any lighter, has it?"

"Did you expect it to just go away?"

"No," Tony replied, his voice low, "I never expected it to go away." Tony's eyes became distant, as if he were seeing some far-off scene. "I dream about it," he said. "I dream I'm there in the bedroom when he breaks in — no, it's not what you think. My legs are like concrete, so heavy I can't move. I see him come through the window and stand up straight, hardly breathing, waiting for his eyes to adjust to the dark. When I shout to Giselle, she doesn't hear me, but *he* does. I shout many times. He turns his head and looks at me, somehow knowing I can't move, knowing she won't hear me; then he takes out the knife and walks to the bed. I wake up and I'm still screaming. Giselle must have screamed like I do in my dream, with no one but him to hear."

"Old ground, Tony. There's no use going over and over what's done."

"I can't help it, Sheen." Tony twisted another finger, but the knuckle didn't crack. "Did you see what he did to her? Did you see her face? He cut her so badly."

"I saw it, Tony," Sheen said softly, but his memory of the woman's face was overshadowed by his memory of the dark batture, the pulsing tugboat diesel, the man's face contorting grotesquely as the small-caliber bullet entered his ear.

"They never should have let him go. They should have held him on *something.*"

Sheen looked past Tony at the shopping center's pastel pink facade. "You can't beat up a suspect in the interrogation room and expect the confession to hold water. They didn't have any choice — the confession was all they had."

"But that's why he confessed to me."

"You should never have gone near him," Sheen said, his voice sharp. "*Never.* You knew better. *You* made the mistake."

"He didn't just cut her face, Sheen."

Sheen looked at Tony, and his voice softened. "I know that, Tony, but he wasn't after you or Giselle in particular — he didn't know she was a cop's wife."

"That's supposed to make me feel better? Once he put it together, he used me too."

"You gave him the opportunity. He was sick, but he wasn't a fool. It almost worked." Sheen raised one shoulder and dropped it in a resigned shrug that conveyed a great weariness. "You're lucky you didn't get sued for the beating you gave him. *You* made the mistake," he said again.

Tony twisted his ring finger, and the knuckle made a sickening grating sound before it popped.

"I know," he said, his voice very low, a whisper. "That's why in the dream I can't move: I know everything I do will come out wrong. Sometimes I feel that I must get it straight, somehow."

Sheen turned on the seat and looked at the shimmering waves of heat rising from the dark hood. He spread one hand over his face and pulled down, stretching the skin and pulling it taut.

"Are you going to confess?"

Tony looked down and did not reply. He put his arm on the seat back, his hand near Sheen's headrest.

"You can probably cop a plea," Sheen said. He spoke in the casual manner of a disinterested counselor. "When you explain the mitigating circumstances, they're likely to reduce the charge. The media are a factor, but a good attorney will bring out the fact that you were a husband first, a policeman second. So you cop to manslaughter, live through prison, and you're back on the street in five years — if they don't figure out that the other killings were blinds. If they *do* figure it out, you'll fry."

Sheen turned his head and looked at Tony Avila directly. His eyes were as hard and as cold as his voice. "Keep it a personal problem."

Tony Avila leaned forward. Two fingers of his right hand slipped under the headrest and made contact with the handle of the derringer.

"Are you threatening me, Sheen?"

"How can I threaten *you,* Tony? You're the cop. I'm the one they think is the murderer, the vigilante. I'm advising you to keep it a personal problem, but you make up your own mind. If you have to do it, do it, but give me a week's jump — you owe me that much. The courts frown on complicity, even unwitting complicity."

"You know I'm not going to cop, Sheen."

"No, I don't," Sheen said, and looked at him with a directness that was frightening. "I don't know that *I* won't. Sometimes it gets pretty heavy to carry. But if I decide to do it, I promise you the same thing, a week's jump."

Tony knew Sheen well enough to know that he would not take his own promise lightly, and, relieved, he pulled his hand away from the derringer. If Sheen *did* decide to cop, he would have a week, and many arrangements could be made in a week.

"Enough," Tony said with finality. "What do you need? I got to get back to the office."

Sheen pushed in the dashboard ashtray, then pulled it back out. "Have you ever heard of a guy street name Profit?"

"White guy? Deals coke? What you need with him?"

"My business."

Tony's deep brown eyes studied Sheen's face. "I hope you're not too close to him, Sheen. He's a punk. I know that for a solid fact."

"From what source?"

"From the casebook. I never worked it, but we had a client who was going to give him up. We played it by the numbers, one, two, three, nothing to it; then, just before the bust, the client goes rabbit, nowhere to be found. No information, no bust. The end." Tony shrugged. "It happens. I guess she got scared."

Sheen's head jerked up.

"What was her name?"

"I don't remember — it's been a while. She was real pretty, though: big brown eyes, curly hair."

"Was her name Andrea?"

"It could've been," Tony said, and shrugged again. "I don't remember. The punk got himself popped anyway — yesterday, I think."

With his forefinger Sheen pressed his lower lip hard against his teeth, using the sharp pain as a focus.

"How badly?" he asked.

"He's down, but he's not out, not yet. We had some problems." Tony held up his hand, palm flat and fingers extended as if he were about to stop a swinging door. "Don't ask about the problems. They embarrass me."

"Was the same woman the informant?"

Tony rotated his raised hand until the palm turned up in a gesture of uncertainty. "I don't think so, but it wasn't my case."

"I want to see the file."

"You in that deep?" Tony asked. When Sheen didn't reply, he added, "You're a fool."

"I'd still like the file."

Tony shook his head. "I can't get it. Maybe in a couple of weeks, but right now it's with the new grand jury."

"He was just arrested last night."

"He never should have been, I hear. Anyway, that's all I know. The file was sealed and passed to the grand jury — I only know that much because I was in the office when the federal marshals arrived with subpoenas." Tony rapped a knuckle against the plastic wood on the dashboard. "I will say this: I'm glad as shit I was nowhere near that bust. Heads are going to roll. Call me in a couple of weeks, and I'll give you the details."

"Is Profit going to walk?"

"Nobody knows." Tony looked at his watch, turned, and put both hands on the steering wheel. "I gotta go, Sheen. I'm wasting the taxpayers' money."

"I *will* call you, Tony," Sheen said, and opened the door.

Tony replied, his voice oddly challenging, "Do that, amigo."

He put the blue police light in its magnetic holder on the dashboard, and as soon as Sheen had gotten out and closed the door he stomped on the accelerator and twisted the wheel. The police car spun in a tire-squealing turn toward the exit.

For a long moment Sheen stood motionless, alone in the empty corner of the parking lot. He ran his fingers through his hair. His face showed a curious mix of discordant emotions.

6

AS THE sun dropped behind the surrounding trees and the shadows lengthened across the open clearing, it seemed to Profit that the friendly quality that made the yard seem an oasis in the thick pine forest was changing: the tall trees began to form a dark, formidable wall that enclosed the yard and gave it the confining quality of a pen. Profit took a long swallow from the beer in his hand, emptying it; he turned away from the window and threw the bottle at the open compactor drawer. When it missed and clattered on the floor he slapped his thigh in frustration.

Profit was alone. Debbie was gone. Despite his anger when he had discovered her empty closet, when he had seen the uncluttered bathroom shelves and the plastic trash bag topped with odd scraps of paper, old cosmetics, and photographs torn in two, he had felt a peculiar emptiness, a hollowness, and he realized that he missed her. He retrieved the beer bottle and set it on the counter.

"The rats think the ship is sinking," he said out loud, without rancor, "but it's not." He got himself another beer from the refrigerator before he returned to his game.

Although he knew he was not technically very good at it, Profit played chess. The chessboard balanced on a waist-high wooden stool in the middle of the floor, he walked around and around it, standing first on one side, then on the other, playing against himself. Each move was punctuated by the sharp click of a stone piece on the stone board, and as if the click were that of a switch in his mind, Profit then moved mechanically to the other side of the board. The game seemed to refresh him, to exercise that part of his mind he valued most, and Profit had tried to nurture the self-contradictory ability to split his consciousness and genuinely to want one side, then the other, to win. When at the end of a game he felt simultaneously triumphant and defeated, he knew his concentration had been complete and that he had successfully compartmentalized adversarial positions. The only crutch he allowed himself was the chess set: the board and the pieces were gray and tan, neutral colors that blurred the distinction between the black side and the white side. He played with the undiluted narcissism of a boxer sparring with his own reflection in a full-length mirror.

When the phone rang, Profit moved so abruptly to answer it that his hip bumped the corner of the chessboard, and it fell to the floor with a heavy thud. Chessmen scattered. Profit said only, "I'll call you back," and hung up the phone. He had been expecting the call, and the keys to the truck were already in his pocket. He put the chessboard back on the stool, but he left the scattered pieces on the floor.

The fading light was deceptive, and Profit had trouble seeing the road well enough to anticipate bumps. Twice his head hit the roof before he stopped and put on his seat belt. Unnoticed, an empty soft drink can rolled back and forth across the worn rubber mat on the floor on the passenger side.

On the orange brick side wall of a two-pump gas station, there was a pay phone. Profit pulled in as close as possible to the phone and parked the truck. After he had dialed the number to Miami, he leaned back against the hood; the engine was hot, and he was sweating before the call was answered.

"Hey, how are you?" he asked when the line clicked open. The connection was poor, and he heard his own voice echoing down the line.

"Better than you, I hear," was the reply, the words distant and mechanical.

A pickup truck turned into the station and stopped nearby. A teenaged boy in a cowboy hat opened the driver's door, turned on his seat, and glared at Profit.

"That depends on what you heard," Profit said, volunteering nothing. He faced the wall, ignoring the cowboy who wanted to use the phone.

"For one thing, I heard you were in jail."

Shit, Profit swore to himself, then asked, "Was Debbie working for you?"

"That is not the matter that concerns us," Moses replied. "Tell me about your arrest."

"Have you seen her?"

There was a pause before Moses answered, and five quick tones beeped faintly on the line.

"Yes, I have seen her; no, she was not working for me. I will not ask again about what has happened to you."

With the key to his house Profit scraped a jagged line on the soft brick wall.

"It's under control."

"That's a first."

"Hey," Profit snapped, "do you want the story or not?"

"Sincere apologies. Please continue with your story."

On the two-lane highway in front of the gas station a dark blue Ford passed at high speed. Profit watched the red taillights fade as the car moved quickly into the distance.

"They kicked the door on my work apartment at about four in the morning. There was hardly anything there, less than two ounces and some equipment — the total loss was less than five thousand dollars. I was released as soon as the paperwork was done. It's an occupational hazard, Moses. Big deal. It's my problem."

"Yes, it is your problem. What concerns me is not *how much* was lost but *why* anything was lost at all. I hear you have a cop working for you, a man named Vicedomini."

"You hear a lot."

"If I don't look after my interests, who will? It is my practice to keep an eye on all my chippies."

"Fuck off," Profit answered, his voice sullen but not challenging. "There's no connection."

"But isn't it very much a coincidence?"

"No, it's not. Think about it. If he were still a cop, why would he pop me after just one run? He was a uniform, anyway. And he's still working for me. Why wasn't he brought in after the bust?"

"You're asking me questions; you're supposed to be giving me answers."

Profit leaned heavily on the key and gouged deeper into the brick wall. Orange dust coated the back of his hand.

"You're blowing it, Profit," Moses continued. "You've had a very good thing, and you've had it too easy. You must learn certain rules of business. Your friend is a liability. He has been very expensive already. It will only get worse."

"As long as it doesn't get back to you, it's not your business. You do what *you* have to do, and I'll do what *I* have to do. I *always* hold up my end. Always."

Moses's voice was calm and unruffled, patronizing. "Now there's a good boy. I'm glad we agree that *something* has to be done." Again the five quick tones sounded faintly. "When will you be down this way again?"

"Soon," Profit said. He started to add, "Tell Debbie to call me," but he thought better of it.

"Between now and then, try to avoid coincidence, Profit," Moses said, and broke the connection.

Profit listened for a moment to the dial tone and thought of the small house Moses used for storage, of the garbage cans filled with cocaine and the pungent medicinal smell that pervaded the air, a smell he associated with money — and retirement.

"On schedule," he said softly to himself.

He brushed the orange dust from his hand, wiped the key on his pants, turned away from the phone. He looked at the young cowboy and shrugged apologetically. As he stepped around the truck, he slapped one hand on the hood in a ringing gesture of satisfaction.

That same evening, Sheen sat at the desk in his bedroom and delicately cut his model into pieces that would fit into the trash. The razor-sharp X-acto blade sliced unevenly through the soft foam-core board and hard glue. Small curls of cardboard like little hairs littered the desk.

Andrea was furious. She stood next to the desk with her arms crossed and her feet apart, toes out. Her brown eyes were as hard as marbles.

"There isn't only one obligation," she said. "You have others: to *yourself* and to *me.*"

"I can maintain all three," Sheen replied evenly, "and he needs help."

"You'll throw your life away for him. Can't you see what he is?" She rapped her knuckles on the desk. "Look at me."

Sheen put down the X-acto knife and with the heel of his hand wiped the desk, pushing the small curls of cardboard into a pile.

"He's a friend."

"No! You're his friend; he doesn't know what it is to be a friend. He's out for himself and for himself only. That's something you better remember. He's using you. He uses *everyone.*"

Sheen pushed the pile of cardboard shavings off the corner of the desk into his other hand and squeezed the prickling, pulpy mass into a ball.

"Even Profit wouldn't bust himself," he said softly.

"You don't think so? Then you *really* don't know him. He'd have himself arrested — he'd have his mother arrested if he could make money from it. He ruins people for fun, and he needs something from you. He'll sell your friendship across the counter." Andrea turned away from the desk. For a moment she could get no other words out, then she said, "God, I regret I ever let you meet him."

"What does he need from me?" Sheen asked. "What can he get?"

82

Andrea turned back, and in her eyes there was a plea. "I'm begging you not to work for him. Isn't that enough?"

Sheen did not reply. The cardboard was doughy in his hand, and he dropped it in the trash.

Andrea stood in front of him, so close that her thigh was against his knee, and when she spoke her voice was low and hesitant, the words formed with difficulty.

"Before I met you I went out with a guy named Hal — you've heard me talk about him. He was very special to me. Hal was a big man, twice as big as you, but he was as gentle as he was big, even-tempered, soft-spoken. He was a carpenter." Andrea's eyes brimmed, but her voice became stronger and took on a matter-of-fact tone. "After I came back from Europe — after Profit had played that little game — Profit hired Hal to build his kitchen. Hal was happy working with his hands, and he did beautiful work. But Profit had him out in the country for two months. He started him on cocaine and started him on fast money, and Hal couldn't handle it. It was new to him, exciting and different, and it became his life. I wasn't much help because it was new to me too. I didn't see what was happening."

Andrea's eyes fixed on the X-acto knife. She reached out and turned it so that the tip of the blade pointed at herself.

"Hal started shooting the coke, then running coke and heroin, then just heroin. Have you ever watched that happen to someone you love? Have you ever seen that hunted look in a junkie's eyes, or seen a powerful man drop fifty pounds and look like an inmate in a concentration camp before he shoots himself so full of shit that he doesn't even notice the end of a scaffolding? He fell forty feet onto a brick patio."

Andrea looked directly at Sheen, and in her eyes there was a hard, brittle glint. "Do you know why Profit played *that* little game? Because he wanted Hal out of the way long enough to fuck me."

"And you think that's what he wants now?"

"You don't see it at all, do you? He lives his life through other people. He doesn't want me, he never wanted *me*, he

83

wants a part of us — that's what he needs from you, that's what he can get. He's already getting it. We're here talking about *him.*"

Sheen rubbed his open palm on his knee, and he felt the dust from the cardboard roll into tiny balls.

"Why do you still see him?"

"I don't know!" Andrea shook her head roughly, and a tear flew out of the corner of her eye. "I guess because I know I can handle it, or maybe because I'm just waiting to see him get his own."

Sheen looked closely at his palm, then he looked up and said, "Is that why you were going to give him up to the police, inform on him so you could see him get his own?"

For a moment Andrea stared at Sheen without comprehension, then she drew back as if she had been struck, and her face crumpled. She made her hands into fists and seemed to pound an invisible wall.

"I hate him. I hate him. I hate him."

She turned abruptly and went into the bathroom. Sheen heard her crying, but he stayed in his chair, his eyes fixed on some point only he could see.

"Even Profit wouldn't bust himself," he repeated quietly.

When Andrea came out of the bathroom, she was dry-eyed, and her face was a resolute mask.

"Are you going to work for him?" she asked, her voice clear.

When Sheen didn't reply, she stepped close to him and put her arm across his shoulders.

"I love you, Sheen, really I do, but I won't stay here, not for this." She moved away, took off the watch Sheen had given her, put it on the corner of the desk. "Give it back to me when you can keep your promise," she said.

Sheen did not reply, and he did not move. He heard her closet door open and the sounds of hangers clicking on and off the rack. He heard the dresser drawers open and close. He did not know why he was being so obstinate, when he knew he was wrong.

He stood up, put both hands in his pants pockets, and said, "I love you too, Andrea."

Andrea closed her suitcase and snapped the clasps.

"You don't have to leave," he said. "I'll be back in a couple of days."

Andrea lifted the suitcase from the bed and stood it upright on the floor. She walked up to Sheen and hugged him tightly, then put both arms around his neck.

"I *do* hope you come back safely," she whispered. "I *really* hope so."

She took her arms from around his neck, retrieved the suitcase, and walked out through the living room. At the front door she turned and waved.

Sheen smiled briefly and waved back. "See you in a couple of days," he said.

Andrea shut the door quietly but firmly as she left.

For a long moment Sheen stared at the door as if it might open again; then he went back into the bedroom. He picked up the small rectangular watch from the desk — it still felt warm — and put it in the top drawer of the dresser before he reached into the second drawer and took out his Colt .45 Gold Cup.

The pistol was a solid, balanced weight in his hand, something he knew he understood. He released the magazine, locked the slide to the rear, checked the chamber, released the slide. The simple procedure was reassuring, each step part of a predictable sequence. He laid both the pistol and the magazine on the bed. Beside them he placed a change of clothes and his flight bag. His flight departed in less than an hour.

Sheen packed carefully, straightened the apartment, connected a timer to the bedside lamp so that it would turn on at dusk and off at dawn. On the desk he left a brief note for Andrea.

At the airport, Sheen downgraded his ticket from first class to tourist. He was among the first to board, and he sat in a window seat at the very rear of the plane. Airborne and at cruising altitude, he felt the drone of the engines balancing the hum in his ears.

When Profit saw the gray BMW with Florida license plates turn into the diner's parking lot, his first impulse was to run, but a numbing fear held him motionless. His mind raced but produced no result, like a tire spinning on slick red clay. The BMW momentarily stopped behind his truck, then moved slowly forward and parked at an angle across two spaces.

Ronnie Fraiche got out of the car, looked through the diner's plate glass window, saw Profit, jerked his chin toward him in a gesture of recognition. Profit slumped back in the booth.

Fraiche's head seemed to swivel rather than to turn as he entered the diner and appraised it with obvious distaste. Halfway down the counter he stopped to look at the sliced apple pie that was beneath a clear plastic cover. One hand went to his mouth and pinched his lower lip. He slid into the booth across the table from Profit and wiped the table's plastic surface with a paper napkin before he leaned forward on his forearms.

"What the shit do you come out here for?" he asked, his voice matching his sour expression. "Look at this place. Have you seen that pie?"

"I like it," Profit said, and shrugged. "Why do you have Florida plates on your car?"

The judge looked surprised. "Taxes," he replied. "It's not my car — it's leased, registered to the company in Miami. Nobody should *own* a car."

Profit looked at the judge, his eyes wary and skeptical. "How did you find me?"

"Easy. The narcotics people have a file on you that looks like an encyclopedia. It names this place, says you hang out here sometimes, like if you can't sleep or have to make a call."

Involuntarily Profit's eyes shifted to the gas station across the street and the pay phone that hung on the orange brick side wall.

"You didn't answer at your house," the judge continued, "so I took a chance you'd be here."

"I thought you would be avoiding me like the clap."

"I should be," the judge replied, swiveling his head to look over his shoulder. "I'm crazy to be here." His voice dropped to a whisper. "Your phone is as hot as a two-dollar pistol."

Profit picked up a white plastic spoon that had come with his milk shake and bent it into an arc.

"So tell me something I didn't already know."

The judge's eyes flashed with anger. "You mean you knew your phone was tapped? And you're still making calls like that? Even to me? You bastard — "

"We set a time, so what?" Profit broke in. "It could've been a court date."

The white plastic spoon snapped unexpectedly, and they both looked at it. Profit scraped the jagged end of the broken handle on the table, as if he were taking notes.

"Can they do that?" he asked. "Legally tap my phone?"

Ronnie Fraiche's heavy black eyebrows were a solid line low across his forehead. His anger was evident, but his voice was deliberate and even, the voice of a man accustomed to applying formal rules to distasteful affairs.

"No, they can't, not legally, not in this state, but they got carried away and they've been doing it anyway. Apparently it's been going on for a long time: the police have been running illegal wiretaps and attributing the information to confidential informants. Handled right, informants are protected, so it was a tight package. Some little fart in the district attorney's office found out and unwrapped it to the U.S. attorney. The U.S. attorney is going after it with everything he's got — and believe me, he's got plenty. He convened a grand jury so fast the jurors made vapor trails getting to the courthouse."

Profit dropped the broken spoon on the table.

"So what does that mean to me?"

Fraiche leaned back in the booth. "It means the charges against you will be dropped."

"No shit," Profit said, and the corners of his mouth turned

up in a cautious grin. "But they got me pretty solid, Ronnie. They had a warrant. They got me with the coke in my house — "

"None of that matters. You never heard of the exclusionary rule? You ought to know these things — you in particular. There are rules that precede and follow an arrest. Once one of the rules is broken, everything that comes after it is disallowed — like in football, once you step out of bounds, the rest of the play is off, no matter what. The police stepped *way* out of bounds running illegal wires. The district attorney is nol-prossing cases like they were diseased."

"I like that law," Profit said. Although it didn't change his plans, it did make the plans less expensive. "Will they give back the evidence?"

"Be a clown with somebody else, Profit," Fraiche said. He stood up angrily, his patience gone. "I put up with you because you've got good stuff, but you're a pain in my ass. I came out to this pasture to tell you to lie low, you've got problems, and while I'm looking out for you, you're making jokes and calling me on a phone you know is tapped. Don't call me again, not from *any* phone."

Profit cocked his head to one side, and his lips pulled tight in a mocking grin.

"You didn't come out here to tell me to lie low. You came to put distance between us, to cover your own butt. You're nervous, Judge. Take a Valium, or call someone who cares."

Ronnie Fraiche's eyes flashed with anger. His words came out slowly, heavy with contempt. "You think you're so cute, it's too bad they didn't pop you when they *did* have an informant."

Profit's eyes widened, but the grin remained fixed on his face and he said nothing.

Fraiche leaned down and put both fists on the table. "And Profit, if you plan to take somebody off, use a different phone. That one," he said, pointing at the gas station across the highway, "is a direct line to the U.S. attorney."

"What?" Profit was stunned. His mouth opened and closed dryly, the grin gone. He reached out and grabbed Fraiche's arm before he could turn away. "They tapped the pay phones too?"

"Something you didn't know? Where's the joke? Where's the snappy comeback, Profit? You think you're dealing with morons? They've got people who've been working narcotics for twenty and thirty years. They don't miss tricks. They see you using the same pay phone over and over, they know you're doing business — of course they're going to tap it." Fraiche pulled his arm free from Profit's grasp and stood up straight.

"Who has the tapes?" Profit asked, his voice tinged with panic. "How many copies are there?"

Ronnie Fraiche snorted. "The new grand jury has the tapes. I saw a copy of the transcript; copies are around if you know the right people." His voice suddenly took on a brutal edge. "Try to lever me, Profit, or try to bring me into the stink, and I'll have a copy of that transcript on the next plane to Miami, to the *friends* you intend to rob. Let's see how well *they* like your jokes."

For a long moment Fraiche stared at Profit, trying to determine whether or not his message had been understood, but Profit did not seem to respond at all. His eyes were watery and vacuous. His jaw was slack. Ronnie Fraiche turned on his heel and left the diner.

As if he were deep under water, under great pressure, Profit moved his hand in a slow arc to his face and pressed against his eye. He turned his head and watched the judge get into the gray BMW with the orange and green Florida license plates.

"Holy shit," he said softly, and his hand dropped from his eye and rubbed his cheek. "Holy shit," he said again, an odd sort of litany.

7

SHEEN WAS ahead of the schedule he had set for himself, and after he had crossed the Golden Gate Bridge, he turned onto the road that led to the scenic outlook on the north side of the bay. The curving drive turned him back in the direction from which he had come so that he faced the bridge he had just crossed. The Golden Gate's odd orange lights faded into the looming Presidio shadows, and unconsciously his eye followed the sweeping curve of the massive cables arcing away into darkness.

Across the bay, past Alcatraz, San Francisco sparkled. The individually hard and brittle pinpoints of light formed a brilliant cluster that was somehow soft. Sheen got out of the car and stood by the low stone fence that bordered the outlook. He felt intensely alive, his nerves as taut as strings that produce high notes. The air was crisp, and the wind seemed to anticipate him, blowing in his face no matter which way he turned.

He saw a small boat crossing the bay, rolling violently on the black water beneath the bridge. *An unwise voyage,* he thought, and surrendered to the cold wind and got back into the car.

Sheen's instructions were straightforward: wait in the Sausalito Howard Johnson's parking lot between nine and nine-thirty; take delivery of a prepaid package and send the package on to New Orleans by any service other than the mail. While Sheen knew that the northern California coast was providing new points of entry, still it seemed rather inefficient that Florida cocaine was delivered to California while California cocaine was sent to Louisiana. "It sounds like a government operation," Sheen had joked when he first had heard Profit's instructions, but he didn't like it. He didn't like being alone, and he didn't like handling drugs. He didn't like being in a situation where he had to trust someone whom he had never met.

He moved to the middle of the front seat, took off his jacket, slipped on the shoulder holster. The big Colt, cocked and locked, protruded slightly from beneath his armpit. When he moved into the driver's seat, the barrel end rubbed against the seat back.

Sheen had rented the largest car available at the rental agency, and he drove the big Plymouth smoothly, so that it seemed to set its own speed. Past the Howard Johnson's, he parked in a convenience-store parking lot. Traffic was sparse; only an occasional streetlight punctuated the darkness. He knew the location was well suited for a hit-and-run: sporadic lighting, irregular traffic, a short run to the freeway and a quick escape. But for the same reasons it was also a good place to make a delivery. He got out of the car, opened the trunk, disconnected the brake lights, slammed the trunk closed. Before he pulled shut the driver's door, he tapped the brake pedal to be certain he had disconnected the correct wires; no taillights showed, even with the engine in gear and the headlights switched on. Satisfied that the car was difficult to see from behind, he pulled his seat belt tight. At exactly nine o'clock he drove into the Howard Johnson's parking lot.

He circled the lot twice before he chose a spot and backed in carefully. The space was tight for the big Plymouth: he wouldn't be able to open the doors, but no one would be able to walk up beside him, either. He was beyond the pool of bright light at the motel's entrance but not so far back that the car was in deep shadow. He clicked the headlights to bright before he switched them off and put the wheel to the left. The car was in gear, motor running. He put the Colt under his leg and his hand on top of the wheel.

The engine hummed softly at idle. A valve clicked monotonously. Sheen checked the rearview mirror, then the windshield, then the rearview mirror. The heater blew warm on his feet. The first bullet passed under his arm and smashed through the dashboard. In the same instant he heard another bullet hit and a shattering pain screamed through his hand. Sheen collapsed onto the seat and mashed the accelerator. The car jumped into a smoking blind turn; the wheel kicked hard as the Plymouth sideswiped a parked car. For a terrible moment, as metal ripped, it seemed the engine had stalled, but he twisted the wheel violently and the car shook itself free and accelerated, bouncing over the curb. The rear window disintegrated in a shattered mosaic. Heavy hammer thumps slammed the trunk. The car vibrated savagely as Sheen fought it onto the street, flat out toward the freeway ramp. His hand felt like it had been caught in a chainsaw; he jammed it down into the flight bag, pushing as hard as he could against the packed clothes. Behind him, headlights were coming up fast. He turned onto the freeway ramp in a tire-searing drift, then pushed both feet down on the brakes. Because no brake lights showed, the following car nearly ran into him before he stomped on the emergency brake and spun the wheel. The big Plymouth shuddered and squealed into the turn as a low gray Corvette whipped past, wisps of smoke burning from its tires as it braked. Sheen accelerated hard back down the ramp. The clothes in the flight bag were warm, sticky wet. Sheen knew he was losing too much blood. He tried to think, but all he could remember of the area was the bank where Profit had gotten the checks. The Plymouth was rattling. The oil caution light blinked red. He knew he didn't have much time. He raced along the twisting road into Sausalito, and finally he saw the bank and swerved out into oncoming traffic, swerved back, and aimed the car at the bank's front doors. There was a stunning impact, a strangling tension on the seat belt, the sound of crumpling metal and shattering glass; then there was the sweet, distant sound of the bank's alarm. Sheen heard concerned voices and a nearby siren. He lay his head back on the seat and blacked out.

The blackness was liquid, uneven, fading in and out like a tremolo. There were shadows that murmured urgently, instructions he could not understand. He felt himself lifted, again and again.

"Leave me alone!" he heard someone shouting.

A strap pulled tight across his chest.

There was a confusing moment of intense white light, a moment when the shadows focused and he saw starched white uniforms, purposeful faces, coarse black hair on the back of a hand; then there was a sharp jab in his arm and a glow gushed through him, deepening the blackness and making it even, soothing, warm.

When he next awoke enough to focus, a nurse spoon-fed him cereal. Through a deep haze he saw sunlight through the windows. He nodded in appreciation to the nurse, and a sharp pain shot through his shoulder, a pain that dissolved the haze. He lay still and savored the soggy-crunchy texture of the cereal. He saw that his right hand was wrapped in a massive bandage. He swallowed, and before the nurse could assemble another spoonful from the bowl, he asked, "Will I live?"

The nurse's kindly face softened into a smile.

"Oh, yes," she said. "How are you feeling?"

"Fine," Sheen replied, and shook his head, refusing the spoonful of cereal she offered. "What's the damage?"

The nurse put the spoon back in the bowl, took a napkin from the tray, gently wiped his mouth.

"Your doctor will have to tell you that," she said, soothingly evasive. "You're a very lucky young man, though, not to have been hurt more badly. I drove past the bank on my way to the hospital, and when I saw that car, I thought someone had been killed for sure."

"Very lucky," Sheen agreed.

The nurse moved the tray from the bed to the bedside table. "The police want to talk to you. Do you feel up to it?"

"Do I have a choice?"

"Probably not. They can be *so* persistent." She clasped her hands together in front of her chest. "Can I get you anything else?"

"How about something for the pain?"

"I'll see what the doctor left for you," she said, and she turned away and went out.

Sheen rolled his head to one side to look out the window, but the corner of a pillow blocked his view. When he tried to move the pillow out of the way, the tube running into his good arm pulled tight, too short to allow him to reach behind his head. He closed his eyes and counted the dull pulses throbbing in his hand. When he heard the faint swishing sound of the door, he opened his eyes slowly, reminding himself to ask the nurse to fix the pillows.

Two men in suits stood at the foot of the bed. Sheen felt a quick, paralyzing fear: he was trapped, pinned to the bed, helpless. One of the men showed a badge, and the fear passed.

"You had quite a night," the shorter of the two men said. He seemed as broad as he was tall. One eyebrow was split by a short white scar that cut diagonally through it, and the base of his nose was thick with the lumpy cartilage of an unattended break. The taller man was thin, his face dominated by a drooping brown mustache that only partially concealed prominent, protruding front teeth. His hair was brushed straight back from his forehead; his hairline formed a sharp V that made Sheen think of a ferret.

"I'm Ridell," the shorter man said, then jerked his thumb at the taller man. "This is Gossett."

Sheen struggled to sit up on the bed, but without the use of his arms he could manage only to bunch the pillows with his shoulders and incline his head.

"I suppose by now you know my name."

"You had a police I.D. in your pocket, Vicedomini," Gossett

said, his voice as pointed as his hairline. "You're not supposed to keep it after you quit."

"It was lost," Sheen lied thinly, then smiled. "I didn't arrest anybody, and look at the service I got."

Ridell returned the smile and pulled a chair close so that he could sit by the bed. Gossett remained standing, his dark brown eyes fixed on Sheen's face as if it were a target. Sheen knew instinctively that Gossett and Ridell had been partners for a long time. He had seen it often before, the way the personalities fit together, working both sides of the subject of an interview like the jaws of a pair of pliers.

"Did N.O.P.D. verify me," Sheen asked, "or have they written me off completely?"

Ridell reached into his inside coat pocket and took out a green-and-white-striped strip of paper that was perforated on both ends.

"Two years with the New Orleans Police Department," he read out loud. "Third in your class at the academy."

"I flubbed the test on parking violations."

"Sixteen months in uniform in the housing projects. Two awards for valor under fire. Three pistol range records — one of which, by the way, was broken two weeks ago."

"The bull's-eye," Sheen said. "I never could hit a target if it didn't move. I still can't."

Ridell folded the strip of paper neatly and put it back in his pocket. "They haven't written you off — "

"But *somebody* nearly did," Gossett interrupted. "So far we've gotten four slugs from the car. At least three more passed right through."

Sheen was startled.

"What size?"

"They were .44s. The slugs came from two different guns — and nobody heard any shots."

"I didn't either," Sheen replied without thinking.

Gossett put both hands on the metal rail at the foot of the bed and leaned forward. "Silenced auto-magnums are pretty specialized equipment, Vicedomini. What kind of people have you been hanging around? What are you doing out here?"

Sheen looked at Gossett with slow, sleepy eyes that he hoped hid his apprehension.

"I'm on vacation," he said. "I had a few days coming to me — "

"Right." Gossett cut him off. "We already called your office."

"Your supervisor was surprised to learn that you were in California, Sheen. You told him you were going camping."

"I changed my mind."

"You always carry a piece?"

"I got in the habit. When was the last time you went out without one?"

"*I'm* a cop."

Sheen shrugged. "Anyway, it wasn't on my person."

"The shit." Gossett spat out the words. "Now tell me you're just fruit for shoulder holsters. How about some straight answers, Vicedomini?"

"Anything I can."

Sheen looked first at Gossett and then at Ridell. Ridell nodded at him encouragingly; Gossett glared at him with undisguised contempt. When he spoke, Sheen looked between them at the wall.

"I'm on vacation," he said again.

Gossett threw up his hands in an unmistakable gesture of disgust.

"Here, I'll save you some breath: you got this sudden urge to see San Francisco, so you changed your camping plans. You took the first flight out, rented a car, and were about to check into the Howard Johnson's when you got jumped for no reason."

Gossett stopped and let the silence grow tense.

"That's about it," Sheen said finally.

"I'll give you a better story, Vicedomini. You're out here on business. You're making either a pickup or a delivery — it was probably a pickup since you didn't have much time

96

to drop anything and the car is clean. I can even tell you *what* you were supposed to pick up, I just don't know how much. Maybe you didn't know, either — maybe you didn't know how sour it was on this end — but you were expecting something. The taillights were disconnected on your car, and you were carrying a cannon. Maybe you didn't even know who you were supposed to meet, in which case you're not just a fool, you're also working for somebody else. That spells interstate conspiracy. You're a delivery boy in a world of shit. You like *that* story?"

Sheen had been on the other side of too many interrogations to feel intimidated by Gossett. He knew that other than the fact that there had been a pistol in the car, they didn't have anything. Conjecture didn't go to court.

"I'm on vacation," Sheen said again.

Gossett slapped the metal rail at the foot of the bed. "Your ass hurts. Keep going with it, Vicedomini. Ask us why we're not out looking for the *real* criminals."

When Sheen looked at Gossett, his eyes were no longer slow and sleepy. "I'm not trying to insult you, Gossett."

Ridell held up one hand. "You're just not saying anything, right?"

Sheen rolled his head on the pillow and looked at Ridell. "Are you going to charge me with the pistol?"

"No," Ridell replied, and took a thick brown plastic wallet from his inside coat pocket. The green and white strip of computer paper came out with it and fell loose toward the floor, fluttering. With a punchlike, jabbing thrust, his left hand flashed out and snagged it; he saw Sheen watching him, and he grinned self-consciously as he took a business card from the wallet and wrote on the back of it. "Consider the lack of a charge a courtesy for an ex-cop. You can claim the pistol from our office when you're up and around."

Ridell put the business card on the bed, stood up, returned the chair to its place near the wall.

"You might as well have it as a souvenir," Gossett said, and pushed himself away from the metal rail at the foot of the bed. "You sure can't shoot it, not with that stump." With his forefinger he pointed at the bandage on Sheen's hand.

Sheen felt the blood drain from his face.

Ridell gave Gossett a sour look, then said to Sheen, "You'll be all right, buddy. It's not a stump. You got plenty of fingers left. I wrote the report number on the back of the card."

Sheen did not reply. He closed his eyes and lay his head on the pillow, pretending to rest. He heard the click of heels, the door's faint swishing, a loudspeaker in the hall. He lay still until he heard the muffled thump of the door meeting the rubber stops in the door frame, then he rolled onto his side and began to tear at the bandages on his hand. He unwrapped layer after layer of gauze, ripping at the tape and the knots with his fingers and his teeth. Blood was dripping past his elbow when he came to the thick cotton pads. His whole arm throbbed furiously. He grabbed the edge of the pads and yanked. Pain blinded him. He clenched his jaws tight, and after a moment he was able to open his eyes. But he could not believe what he saw: his little finger and half of his ring finger were gone. Ragged stitches were sewn directly over the joint and the knuckle. Swollen stumps were all that remained of the fingers.

His body convulsed.

When the nurse returned with his pill, Sheen was unconscious, his arm extended straight out from his side, rigid, as if he held something hateful.

During the day that followed, Sheen intermittently felt pain in the missing fingers, a deep aching throb in the fingertips he knew were gone. Ghost pain, his doctor explained. It was common and to be expected. But Sheen found the pain unsettling: he could not understand how something that was not there could cause a tangible feeling.

Thirty-six hours after he had been admitted, he left the hospital, took a taxi into San Francisco, and checked into a small motel. The residual effects of the hospital-administered drugs created a soft haze around him, an intensely private, introspective vision that he could not seem to focus. He slept for twenty-four hours, and when he awoke the haze was gone, dispelled, it seemed, by a single-minded purpose: confront Profit.

Both his thoughts and his actions were directed by that purpose, and he proceeded in a set, mechanical way, concerned only with the efficiency of his movements. He retrieved his pistol, took the first available flight to New Orleans, rented a car, bought supplies. Only when he was in the woods less than a mile from Profit's house did it seem he had moved too quickly, *too* efficiently, and he sat on a soft mound of pine needles and leaned back against the rough bark of a towering pine tree. Low clouds passed in front of a quarter moon. The air was soft and sensual. The pain in his hand was a dull throb.

Sheen did not have a plan. He assumed that Profit had bought protection — at the very least he expected to encounter an elaborate security system — but he did not think the potential problems were significant.

Sheen stood up by pushing against the tree, and a small piece of bark went down his shirt. He shook his shirt by the collar, and reflexly reached with his right hand for the gas can; but the two fingers that protruded from the bandage were not able to hold the fifty-pound weight. He untucked his shirt to allow the piece of bark to fall out and carried the gasoline in his left hand as he continued on toward Profit's house.

His arm grew tired, and Sheen began to count his steps, allowing himself a brief rest period every two hundred yards. Each time he put down the heavy gas can, he swung his arm in a wide circle, flexed his back, rubbed his knee where it bumped the metal rim of the can. He walked parallel to the road, guiding himself first by the low moon, then by the glow from the lights.

High-intensity floodlights on the perimeter of the clearing around Profit's house were directed inward and made a brilliant pocket of light that reminded Sheen of a Little League baseball field lit for a night game. In the middle of the clearing, the house seemed unnaturally quiet: there was no activity; no inside lights were on. Sheen moved around the circumference of the clearing until he was near the corner of the house that was closest to the woods. He put down the gas can and sat on it, waiting for the strength to return to his arm. Behind him crickets in chorus made a pulsing sound that started low, inflated in crescendo, stopped suddenly.

In front of him, in line with the corner of the house, was a tall pine tree, and when Sheen moved across the clearing he ran first toward the tree itself and then into the black stripe of shadow it cast. At the corner of the house he stopped, listening, before he lay down and worked his way under the house, moving himself by pulling with one elbow and pushing with his feet and knees. When he was beneath the living room, he opened the gas can, lay it on its side, and began to crawl to the opposite corner of the house. The metal can made a soft grating sound on the hard dirt; the pink liquid made a soft gulping sound as it poured. He stopped once to saturate a pile of scrap plywood that had been tossed carelessly beneath the kitchen. The fumes from the gasoline were heavy and pungent in the still air.

Sheen crawled from beneath the house and moved quickly across the clearing into the woods. In the shadows he walked the length of the house until he was near the exposed outside water heater. His clothes smelled of gasoline, and his thigh burned where gasoline had soaked through his pants.

Awkwardly, he took the Colt from the shoulder holster with his left hand, pulling it down rather than sideways so that it would not point at his chest. He held the pistol with his left hand and used a tree to steady his aim. The safety clicked off with a familiar sound. For a moment, as he aligned the front sight blade in the rear sight notch, Sheen had a sense of timelessness, of years bridged by the identical repetition of a single action; then the pistol jumped, surprising him, and the concussing force of the shot slapped his face.

His knuckles scraped painfully against the tree's rough bark, and, triggered by the sound of the shot, a wailing alarm sounded. Sheen braced his hand and fired again. The heavy shots echoed, rolling through the woods. Sparks exploded from the base of the water heater. The cover blew off the open gas pilot flame.

The gasoline did not ignite.

The alarm wailed, high-low.

Sheen moved quickly to his left and put the pistol on the ground as he fumbled with the second magazine. The barrel hissed, hot against the damp pine needles. He looked up when he heard a sucking *whoosh,* like a huge oven igniting, and he saw the house explode into flames. A giant ball of black smoke mushroomed past the flames, which were already higher than the roof. In the thick smoke, embers and sparks shot upward.

Sheen held the pistol between his feet to reload it, squatting over it like a peasant in a rice paddy. The electric lines to the house parted with a fizzling, popping sound, and the wailing siren stopped abruptly. As Sheen again moved to his left, the orange-yellow light from the fire diminished as the gasoline was expended and the wood settled into a solid, slower burn. Though the lights had gone out, it was still as bright as day.

Sheen tripped on the root of a tree and fell, absorbing the shock by rolling from elbow to shoulder, cradling both his injured hand and the pistol. Briefly he lay flat on his back, devising a way to stand without letting either hand touch the ground. Overhead the thick smoke billowed toward the low, churning clouds. He walked more slowly after he got up, and watched his feet. When he was one-third of the way around the perimeter, he saw Profit standing motionless in the clearing, facing the house.

Profit was barefoot and shirtless, dressed only in a pair of cutoff jeans. His shoulders were rolled forward, and his back was bent as if he were about to drop to his knees, as if the weight of his own body were too much to carry. In his right hand he clutched his brown leather attaché case; it swung to and fro loosely, a pendulum on a short, limp arc.

Sheen moved close behind him before he pushed through

the brush and walked into the clearing. Even though the flames were at least fifty yards away, he felt his eyes dry and the hair on his skin singe.

"So, what have you been up to?" he shouted over the roar of the fire, brutally mimicking Profit's standard greeting.

Profit turned slowly away from the fire to face Sheen. His expression was vacuous. His lips were parted slightly, moving fitfully but making no sound.

"Are you right-handed?" Sheen asked.

Profit looked at him with eyes that were dull and glazed, and did not reply.

Sheen raised one shoulder and dropped it, then his wrist moved slightly and he fired once.

The bullet seared across the back of Profit's hand.

Profit dropped his attaché case and fell to the ground, clutching his hand to his chest.

"It hurts, doesn't it?" Sheen shouted, and held up his bandaged hand as if it were a weapon. Then he moved forward, picked up the attaché case, and moved back.

Profit rolled onto one side, pressing his hand between his upper arm and his ribs.

Sheen squatted on his heels and laid the attaché case flat. He put the pistol on the ground next to it, within easy reach, then opened the case and sorted through the thick sheaves of large-denomination bills, his fingers moving without haste, probing, stacking and restacking the packets of bills, feeling the lining. In the soft leather file pocket he found Profit's thick, rubber-band-wrapped address book, and he put it on the ground beside the pistol, closed the case, and stood up.

"I'll keep this for insurance," Sheen said, waving the address book at Profit. "Call off the hit, or next time I'll keep you in the house." The words held a hard certainty that was brutal in its matter-of-factness.

Profit pushed himself up until he was kneeling. His expression was no longer vacuous. His eyes reflected the raging firelight.

"I didn't order the fucking hit. *I* didn't order it. Miami called it. *Miami.*"

Sheen picked up the attaché case with one finger of his bad hand.

"It's all the same to me, Profit."

Profit stood up, squeezing his right hand with his left, his body bent in the middle. "This is a cover, isn't it, an excuse to take me off? You don't care about the hit. You want the *money.*"

With a slow movement of his head, Sheen looked at the attaché case, then back at Profit. "You're pitiful," he said.

Moving sideways so that he faced Profit as he walked around him, Sheen moved so close to the fire that the heat singed his hair and burned his skin. With a spinning motion, flinging his arms straight out from his side as if he were throwing a discus, he threw the attaché case at the house.

"No!" Profit shouted.

The leather case sailed on a long, slow trajectory that dropped it deep within the flames.

"Call off the hit," Sheen repeated.

He moved away from the heat, away from Profit, and started down the red dirt road that led to the highway.

8

SIX HUNDRED feet above the street the wind hit the skyscraper in gusts. Deflected down the tower building's flat face, it swept past the lower floors in a swirling downdraft; deflected again by the pavement and embroiled by the heat that made it rise, on the street the wind was a squally, whistling force that came unexpectedly from any quarter. Skirts blew flat against stockinged legs and suit coats became comic trailing capes. Water in the plaza's fountain blew horizontally, first one way, then another, pivoting like an airport's wind sock; wet spray darkened the brown tiles, moving along a constantly shifting radius.

Sheen sat on a wooden bench that was on the circumference of the stain, his brown paper lunch bag tucked securely beneath his leg. He was fascinated by the water: the fountain was enduring, even though its definition turned to mist. Somehow it seemed to have the same unsettling quality as pain from fingers that were not there.

Sheen had adapted quickly to his hand's diminished capacity, and in compensation he had learned that he was effectively ambidextrous. Although he was still self-conscious about his hand's appearance and often kept it hidden in his pocket, he was himself no longer repulsed by the sight of it. There were even some advantages: he discovered that when he shaved in the mornings before work, holding the razor by two fingers gave a delicate feel to the stroking motion and, incredibly, a closer shave.

The sun was warm on his face, and he closed his eyes and leaned back on the bench, his hands resting lightly in his lap, the glowing light behind his eyelids making his thoughts wander pleasantly. It had been two weeks since he had seen Andrea. Although he spoke with her daily on the phone, he had neither visited her nor allowed her to visit him. He had been in a car wreck, he said, and he was adamant about their separation, insisting that he needed time to heal. Sheen was concerned that Profit would make another attempt on his life, and he did not want Andrea near if something did happen. But with each passing day the likelihood of trouble lessened. Another few days and he would bring her home.

Sheen had decided that he would ask Andrea to move in with him. He had money in the bank, and if they saved the money she spent on rent and utilities, she would be able to quit work and go to school full-time. The prospect pleased him. As Sheen stood up from the bench and put his lunch bag in the trash, he realized he was not so reluctant to go back to his office. Unaware that he was doing so, he hid his hand in his side coat pocket.

In his office, Sheen poured himself a cup of coffee before he began to work, and idly he watched the steam rise from the coffee's shiny black surface. On the telephone on his desk one of the square, clear plastic buttons blinked, then stayed lit briefly before it began to blink again and his buzzer sounded once. The bandage on his hand had been changed to a small cosmetic dressing, and Sheen easily picked up the phone receiver with two fingers and a thumb.

"Sheen?" the familiar voice asked. "Is that you?"

"Andrea," Sheen replied, and shifted the phone to his left ear. "I was going to call *you*. I was thinking about you while I was at lunch."

"This isn't Andrea, Sheen. This is Becky."

Sheen was not surprised: often on the phone he confused Andrea's voice with her sister's.

"Hi, Becky," he said, and leaned back in his chair, causing it to squeak. "This is a nice surprise. What's up?"

There was a long pause before Becky spoke again, and in the humming silence there was an odd, strained quality that made Sheen sit up straight, listening intently.

"Sheen, I don't know how to say this well: Andrea is dead. I'm at the hospital now. I just saw her. She was riding her bicycle home from school. A car went out of control and hit her."

Two piles of paper on his desk came into bright focus. One was neat and orderly; the other needed sorting. He heard his voice, out there, reasonable.

"Which hospital?"

"The emergency room at Charity."

Becky was so calm.

"I'll be right over," he said, and gently, as if it were very delicate, he put the phone receiver in its cradle before he stood up, looked around, walked out of the office.

Small things held his attention. The coins jingled in his pocket; the orange elevator button was warm to the touch. He realized his nails were pressed deeply into the palm of his hand.

Outside, he walked stiffly to the corner. He stumbled twice because his feet did not seem to lift correctly.

He saw a taxi, and he flagged it.

"Where to?" the driver asked.

"The hospital, please," he said softly.

"There're only about twelve of 'em, pal."

"Charity," he said, and closed the door.

The taxi ride passed in one long moment, a collage of images and colors he did not seem able to integrate.

Becky met him at the top of the hospital's white concrete ramp and hugged him briefly, clutching the sleeves of his jacket.

"Where is she?" he asked.

"She's here, but they're getting ready to take her to the coroner's office."

106

The sliding glass doors opened electrically, and they walked through.

To the right of the doors there was a row of tables. Each table was surrounded by a white curtain hung from a shiny metal rail. Some of the curtains were open; others were closed. Near the third table he came to, Sheen saw Andrea's tennis shoes on the floor. One lay on its side, and he saw that the sole was worn smooth on the heel.

"You should have new shoes," he said, and he bent over to place the shoes neatly side by side before he stood up straight and slid the curtain open.

A white sheet was draped over her. Gently he took one corner, lifted it, and pulled it back. It looked like Andrea, but the warmth had left her, and it was obvious that Andrea was not there anymore. A thin yellow fluid had dripped from her nose, and there was a small trickle of blood on her forehead.

"You must have hit your head," he said, and with his fingertips he brushed her hair away from the cut.

Her skin was cool, already bluish.

He lifted the sheet back over her.

He turned in a circle, away and back; his hands rose and fell at his sides. He saw her backpack on a chair, and he picked it up, sat where it had been, and put it on his lap. For no reason he looked through the backpack: inside there were three books, a notebook, a wallet. In the wallet's change pocket there were three pennies and a hair band. Suddenly his heart blew out of him, and he felt a roar. He felt a pounding. He realized he was beating the arm of the chair, but he could not make it stop. His eyes were full, and he could not see. He sat forward, his back bent, his face in his hands. It came in him again and again in huge waves, and he could not make it stop.

Suddenly calm, he realized that Becky was sitting next to him, her legs folded under her, a box of tissues in her lap.

"I'm not much of a help, am I?" he said, and it took him again.

Her dress was wet beneath his face.

He felt her speaking, but he did not hear the words.

Two men were standing at a polite distance. Becky went to the ambulance attendants, and they spoke softly.

A stretcher on wheels rolled past.

Sheen felt Becky next to him.

"I'll ride with her," he said.

"No, you won't," she said firmly. "You'll stay with me."

Sheen looked at her, and he saw that her eyes were the same soft brown as Andrea's.

"Please," she said.

The sobs started in his chest.

Outside, the heat of the day had passed. The evening would be cool.

In his apartment, Sheen made coffee. Becky and he sat quietly at the kitchen table, listening to the coffeemaker gurgle and hiss. They had run out of things to say. The apartment looked the same, but it felt so different. There was a huge emptiness. Sheen thought Andrea should walk through the door and see Becky and him sitting together. *Alone with my sister, eh?*

Shared possessions were everywhere. Each one already was a memory. He read them like a book.

The blender bowl was cracked. "Don't put a spoon in it," Andrea had said, too late.

A corner on the table was dented. They had laughed because they had both tried to pretend that the table wasn't heavy, then they had pushed together and jammed it into the wall.

A pot had a broken handle.

The memories were distinct; one led to another. He did not notice when Becky left. He stared at the cutting board and saw Andrea chopping deftly. He closed his eyes.

He had met her late one night when he had been on patrol, driving the same block over and over, waiting for something to happen. Her car had had only one headlight, and he had stopped her to tell her so and to tell her that the housing project at night was not a safe place, particularly not for a woman. But before he could give her the warnings, she had begun to lecture *him,* telling him that if he would go out and do his job rather than stopping women for the crime of being alone, maybe the other headlight would not be stolen too; of course she knew the projects were unsafe, she was not sightseeing, she was lost, and *if* he could give her directions, and *if* he could get tickets to the ballet, *then* he could take her to dinner.

Sheen had not been able to believe his good luck. He could remember the unsettling, awkward feeling of standing beside her car in the harsh glare from his headlights, both hands in his pockets, rocking back and forth from heel to toe because he did not know what to say.

He could remember getting back into the police car and realizing how empty his life was. Before the ballet they had gone to dinner; within a month he had asked her to leave a change of clothes in his apartment.

In his closet, the hems of the dresses she had left behind brushed the top of his tool box.

Sheen felt an overwhelming loneliness. It was pervasive, almost tangible, and nothing he did seemed of consequence, nothing mattered. He moved through each day by rote; events unfolded as if they were being shown in some distant movie.

"I have to see it through," he said over and over.

On his right wrist he wore the small gold watch he had given her. He quit his job. He closed the blinds and the curtains, and hour after hour he sat on the couch in the dark apartment and stared blankly at the wall.

He tried to use his reason. The loneliness deepened.

He knew scientists said nothing was ever completely destroyed — that was a reasonable thing. Where was Andrea? She was alive *in* him; she was dead *to* him. She was dead. The words sounded hollow, like a pebble hitting the surface of a deep pond. He saw the stone sink out of sight long before the ripples ceased. He knew she was not completely gone; she was dead. The words sounded hollow, like a heavy door closing. She was dead.

"What will I do?" he asked himself, and he remembered the time he had asked her the same question.

When the trouble had begun at the police department, when it had become painfully obvious that Tony Avila intended to make him the scapegoat for his vengeance, Andrea had told him to quit, even though she did not know the reason for the trouble. He remembered how she had drawn the corners of her mouth down thoughtfully and furrowed her brow, and he remembered the way she had sat, her elbows on the white maple table, her fingers twisting a loose strand of hair, her head cocked to one side, hearing more than just his words.

"It's making you unhappy — that alone is reason enough to quit. Is being a policeman *that* important to you?"

"But what will I do?" he had asked.

"That's the easy part," she had replied. "You'll look for work. I'll help you. It'll be fun!"

"Right," Sheen had said ironically. But in a way it *had* been fun.

Every morning Andrea had written down for him a specific goal: "I will have two interviews today," or "I will phone ten places today." He remembered the yellow legal pad next to the phone, the looping roundness of her writing; the notes always ended "Get to it." She had broken the overwhelming whole of the work search into daily bites, and although some of the bites had been hard to swallow, overall the process had become palatable.

In the evenings she had read and reread the paper, pretending that she was a machine programmed to search out and respond to ads. She made a whirring noise as she typed his résumés, and she beeped when she saw an ad she thought was attractive. As Sheen followed her lead and tried to make the search into a game, his dread gradually changed to an odd fascination. He saw that each ad carried, beyond the printed information, the potential for new experiences: new offices, new work, new people. He began to respond to a wider variety of ads, and a latent eagerness showed on his applications. By the time he was rewarded with employment, he had grown almost fond of the routine.

He remembered the day he had told her that he had gotten a job — a good one, he believed, one he could live with. She had hugged him so tightly his neck had cracked. "I'm so proud," she had said, her eyes bright.

"What will I do?" he asked himself.

Hour after hour he sat on the couch in the dark apartment and stared blankly at the wall.

Becky called him twice, once to ask him how he was and once to ask him to drive her to the funeral.

"Fine," he answered the first question, and "Okay," he answered the second.

At the front of the church, the dark wood casket was covered with flowers. Ushers moved quietly up and down the aisles. Sheen sat alone in the middle of a pew. He was determined not to cry, and to distract himself he counted the panes of glass in the windows, the candles by the altar, the number of pieces in the stained glass panels. When the pastor began the service, Sheen concentrated on the sonorous, lulling sound of the voice and allowed the words to run together, indistinct, unimportant, like smoke caught and carried by a breeze. He forced his mind to wander, to shift itself away, and he remembered another time when words had formed indistinct sounds. He smelled the smoke.

He remembered that a light haze had covered the far hills and that three helicopters in formation had thumped past in the valley, their dark green color making them little more than movements in the shadows on the valley floor. He remembered that he too had been part of a formation, one in a line of men dressed in splotched green camouflage uniforms.

"We beseech Thee, our heavenly Father, to take these young men unto Thy peace; to grant to them the peace they fought for others to have, a greater peace, one they may know only in Thy hands."

111

"Give them what they really want," Bolduc whispered beside him, "a greater piece of ass." The squad leader grinned, and as he leaned close to Sheen to comment, the grenade launcher slung across his back clanged noisily against the grenades on his belt.

"And may these men gathered here remember their fallen comrades as they go again to do battle. In their memories of their friends may they find Thy strength as they take up their swords in Thy work."

"Sword, my ass," Bolduc whispered, and patted the grenade launcher. "White fucking phosphorus, I tell you what. Willie Peter make you a believer."

"Let us pray. The Lord is my light and my salvation: whom shall I fear? The Lord is the protector of my life: of whom shall I be afraid? If a battle should rise up against me — "

"Call the Army, the Marines ain't home," Bolduc said.

" — in this I will be confident. One thing I have asked of the Lord, this I will seek after: that I may dwell in the house of the Lord all the days of my life. Amen."

A low murmuring: "Amen."

"While we're assembled," the chaplain said before anyone could move, "I've been asked to speak to you about our performance in recent weeks."

"Here it comes," Bolduc said, nudging Sheen.

"As you all know, these past several weeks have seen our body count drop drastically. I don't know the tactical reasons why so few of the enemy have been killed — tactical matters are best left to those more knowledgeable about such things — but I do know this: we cannot allow our friends, our comrades in arms, to have died in vain. We cannot allow their deaths to be meaningless."

"Meaningless," Sheen repeated to himself.

His right hand clasped his left wrist, and his back was bowed. He looked up, comprehending slowly where he was, and why. Among the people he recognized slightly was Becky, who was dabbing her eyes with a handkerchief. Suddenly it seemed that the air in the church was too close, the smell of the flowers too thick and nauseatingly sweet. He sat up and loosened his tie, but that did not help.

Sheen stood up, glanced around uncertainly, and sidestepped away from the center aisle, away from the crowd and the sonorous sound of the pastor's voice. The heavy leather sole of his shoe bumped loudly against the leg of a pew, and for a long moment he felt curious, disapproving glances. He heard the slight hesitation, the momentary interruption of the eulogy. He felt a clammy sweat on his face and under his arms.

At the side door, with one hand on the doorknob, he paused long enough to catch Becky's eye and to wave goodbye. Becky acknowledged the wave with a sad smile and a nod that showed she understood. Their eyes locked; when Becky turned away, Sheen knew he would never see her again.

Outside, the day was cool and very clear.

On his way home Sheen stopped at a convenience store to buy groceries. As he pushed open the door of his apartment with one arm, a box of cereal fell to the floor. He stooped down to pick it up, stood up, and an odd thing happened: his perception seemed to shift, and he saw his living room as if he were an infrequent visitor. The space was at once both vaguely familiar and largely unknown — he seemed to know where things were, yet he had no idea why they were as they were. The records by the stereo were an odd combination: classical, country, jazz, rock and roll, new wave and rap music, in no particular order. Similarly, the books on the shelf were eclectic: fiction, nonfiction, books of photographs, books of paintings, even books written in ancient languages — all were randomly arranged, without apparent order. Sheen put the bag of groceries on the coffee table and investigated further.

The bedroom was austerely furnished. There was a low, unmade bed and a television set on the floor; there was a drafting table, a metal stool, a dresser in one corner. Shoes and clothes were scattered where they had been dropped. Despite the superficial mess, however, Sheen recognized an underlying order, an efficiency in the arrangement of the furniture. For a moment he did not understand why dresses hung in the closet.

In the top drawer of the dresser, a small jar contained silver change; in the second drawer, beneath the shirts, he found a heavy wooden box. The box was worn on the corners and along the bottom edge, as if it had been moved and carried often, and a name was engraved on a small brass plate. "Vice-domini," he read out loud, enunciating each syllable, and he sat on the bed, put the box in his lap, opened it slowly.

The box was lined with blue velvet, and in a shallow recess, a pistol fit snugly.

In his hand the pistol was heavy and familiar, solid and reassuring, an anchor. He moved it in a slow arc, back and forth in front of his face, and his eyes seemed to follow automatically, effortlessly aligning the front sight blade in the rear sight notch. He put the pistol back in the box and closed the top so quickly it was somehow disturbing.

Sheen walked back into the living room and picked up the bag of groceries from the table. As he did so, he realized that the air in the apartment was musty, and he went to open a window. He twisted the lock with his free hand; just then his eyes fixed on the framed certificate on the wall, and he seemed unable to look away, entranced, as if he were for the first time seeing the bright blue letters and official gold seal of the city.

"For valor," he read out loud, and suddenly he remembered the events for which he had been given the award — remembered so vividly that it seemed he was again standing on the black asphalt basketball court, his heart seeming to pound as loudly as the basketball that bounced beneath his hand; his other hand was on his service revolver, the black Colt that was worn on the barrel end and the trigger guard from where it had rubbed against the holster over and over, draw and fire, draw and fire. He remembered the rage on the man's face as he had burst through the door onto the balcony, screaming before he began to shoot, "Quiet! Quiet! Quiet!" And he remembered that the sound of the bullets passing overhead had seemed louder than the sound of the shots. His eyes had automatically aligned the sights, and his finger had squeezed the trigger so gently that the sound of his own shot surprised him. The man's head had snapped back, and he had collapsed.

Sheen remembered the sadness he had felt, the overwhelming sense of futility. Courage, he remembered thinking, is not only the ability to meet the enemy but also the ability to face yourself afterward.

I survived the sadness then, he thought, *and I will survive it now,* and with that thought his perception shifted again. In that moment, the loneliness and the hurt coalesced and created an impelling determination, a ferocious indifference.

Sheen turned away from the award, raised the window, and put his free hand on the sill; he leaned out and breathed the fresh air — suddenly it seemed that the apartment smelled like a penned animal's cage.

Heat shimmered in waves from the hood of the dark blue Ford. Tony Avila nervously drummed his fingers on the steering wheel. His dark cheeks were flushed. He took a final pull on his cigarette, leaned forward, stubbed it out with a pounding motion that rattled the dashboard ashtray.

Next to him, Sheen was twisted on the seat, looking at him with undisguised anger.

"Look, Sheen," Tony Avila said, trying to voice a conviction he did not feel, "I'll tell you what's in it, I'll even read it to you — I just don't want the file in *your* hands with *you* reading it. I took enough of a chance just getting it. Technically, the file is still with the grand jury. I never worked the case, and I never had any business with this guy Profit. So how's it going to look, me taking the file on him and putting it in your hands?"

"I told you how to cover it," Sheen said. He reached into his pocket, took out the thick, rubber-band-wrapped address book he had taken from Profit's attaché case, held it by one corner, and shook it at Tony Avila. "If anyone asks, I'm an informant. It may even work out that way — there are names in this book that would surprise even you."

"But you're not a policeman anymore, Sheen. If it ever gets to court, it makes a big difference. I can tell you what I want, but nobody outside the department gets to read the files. You know that."

Sheen pinched his lower lip between thumb and forefinger, pulling the lip down, and when he spoke the words whistled through the exposed teeth.

"If it ever gets to court, Tony, it's not going to be because I read the file on a punk."

Tony Avila's eyes widened slightly, and his neck reddened above his starched white collar.

"I didn't mean that," Sheen said, and he turned on the seat and faced the front of the car. He put his elbows on his knees and his face in his hands; with a slow circular motion, he rubbed his forehead with his fingertips. "What do you expect me to do?" he asked, his voice low and passionate. "Her funeral was nine days ago. For nine days I've been sitting on my thumbs waiting for you to get the file, and now that you have it, you tell me I can't read it because you don't want to violate departmental policy." Sheen dropped his hands from his face and looked at Tony Avila with eyes that were angry and challenging. "I could ask for a whole lot more than a file, Tony. I could ask *you* to find him."

"I'm already looking, Sheen — you didn't *have* to ask."

Sheen's breath expelled through his nose and made a snorting sound. "Don't go too far out of your way. I wouldn't want you to violate policy to do it." He put his hand flat on the seat and leaned on it. "Nine days after your wife's funeral, were you still looking? Within a week I'd already delivered the punk to you, and you'd already set up a blind, a *double* blind — you set *me* up, too."

Tony Avila slouched on the seat. "That was different," he

said, his voice low. He started to look at Sheen, thought better of it, looked at his lap. "She was my *wife,* Sheen."

Sheen slapped his palm on the dashboard; it made a sound like a shot.

"You no-nuts bastard! You owe this to me! You think some fucking priest changes how you *feel?*"

Tony Avila did not reply. With his right hand he grasped the ring finger of his left and twisted it. The knuckle made a grating sound before it popped.

Again Sheen slapped the dashboard, but this time it was a gesture of disgust. He sat back against the car door, draped his arm over the seat back, pulled his ankle beneath his knee.

"Read it to me, Tony. Read me the whole file. Every word."

Tony Avila twisted his finger back and forth, forcing bone against bone as he hesitated; then, slowly, he leaned forward and reached under the seat. He brought out the thick file folder and put it on his lap. Without thinking, he pulled back the corner of the folder, creasing the cover into two triangles. He stared out over the hood of the car and handed the file to Sheen.

Sheen took it quickly, greedily, snatching it out of Tony's hand before he could change his mind. For a long moment neither of them moved; then Sheen began to read and Tony Avila reached in his pocket for a cigarette.

"It says here that Profit was busted for less than two *ounces* of cocaine," Sheen said after a minute. "He told me he lost two *kilos.*"

"So he lied," Tony replied dully, the tone conveying a cynical lack of surprise. "It made him feel important."

"Jesus, Tony," Sheen said, and looked up. "Profit knew about the tap. He *knew* his home phone was tapped."

Tony brought one leg up on the seat and turned to face Sheen. "Yeah, that one is hard to figure. It's almost like he set up his own bust. But they foxed him with the other one, the tap on the pay phone. Man, I'm glad I was nowhere near that bust." He twisted around to open the window further.

117

"I wonder why he was going to take off that guy in Miami. Greedy bastard. If he did half the business it looks like he was doing, he was rolling fat."

"You checked the phone number in Miami?"

"*I* didn't, but it was checked. Read on."

Sheen perused the pages quickly — the phone number had been traced to a Cuban restaurant in Little Havana — but the file was inconclusive. Other than the transcripts from the conversations that had been recorded illegally, the evidence against Profit was embarrassingly meager, and the conversations themselves were so veiled and so ambiguous that they were largely indecipherable.

Sheen read the file front to back. The most recent events were first and the first event was last; he slowly read the report with which the file had been opened, the report that an informant had come forward, a white female who claimed knowledge of a cocaine distributor. *Andrea,* Sheen thought sadly.

He closed the folder and dropped it on the seat.

"What do you think?" he asked.

Tony Avila raised one shoulder and dropped it in a gesture of uncertainty.

"I don't know, Sheen. Maybe it *was* an accident."

"Like this was an accident?" Sheen held up his right hand and wiggled the stumps.

"I hear his house burned to the ground, too. You may never know. Profit could have done it, but that other guy, the guy in Miami, Moses, he could've done it, too. If he knew Profit was setting him up, he might have figured it was a sure way to put you after him — then Profit is no problem."

Tony Avila's deep brown eyes studied Sheen's face, and he added, "If that *is* the way it happened, you're dancing to his tune."

Sheen nodded in agreement. "I know," he said. "That's why I'm going to find both of them."

"Yeah? How you gonna do that? You plan to set up an appointment with a secretary? Bump into them at the club?"

"I'll find a way," Sheen said.

Tony Avila slowly shook his head. "You go to Miami, they'll eat you for lunch. You don't even speak the language."

"I *will* find a way," Sheen said again. "All I need is something to sell, something to start me through Profit's connections."

"You're bad when you got a gun in your hand," Tony said, "if there's enough hand left."

"There's enough," Sheen snapped. "*You* wouldn't come out on me."

Tony Avila casually moved his arm along the seat back. "That's true," he said, "I wouldn't."

He looked pointedly out the window, as if something of interest had caught his eye, and waited for Sheen's glance to follow; Sheen's eyes moved only slightly, away and back.

"But I'd make sure I didn't *have* to come out on you, Sheen," Tony continued, his voice calm and placid, almost amused, as he pulled the .22 derringer from beneath the headrest and pressed the barrel against Sheen's left ear. "It's been done before, remember?"

For a moment Sheen was so startled that he could not move, but anger quickly displaced his fear, and he threw open the car door.

"Before you go, amigo," Tony said, the derringer dangling loosely in his hand, "you should know that you've got one other problem."

Sheen's greenish eyes flashed, but his expression was frozen, his lips pressed tightly together, the muscle pulsing in his jaw.

Tony Avila casually put down the pistol and reached beneath the seat; with a fluid flick of the wrist he flung a second file folder at Sheen. The folder bounced off the seat back and landed flat on the seat.

On the cover of the folder was the official seal of the United States Drug Enforcement Administration. On the tab in the upper left-hand corner, a name was printed in precise computer letters: VICEDOMINI, SHEEN.

9

THE HOUSE projected from the face of the cliff and seemed to be balanced on rather than fastened to its thin supports. Beyond and below the house, the open expanse of deep blue water stretched to the horizon, shimmering in the early morning sun. The wind was calm, and sounds carried. A red sports car flashed past on the highway, tires squealing as it braked for a hairpin switchback. When the car was past the turn, Sheen bent both arms and rolled his neck, stretching luxuriously; straightening his arms and twisting his back, he tried to get the stiffness out of his muscles and joints. The ocean air was damp and cold, and he had been quiescent for more than an hour.

With his hands back in the side pockets of his jacket he crouched on his heels two hundred feet up the cliff and across the highway from the house. He continued to wait, and as he did so, again he considered his plan: Sheen intended to steal the cocaine Profit had sold to John and Stuart. He needed the cocaine, he reasoned, so that he could begin to call the numbers in Profit's address book — call the numbers and approach the people, one of whom would lead him to Profit.

Profit, Sheen said to himself, his internal voice even, unemotional. Briefly he wondered why he felt obligated to find Profit, what he hoped to gain. "You have to know where your obligations end," Andrea had said. *The obligation has become a duty,* Sheen thought, *duty to myself, not to her. She is dead.* But he wondered how the duty would affect him, because he knew full well that often enough, you are what you seem to be — and he was about to steal.

Just then he heard the knocking clatter of a diesel automobile, and a maroon Oldsmobile roared up the driveway and turned onto the highway. Behind the wheel, John's posture suggested a grim determination. He was late for the opening of the market.

Sheen waited five minutes before he walked down the steep hill, down the orange dirt driveway, and down the white concrete steps with the low risers and long treads. At the front door, he knocked twice.

From inside the house a vexed voice said, "Just a moment, John."

Stuart did not look to see who was at the door; rather, he simply pulled it open and walked away. By the time the door had bounced against its stop he was already past the foyer, ankle deep in the living room's shag rug.

"I've told you before," Stuart said over his shoulder, his voice reproachful, "you can't leave that hurriedly and expect to remember everything. What is it this time? I *know* you have your glasses."

Sheen stepped into the foyer and closed the door. "But I don't wear glasses, Stuart," he said, and he watched carefully as Stuart turned quickly and clutched at his bathrobe, pulling it close at the throat.

The television was on, tuned to the morning news, and before he spoke Stuart reached down and snapped it off. "What are *you* doing here?" he asked, his voice sour.

Sheen moved further into the room and said, "John didn't tell you I was coming? That wasn't very thoughtful of him."

Stuart's face was puffy from sleep, and he looked exasperated. "He didn't say anything to me — not that John is known for his thoughtfulness. You should have called first, at the very least, before you just dropped by. You gave me quite a start."

"I'm sorry. I *should* have called," Sheen said, nodding agreement, his voice deprecatory, "but there aren't any phones nearby and I was hoping to catch John here. Now I guess I'll have to go back to the city."

"You see how a little courtesy — " Stuart began, then stopped himself. "Well, before you go, would you like a cup of coffee? The pot is fresh."

"Coffee would be nice," Sheen said. In the kitchen, he turned a heavy chrome stool so that he could lean back against it.

Stuart pulled tight the sash on his robe and went behind the green Formica counter.

"Cream only," Sheen said, then added as if he had just thought of it, "Maybe you can help me, Stuart."

Stuart's thinning hair formed a wedge on top of his head. He did not look up as he said, "I certainly don't know how." He poured two cups of coffee, turned to the refrigerator and opened it, turned back with a carton of milk. "John handles *all* the business. He insists on it."

He put a cup of coffee on the counter in front of Sheen, picked up his own cup, and sipped from it delicately.

"But he must value your opinion." Sheen stirred the coffee, held the spoon over the cup, looked at it speculatively. "Profit has been shorting you, Stuart, not by weight, of course, but on quality — weight and quality are the same thing, really. For the money you pay, I can do better, much better."

"John will be very interested, I'm sure." Stuart's tone indicated a polite but detached interest. "He and Profit have never really seen eye to eye."

Sheen tapped the spoon once on the counter. "What I'll do is this: I'll trade you a quarter pound of my coke for four ounces of the coke Profit sold you. You'll see for yourself what garbage you've been serving your friends."

Stuart's lips pursed, and Sheen knew that he had scored.

He reached into his shirt pocket and took out a small square of tin foil.

"Try some of mine," he said, and he extended the packet across the counter, far enough that his offer was clear but

122

not so far that Stuart could accept it without reaching for it.

"Quite the salesman, aren't you?"

"I just think you deserve better than you get."

Sheen smiled when Stuart took the packet because he knew the cocaine Profit had left for Andrea and him was uncut, at least twice as pure as the cocaine Profit had sold to John.

With one finger Stuart hooked the long gold chain that hung around his neck and pulled it up past his ear, until a small gold spoon appeared on his chest. He allowed the spoon to dangle as he leaned forward to open the tin foil; then, retrieving the spoon and holding it between thumb and first finger, he dipped into the packet twice. He stood up straight, inhaled deeply, smiled.

"*That,*" he said, rubbing his nose, "is a delightful experience, particularly after that *other.*"

"It's for you," Sheen said. He pointed at the tin foil and winked. "So let's make the trade."

"Now? I don't know if I should."

"Why not? I'll see John in the city and tell him — we both know how pleased he'll be — and I won't have to make another trip out here. It works well for all of us."

Stuart put his hands in the pockets of his robe and stared absently at the open square of tin foil.

"John *will* be pleased, won't he? Do you have four ounces with you?"

Sheen nodded and stood up.

"It's in my car."

"I warn you, I'm going to test it."

Sheen smiled confidently and made his way to the front door as Stuart moved from behind the counter. Sheen loudly opened and closed the door, but he did not go out; for a full minute he stood motionless in the foyer, then he walked back through the living room and down the hall.

In the master bedroom, Stuart was on his knees in the walk-in closet.

Sheen waited for him to turn away from the floor safe.

"How much do you have left?" he asked.

"Quite a bit," Stuart replied. "We've been saving it. We're going to have a party soon — it will be wonderful to have *good* coke for our guests."

Stuart inched further into the closet and brought out a triple-beam balance scale and a chemical test kit. Two bags of cocaine as large as grapefruits were on the floor by his knees. Preoccupied with his task, he did not notice when Sheen took a pillowcase from a pillow on the bed.

Casually, Sheen squatted on his heels beside Stuart, hefted one bag of cocaine, then the other, and put them both into the pillowcase.

"What are you doing?" Stuart asked. He sat back on his heels and folded his hands in his lap, watching curiously.

Sheen picked up the scale and the test kit and put them, too, into the pillowcase.

"I'm stealing the cocaine, Stuart," he said. He stood up, the pillowcase in his left hand. "I hope you won't make me hurt you to do it."

"If this is a joke, it's in very poor taste."

"It's not a joke, Stuart. I regret having to do it, but I *have* to have the coke. If I can, I'll replace it."

"But why would you do this?" Stuart asked, his tone a mix of disbelief and mounting anxiety. "You can make so much money from John. We're always honest in our dealings."

"This," Sheen said, lifting the pillowcase slightly, "is not for money."

He backed away three steps, toward the door.

"Do you have any guns?"

"Of course not, they're illegal."

Stuart started to stand up, but Sheen motioned for him to stay where he was, and he sat back on his heels. His voice dropped to a pleading whisper, and he said, "Don't do this. John will just die, really. Please, don't do this."

"I'm sorry, Stuart. You'll get more cocaine for your party — and I *will* try to replace this." Sheen twisted the pillowcase so that it wrapped around his wrist. "Don't move until you hear the front door close."

124

Stuart's soft brown eyes were sad and hurt more than angry. "But I thought you were someone of integrity," he said.

Sheen did not reply. He stepped back through the bedroom door, and, out of Stuart's sight, he waited in the hall. After a moment he looked back into the bedroom.

Stuart had shifted his position on the floor. He sat with his legs crossed Indian style; his hands were on his knees, palms up, thumb and first finger on each hand forming a circle. His eyes were closed, and in a low voice he was chanting monotonously.

Sheen turned and walked down the hall, the pillowcase heavy in his hand.

He walked up the steps, up the steep driveway, up the road to the car he had concealed past the switchback. Carefully he packed the cocaine, the scale, and the test kit into his suitcase, then he locked the suitcase in the trunk and began to drive the winding coast highway back to San Francisco. Near the Howard Johnson's parking lot where he had been attacked, he stopped and twisted the rearview mirror so that he could look at himself, but he could see no significant change in the face that peered back at him.

At the airport, Sheen checked the suitcase through to New Orleans, bought himself a cup of coffee, walked slowly down the concourse. When he neared the departure gate, he stopped to look through the large plate glass windows at the idling jet. In the cockpit the pilot was reading a newspaper; on the ground near the middle of the airplane, two baggage handlers were throwing suitcases from open trailers into the baggage compartment. Sheen looked for his suitcase, but he knew it was unlikely he would see it.

Close behind him, a harsh voice said, "I wonder what's in all those bags?"

Sheen looked around so quickly that coffee spilled over his hand. Reflexly he tried to move away from the spill, but he bumped two solid bodies, and the coffee spilled again.

Detective Gossett was on his left, Detective Ridell on his right, standing so close behind him that he was pinned, facing the glass. Sheen turned his head to look at one, then the other.

"I wonder if it's worth the trouble to get a warrant?" Gossett continued, his mouth so near that Sheen smelled his breath, a sour combination of coffee and cigarettes. "Or maybe you've got something in your pocket? What about it, Vicedomini? Should we bother? Or should we just drop a quarter to New Orleans and let them do the paperwork? You on vacation again? Can't think of anyplace else to go?"

Sheen shifted the cup of coffee from one hand to the other.

"I'm leaving," he said.

"Yeah? Maybe you are, and maybe you aren't. How's the hand? I hear you lost more than just your fingers. I feel for you, Vicedomini. I feel for your dead girlfriend."

Sheen twisted to his left, bumping Gossett as he turned away from the window. His mouth was hard around the words it formed.

"You're out of line, Gossett, way out of line."

"And so sensitive."

"We're here to see you off," Ridell broke in. "To make sure that you *are* off."

"Yeah, and to let you know we're on you like flies on shit. Go back to your sewer, Vicedomini. Get *real* dirty, so when the D.E.A. pops you you'll be gone forever — they got such a nice file on you already."

Sheen felt a strong hand grip his arm above the elbow, and he could feel the press of Ridell's solid bulk.

In a low voice Ridell said, "Your plane is boarding, Sheen. Make us all happy: don't come back."

The hand released its grip.

Sheen looked first at Ridell, then at Gossett, then he pushed between them, put his coffee cup in an ashtray, and walked past the ticket agent and down the ramp, resisting the urge to look over his shoulder.

When he looked out the plane's window, Sheen saw Gossett and Ridell on the concourse, watching his departure. Gossett was talking, animatedly gesturing as he spoke, and Ridell was listening, nodding his head to show that he understood. Sheen was certain that Tony Avila had sent them, but he did not know what he could do about it.

A boxlike yellow tractor passed under the wing; a moment later, the airplane lurched and began to roll backward. Gossett stopped talking and stood noticeably still. Ridell rubbed his lower lip thoughtfully.

"Tony Avila," Sheen said to himself, his voice low but emphatic, as if he were making a promise.

When the airplane turned away from the boarding gate, Sheen shook his head roughly side to side, clearing it, then took out Profit's address book so that he could review the names and numbers that were written there.

In the Dallas/Fort Worth airport, while awaiting the connecting flight that would take him to New Orleans, Sheen began to make calls. Repeatedly he explained that he was temporarily taking over Profit's distribution routes. "Yes," he said, "Profit is fine; no, there has not been any trouble. Profit is tired, on vacation, looking for new sources, better quality." Although many of the buyers seemed hungry, by the time his flight was called, only one person, a man named Willie, had agreed to meet him.

"One is enough," Sheen said to himself. "At least it's a start."

At home, Sheen used the small watch he had given Andrea to mark his place in Profit's address book; he stashed the book in the kitchen cupboard with his newly acquired nine hundred grams of cocaine.

From his apartment in the Irish Channel Sheen had to drive through the central business district and the French Quarter to find the small grocery in the Faubourg Marigny where he had agreed to meet Willie. The workday traffic was heavy, and he marked his progress first by blocks, then by feet as he passed the sterile new tower buildings, crossed Canal Street, moved slowly into the French Quarter. As traffic started and stopped, Sheen looked through the windows of shops and bars and through ornate iron gates into open courtyards and dark alleys. The low, old buildings seemed somehow secret, turned inward, and Sheen had the unsettling sense that he was in some complex labyrinth without a center.

On the far side of the French Quarter he found the grocery, parked, got out of his car, and leaned back against the warm hood. He was nervous, uncertain what to expect. He realized that the sun was hot and moved into the shade under a second-floor balcony.

At exactly ten o'clock a dark blue pickup truck stopped at the curb in front of the grocery. Jacked up over huge tires, the truck seemed strong and solid yet delicately balanced; somehow it reminded Sheen of the house on the cliff. Brownish mud was caked on the truck, thick around the wheel wells, splattered as high as the white camper top. The driver's door opened, and a man with long red hair and a thick red beard stepped down from the cab. He was built solidly: sloping, powerful shoulders, big neck, big wrists. He wore blue jeans, a long johns top, a red and white ball cap. His boots were caked with the same color mud that was on the truck.

"You Sheen?" the man asked.

"Yes," Sheen replied, and pushed himself away from the wall against which he had been leaning. "Are you Willie?"

"No, but Willie sent me." The man jerked his head to one side, indicating the truck. "Get in."

"I have my car. I'll follow you."

"Your car ain't going to make it where we got to go, partner. Hell, my truck just barely gets through, itself."

Sheen rubbed his nose with one finger as he considered the situation.

"I'd rather not," he said. "Tell Willie I'll see him in the city sometime."

"Suit yourself," the red-haired man said, giving an exaggerated shrug. "But you're settling into a mighty long wait. Willie ain't been to the city in a year or better."

He reached into his hip pocket, took out a foil bag and unfolded it, extended the bag toward Sheen. Sheen shook his head no, and with one pink, freckled hand the man reached into the bag and pulled out a moist black clump of tobacco.

"Listen," he said. He put the tobacco in his mouth, chewed twice, adjusted the wad in his cheek before he continued. "If Profit sent you, you'll be treated like a prince. If he didn't, you shouldn't be coming anyway. Willie said I should get you, so here I am. But I got to get moving. By noon it's going to be hot enough, and I've got no mind to dawdle into the heat of the day."

"How far is it?"

"About two hours," the man replied, and turned his head to spit a long brown jet of tobacco juice into the gutter, "give or take a bit for sinkholes. My name is Red, by the way."

Sheen watched the tobacco juice ooze down the curb; he rubbed both hands over his face, suddenly feeling very tired. He knew he had to take the risk: one connection would lead to another, and somewhere between the connections, both Profit and Moses were on the circuit.

"All right," Sheen said. He dropped his hands from his face. "I've never been in a sinkhole, anyway."

Red looked at him with an amused smile.

"Well, you won't have to wait long now."

They drove southwest, away from the city. Across the Mississippi River they turned from the four-lane freeway onto a two-lane secondary road. The truck's heavy tires roared on the pavement, making conversation impossible. Sheen had no idea where they were going. Along the roadside the heavy growth of plants formed a solid wall. Red slowed to turn onto a twisting white shell path, then suddenly he left the path.

The truck labored heavily, bouncing over tree stumps and low mounds, sinking unexpectedly in deep mud and sand. Once the truck mired past its axles, and Red looked at Sheen and said, "You're in your first sinkhole, partner." Then he got out of the truck to play out a winch cable and wrap it around a tree. He sank in mud past his knees. Even with the windows closed Sheen could hear the obscene sucking, slurping sound the mud made each time Red laboriously took a step. The winch pulled them free, and for another half hour they bounced on — south, Sheen noted, watching the dashboard compass — before, finally, they stopped in the shade of a huge oak tree.

Sheen felt battered by the ride, and was relieved that they were taking a break. He wanted to get out of the truck to stretch, but when he opened the door, mosquitoes swarmed in. Quickly he pulled it shut.

Red said, his voice surprisingly sympathetic, "The mosquitoes get worse every year, I think. Look in the glovebox, there's some repellant. I'll jump out real quick and get the boat — once we're on the water, the mosquitoes aren't so bad."

Sheen looked around, but he did not see any water. Before he could ask, however, Red was out of the truck. Sheen watched as he walked past the oak tree and almost immediately dropped hip deep, pushed through the high grass, and was gone from sight. It happened so quickly that Sheen was sure it was some sort of illusion. Still he could not tell where the land ended and the water began.

A few minutes later Sheen heard the whine of a powerful high-speed engine, and a flat-bottomed boat seemed to erupt through the tall razor grass. The boat skidded across the tree roots; the rudder pivoted, and the boat spun up beside the truck. Red sat in the back, up high, just in front of the propeller, and he motioned for Sheen to sit on the low front bench. As soon as he was on the bench, gripping the aluminum seat tightly with both hands, the engine whined high and the airboat thudded across the roots, the grass parted, and they were on the water.

The bayou ran through vegetation so thick and heavy it formed dark tunnels and across open fields of low grass; it intersected other narrow channels and canals as wide as rivers. They stopped once so that Red could reach into his pocket for more tobacco, and Sheen breathed deeply, savoring the intertwined smell of growing things and decay. He reached down to pluck the flower from a water lily, and behind him a heavy shot exploded; next to his hand, the dull brown water erupted and splashed over him.

130

"Cottonmouth," Red shouted, "a big one. Look."

Sheen looked, but he did not see the snake. He kept his hands inboard.

A broad mudflat oozed into an open, meandering waterway, and Red opened up the airboat, pushing it, sliding it sideways on the sharp turns. Sheen marveled at how smoothly the airboat slipped across the surface of the water, as if it were greased, or on ice. In the middle of a sharp bend Red cut the engine, and they drifted; just as the boat was about to stop, it bumped a hidden pier. Sheen saw then, buried in the high weeds, the rough-sawn, weathered gray cypress planks that formed a shaky walkway.

Behind him, Red said, "It's been a pleasure."

Sheen looked around uncertainly.

Red pointed down the walkway at a dark pocket of shadows.

"That way," he said. "Tell Willie I'll pass by later — particularly if Freddie's going to cook."

Reluctantly Sheen stood up and stepped onto the pier.

The airboat drifted away. Red waved before he started the engine. The rudder pivoted, the boat turned, and Sheen felt the powerful prop wash as Red accelerated and disappeared around the bend. The engine's drone faded, and suddenly an overwhelming stillness settled. Small insects hummed. Ripples washed against the pier. Sheen found it hard to believe that he was only two hours from the city, two hours from the slow-moving traffic, the sterile tower buildings, the French Quarter. He felt intensely alone and helpless. He was frightened in a way he had never before known — afraid that he would not be able to take care of himself.

Irresolute, he turned and started down the rickety walk.

Past the high grass, centered between two huge oak trees, there was a house on stilts, ten feet off the ground. Surrounded completely by a screened porch, it seemed veiled, deserted, the old wood siding faded to the color of the shadows. On the ground near the walk was an old, rusted metal sign; near that was a discarded outboard motor.

A mongrel dog appeared suddenly, snarling low in its throat.

Sheen froze. The dog's snout was swollen hideously, and the animal seemed unsteady on its feet.

From the porch, someone shouted, "Get!" The screen door slammed. "I said get!"

A short, plump man stood on the stairs that led up to the house.

"You Sheen?" he asked. "Come on in. The dog won't bother you. He was snake-bit yesterday. He can hardly walk."

Sheen saw that the dog's eyes were glazed, and he took a tentative step forward. The dog lay down and put its head on the ground.

"Are you Willie?" Sheen asked as he neared the steps.

"Do I look like Willie?" the man replied, and laughed. Three of his front teeth were missing, and the remaining ones were stained yellow-brown. "You wouldn't know, would you? Nah, I'm Freddie." He wiped his hands on the apron that was tied around his middle. "Willie went to get a turtle — he said we should feed you right."

"When will he be back?"

Freddie gave a now-there's-a-dumb-question look, and said, "Soon as he gets a turtle, of course. Come on in."

Low iron bunks ran side by side down the length of the porch. They made Sheen think of a barracks, but the beds were unmade and the arrangement was haphazard.

"Do you have enough beds?" he asked.

Freddie laughed again. "It was my daddy's idea to get all those. He wanted us to be a lodge — he was touched in the head. I just keep 'em because I only have to change my sheets once a year. I have company a lot, too: it's my cooking. You want a beer?"

Sheen nodded, and Freddie led the way to the kitchen.

Large black cast-iron pots were simmering on an old cast-iron stove. The ancient sink was the color of rust, and the floor was filthy with layers of dirt, grease, and footprints; in stark contrast, the refrigerator and the freezer were new and hygienically white. Freddie reached into the refrigerator and handed Sheen an ice-cold bottle of beer.

132

Sheen held the cold bottle against his forehead before he opened it and took a long, luxurious swallow.

"Where do you get electricity?" he asked.

"You don't ask, and I won't lie. But they got power lines all over this swamp." Freddie gave him a conspiratorial wink. "I got a generator, if anybody asks. I got a phone too, but I guess you know that. Willie gave me the icebox and the freezer. That boy does like to eat, but Bear — that's his brother — he's in another class altogether."

Freddie lifted the lid on a pot and looked inside.

"Say, hand me a bag of ice, would you?" With a long serving spoon he pointed at the freezer.

Sheen stumbled on a broken linoleum tile as he crossed to the freezer. Not seeing a convenient place to put down his beer, he bent over and set it on the floor, then wiped his hand on his pants and raised the freezer door. When he looked inside, he felt a fear that paralyzed him completely and made him unable even to breathe: on top of the ice, coiled at chest level and ready to strike, was the largest snake he had ever seen. The black, diamond-shaped head was as big as a saucer. The black, unblinking eyes were fixed on his face. Both his hands were on the freezer door, over his head, and his chest was a broad, exposed target. For a full half minute he did not move; then with all his strength he slammed shut the freezer door and jumped back.

Behind him, Freddie was doubled up with laughter, one hand over his mouth. He slapped the other hand on the stove and said between fits of laughter, "That damn snake works *every* time."

Eventually he stood up straight, walked to the freezer, and opened it.

"I keep my hides in here."

With both hands he grabbed the snake by the top coil and lifted it up. The snake was frozen solid; exposed to the humid air, its scales developed a thin layer of frost.

"And this snake *keeps* my hides in here — it's what you call a burglary device. Shit, you were pretty good. Bear damn near died. I think he would've killed me if it hadn't been Willie's idea in the first place. Even Bear won't tangle with Willie."

As Freddie put the snake back in the freezer, he kicked over Sheen's beer on the floor.

"Help yourself to another," he said, and picked up the brown bottle from the floor.

"I don't know if I should — there's no telling what's in the refrigerator."

Freddie laughed again and shut the freezer.

"Can't fault you on that. I'll get you one."

Involuntarily, Sheen shuddered as he looked at the freezer and thought of the snake.

"What kind of hides do you keep?" he asked.

Freddie gave him a look that he might have given a less than bright child.

"Why, alligator hides, of course."

From behind them an angry voice said, "You know that boy real well, Freddie?"

Sheen looked over his shoulder. As soon as he saw the man in the doorway, he knew he was looking at Bear: massive shoulders sloped above a huge belly, and chest and arms, up to the top of the shoulders, were matted with dark brown hair, bearlike. The man wore gray overalls without a shirt, and heavy boots. His hair was long enough to be pulled back in a ponytail, but his beard was closely trimmed. It was thicker but no longer than the hair on his shoulders.

"Willie invited him," Freddie said. "He's okay with me."

Bear looked pointedly at Sheen, and in his glance there was a physical challenge: it was a look that dared Sheen to cross him, dared him *not* to back away. Sheen could imagine Bear in the housing projects, bad-ass white man getting off his motorcycle, stomping into the black men's bar, ordering a beer, and looking around in just that way — challenging, daring. They did that sometimes, the ones new to the city, the ones who thought they were *bad*. They had their beers and they left, the smart ones; the others stayed too long and had their faces kicked in. Sheen had seen it before, too often, because he had been called to drag them out of the bars and take them to the hospital, and all the while, if they were conscious, they would say how *bad* they were, how much damage they had done, how much damage they would do when they went back.

Sheen gave Bear a dull look and dropped his glance, watching his hands.

Bear's breath expelled through his nose with a snorting sound.

He said, "Willie don't know him either, you dumb fuck."

Bear reached back through the doorway; Sheen twisted slightly and raised the tail of his shirt so that the handle of his Colt was exposed and accessible. *You do not try to reason with someone like Bear,* he thought.

Bear leaned down, and Sheen saw the handle of a revolver sticking out of his hip pocket. He stepped behind the counter, took out his Colt, and held it beside his leg as Bear grappled with something on the floor, cursed, made a vicious swiping motion with one hand. A large green turtle over two feet long skidded between his legs, sliding and spinning on its shell, upside down. Because its shell had a thick ridge, the turtle canted to one side on the kitchen floor; looking around curiously, it moved its legs back and forth in the air, as if it were swimming.

Very slowly and deliberately, Bear took the long-barreled revolver out of his hip pocket, aimed it, and fired. The shot had a concussing, ringing force; the turtle's head disappeared. Bear put the revolver back in his pocket, but before he walked out of the kitchen, again he looked pointedly at Sheen, his eyes squinting, his message clear.

The outside door slammed shut behind him.

"Bear's all right," Freddie said, "once you get to know him. He won't bother you — and man, look at the turtle we got." He picked up the turtle by one leg and held it high, a prize. "Willie will be coming soon. Take your beer out on the porch. I got to get cooking."

Sheen slipped the Colt back under his shirt before he moved away from the counter.

"Thanks," he said, relieved, not wanting any part of dicing the turtle. "All I need is a beer."

"Help yourself," Freddie said, then laughed. "I guess I'll get it for you. I probably owe you that much."

Sheen smiled then, a genuine smile. For the first time since Andrea's death, he felt he was among the living.

The house was built on a low rise, a small island in the swamp, and from the elevated porch Sheen could see water all around. He felt, beneath his fear, the attraction the swamp held, the heavy stillness, the life. There was a sense of peace, a sense of the natural order of things. He held his beer up to the light and watched the bubbles rise up in it; through the amber bottle, he saw movement in the tall grass.

A lithe, shirtless man appeared first. He took one step into the clearing, then turned and again was lost in the weeds. Bear appeared next. He moved slowly and heavily, a large canvas oyster sack over each shoulder.

The shirtless man appeared again and cupped his hands to his mouth.

"Yo, Sheen, lend a hand!"

Sheen left his beer on the porch, went down the steps, and followed the trampled grass to a second hidden pier where a small pirogue was piled high with supplies. The lithe man came up the landing to meet him. He was not much taller than Sheen, certainly not over six feet. His body was lean, and his skin was tanned to a deep bronze. The cords stood out on his neck and gave the impression of a tautness about him, a tension. He had the blackest eyes Sheen had ever seen, blacker even than the eyes of the snake in the freezer: flat, dull black. His black hair was cut short. Sheen had no difficulty believing that Bear would not tangle with Willie. *Not many people would tangle with Willie,* he thought, *not with any success.*

"Help me unload this stuff," Willie said, and he knelt on the low pier, reached into the pirogue, and handed up a case of beer. There was an easiness to his movements, a certain grace. "Stack it on the walk. Bear will get it inside."

The pirogue was quickly emptied, the supplies piled neatly on the pier.

"Hop in," Willie said, pointing at the pirogue. "I'll show you around."

Sheen hesitated, and Willie saw it.

"It's up to you, Sheen," he said, "but we have to start somewhere." He stood with his hands on his hips, his head cocked slightly to one side, assessing Sheen openly and giving Sheen the time he needed to look back, to make his own assessment.

Sheen could see in Willie a rigorous self-sufficiency. After a moment he saw, or thought he saw, the beginning of a smile, and when Willie rubbed the corner of his mouth, pulling the skin down so a smile would be lost, Sheen liked the gesture, because he too felt it was silly to stand there and stare so openly, as if they both were gazing into crystal balls.

"Ride in the front," Willie said, "or push from the rear."

Unaware that he was doing so, Sheen rubbed the corner of his own mouth, pulling the skin down, and said, "I think I'll ride."

Willie said, "Smart choice," and Sheen caught the quick smile before he turned his head.

Sheen knelt cautiously in the front of the small boat, and Willie stood in the back; with a long pole, Willie pushed the pirogue away from the pier. The long, stroking motions Willie used with the push-pole gave the pirogue a slow, lulling momentum.

After a minute Willie said, "Take off your shirt and get some sun — you could use it."

Sheen turned slightly to look over his shoulder at him, but the pirogue rocked and he turned back to the front.

"Be careful about moving until you get the feel of it," Willie said. "And you *may* take off your shirt; I've seen pistols before. Just don't point it at me." As Sheen carefully slipped his shirt off, Willie continued, "It takes some getting used to, being out here, but it gets in your blood."

Sheen folded the shirt into a square and worked it under his knees to cushion them.

"How long have you been out here?" he asked.

Willie either did not hear the question or chose to ignore it.

"I never did like Profit," he said. "He was always a little too slick for my taste, a little too much the dealer. Hell, I don't even like cocaine, but for a while it makes me feel so good I forget I don't like it."

An undesired treat, Sheen thought.

"But you're not slick enough, Sheen. You're no dealer. You'll only get your ass in a crack."

Sheen raised one shoulder and dropped it. Whether the gesture was meant to convey a difference of opinion or indifference was hard to tell.

"He's gone," Willie said. "You won't find him by running down his connections."

"How do you know so much?" Sheen asked, his tone dull, matter-of-fact.

"It's a *very* tight community. There's a grapevine you would not believe."

"Then you know why, too."

"I know you lost some fingers, and I know you lost your girlfriend."

Willie held the push-pole out of the water and allowed the pirogue to drift.

"I don't think Profit has the balls to order a hit. He twisted and turned so much he lost his spine. You're getting into something you know nothing about, less than nothing. You think you can take care of yourself — we all *think* we can — and you probably handle yourself pretty well; but anyone can get so far from what he knows he really *can't* take care of himself."

Willie squatted down on his heels and pulled the push-pole inboard.

"You see it?" he asked, and pointed over Sheen's shoulder.

138

On a low bank, peering out from the grass, a beaver watched them, wary, ready to flee.

"There's so much life out here," Willie said, more to himself than to Sheen. "Everywhere, I guess."

The beaver slipped smoothly into the water and disappeared beneath the surface.

"Do you make your living dealing?" Sheen asked.

"No," Willie replied. He stood up and again began to push the pirogue with the long pole. "I used to be pretty active, but it wore off. For a while dealing seems glamorous, then you realize you're invisible: no one sees you, they see only what you're bringing them. And that makes you crazy."

Sheen looked around, hoping that Willie would elaborate, but Willie was twisting the push-pole to free it from a snag.

When he turned back, Willie concluded by saying, "I'll turn an ounce or two for friends, at cost — and *that's* not dealing. Sometimes I have a party."

Sheen thought of Stuart sitting on the bedroom floor, of the eyes that were sad and hurt more than angry, of the party plans he had interrupted.

"Do you have money stashed?"

"You mean, how do I afford it? Look around, Sheen: alligator, nutria, mink. Money is the easy part."

Willie lifted the long pole out of the water and swung it in a wide arc before slapping it down hard.

"I could do without the snakes, though."

"Me too," Sheen said dryly.

Willie laughed a deep laugh then cut himself short.

"Sorry," he said. "I should make Freddie stop his snake-in-the-freezer gag, but he gets such a kick out of it. I thought Bear had had a heart attack when Freddie pulled it on him."

Sheen wiped off the water that had splashed on his arm.

"If you see Profit, will you tell me?"

"Probably not, but it's just as easy to say that I will — I won't hear from him. Profit fucked up and not just with you. By now he's so far underground he's buried."

139

Sheen started to say something, and Willie added, "I don't mean dead." He pushed the pirogue toward shore, and the bow of the boat bumped the hidden pier: they had circled the whole small island.

Sheen held on to a cypress plank and stood up, bending over so that he would not lose his grip.

"How would you find him?" he asked.

Willie stepped onto the pier and looked at Sheen directly, his eyes flat black.

"I wouldn't bother," he said, his tone conveying both a statement of fact and a warning.

Together they lifted the pirogue out of the water and laid it upside down on the pier. Willie stepped over it, started down the pier, turned back to Sheen.

"I don't guess you brought anything with you?" he asked.

"You just said you don't like it."

"I also said I forget," Willie replied, and he smiled warmly, stretching his lips and exposing an even row of very white teeth.

For a moment Sheen did not understand why the smile was disconcerting; then he saw that Willie's smile in no way touched his eyes. They remained fixed and level, flat black, without any emotion whatsoever.

"Well, *if* you brought some, don't bring it out until later. You're going to want your appetite: Freddie can cook. I should have a belly as big as Bear's."

Sheen nodded curtly, showing that he understood, and ran his tongue over his lips, which seemed suddenly very dry.

In one corner of the kitchen Bear sat on a low wooden stool and shucked oysters, twisting the blade of a heavy knife until each dark gray shell cracked, throwing the top half of the shell into a washtub, and scraping the bottom half, the half with the oyster, until the gray, jellylike meat was loose, floating in its own juice, ready to eat. Every third shell he cracked he held up to his mouth and sucked, slurping down the oyster without chewing it; clear juice ran out of both sides of his mouth and dripped down his beard. Freddie stood at

140

the counter dicing wild onions and snapping green beans, and every time Bear ate an oyster, he gave the count: "Three dozen, three; three dozen, four." Every so often he took one of the shells Bear put on the counter and had an oyster himself, sucking it through the gap in his teeth and smacking his lips contentedly.

When the alarm triggered, neither Bear nor Freddie so much as flinched, and for a moment Sheen thought the sound was in his head. High and low tones alternated quickly, deafeningly, vibrating the walls and the floor. Bear continued to shuck oysters. Next to his feet, beer bottles clattered nervously on the floor. Willie moved by so quickly he was a blur, and Sheen followed.

The alarm stopped.

Behind the kitchen a short corridor turned to the left, and a heavy door was open. Sheen stopped short, amazed by what he saw through the door: a small, windowless room no more than ten feet square was brilliantly lit; on three sides of the room, there were consoles of electronic instruments. At least a half-dozen LED displays showed different numbers in glowing red digits. An oscilloscope pulsed, its soft blue line changing rapidly from jagged to smooth. Dozens of indicator lights glowed in different pastel colors. Willie was punching soft-touch buttons so quickly it looked as if he were playing a piano. He looked over his shoulder and saw Sheen.

"Listen," he said, his expression blank as he concentrated, jerking his chin to indicate direction. "That way."

Sheen listened intently, then said, "I don't hear anything."

Willie pulled at his ear and turned a knob on the oscilloscope. "You will."

It was very faint, off in the distance: the sound of a helicopter at low altitude. And it was audible only a moment before it faded.

Willie touched more buttons, watched the numbers change, turned back to Sheen.

"This is my telephone," he said, and he grinned, but the expression was forced. "And my hobby: ham radio. I can talk

141

with anybody on this side of the planet — if I catch a good bounce, the other side too. I put out more watts than the local commercial stations, but I never have gotten around to getting a license. So I monitor local outputs."

"The alarm?"

Willie nodded. "If it's mobile and it gets close, the alarm sounds."

"If you're not broadcasting, what difference does it make?"

"If I'm not broadcasting, none." Willie pointed at a small video display terminal. "But I have programmed automatic responses — that's how I keep in touch with my regulars. Or maybe Bear starts screwing around and leaves an open microphone. It's better safe than sorry, anyway. The F.C.C. comes down pretty hard on us amateurs, and I'd hate to lose all this stuff."

Willie took a step toward Sheen, indicating that he was ready to leave.

"How does the telephone tie in?" Sheen asked.

Willie's lips pursed just a fraction.

"Alternating microwave scans," he said. "Do you know anything about electronics?"

Sheen shook his head. "No."

"Then let's just say I borrow from Ma Bell what she's not using at the micro-moment." Willie took another step toward Sheen and reached past him to turn off the lights. "Nothing about it is complicated." He motioned for Sheen to move back so that he could close the door. "You pick it up as you go along — it just takes a while to get the swing of it, like anything else. I started when I was a kid."

Sheen wanted to ask another question, but before he could, Willie said, "Let's eat. I'm starving."

As Willie shut the heavy door, Sheen sensed that he was also shutting the door on further discussion of his radio, dismissing it as unimportant, a personal quirk. But Sheen had seen in his expression a hesitancy and an aggravation that let him know the radio was more to Willie than an amusing diversion, more than a hobby. Willie stumbled over Sheen's foot but did not seem to notice; just then his expression was a mix of displeasure and preoccupation, an expression Sheen was sure would not last long.

The contrast between the kitchen and the radio room was so stark that it seemed as if the short corridor separated eras as well as rooms. In the kitchen the single bare bulb that hung from the ceiling made a dim yellow light that illuminated a tableau: Freddie looking over his shoulder and smiling, the large gap in his teeth filled by an oyster, the gray, shiny mass quivering between his lips; Bear, clear juice dripping from his chin, looking down between his fat thighs, intent on cracking the shell he held against the top of the stool; the turtle's blood still splattered on the floor, the sink the color of rust, the wallpaper peeling in patches. Into that scene Willie walked casually, slowly, one hand in the pocket of his jeans. But there was nothing slow about the way he hit Bear, twice, in one extraordinarily rapid movement. His fist hit first, directly between Bear's eyes, then his forearm followed as Bear's head snapped back. The forearm caught Bear squarely on the nose, and there was a sickening, grating crunch. Willie, with his other hand still in his pocket, bent at the waist, put his mouth near Bear's ear, and said in a whisper so harsh it sounded like a hiss, "Don't *ever* touch my phone."

Bear stood up slowly, the heavy oyster knife clutched in his hand, a thin line of blood dripping from one nostril. He was half a head taller than Willie and twice as broad, and he gave him the look he had given Sheen, challenging him, daring him. Willie moved back a step, not giving ground but preparing himself. He drew his hand out of his pocket and stood up straight, his eyes flat, dull, black, emotionless.

For a long moment they stood like that, poised, then Bear reached down beside his foot, twisted the neck of the burlap oyster sack, lifted it, and left. The screen door slammed shut behind him.

Willie looked at Sheen, and said, "One day he'll get his arms around me and break my back," and he smiled that same warm smile that did not touch his eyes. Then he straddled the stool, dragged the second sack of oysters near, and sat where Bear had been. Freddie handed him an oyster knife, and he began to open oysters.

Sheen leaned back against the counter and sipped a beer, listening to the cracking and scraping sounds. He had the strange sense that the exchange had been a show, a display. The question was, to what purpose?

They ate turtle stew, fried alligator, snap beans, corn bread, and turnip greens. After dinner Sheen brought out the ounce of cocaine he had stashed in his boot. They drank Dixie beer from long-neck bottles and tooted cocaine through a hollowed-out boar's tusk. At midnight Sheen lay down on the end bunk and tried to get to sleep, but he was wired and sleep was elusive. Dreams came and went. Insects hummed against the screens. Once during the night he heard muted conversation in the radio room. The language seemed foreign, oddly accented, but he listened only for a moment, then a dream overtook him.

In the morning both Willie and Bear were gone. Red returned with his airboat and took Sheen back across the swamp then back into the city, letting him out on the curb where he had picked him up twenty-four hours before. When the dark blue pickup truck had gone, returning, he assumed, to the swamp, Sheen opened the small bag of fried alligator Freddie had insisted he take and looked at it closely, as if examining it for clues.

10

IN HIS dark apartment Sheen put his head down on the kitchen table and cried. He felt lonely, purposeless, afraid of shadows and quick movements. He knew his mood was largely the residual effect of the cocaine he had snorted the night before. "It's *all* the cocaine," he said out loud, but the knowing did not diminish the feelings.

Deep down, he felt it didn't matter. Andrea was dead. Nothing he could do would bring her back. The void she left was too big to be filled by revenge, but he felt revenge was all he had, all he could do, his *duty*. He realized then that the end of the search frightened him more than the search itself.

He washed his face with cold water and poured himself a large tumbler of Scotch. When he checked his answering machine, he was surprised to hear five messages requesting him to return calls. All five messages had been left by people listed in Profit's address book.

The boutique had opened in a hastily prepared cottage, but as it had become more chic and more pretentious, as the owner had tapped further into the pool of idle women from Dallas and Houston who liked nothing better than to fill a day by jetting to New Orleans to shop, it had moved to a renovated Italianate mansion. The rectangular front windows had been exchanged for thick, round pieces of glass that softly distorted the displays so that the mannequins seem to float, isolated in lush high-fashion bubbles. Inside, the store itself was a display, a series of small rooms made up to resemble luxurious boudoirs. The clothes were hung in closets and draped over velvet settees; accessories and jewelry were laid out on antique dressing tables or on bureaus with white marble tops. The atmosphere was hushed and subdued, the lighting indirect and very soft.

Sheen felt conspicuously out of place.

A soft voice asked, "May I help you?"

The woman's hair was swept up and back, away from her face, and her shoulders were made to look square by the blouse she wore. She had dark, aggressively innocent eyes.

"I'm looking for Elaine," Sheen replied.

"You must be Sheen," she said. "Elaine is expecting you."

Sheen followed her the length of the store. Her blouse was translucent, and she wore it with a natural sexiness, loose, so that dark subtle shadows moved as she moved. When she turned back to him and said, "Through there," pointing at a dark wood door, her blouse flared open momentarily and Sheen saw enough to know that she wore nothing underneath it.

"My name is Marty," she said. "If you are who I think you are, we'll see each other again."

"That will be nice," Sheen replied. He put his hand on the brass doorknob, but before he turned it, he looked over his shoulder and watched her walk away.

On the other side of the door, a short corridor led to an opulent office. The walls were of sandblasted cypress. The furniture was chrome and leather. Elaine sat behind a large oval of thick glass that seemed to float three feet above the floor, running one long red fingernail down a page of figures. Her eyes followed her fingernail, and she held up her other hand in a gesture that said "Wait"; when she looked up, her timing was so perfect, her face so expressive of the busy executive who interrupts her day for *you,* that Sheen wondered if he was indeed in an office or simply in a space made to resemble an office just as the display spaces were made to resemble boudoirs.

"You're Sheen?" Elaine asked. "Darling, I am *so* glad to see you."

She stood up and moved from behind her desk, leaving one hand on the glass and allowing it to move beside her, coyly tracing the ellipse she walked. Her dress was made of white lace, and she wore a long rope of pearls and a broad-brimmed white hat trimmed with more lace. Her eyes were made up to look larger than they were, and softer.

"It has been dry, dry, dry, and Profit is nowhere to be found. When you see him, you tell him for me that I am more than a little piqued. He knows how important it is to me. I simply *must* keep my customers happy, or someone else will — and we don't want that, do we? It is hard to be too, too angry. Profit is such a dear. But life must go on, and here *we* are."

Elaine stood close to Sheen and looked at him directly. He saw that she was older than she tried to appear — substantially older. Her perfume floated around her in thick jasmine waves.

"How soon do you think I could get something?"

"It's not very good."

"My dear, baking soda is better than nothing. You're new at this, aren't you?" Elaine reached up with both hands and straightened Sheen's collar, adjusting it slightly and running one long fingernail lightly along the side of his neck as she did so. "You poor thing. You must *never* tell me it's not very good. Tell me it's the best, so I can tell my customers the same thing."

Sheen moved one shoulder nonchalantly.

"It's the best," he said.

"There, that wasn't so hard, was it? And now *I* don't have to lie, not that I'm a virgin. I need five ounces, but if it's not very good, you'll be a dear and give me six ounces for the price of five, won't you?"

"But Elaine, I just told you, it's the best."

Elaine laughed easily, but her tone took on a derisive edge. "My, we learn quickly, don't we? How bad is it?"

"Judge for yourself," Sheen said. "I'm no chemist."

He took a small square of tin foil from his shirt pocket. Before he extended the sample to Elaine, he readjusted his collar in an exaggerated way she was sure to notice.

Elaine took the packet.

"It doesn't matter. Bring me five ounces. When can you get it here?"

"As soon as I can," Sheen replied. "I'll make you this deal, Elaine: I'll give you the sixth ounce; in return, if you see Profit, you give me a call."

Elaine crossed her arms and cocked her head to one side. "That sounds ominous. What if I refuse?"

"I'm not asking very much — a telephone call no one will ever know you made." Sheen dropped his chin and looked at her from beneath his eyebrows. "If you refuse, you'll find out what 'dry, dry, dry' *really* means."

Elaine gave him a skeptical look that carried with it mild distaste. She turned to her desk, and from her purse took a sealed white envelope.

"Half in advance," she said, turning back and extending the envelope to Sheen.

Sheen did not look at the envelope. He allowed her to hold it between them in midair.

"I know it would never happen," he said, "but if you did see Profit, and somehow you forgot to call . . ."

Elaine dropped her arm to her side; with her other hand she traced an *X* between her breasts.

"Cross my heart," she said dryly.

"Do not take me lightly, Elaine. I know where you live."

Elaine placed the envelope on the front edge of the desk and stood behind her chair.

"I want to see him too, my dear," she said. "There's a small matter we have to discuss, a pyramid."

From the way she said it, Sheen knew that she had used

the word advisedly, to see its effect. When he did not reply, she pulled the chair away from the desk and sat down.

"You may deliver my merchandise to Marty. I'll call you if I see Profit." Her tone left no doubt that their business was concluded.

Sheen picked up the envelope from the desk, folded it in half, put it in his hip pocket. Soundless on the thick carpet, he left Elaine's office.

On his second trip through the boutique, Sheen noticed that the walls of the small rooms were really only panels, temporary, easily moved. Through a crack between two of them he saw a middle-aged woman, naked except for brief panties, standing in front of a long mirror using both hands to drape necklaces around her throat. At the front door Marty was leaning against the door frame, looking out. A light rain had begun, and the street was shiny and wet.

When he was near, she turned her head slightly and looked at him.

"You shouldn't peek into a lady's dressing room," she said.

Her features were sharp but not delicate. She wore more make-up than Sheen liked, but there was fun in her eyes.

"Why did she get undressed to try on necklaces?" he asked.

"She didn't," Marty replied.

Sheen waited for her to explain what she meant, but after a moment it was clear that she thought her answer sufficient.

He said, "I'm supposed to meet you later. Do you want it brought here?"

"That's good news." Marty turned to face him. Her hair was dark brown with reddish-orange highlights that glinted even in the dull light. "Yes, here. You wouldn't believe the difference it makes in sales."

"Quite a marketing strategy."

Her eyes surprised him. When she said, "It works," the mischief left them, replaced by an unmistakable hardness; then they changed again and became self-reproachful. "But sometimes it makes me feel sleazy. I guess I'd feel worse if the customers really couldn't afford it. We close at nine. Will you be back by then?"

"I can be," Sheen said.

"After you've dropped it off, would you take a walk with me? It doesn't matter where. I don't get to walk very often, not at night."

"A walk would be nice," he said.

He had the sense that the awkwardness was mutual, and he pushed open the door. When he turned back to say goodbye, he saw that Marty had moved as quickly as he. She too had turned, and she was walking back into the store, the subtle shadows of her blouse moving as she moved.

The power lines hummed overhead, crackling in the light rain. The street was lined with widely spaced houses built in various styles, but the purple streetlights made colors monochromatic; and from the street one house looked like another, looming silhouettes behind high fences.

Before she had left the boutique, Marty had changed clothes. She still wore the blouse that made her shoulders look square, but with it she wore faded jeans and sneakers. She had removed most of her make-up, and her hair was brushed back rather than up in a softer and less angular style.

Sheen said, "Marty is an unusual name for a woman."

For a long moment she did not reply, and it was there again, the awkwardness.

"My older brother did that to me. He said there were too many Marlenes — I think he wanted a baby brother."

"Where is he now?"

"He's dead. He stepped on a mine in Vietnam."

"I'm sorry."

"Don't be. It was a long time ago, and it was what he wanted — not to die, I mean, but to go. He said it wasn't much, but it was the only war we had. Dumb kid. Looking for adventure, I guess."

There was a strange quality to the silence that followed, an expectancy that made Marty continue.

"I've never forgiven him for getting killed. He got off so easily. I hope he found his adventure."

Sheen wondered how they had gotten so deep so quickly.

Marty said, "Is that what you're after? Adventure?"

Sheen replied, "Adventure used to seem important to me; now I'm trying to learn to live with myself." He took a long step over a pothole filled with water. "Distractions aren't always as self-indulgent as they appear."

Marty looked at him skeptically out of the corners of her eyes, and Sheen knew instinctively that the source of her wariness was emotional, not intellectual.

"I wanted to teach Latin," he said, "but I couldn't afford to go to graduate school . . . That's not entirely true: if I had wanted to go badly enough, I would have found a way to pay for it."

"Are you Catholic?"

"No," Sheen said, and smiled. "Latin was around long before the Catholics. I'm not pagan, either."

He looked at Marty and saw her grin, the corners of her mouth turned up just enough to lessen the skepticism in her eyes.

"I liked the way the words fit together so exactly," he explained. "They're right or they're wrong, no equivocation. Something about it is solid and secure. Actually, the best teacher I had was named Goldstein — I don't think he was pagan either."

Sheen smiled again to see if Marty would smile back, and she did, a warm, indulgent smile.

"So what happened?"

"I don't know," he said. "I needed more, I suppose."

He put one hand out from beneath the umbrella they held between them and waved it back and forth, palm up. "It's stopped raining," he said. He moved the umbrella to one side and closed it; but when he tapped the metal tip on the ground, it popped back open. He closed it again and fumbled with the strap, and Marty saw the quick shift in his mood, the sudden aggravation that bordered on anger, the missing fingers that made a simple task difficult.

Unaware that he was doing so, Sheen glanced at her furtively and hid his hand in his pocket.

"I wrote an article," he said, too quickly. "In order to publish it, I was required to go through the whole M.L.A. index to be certain no one had already written the same thing — but I knew no one had, not *my* article. I lived in the library for three weeks. No one had written the same thing, but the process made the language seem out there, outside of *me*. Does that make any sense? I wasn't allowed simply to respond, to note something I found interesting, and I didn't want limitations imposed on my responses." Sheen tapped the umbrella on the pavement. "I may have been wrong."

Marty pinched her lower lip between her teeth thoughtfully.

She said, "Why don't you go back to school and see whether you were wrong or not?"

"I may."

Marty allowed him to bear the burden of the silence that followed, a silence punctuated by the sound of their shoes squishing rhythmically on the pavement.

"I may," he said again.

"*If* you don't get caught."

"Dealing cocaine is not a career for me."

"I don't mean caught by the police, I mean caught up in it. It's a very seductive occupation — being caught by the police isn't the only consequence."

Sheen used the tip of the umbrella to spear a wet leaf.

"Sometimes you have to do what you think is right, regardless of consequence." He tried to spear a second leaf, but it remained stuck to the wet pavement. "Sometimes an extravagant response is the only way to show you have any feelings at all."

"I don't follow you."

Sheen stopped and turned toward her. His face was set and hard.

Marty looked back at him with dark eyes that were steady and calm.

"I want to find Profit," he said. "He killed someone I cared about. This is the only way I know to find him."

For a long moment she held his gaze, then she turned and started again down the street. When he fell into step beside her, she asked, "What did you do when you got out of school?"

Sheen's reply was offhand, a bit too casual. "I was a policeman."

"No limitations there."

"They're defined, and they apply only to actions, not to thoughts or feelings. Once you learn the rules, there's a freedom."

"And a security."

Sheen nodded agreement, but the thought took him by surprise.

"Why did you quit the police — assuming, that is, that you *did* quit?"

Sheen pulled his ear absently. "I don't know. It lost its glow, I guess."

"When I started with Elaine, I thought there was a glow about her. She's very shrewd — too shrewd, sometimes." Marty gave him a look that might have been a warning, then glanced back up the street. "My apartment is around the next corner."

"Elaine mentioned that she wanted to see Profit about a pyramid. What did she mean?"

Marty's eyes narrowed, but her voice was resigned. "I don't know. They make deals on top of deals. Profit has cash. Elaine knows people." She turned toward him but did not stop walking. "What will you do when you find him?"

Sheen took his hand out of his pocket and extended it between them, palm up and flat.

"I let him go once," he said.

To his surprise, Marty took his hand in both of hers and examined it closely, turning it over and back to look at both

153

sides. When she let go, Sheen quickly put his hand back in his pocket.

She did not speak until they reached the corner and were standing directly beneath the streetlight, in the circle of purple light it made. Then she said, "You're a strange man: frustrated Latin teacher, ex-cop, cocaine dealer — three contradictions. Do you think you'll ever find whatever it is you want?"

Sheen did not reply. He saw that she was looking at him and shifted his gaze.

"Well, here I am," she said, and pointed across the street at a short flight of stairs. "Thank you for the walk."

Sheen did look at her then, and he saw that her expression was open, not accusing.

"Would you like to go to dinner sometime?" he asked.

"Yes," she replied. "I'd like that."

She stepped up on the curb, leaned forward, and kissed him lightly on the cheek.

Sheen watched as she walked inside. At the door, she turned briefly and waved. A moment later he saw a light go on, but the curtains were drawn, too heavy to see through.

Before he went home, Sheen made one more stop and sold another six ounces of cocaine. In his apartment he put all the money he had made that day on the bed and deliberately mixed it into a loose pile so that he would have to recount it, one bill at a time.

As if he were playing a card game, holding a wad of money in his left hand and dealing it out with his right, he separated the bills by denomination and made neat stacks. As he sorted, watching both his hands and the money, he noticed that his injured hand gave him little trouble, of itself. Rather, the difficulty came when his memory directed his hand to do something it was no longer able to do. Refusing to acknowledge the missing fingers, his memory continued to assume a dexterity that no longer existed. Sheen realized then that it was his mind, more than his diminished capacity, that caused his problems. His memory did not seem to be able to distinguish between past and present. It was to Sheen an odd thought, but it pleased him: after all, he could do something about his memory.

When he had laid out the money neatly and counted it, when he saw to his own satisfaction how much was there, Sheen momentarily felt exhilarated. It was as if someone had given him something for nothing — and yet he had earned it — and there was in the whole process a feeling of freedom, a feeling of having won something. But the exhilaration reminded him of the small post office in Sausalito, of Profit next to him in the car, handing him envelopes, watching him closely. Suddenly he clearly remembered Profit's face, the speckles of gunpowder around his eye, the way he pressed the heel of his hand against them, the exact tenor of his voice, so emphatic it was almost bitter as he said, "Poverty is a disease." Sheen looked again at the money on the bed. He did not know what it could bring him. He did not like its source. He knew he had to get a safe deposit box.

There were three solid knocks on the front door; a short pause; two more knocks.

Sheen quickly collected the neat stacks of bills from the bed and hid the money in a pillowcase, stuffing it beneath the pillow.

The doorknob rattled, twisted back and forth.

With the .45 in his left hand, Sheen looked into the living room, his body concealed behind the door frame.

He called out, "Who's there?"

"It's Willie, Sheen, Willie from the swamp."

Sheen was surprised, but he was also relieved — Willie at least was someone he knew. Quietly he crossed the living room and twisted the key in the lock.

The door slammed open against his shoulder. He stumbled backward. Before he could fall two hands were on his wrist. A thick arm was around his throat. Sheen dropped his weight, forcing the arm to bend to lift him, then he pushed upward and threw back his head. He heard a solid crunch and a sharp exhalation of breath, and he twisted free. The .45 clattered loose on the floor. He rolled under the hands that were still

155

holding his wrist, and they lost their grip. On his feet quickly, he froze: Willie had the pistol.

Sheen was not sure which arrested him more, the fact that Willie had the pistol or the sight of him in an immaculate gray suit, starched white collar high on his neck, subdued dark tie knotted perfectly.

"Sit," Willie said. He pointed at a chair with the pistol. "Keep your hands in my sight."

Sheen said, "I'll save you some trouble. The money is in the pillowcase on the bed."

"You should get a safe deposit box," Willie said evenly. "I'm not here to steal your money. Please, sit down."

Willie turned his head slightly, and Sheen followed his glance to see Bear, one hand over his face, standing near the corner.

"It's my goddamn nose again," Bear said, his words muffled by his hand.

A second man, short but very wiry and muscular, like a gymnast, got up from the floor. Willie nodded once, a barely perceptible movement of his head, and Bear and the wiry man moved in unison and began to search the apartment. Sheen knew from the coordination of their movements that they had practiced the door as well as the search: Bear had kicked high, near the lock, and the wiry man had jumped low for the weapon.

Sheen sat down on the chair Willie had indicated and put his forearms on the armrests, his hands in his lap. Willie sat down across from him, on the couch. He sat hunched forward, his elbows on his knees, the .45 held loosely, the barrel dangling between his calves.

The apartment was searched quickly. The wiry man whispered in Willie's ear. He spoke rapidly, in Spanish, and once his eyes shifted and he looked at Sheen, as if for emphasis. Willie nodded again, and the man went to the door. He held the door open for Bear — an oddly formal gesture — then went through himself and closed it quietly.

"They give you their compliments," Willie said, "and I add mine. Your reaction time is extraordinary."

156

"You are in my house," Sheen said, the forced matter-of-factness of his tone revealing his anger. "What do you want?"

"First, I want to apologize for the . . ." He paused, considering what word to use. "Intrusion. A precaution. I'm sure you understand."

Sheen watched as he released the magazine from the pistol and put it on the table. With a rapid back-and-forth jerk, he pulled the slide on the pistol to the rear and caught in midair the bullet ejected from the chamber. Pleased with his display of dexterity, Willie put the pistol on the table too, and stood the bullet next to it. He unbuttoned his suit coat, sat back on the couch, crossed his legs.

Sheen realized then that Willie's entrance had not been a precaution; it had been a display of power and control not unlike the display he had made after the open microphone had triggered the alarm in Freddie's cabin.

"That is a beautiful weapon," Willie said. "What is the purpose of the small ports in the barrel?"

Sheen did not reply, and after a moment Willie sat forward again, his elbows on his knees. The smugness left his face. He addressed Sheen pointedly.

"I am here secondly," he said, "to inform you that Moses would like to meet you. Moses feels a meeting would be advantageous to you both."

Sheen's eyes widened slightly, and a muscle jumped in his jaw. He had to control the urge to say "Damn." He knew he should have seen the connection between Moses and Willie. Willie had even told him: "It's a *very* tight community."

In an attempt to cover his surprise, he said, "Tell Moses I'll see him when *I'm* ready."

Willie gave him a knowing look, picked up the bullet he had put on the table, rolled it back and forth between his palms.

"Do not be too hasty to refuse his offer, my friend. Moses has helped you a great deal already. He can be of enormous benefit to you in the future."

"Moses has helped me how?"

"For one thing" — Willie tapped the bullet on the table for emphasis — "he replaced the kilo of cocaine you stole, so John did not send people to break your back."

Sheen felt a chill run up his spine and, oddly, a hot flush in his cheeks and ears.

"That's bullshit. John doesn't have that kind of juice — not some broker."

Willie replied with exaggerated patience, as if he were addressing a child. "You cannot believe that, Sheen. If a man is able to drop fifty thousand dollars for his recreational drugs, certainly he is able to hire two like those." Willie jerked his chin at the door.

"I thought Bear was your brother."

Willie arched one eyebrow slightly, dismissing Sheen's remark as unworthy of comment. Again he tapped the bullet on the table.

"Consider another thing: where all of a sudden did *you* get so many connections? People coming out of the woodwork, calling you?"

Sheen took a deep breath and held it, allowing the air to escape very slowly.

"Moses, too? Why?"

"Why not? Moses needs someone to replace Profit, and you seem to be the logical successor. You know the city. You know some people. You're already making connections, and you have the balls to follow through. Don't blow it, Sheen. It's being handed to you, a franchise many people would kill for."

Sheen looked at Willie directly, pointedly.

Willie shook his head. "Moses did not kill your girlfriend. Meet him, you'll see for yourself: it's not his style. Cross him and he comes after you — that I guarantee." Willie put the bullet back on the table. "What have you got to lose by meeting him, Sheen? You're looking for him anyway. He's not going to come to you."

Sheen rubbed his chin thoughtfully and curled his lower lip over his teeth.

158

"What are you in this, Willie?" he asked.

A trace of caution appeared in Willie's black eyes. He looked at Sheen openly, but his face was a watchful mask.

"I work for Moses, at his discretion. Because he trusts me, I have many duties."

"Duties that include radio communications?"

Willie's expression remained bland.

"Trust is a strange thing. It expands to fill a need." He reached into an inside coat pocket and brought out an airline ticket, which he carelessly flipped onto the table. "I took the liberty of booking you on a flight. Someone will meet you on the other end."

"What if I don't show up?"

"No harm will come to you, if that's what you mean." Willie got up from the couch and stood looking down at Sheen. His eyes were level and very hard. "But if there is no trust, the need will disappear. You will not be able to get more cocaine. You will not make any more connections. The connections you have made will be broken." Willie's voice dropped and became more emphatic, each word clearly enunciated. "You will never find Profit."

For a long moment Willie and Sheen looked at one another, then Willie stepped around the table and walked to the door. His hard heels made a sharp, certain sound on the bare wood floor. The door closed solidly behind him.

Sheen moved to the couch and sat where Willie had sat. For a moment he studied the airline ticket, flipping through the thin sheets of gray paper and red carbon paper and reading the square, impersonal characters of a high-speed line printer. The ticket gave him a first-class seat on a direct flight to Fort Lauderdale. The plane left at ten the next morning.

Idly he picked up the pistol from the table, inserted the magazine, and released the slide, chambering a round. He saw that he had forgotten the bullet Willie had left on the table, so he dropped the magazine back out of the handle. With a rapid back-and-forth jerk, he pulled the slide on the pistol to the rear and tried to duplicate Willie's catch of the bullet ejected from the chamber; but the mutilated hand holding the pistol did not have the strength to hold it steady, and the bullet flew wild. It flipped over the table, hit the floor, and bounced before it began to roll with that distinctive sound a round metal object makes when it rolls over wood — a sound that seemed to mock him.

11

Except for the lawn, from the outside the property seemed abandoned. The red canvas window awnings on the house had faded to a rusty pink. The stucco was aged and yellowed. The red tiles on the roof were chipped and broken in places. But around the inlaid stepping stones and the scattered palm trees the lawn was a rich carpet, impeccably trimmed, as luxurious and flawless as a putting green.

Inside the house, the ceiling of a long gallery was rounded. The arches over the windows flared into the curve, and the shadows overhead were conical. The floor was made of heavy, dark blocks of polished stone, uneven but cool. Three steps down from the gallery, the living room was huge, stately. The ceiling was very high and decorated with ornate, hand-carved wood panels. Curtained windows and glass doors softly diffused the sunlight and subdued colors; still, the red leather furniture and bright red shag carpet were startlingly bright, clearly out of place.

Sheen stood by a window and looked out at the manicured lawn, and past it at the private beach. The sand was dazzlingly white. The translucency of the curtains reminded him of the blouse Marty had worn the night before. Behind him stood two tense, swarthy men in suits. For a while he had watched them watching him, their dark eyes hard and dull, moderately curious, but he had turned to the window because he had seen them before, or ones just like them, and the view out the window was more pleasing.

When he heard footsteps, Sheen turned away from the window. He was momentarily blinded by the glare, the center of his vision a yellow-blue blur.

"I am very glad you decided to accept my invitation."

As Sheen's eyes adjusted, Moses came into focus. He was slender and dark. His eyes were dark and deeply set. He wore light-colored slacks, pleated in front, and a slightly oversized bright red silk shirt that draped his thin chest loosely and showed the outline of an undershirt beneath.

"We have very much to discuss. Would you care for a drink, or some iced tea?"

Sheen shook his head. "No."

"The iced tea is very good in the heat," Moses said. Without turning his head he held up his left hand, fingers extended in a *V,* and said to the men in suits, "Bring us two glasses of iced tea. Perhaps my guest will change his mind."

The men moved quietly out of the room.

Moses brought down his hand. "Please, sit down," he said to Sheen. There was a whippetlike quality about him, very bony and gristly, all cords and lean muscles, quickness without real strength.

Sheen moved around the couch and sat on one end of it. Moses sat opposite him on one of the red leather chairs. Between them there was nothing but four feet of bright red shag carpet. When Moses crossed his legs, he exposed a thin tan sock with white ribs.

"In one way," Moses said, "I know very much about you; in another, I know nothing at all. I thought you would be a bigger man, taller. Reports are so often misleading. The imagination fills the spaces between the facts."

A houseboy in a starched white jacket entered the room carrying two tall glasses of iced tea on a silver tray. When he reached them, he bent long enough for Moses to see the glasses and nod approval, then he placed one glass on the side table next to him and one next to Sheen. From under

162

his arm he produced a thin, rectangular wooden box; he opened it and offered cigars to them. As he did so, the silver tray slipped and fell onto the carpet near Sheen's feet. Sheen started to reach for it to hand it back to him, but the houseboy gave him a look that stopped him, a pleading look, his eyes wide with too much fear.

Moses did not look at him. He took a cigar from the box and said to Sheen, "The cigars are Cuban, of course — as am I." He held the cigar under his nose and breathed deeply, with evident satisfaction. "You are yourself dark enough to be Cuban."

The houseboy picked up the tray from the floor, and Moses did look at him then, with a cruel, assessing look that made Sheen understand the fear he had seen in the young man's eyes.

"I am *not* Cuban," Sheen said sharply.

Moses looked back at him, misinterpreting the sharpness in his tone. "I did not order the attempt on your life."

"I can live with this," Sheen said. He held his hand just slightly above the armrest, palm in and up, fingers and stumps spread.

"Nor did I order your girlfriend's death."

Sheen put his hand down and watched the houseboy leave. "Maybe they were just happy accidents: muggers and a careless driver." The houseboy gave Sheen a furtive look he could not read, and he shifted his gaze to Moses.

"In your place I believe I would feel the same way, but you must look for the intersection of coincidence." Moses held the cigar by one end and moved it as he spoke, as if he were conducting his words. "Profit wanted you dead in order to put pressure on me: it would look as if I had done something I had not. When you survived the attempt on your life and burned his house, he wanted revenge."

"That's one possibility. The other is this: you set up the hit on me to protect the connection to you. When that didn't work, you ordered Andrea's death to put me after Profit."

"I would have been more direct. I would simply have elimi-

163

nated Profit. But there was no need for that. Profit was very indiscreet on the phone. I knew there was no informant, and I knew that he had arranged his own arrest to sever his ties to me — not very original, but effective. Therefore I was not surprised to learn that he was planning to rob me." A brief, confident smile flickered across Moses's face. "Planning to *attempt* to rob me. All I had to do then was to cut him off. Any further action would have been unwarranted, useless — worse than useless, because further action would have posed a new set of problems." Moses reached into his pants pocket and took out a small silver trimmer. He positioned it on the rounded end of the cigar and looked back at Sheen. "You see, to sever ties is also to cancel obligations. Profit was making some very bad investments. He did not think I would find out so quickly." Moses squeezed the trimmer, and it cut with a click. "But he forgot that *his* connections are *my* connections as well."

"I *will* learn the truth," Sheen said, trying to convey a certainty he did not feel.

Moses lit his cigar with a thin gold lighter and blew a long, slanting plume of smoke at the ceiling. "Yes, I believe you will, and I wish you luck on your odyssey. But my concern is more immediate. I must replace Profit quickly, or the connections will disappear. As any salesman will tell you, connections need constant attention. People move. They change their phone numbers. They stop to think and find new suppliers. The routes he serviced are very lucrative. I do not want to lose them. You already have one foot in the door. What will you do?"

Sheen rubbed his lower lip pensively, then shrugged.

Moses looked thoughtfully at his cigar, licked his forefinger, rubbed a spot near the ash where it was burning unevenly.

"Forgive my presumption," he said, "but I think you *are* certain what you will do — or you would not be here. You think that in order to find the killer of your girlfriend you must remain close to me, and you must find Profit. I offer you a way to do both. And we will both make very much money while you are doing it."

164

Sheen ran his hand over the leather arm of the couch, one finger probing a seam. He wanted to know what Moses was thinking, and he wanted to keep him talking. He said, "You mentioned that Profit was making bad investments. What were they?"

Moses took a deep pull on his cigar, studying Sheen. When he exhaled, smoke billowed around his face and his eyes squinted so that only a dark gleam was visible between the lashes. "Yes," he said, "the investments explain very much." He waved away the smoke, put the cigar in an ashtray, and rearranged himself in the chair so that his head was in the crease between the back and the wing, his thin shoulders composed in the corner. "Everyone in my business makes money in two ways: they buy for less than they sell for, as does any salesman, but they also — and this is what makes this business so unique — sell more than they buy. I may take one pound of merchandise and make it into two. The men to whom I sell do the same thing, as do the men to whom *they* sell, and so on. One pound may eventually become eight pounds, though the purity of the original product may decrease from ninety percent to less than ten — it does not matter. If you drew that sequence in a diagram, the diagram would resemble a pyramid. *I* would be at the top." Moses gave Sheen a thin smile that faded quickly. "That is the normal course of distribution, and everyone is very happy. But Profit thought he could build a second pyramid within the normal one. He offered to jump his customers up a step in purity if they met two conditions of the sale: a cash advance above the cost of what they were buying, and two new buyers. The new buyers also had to advance cash, half to the recruiter and half to him. The advance up Profit's pyramid came in purity. New recruits paid so they could profit both from the increased purity and from the cash advances of those who joined after them."

"You mean," Sheen interrupted, "that Profit admitted he was cutting the cocaine he sold?"

"Of course," Moses replied. "That was the strength of his plan. He brought out into the open what everyone knows but no one admits. Cocaine cut with honesty is a unique blend, don't you agree?" Moses smiled, leaned forward and picked up his tea, settled back in the chair. "Alas, each time one group was due to rise a step in purity, Profit had to add a new level to the bottom of the pyramid, a level twice as large as the one that came before." Moses moved the glass of tea with a circular motion, and the ice tinkled.

"It could not last. Eventually he would have needed a very large amount of merchandise at one time so he could collect from everyone at once. His new recruits would get nothing. His upper levels would have promises of more to come. He would collect twice from them, and the second time they, too, would have only promises, no cocaine. He would keep the cash from the cocaine he sold, from the cocaine he promised, and from his new recruits. Honesty is the best policy." Moses lifted the glass of tea but stopped it halfway to his mouth. "I'm sure it would have made a very tidy sum, and who would have complained — or rather, to whom would they have complained?" He completed the movement of glass to mouth, took a sip of the tea, put the glass back on the side table. He saw that the glass had made a dark, wet circle on the thigh of his slacks, and he brushed at it lightly before he looked back at Sheen.

"But while he was building this second pyramid, Profit had to cover his obligations. He had both to prove his credibility and to instill the greed that made his scheme work. And it was breaking him. He was being forced to deal without cutting — without cutting as much as he was accustomed to, anyway — and the cash advances were not covering the increase in his costs. He knew I would not extend him credit in the amount he needed. I believe he hired you with the idea in mind to steal cocaine from me. Then he had himself arrested. That temporarily canceled his obligations so he would have time for his preparations. Everyone in the pyramid would use up what cocaine they had. Simultaneously they would all be hungry. I would not expect him to fulfill his normal duties, and presumably I would be unprepared for his attempt to rob me."

Sheen slowly shook his head.

Moses asked, his voice insinuatingly patient, "Is there something you do not understand?"

"No," Sheen replied, "I think I *do* understand." His tone conveyed a weariness that showed in his eyes. "If you knew what he was doing, why didn't you stop him?"

"For what reason?" Moses's eyebrows lifted smugly. "While he was building his pyramid, Profit was turning over a very great amount of merchandise. I was making very much money from legitimate sales to him. What he did with that merchandise was his business."

Sheen spread one hand over his face and moved it down to his throat, pulling the skin taut over his jaw. "Profit had himself arrested to create a delay?"

"The arrest was to create time for his preparations," Moses replied politely. "The *method* of the arrest was for your benefit. By making you think there had been an informant — you, of course, being the one likely to have been that informant — he hoped to pressure you to help him rob me." Moses gave Sheen the same assessing look he had given the houseboy.

Sheen returned Moses's look with an expressionless stare. "Why didn't he make his score?"

Moses picked up the glass of iced tea and sat it on the dark circle on the thigh of his slacks. "He lost his nerve. Profit knew it would be very risky to rob me. My security is excellent." Moses took another sip of the tea, moved the glass away from his mouth, and slanted the rim toward Sheen in emphasis. "But Profit is clever, very quick to change plans. At times that is a great asset. He could reduce his risk: if he had you killed, it would put me in a difficult situation. As I said, it would look as if I had done it. He would use that to his advantage to try to get the cocaine he needed." Moses shrugged. "Perhaps he was not certain of your help."

"But if I *had* been killed, he would have been as suspect as you."

"What did he have to lose? What he hoped to gain was more credit from me. One way or another, he had to have cocaine." Moses smiled thinly. "He showed how little he knows me."

The houseboy appeared in the doorway and stood indecisively. Moses waved him away, flicking his wrist irritably.

"But then you were not killed," he continued. "Profit had no hope of credit from me. You would not help him, of course, and he could rob no one. He could get no cocaine, and his pyramid was collapsing. Months of work and a fortune were slipping away from him. He was already cornered and angry when you burned his one remaining asset, his house."

Sheen thought of the sucking *whoosh* the house had made as it ignited, the intense heat, the smell of the burning gasoline, the raging fire reflected in Profit's eyes. He remembered the brown leather attaché case sailing on a long, slow trajectory deep into the flames.

He heard Moses say, "Profit came to value revenge more than money — actually, it was all he had left — and your girlfriend was the one to suffer. Or perhaps *you* are the one to suffer; that I do not know."

Sheen rolled his head back, then forward, and for several seconds he stared at the red shag rug. The story was convoluted enough to be true. It matched Profit's penchant for misdirection perfectly. But there were two things that didn't fit. Why would Profit lose his nerve so late in the game? The pyramid must have taken months to construct, and he could have pulled out at any time, writing the losses off to a bad investment. The other thing was more obvious: Profit would never value revenge over money.

Sheen looked up and said, "How can I step into his place? The buyers must be furious."

"Quite the contrary," Moses replied confidently. "For a brief time all but the newest recruits had a very happy circumstance, a pyramid that worked. You simply ignore their good fortune and bring them merchandise of the quality they deserve for the quantity they are buying. They may seem disgruntled, but they were not entitled to that which they were getting previously, and they know it. They will never again have such deals. By now they are very hungry, which, as I said, is why you must decide quickly what it is you are going to do."

Sheen looked at Moses with eyes that were curiously hard. "I heard what you said."

12

IN THE next several months, Sheen learned patience. He learned that dealing was waiting: waiting for phone calls, waiting for cash, waiting for customers, deliveries, airplanes; waiting for miles to pass as he drove back and forth, New Orleans to Miami, Miami to New Orleans, the cocaine locked in the trunk, secure from a random search. Sheen learned that no matter how intricate his preparations, no matter how certain his plans, more often than not he had to change those plans, to construct contingencies because a phone was busy, a flight was canceled, a bank was closed. The series of small delays, individually unpredictable yet consistent in the aggregate, always led to a wait. He watched a lot of television. He read books and magazines. He worked crossword puzzles, and he taught himself chess. When and if a wait paid off, it precipitated a frenzy of activity; he did not like to hold longer than was absolutely necessary. But despite the delays and the bursts of nonstop activity, it seemed to him that the days ran together like a seamless roadway he was passing at moderate speed, blurred if he looked at it closely, clear farther off.

There was a hotel in Old Miami Beach he liked very much. It was an old hotel, built in the 1930s, that had touches of Art Deco modified in the peculiar, flamboyant south Florida way. The carpets in the corridors were worn and smelled of mildew and the paint was old and faded, but the air conditioning worked, and there was a room on the fourth floor that had a generous corner balcony with a flat balustrade wide enough to hold a plate of food and a cold rum drink but low enough that it did not obstruct the view. The view was pleasant, across the pool and the beach to the ocean, and often he put a lounge chair next to the balustrade and sat there, looking out. Sometimes for brief spells he forgot about his drink, then, when he reached for it, he found the glass covered with sweat, the ice cubes melted, water floating over the rum, and he would get up to make himself another.

Sitting there on the corner balcony, he allowed himself to unlock his memory. Andrea was dead, but it was all right to think about her. He still felt the sadness, but it was not so painful, not unbearably so.

He remembered one clear Sunday afternoon when they had gone together to the French Quarter. They did not have much money, but what they had they decided to spend on food. In the window of a restaurant they had seen a huge kettle of boiling crayfish, and they had bought two pounds and taken them to the levee to eat. The bright red shells had been hot, and the meat in the tails had been warm and succulent. *That was a good day,* he thought. Ships had glided past soundlessly on the river. On the breeze there had been the smell of freshly ground coffee.

One very cold day when the temperature had been near freezing Andrea had borrowed bicycles. They had bundled themselves up and ridden through the Garden District looking at the big old houses, then back to the Irish Channel and a neighborhood bar where they had drunk cheap brandy until they were flushed and warm, peeling off layer after layer of clothes. *That too was a good day,* he thought.

There had been many good days.

But Sheen made it a rule never to think too long, never to remember too much, and sometimes he left the balcony while the sun was still high and retreated into the dark room with the faded paint and the air conditioning that worked very well, the room very cold after the heat.

For three days nonstop he had made his rounds, met the buyers, collected the money. Elaine's boutique was the last stop he would make before he went home and went to sleep. On the porch he looked at his reflection in the display window. His eyes seemed dark, but so was the glass. Behind the glass a mannequin seemed to float, isolated, and to eye him coolly.

Marty saw him and waved. Sheen saw that she was busy with a customer, returned the wave, and walked past her to the back of the store.

Elaine seemed to know that he was coming, and she was already out from behind her desk and moving toward him as he entered her office. Her dress was black with a slash of red across the front. Her hair was pulled back away from her face, and she wore a broad-brimmed black hat. When she stopped, one hand on her hip, one foot turned out, she looked just like the mannequin in the window, but her expression was not so cool.

"Dear Sheen, you *do* look a mess, but I suppose by now I should be used to it. I know I'm always the *very* last on your list. Why is that?"

Sheen raised his eyebrows and pursed his lips. "I guess I save the best for last, Elaine," he said, his tone as dry as he could make it.

"Then I'll have to stop being your *best*. You called three days ago. Three days."

Sheen turned a chair to face her and sat down in it. He was tired, and for a moment, as he lifted his briefcase into his lap, he closed his eyes.

He heard Elaine say, "It is hard to be too, too angry. You're always such a dear when you *do* finally arrive. Six ounces for me?"

The clasps on the briefcase popped open with a distinctive *click-click*.

"You should buy by the pound, Elaine. It would save you

a lot of money, and it would save me a lot of bother."

"My dear, I would like to buy by the kilo. It's just a matter of money — or credit." She looked at him pointedly.

Sheen ignored the look and handed her a sealed plastic bag. "It's the very best," he said. He closed the briefcase and put it on the floor.

Elaine took the bag and hefted it, moving it up and down as if her arm were the arm of a balance scale. The bracelets jangled on her wrist. She turned away from him, put the bag on her desk, turned back, her expression much softer, and knelt by the chair, her hands resting lightly on Sheen's arm, her face close to his.

"You know, Sheen, there are other ways for us to do business together — and it would be such a natural thing."

Sheen rolled his head until his chin was resting on his shoulder. In a very tired voice, he said, "Don't start today, please. I'm exhausted. I just want to go home."

"*That's* not what I meant," Elaine replied. With one long red fingernail she traced a vein on the back of his hand. "It's just that I know so many people, and you have such wonderful connections. We should make more of our natural resources." She smiled at him coyly.

Sheen slouched down in the chair and closed his eyes. The wide brim of her hat touched his ear, and he brushed at it, annoyed.

"Sure. We should start our own pyramid."

He felt her response in the sudden, angry pressure on his arm.

Elaine stood up, crossed her arms, rocked one foot back on her high heel so that the sharply pointed toe of her shoe aimed directly at him.

"Do you read the newspaper?" she asked, her voice cutting.

Without opening his eyes, Sheen shook his head.

"Well, if you did, this last week you would have read that the Coast Guard has been collecting bales of marijuana. Dozens of them have been found floating in the Gulf. A ship either sank or abandoned its cargo. The bales weigh five hundred

173

pounds each, and they're sealed, watertight. Some are still floating around. Others have washed ashore. I know a man who has two of those bales, and he doesn't know what to do with them."

"I'm not interested," Sheen said. "I wouldn't know what to do with them either."

Elaine gave him a withering look, then continued as if he had not said anything. "The man works on a shrimp boat. He's a hick from Mississippi. Offer a hundred dollars a pound — three times that would be a bargain. I can sell one hundred pounds immediately. Within twenty-four hours you'll have one-third of your money back, and you'll have nine hundred pounds left to sell. You have other connections, ask around. People rarely use just one drug."

Sheen pushed himself up in the chair and propped his head on his hand.

"Why don't you do it yourself?"

Elaine, her arms still crossed, tapped her finger on her elbow.

"I don't have the cash to buy that much, and it's all or nothing. The man is nervous. He just wants to get rid of it, and he won't break the bales."

"What's in it for you?"

Elaine smiled a thin, hard smile. "As the broker, dear heart, I earn a commission: twenty-five percent of the net."

Sheen yawned tiredly and rubbed his hand over the stubble on his cheeks. "Offer him seventy-five thousand."

Elaine's eyes went wide. "That's ridiculous. One hundred dollars per pound is insulting enough."

"Seventy-five thousand dollars in a briefcase makes an impressive sight, Elaine. He won't be too insulted when he sees it." Sheen sat forward in the chair and put his hands on his knees. "Anyway, that's all I'll go. Anything over seventy-five thousand is up to you. *I* should be offered that kind of money for something I found floating in the water." Sheen pushed himself to his feet. "How do you know him?"

"His girlfriend has expensive taste in clothes."

"So give him a line of credit."

174

Elaine smiled wanly. "Maybe I will," she said. She turned to her desk, picked up a thick, white envelope, turned back to Sheen. "I'll call you this evening."

Sheen bent both arms and stretched, arching his back and yawning again as he did so. "Not this evening. Tomorrow. Tonight I'm going to sleep."

Elaine tapped the thick envelope on an open palm. "You are being too, too difficult, Sheen. I told you he's nervous. If we don't move quickly, he's likely to dump it back in the Gulf."

She held the envelope out to him, and he took it; without looking at it, he put it in his hip pocket.

"You can try," he said. He bent down and picked up his briefcase. "I'm a pretty sound sleeper when I'm this tired."

"Once it's arranged, how long will it take to make the transaction?"

Sheen raised and dropped one shoulder uncertainly. "That depends on the arrangements. I can have the money tomorrow — the truck too. It will probably take a day after that to negotiate your commission down to where it belongs."

Elaine's sour smile flashed on and off. "We can haggle later, dear. I know you're so very tired."

In her eyes was a mocking disdain, but before he turned to leave Sheen smiled at her, a genuine smile, amused and almost friendly.

Elaine turned away from him and moved behind her desk. When her office door closed, she twisted her chair to one side and lifted the top of the low cabinet near her desk. On the closed-circuit television monitor concealed there, she watched as Sheen walked the length of her store. Despite the dim light in the boutique, the image was clear, his white shirt pale gray on the screen. He stopped and spoke briefly with Marty, and it entertained Elaine to watch him look around before he kissed her quickly on the cheek, a perfunctory kiss that revealed familiarity. When he left the store and was out of range of the camera, she twisted her chair back to her desk and picked up the phone.

With the underside of her fingernail Elaine stabbed the square buttons, careful not to chip her nail polish as she pressed the number to Miami. There was an unusually long delay, and she heard odd, hollow, clicking sounds on the line. She held the receiver against her shoulder and took off her earring as she waited for the call to go through. The earring was in the shape of a small silver seashell, and she worked the clasp between thumb and first finger, nervously squeezing the delicate spring-tensioned pivot open and closed.

"Hello," she said.

There was no reply.

"Hello, I'm calling for Moses."

The circuit clicked open. The connection made the voice that answered sound distant and mechanical, as if she were listening to a machine, or calling overseas.

"Yes, Elaine," the mechanical voice said. "This is Moses. How did he respond?"

Elaine sat back in the chair and crossed her legs as she spoke. "He did just what you said he would: he agreed to seventy-five thousand. Does he have that much on hand?" She heard her own voice echo down the line.

"How soon?"

"I said I would call this evening," she replied, irritated that Moses had ignored her question but knowing not to ask it twice. "He'll have the money tomorrow."

"Was he tired?"

"Yes, he is exhausted."

"Good. I have already decided on a place."

Marty sat on the edge of the bed and watched Sheen as he slept, his eyes moving rapidly back and forth, his body rigid, his arms tense at his sides. She had learned not to wake him by touching, so instead she spoke to him in a low voice. Marty liked to watch him wake. She liked to feel her voice bringing him to life. And she liked to hear what she had to say: until she began, she never knew what would come out, what was really on her mind.

"When I was young," she said, her voice low and even, "after my brother died, I wanted to live behind a waterfall. I can still hear the sound I thought it would make, the roar, the thunder that never stopped. I pretended that my room at home was a cave carved in the rock. The cave was damp and dark, and there was a metallic smell of minerals so rich it was a taste, like when you put a penny in your mouth and drink water — my brother taught me that."

Sheen didn't move, but she knew that he was waking. She saw the change in his face.

"I think I liked the idea of living behind a waterfall because I so wanted the rain, rain from dark clouds that hid the sun — you see, I didn't want the sun. I wanted days as dark as night. I missed my brother very much."

Beside the bed, the phone rang. The sound was startling, intrusive. Marty grabbed it quickly and held the receiver tightly between her palms, covering the mouthpiece.

Sheen rolled onto one shoulder, awake, and twisted his head to look up at her. "I was almost awake," he said sleepily. "I heard you talking, but I couldn't understand the words — they were just sounds."

Marty held the receiver out to him and said, "I know."

She leaned forward and kissed him lightly before she pushed herself away and started to stand up; but Sheen held onto her belt and pulled her back down next to him.

"Stay here with me," he said and took the receiver. "It's just Elaine."

Marty shook her head. "No, it isn't. It's a man."

Sheen raised his eyebrows and cocked his head to one side as if to say, "So?"

"Hello," he said into the phone, looking at Marty with dark, sleepy eyes.

"Hey, amigo," Tony Avila said. "I haven't heard from you in a while. How have you been?"

Marty saw the sudden change in Sheen's face, and she knew that the call was trouble.

"Fine," Sheen replied warily, pushing himself up until he

was sitting, his back against the wall. "What have you been up to? Have you been promoted yet?"

Tony Avila chuckled. "Not yet, but I got something nearly as good. I'm paying off an old debt." The amusement in Tony's voice deepened. "A friend of yours applied for an occupational license. He's going into business selling smoke alarms — kind of a new line for him. His fingerprints set off the computer on my flag." Tony Avila paused for a beat. "Do you want Profit's address as of ten days ago?"

13

RAYTON WAS a small town a hundred miles northeast of San Francisco and thirty degrees hotter, a mining town that had remained after the Gold Rush miners had gone, a town heralded by a hand-lettered sign that warned LAST GAS FOR THIRTY MILES. The highway sloped down gradually into an arid valley where a hot wind whipped low gnarled trees and made roadside trailer homes rock noticeably. Off in the distance there were mountains.

Downtown was an assortment of old brick buildings built wall to wall. There was an old hotel, a dry goods store, a movie theater with a broken marquee. The main street ran parallel to the highway, and past the brick buildings and the squat stone courthouse set a little apart, the street widened and there were the usual low glass bank, quarter-acre gas station, and drive-up restaurant where local teenagers circled twice before parking. One intersecting street led to the two bungalow-style motels and subdivision flags farther on. Another led to the schools and the church. A mile past the church, before the road began to ascend out of the valley, Sheen found the address Avila had given him.

The house was in a humble neighborhood of single-story frame houses. In the street there were automobiles on jacks, awaiting repair. During the day Sheen watched as barefoot children in dirty T-shirts and hand-me-down jeans chased each

179

other, weaving in and out of the laundry hung on clotheslines to dry. At night he saw men sitting on their stairs beneath dim porch lights, drinking beer, arms over knees, quart bottles dangling in their hands.

When Sheen first saw Profit come out of the house and get into a three-year-old Ford, his reaction was very cool, tempered by determination. He followed him for two days. He followed him to his shop; three large plate-glass windows made up the storefront in the old brick building, and through them Sheen could see bare fluorescent tubes on the ceiling, gray metal shelves, a worn Formica counter. He followed him to the fast-food restaurant where he ate hamburgers for lunch and dinner. Profit appeared relaxed, quick to stop to talk with acquaintances, slower in his walk. The application for the occupational license read "to sell, service, and repair smoke alarms." Sheen knew it was a cover, but he did not know what the cover concealed, what was possible in this small, desolate town. On the second night he went to a motel and slept for five hours, but before dawn he was back in front of the house.

Profit knew he was being followed. Rayton was too small, the traffic too sparse, to allow whoever was following him to go undetected, even at the prudent distance he kept the car. Once or twice Profit was tempted to double back quickly to catch a glimpse of whoever it was, but he didn't really want to know — there were several possibilities, none of them pleasant. He was intrigued that he had been found, and in a way he was flattered that he still warranted the attention. Profit was tired of hiding, and he tried to convince himself that he felt some relief, but he wished he felt more relief and less fear.

Just as the sun came up on his third day in Rayton Sheen used a wire coat hanger to unlock the passenger door on Profit's car, then he sat down on the ground, hidden between the car and a nearby clump of untended bushes, and waited. Two hours later he heard a door slam. He heard footsteps on the sidewalk and the driver's door open and close. He waited until the engine started and dropped back to idle before he yanked open the door. Before the door had rebounded on its hinges he was in the passenger seat, facing Profit, the .45 in his hand.

Profit started, instinctively twisting away.

"Keep both hands on the wheel," Sheen said evenly. "Drive away, slowly."

Profit looked at the .45 in Sheen's hand, but he did not look at Sheen. Very deliberately he put the car in gear and allowed it to roll backward, out of the driveway.

"Where to?" he asked when they were on the street.

"I'll say as we go," Sheen replied. He looked at Profit carefully, studying him, wanting to know what he knew. Profit's eyes flicked back and forth nervously. "Get on the interstate. Use your turn signals."

At the end of the street Profit turned right. The morning sun was low, and the car passed in and out of long shadows. A wheel bearing was worn and made a rough scraping sound as the wheel turned.

"I thought it might be you," Profit said tentatively. When there was no reply, he added, "How did you find me?"

The long shadows made Sheen think of the first time he had ridden in a car with Profit: the Porsche whining at high speed, the airport growing larger in the distance.

"Your new business," Sheen replied, giving the words a hardness he did not really feel.

"The license application," Profit said, nodding his head to show that he was not surprised. "I knew better, but I had to do it. I was hoping they just filed it somewhere — I guess they *do* check it out."

"It's a good cover," Sheen said. "Too bad."

Profit glanced at Sheen. "It's not a cover" — he moved his shoulder forward and back, a gesture of concession — "it's what I do. I sell smoke alarms now." He seemed embarrassed by the admission, and he continued quickly, explaining the circumstances as if they explained him. "I had to do something, and it couldn't be coke. Moses cut me off from my supply. You cut me off from my connections. What money I had you burned with the house. Shit, I had to sell my watch to get enough money to drive out here."

Sheen looked at Profit's wrist and saw a fat stainless steel Seiko where before there had been a slender gold Omega. On the back of his right hand a long red scar angled from little finger to thumb, like a thick welt raised by a heavy cane.

"I sold the Porsche to get the shop started. There's a new law that requires smoke alarms in new houses." He shrugged. "I know how to sell. I get by."

Sheen looked directly at Profit, waiting to catch his eye, and then asked, "Did you kill Andrea?"

Profit pressed his lips together and shook his head. "What do you want, Sheen, a confession? No, I did not kill Andrea. But what difference does it make? Anything I say now is a song and dance." Profit returned Sheen's direct look. "I wanted to kill *you.*"

"But you didn't have the balls, so you did the next best thing."

"I didn't have the money to do *anything.* What I did have was in the attaché case, and you burned that. The rest was out."

"In the pyramid?"

"You know about the pyramid?" Profit twisted his hands on the steering wheel. "Yeah, I guess Moses made a point of telling you. Man, I hate being a sucker." They were passing the old brick buildings that made up Rayton's downtown, and Profit jerked his chin forward and to one side. "There's my shop," he said.

Sheen did not look away from Profit's face; he had already seen the shop.

Profit looked back and said, "Did Moses tell you it was *his* pyramid?"

Sheen replied, his voice patronizingly calm, "You can do better than that, friend — you've had enough time. Moses put me on your rounds. He's maintaining the connections, not burning them."

"Only because he lost his nerve."

182

"Why would Moses be afraid of anybody *you* know?"

"He's not afraid of anybody I know. He's afraid of the people *he* knows."

Ahead of them was the interstate overpass. Profit lifted his hand from the steering wheel just enough to wave a finger left to right as he asked, "Which way?" He heard the safety click twice on Sheen's pistol.

"Take a left," Sheen said, "toward San Francisco."

As they gained speed on the entrance ramp the intermittent scraping sound from the right rear wheel became a continuous rasp.

"You think Moses is top dog," Profit said, his voice raised slightly, whether to compensate for the noise or from fear, it was hard to tell. "But he's on a short leash and a choke chain. Moses is a Marielita."

When Sheen did not say anything, Profit assumed that he should explain. His eyes flicked back and forth from the highway to Sheen.

"In the nineteen eighty Mariel boatlift," he began, "one hundred twenty-five thousand Cuban refugees traveled to Florida. Think about that. Castro did. He saw a chance to empty his prisons and to infiltrate as many agents as he could recruit. As many as three thousand of the Marielitas are agents. Cuba's strapped for cash, so let's say Castro ordered a third of those agents to deal — cocaine, marijuana, whatever. One thousand dealers. Even a tenth that many would be a powerful force. Profits? In the billions. Castro imports wholesale from Colombia, hop-skips it to Florida. From Castro's point of view the question wasn't why, but why not? What's he got to lose? His people can't even afford gasoline for their cars, if they have cars. He even makes money by charging for exit visas."

Sheen interrupted, his voice dry. "Did Moses come over then, in nineteen eighty?" He was not there to discuss Castro.

"No, Moses was already in place, but he was a captain without a ship. Eventually he would have gotten his own recruits, but the Mariel boatlift gave him a whole navy. Just the same, the agents can't do *all* the dealing. Too many gringos

183

are afraid of spics. The agents don't know the people, the young white people with the cash. So he recruited me, one among many. Moses is just an executive in the network. Ask your friends with the D.E.A. or the police. The whole country is divided up into regions. Now he's recruited you — you might as well have a paycheck signed by Fidel."

For the first time since he had gotten in the car, Sheen lowered the pistol. He laid it across his leg, still aimed at Profit.

"Man, has it worked out for Castro. We've resumed normal immigration practices with Cuba — more than twenty thousand Cubans a year are allowed to settle here. He makes thirty million a year selling exit visas. All he had to do was to take back three thousand violent psychos who should never have been let out of their cages in the first place. Be glad you didn't buy real estate in south Florida. It'll never be the same." Profit looked at Sheen and saw the impatience in his eyes.

"Moses isn't too greedy," he continued quickly, licking his lips once, "but he's in a very frustrating position. He takes the risks, and Cuba takes the money. He's allowed to keep enough to live well, but compared to what he's making, it's a pittance. He wants money he can keep. He came up with the idea for the pyramid and hooked me on it. *I* was greedy. I liked the idea of retirement. But when it came down to the final play, he got scared. The smell of something like that is enough to make the Marielitas chop your balls, literally. He didn't know what I'd do, and he knew I had to do *something*. The pyramid was about to collapse. At the very least he would get slapped for not watching me closely. If I drained the pyramid and split, he was in a real bind; the whole route was gone, not temporarily, permanently. And I was getting desperate. My money was *out.*" Profit shifted his gaze to Sheen. "That's when I recruited you."

Sheen's eyelids drooped skeptically, and he said, "You don't sing and dance. You play symphonies."

"You might as well hear me out," Profit said. "San Francisco is another ninety minutes."

184

Sheen said, "We might not be going that far."

Profit thought about that for a moment, then twisted around further, pushing his shoulder into the seat, talking to fill the silence. "You were a natural. Whatever I did I needed protection, and it had to be from someone outside the circuit. That's not so easy to find. I overpaid you the first trip to get you hooked, but you got skittish anyway. I needed time, and I needed you."

Sheen curled his lower lip over his teeth and bit down on it, shaking his head slowly. "You *did* set up your own bust. I heard it from two sources, and I still couldn't believe it."

"It was the only thing I could do. Moses was on my back. The pyramid was on my back. You weren't around. I felt like a kamikaze pilot who had been drafted."

A truck blew by them on the highway, going at least thirty miles an hour faster than they were. Its wake pushed them to the side of the lane, and Profit quickly turned to the front, holding the wheel steady and correcting for the sudden blast.

"Son of a bitch," he said, looking at the rapidly disappearing truck. He checked the rearview mirror and saw that there were no other trucks behind them before he continued. "The bust took the pressure off. What I didn't figure was how fast Moses would put it together. Debbie helped him there, I'm sure. The other thing I didn't figure was the tap on the pay phone. I only needed two or three days to collect the money that was out, but while I was at it I needed you with me, just in case." Again he moved his shoulder forward and back, but this time it was a gesture of apology. "I never have been too good with guns."

"Do you think it would have come to that?"

"I don't know — maybe, maybe not." Profit skipped on so quickly, the answer was evident. "The bust was both a shelter and a lever. See, even after my arrest, Moses couldn't kill me outright. I was too valuable a connection, and somewhere along the line he might have to explain it. As far as I was concerned, sending you to San Francisco was straight except that you weren't picking up coke, you were picking up cash, the first of my collections. I didn't trust you enough to tell you. Cash can have strange effects. When you got back, I was going to take you with me as I made the other collections. It would've taken two days to drain the pyramid. Two lousy days. I'd already made the calls."

The corners of Sheen's mouth drew down thoughtfully. He ran his hand through his hair, front to back, and asked, "Why did Moses try to kill me, assuming that it *was* Moses?"

Profit looked at Sheen with eyes that were serious and earnest. "Believe me, Sheen, if Moses had tried to kill you, you'd be dead. But he didn't want you dead, he wanted you angry. You were guaranteed to come after me. You didn't even know who he was. I'd have to beat feet for sure. The big surprise was I didn't run, and you didn't kill me. I didn't run because I figured I could make you understand what was happening; why you didn't kill me, I don't know. Anyway, once the house burned the game was over. As far as I was concerned I *did* have to leave. It was out of my league. I disappeared, but Moses needed to be certain that I stayed gone. The easy solution was to keep you after me. That's why he killed Andrea, and here you are. It worked."

"How did he explain killing Andrea?" Sheen asked, a weariness in his tone.

"As long as she wasn't making money for the network, it wasn't important enough to need an explanation. They're a rough bunch, and remember, they're Cuban — they have funny attitudes, especially about women." Profit squared his shoulders, rolled his neck, and pushed his cheek down against his upper arm to rub the speckling of gunpowder around his eye without taking his hands from the wheel.

When Profit said, "It wasn't important enough to need an explanation" — not *she* wasn't important enough, *it* — Sheen felt a cold anger, an anger that led him to disgust.

Beside him, he heard Profit say, "You must have used my address book to come after me. Otherwise you would never have met Moses. I wish I had seen his face when he figured out you had my book. He must think he's having a bad dream."

"Why?" Sheen asked.

"Because," Profit replied, "this whole pyramid thing is like chewing gum on his deck shoe: he can't get rid of it. And it's deadly. Once Moses knew you had the addresses and were making connections, there were only two things he could do: off you or use you. If he kills you, he's back at square one, explaining away his life. He has to use you, and you're a link back to me. I hope you're getting good prices, boy. And you, you're in the middle of a minefield you never knew existed."

There it is, Sheen thought, looking away. *I can believe that Moses killed her to achieve an end or that Profit killed her for vengeance.* A sour taste rose in his throat. He turned to the front, put the .45 in the holster on his hip, said, "Take the next exit." Suddenly and very badly he wanted to get away from Profit.

Profit's mouth opened and closed. The next exit was five miles up the road. Small beads of perspiration broke out on his forehead. His skin was pale. Out of the corner of his eye he looked at Sheen slouched low in the seat, both hands in the pockets of his light jacket, his head turned to look out the window. Profit looked back at the road and watched the white lane stripes pass.

On the exit ramp Profit started to ask which way he should turn, but he decided to wait for Sheen to speak first.

Sheen said, "Stop near a gas station. I'll get out and walk."

Profit's head jerked around and he studied Sheen's face, seeing in it the irresolute lack of purpose. Relief came in a rush. He felt weak, almost grateful. He smiled tentatively, and said, "You won't have to walk far. Your friends are right behind us."

Sheen looked at him with eyes that were dull and lifeless. "I'm alone," he said.

Profit jerked his thumb over his shoulder. "I thought they

were with you. They've been behind us the whole way."

Sheen pushed himself up in the seat and turned to look behind them. There were two men in the red car that was following, but they were too far away to be recognized. Sheen shrugged indifferently and turned back to the front.

Profit turned into the gas station nearest the exit, and before the car had come to a complete stop in front of the pumps Sheen opened the car door, got out, slammed the door behind him. In the gas station he thumbed through the thin Yellow Pages, found a number, called a taxi. When he asked the station attendant for change to make a second call, through the window he saw Profit's car going back down the interstate toward Rayton, and he watched until it disappeared, indiscernible among the other cars slowly descending into the valley.

With the change he got from the station attendant, Sheen called Marty.

"Are you up?" he asked when she answered, picturing the way the sunlight seemed to make the white curtains glow in her corner apartment.

"Of course. It's after nine here."

After a long pause he said, "I saw Profit. I talked to him, that's all."

"Are you okay?"

"I feel tired. I'm very tired."

"Come home, Sheen," Marty said.

Outside, on the two-lane street in front of the gas station, the red car that had been following on the highway flashed past. Detective Ridell was driving. Detective Gossett was in the back seat, steadying a pair of binoculars on the windowsill and looking through them.

"That's him," Gossett said. "Goddammit, that's him." With disgust he threw the binoculars on the floor and sat forward, draping his arm over the seat back between the headrests. The police radio squawked, and he said to Ridell irritably, "Turn that thing off."

Gossett watched the gas station pass, his glance shifting from the side to the rear window.

"Shit," he said. "I thought we had them both." His voice was angry, vicious. "Vicedomini kills his punk friend, and we get Vicedomini." His open hand slapped the seat. "Shit. Stop somewhere. I want to call Avila."

14

THE CONFERENCE room was on the twentieth floor of a tower building nine blocks out of New Orleans's central business district. Because there were no other tall buildings nearby, the view was unobstructed, and through the windows it was possible to see three bends in the Mississippi River. In the midmorning sun the river was shimmering gold. Tugboats, barges, freighters, tankers, and riverboats of all sizes and types followed the river's meandering, deceptively placid course.

The room was no larger than a standard office, but it seemed larger because it contained only a single table, three feet by seven feet, around which there were eight chairs, three on each side and one at each end. The table had a brown plastic surface made to resemble wood. The chairs were heavy white oak, the sort often found in waiting rooms. The carpet was dark gray and thin, with a texture not unlike an old bath towel.

Tony Avila sat at one end of the conference room table, nervously twisting the index finger on his left hand, unaware of the grating sound made by the bones in his knuckle. On the wall behind him there was a plaque bearing the official seal of the United States Drug Enforcement Administration. Underneath the plaque large black letters read REGIONAL OFFICE.

Avila did not know either of the two men who came into the conference room. The man who introduced himself as Special Agent William Dryden was about fifty years old, and he was very thin. His shoulders were stooped, as if he had carried too much weight for far too long. He had bright blue eyes that flashed between a high forehead and high cheekbones. His hair was dark blond. He wore a rumpled blue seersucker suit, dark tie, glasses with brown frames, and lace-up black shoes. The other man — Agent Dryden introduced him only as Red — was in his early thirties, powerfully built, and had long red hair and a thick red beard. He wore blue jeans, a dirty long-john top, a red and white ball cap pushed back on his head. His boots were caked with tan mud that had cracked and split as it dried.

Dryden dropped a file folder on the table, and Tony Avila saw the name on the tab in the upper left-hand corner: VICE-DOMINI, SHEEN.

When all three of them were sitting, Dryden spoke to Avila, his voice crisp yet resonant with authority. "Thank you for coming, Detective. I realize you're on your own time, and I appreciate it. I'll try not to waste it."

Tony Avila thought William Dryden looked more like an accountant or a banker than a D.E.A. field agent. *A very cold banker,* he thought, *a man unlikely to give you credit.*

Dryden asked Red, "How badly do we need Vicedomini?"

Red replied without hesitation, "He's the key to the whole operation." He sat forward, put his arms on the table, adjusted a bulge of chewing tobacco in his cheek by pulling his mouth to one side. "The Marielitas have divided the country into five regions. In each region there are five cocaine distributors. Each distributor has his own company; each company operates independently, within an assigned area. Geography makes the southeast the most active region. Cuba is close. The coastline from Florida to Texas is a smuggler's dream. In gross receipts, New York–New Jersey is second; the west coast is third. Penetrating the lower distribution echelons isn't difficult — they routinely hire outside people, usually locals. But stepping up

191

from there has been impossible. The Marielitas have their own language and their own customs — it's a very closed society — and they have only one punishment: any offense brings death."

"How did Vicedomini manage it?"

"Unknown," Red replied, turning his head from side to side, obviously looking for something. His glance fixed on a white Styrofoam coffee cup that had been left on the windowsill. He got out of his chair, retrieved the cup, turned his back to the table, and spat tobacco juice into it. He carried the cup with him to his chair and put it on the floor beside his feet. "Sorry," he said, an embarrassed look on his face. "I've been in the swamp so long, I've kinda gotten used to it."

Agent Dryden smiled a thin, indulgent smile that did not touch his eyes. "Can you speculate about how Vicedomini penetrated above street level?"

Red shrugged. "He may have some sort of lever, or he may simply be a very successful dealer. The important thing is, he *is* in place. He has immediate access to a distributor — a distributor is up two levels from the street, once removed from ever even *seeing* cocaine. At present we know four of the five distributors in our region." Red shifted his glance doubtfully to Tony Avila, then back to William Dryden. "Three weeks ago it was decided to take out the fifth distributor on conspiracy, just to see what would happen. His company operations were interrupted for less than a week, and we still don't know who replaced him. That's why we know only four of the five."

William Dryden said, "Maybe you should have taken all five distributors at once."

"We considered that possibility, but rejected it. One bust could be attributed to simple carelessness. Five simultaneous arrests couldn't. They'd have known the extent of our surveillance, and we wouldn't have gained as much as we lost — five can be replaced almost as easily as one."

"If they're so easily replaced," Avila interrupted, "then someone is in charge of *them.*"

192

Before he replied, Red looked questioningly at Dryden. The special agent gave a barely perceptible nod of his head, giving him approval to continue.

"Our assumption is that there is one man in charge of each region. That assumption is based upon both their method of organization and the findings from our electronic surveillance." Red cupped one hand in the other, fingers wrapped around his fist. He was reluctant to divulge information to an outsider. "The organization is paramilitary. Number is inverse to rank. There are many privates, fewer NCOs, a handful of officers, one general. The distributors are equivalent to field-grade officers. The NCOs are dealers. The privates are bodyguards and chauffeurs. Within each region there is only one communications center, and, we believe, one general."

"That's where you are, Red? In a communications center?"

Red shook his head. "I'm *near* a communications center, Mr. Dryden, not *in* one." He sat further forward, shifting his weight onto his beefy forearms. "The communications center is way out in the swamp. I come and go in the area as a neighbor, and I run a few errands for the man in charge, a man named Willie. Their equipment is very sophisticated — rapidly alternating microwave bands, random computer codes — but essentially there are many channels in and only two out. One of the broadcast channels is beamed directly to Cuba, received by the Ministry of the Interior."

"How do you know that?" Avila interrupted again. He wanted to show that he was alert, an asset to the operation. To work with the D.E.A. on a major operation would guarantee his promotion. And he didn't care how many dirty looks he got from the man assigned to the swamp end of it. "How do you know it goes directly to Cuba?"

Again Red shifted his glance, looking at Avila with light brown eyes that were both questioning and challenging. The glance ran over Tony, taking in the off-the-rack chocolate-brown suit, the cheap yellow tie, the powder-blue shirt. His eyes shifted back to Dryden, and he asked pointedly, "Does he have clearance?"

Dryden waved one hand in a gesture of unconcern. For his own reasons he chose neither to assuage Red's doubt nor to reinforce Avila's position, but subtly encouraged the budding antagonism between them by pretending not to notice it. "It's not important. Where does the second channel go?"

Red leaned down, picked up the cup from beside his foot, spat into it, and put it back on the floor.

"We believe the second channel goes to the man in charge of the region, the general, and if we can find *him*, we can take out their whole command. While we're at it, we'll decimate their army. It will break their backs."

"What about the other regions?" Tony Avila asked.

Red looked at him with disdain, his lips pursed as if he were again about to spit. "We're assigned only to *this* region, Detective."

Dryden took his pipe out of his mouth. He laid it on the table, aligned it carefully, parallel to the edge of the folder in front of him, and said, "You met Vicedomini, Red. You've seen his folder. What do you think of him?"

"I only met Vicedomini briefly, Mr. Dryden. I picked him up in the city and brought him out to the swamp. The next day he took the return trip. It's hard to say — "

"Sheen's not that hard to figure," Tony Avila broke in, "not if you know him." He sat forward and put his forearms on the table, consciously imitating Red's posture but unaware that he was nervously twisting his index finger as he did so. "It's probably hard to read his folder and not think he's savage. But don't get him wrong. He's not savage by nature, it's what he becomes when he has a reason — and he seeks out the reasons."

"I'm not sure I follow you," Dryden said.

Tony Avila released the finger he had been twisting to point at the thick file folder on the table.

"One of his shootings with the department," he said, "was a loony-tune with a rifle, a guy shooting out of a window. Sheen wasn't sure the guy was shooting *at* anything. He thought maybe the guy was just making noise, getting himself some attention. He held up the whole scene until the rounds started coming in close, then Sheen took him himself. You see how it fits? He was the first there, seeking it out, but he had to be sure before he did anything. Once he understands what he has to do, he does it. He gets a blank look, like he's on another planet. And he just does it."

Dryden thought about that for a moment, then asked, "Is it what he *has* to do, or what he thinks it's *right* to do? The distinction is important."

"Sheen is stubborn," Avila replied. "You can't force him into anything."

"Whether or not we could force him," Red added, addressing Dryden as if Avila were not there, "to be of use to us, he has to cooperate. He's in; we're not. He'll have to help us every step of the way — it has to be a carrot, not a stick."

"Do either of you have any suggestions about what to use as a carrot?"

A silence followed Dryden's question. Red again shrugged, and Avila squirmed on his chair, uncertain whether or not to say what he was thinking.

William Dryden looked at him with eyes that were expectant and not very patient.

"There's only one thing you can use," Avila said finally, his voice low. "Give him his girlfriend's killer."

There was a feel to the silence that greeted his suggestion that made Tony wish he had not said anything. He sat back in his chair, put his hands in his lap, and twisted his finger.

Dryden said to Red, "Thank you. I'll review the files and let you know this afternoon how we'll proceed. Good work."

Red nodded once curtly, picked up his spittoon-cup from the floor, stood up. Before he turned to leave he gave Tony Avila a long look filled with contempt, a look Tony felt but did not return. The door closed quietly behind him.

Tony started to say something, to explain what he had meant, but thought better of it. Dryden seemed preoccupied, distracted by a thought as he looked out the window at the river, his expression curiously unformed. Then, as if to conceal the thought, he took a cleaning tool from his pocket and picked up his pipe. The metal tool made a scraping sound in the wooden bowl.

Looking at his pipe as he cleaned it, he said, "I wanted you here, Detective, for two reasons. First, you worked with Vicedomini. You know him. I have to make a difficult decision. Bringing a civilian in on an operation always presents a risk, regardless of his background — and I have to make my decision quickly." Holding the pipe by the stem, the special agent turned it upside down and thumped the bowl against his palm three times. He cupped the tobacco that dislodged, dropped it in a red metal ashtray on the table, and ran his palms against each other, lightly touching in a fussy, dusting motion.

"Second," he continued, "I wanted you to understand the scope of this operation. The drug-dealing faction of the Marielitas is accumulating huge amounts of cash. Their brutality is well documented. Last year in Miami alone there were one hundred thirty-three drug-related murders reported — we suspect nearly three times that many took place and were *not* reported. Eventually the Marielitas will begin to use their cash. They'll diversify their markets. Within their own ranks they'll encourage competition, and at the same time they'll eliminate legitimate outside competition. If we allow that to happen, the Marielitas will be entrenched in our market system as deeply as a cancer, a cancer that will make the Mafia seem pleasant by comparison — not an appealing scenario. If Vicedomini comes in, we may have to use you as his contact. He may request it. Civilians often want someone they know. A friend."

Tony nodded gravely, showing both that he understood and that he agreed, confirming his status as Sheen's friend.

Dryden slowly reached forward and put his hand down flat on the file folder in front of him.

"Now let me run down an unrelated scenario," he said, his words taking on an edge. "A policeman's wife is brutally murdered. A tragedy."

Tony felt the blood drain from his face. The muscles in

his jaw went slack, and his mouth dropped open involuntarily.

"Naturally enough," Dryden continued, his words gaining emphasis from the dullness of his tone, "the policeman comes unglued. He wants to kill the killer — and probably will. But he's emotionally upset, likely to botch the job and to get caught. He appeals to a friend for help. The friend says wait and see, maybe the courts will handle it. Predictably, however, the killer is turned loose; forced confessions don't usually hold up. The killer was smart. He confessed to that same policeman, hoping there would be some abuse and knowing he would walk if there was. Now that policeman's friend has a decision: to take care of the killer himself or to let his friend do it and botch it. Who set up the blinds, Avila? The other killings?"

Tony Avila realized that his mouth was open, and he closed it. He slouched down in his seat until the table was in line with his shirt pocket.

"Is this on tape?" he asked.

"This is between you and me," Dryden replied, his voice deceptively calm. "I have to know about Vicedomini."

"Do I get immunity?"

"Goddammit, you get *nothing.*" William Dryden slapped his palm sharply against the file folder. In the closed room the slap sounded like a small-caliber shot. "I need the information now. Do *not* make me get it later."

There was fear in Tony Avila's eyes, but it was fear mixed with cunning. He knew Dryden was guessing, linking fragments into a likely sequence — the fact that he thought Sheen had killed his wife's murderer showed that — and he knew he had to take the risk that Dryden would not go to the D.A. with conjecture, because he wanted Dryden to use him on the operation, and to use him he had to want Sheen. *If he had ever been on the street,* Tony Avila thought, *he would know that a man straightens his own house.*

He said, "I set up the blinds. Sheen didn't like it. He said I had the killer, leave it alone. But it was too obvious. It *had* to be covered."

"Too obvious for whom?" Dryden asked, his voice cutting, allowing the question to hang. After a moment he took off his glasses and pinched the bridge of his nose between thumb and first finger, wearily rubbing the oval red spots made by the frames. He replaced the glasses and opened his eyes. When he spoke again, he resumed the flat tone he had used previously. "So the friend is set up to fall three times, but it works. All of it works. No one is caught. No one goes to jail. But later, because of a similarly tragic situation, that same friend *needs* a friend. He goes to the policeman. The policeman is nervous — he doesn't like any links to the unsavory past. So what does the policeman do? He sets up his friend again, sets him up to kill in front of other policemen. No more links to the past." William Dryden looked at Tony Avila with repugnance. "You disgust me. You make me want to be physically ill. How do you live with yourself?"

The special agent stood up, kicking his chair back as he did so.

"Here's a third scenario for you, Avila. A narcotics cop in New Orleans is caught with a kilo of cocaine concealed in the trunk of his car. The cop denies any knowledge of it, but the D.E.A. runs it down and word gets out that it's a kilo that was stolen just before a certain Marielita distributor was arrested. If I were a Marielita, I would come to the conclusion that the distributor had been taken down to cover a theft. If I were a Marielita, I would be very agitated. And there are many variations possible on that theme, if you get my drift. In jail or out, you're a dead man — and the world is a better place for it. Even these animals, these Marielitas, have loyalty to something more than their own ass. I should sell you for dog food, Avila, but I need this operation."

Dryden walked around the table and stood behind the chair on which Tony was sitting. He leaned down and spoke directly into Tony's ear, so close that Tony smelled the tobacco smoke in his jacket and felt his breath on his cheek.

"If Vicedomini comes in, and if I have to let you work with him, you will be his guardian angel. You will be his devoted friend. He scratches his finger, and you're there with a Band-Aid. He stubs his toe, and you're so close *you* feel pain. Am I understood? I catch word of anything, *anything,* and I'll yank your string so fast you'll drop your fillings." Dryden stood up straight. "Get out of my sight."

Tony Avila slowly pushed himself to his feet and turned to face William Dryden. Their eyes locked and held, the broad powerful detective confronting the thin government agent with a look that said, "I'll catch you on the street someday, and that's a promise"; and the agent, unmoved, returning the look with blue eyes as hard and shiny as the glass in the frames in front of them.

Tony Avila turned on his heel, yanked open the door so hard it slapped back against the wall, and was gone.

Dryden stared after him, then went and closed the door. He sat in the chair Tony had vacated, slouched low just as Tony had, and pulled the file across the table, turning it so that he could review it again. He felt his heart pounding, and before he opened the folder he took a deep breath through his nose, flaring his nostrils and stretching his lips. Momentarily he wondered if he had overplayed his hand.

Exhaling slowly he opened the file and looked at the two black-and-white photographs stapled to the inside of the cover. Both photographs had been taken through a very long lens that compressed distance, and both had been greatly enlarged for printing so that there was a grainy texture to them, the individual dots composing the pictures clearly visible. In the first photograph Sheen Vicedomini was getting out of a car from the passenger side, leg bent, one foot on the pavement, hand on top of the open door, simultaneously pushing and pulling himself out of the car. In the second Sheen was standing outside the door to a house, putting a key into the lock. He had a large grocery bag under one arm, and his head was twisted around to look over his shoulder; he seemed to be looking directly at the camera. William Dryden studied the two photographs at length.

*　*　*

In Marty's apartment Sheen was sitting on the couch looking at the large corner windows and enjoying the way the sunlight seemed to make the white curtains glow. Every now and then a soft breeze came through the open windows and made the curtains move slightly.

On the other end of the couch, Marty sat with her ankle under her knee, her elbow on top of a cushion, facing him and trying to read his expression.

She said, "You don't *have* to do it."

"I know," Sheen replied. He rolled his head toward her without removing it from the cushion against which he was resting, and his cheek sank into the soft fabric. "What do *you* think?"

"What I think isn't important."

"It is to me," Sheen said. He extended his hand and took hers.

Marty looked down at their intertwined fingers, and her face was much softer than it had been a moment before.

"It's easier to tell you what I think when you're asleep."

"Sometimes I just pretend to be asleep."

"I know," Marty said. She took back her hand and picked a piece of lint from the cushion between them.

"What would *you* do?" Sheen asked.

"I'm not you. I'm not the one who has to go to Miami." In her eyes was uncertainty, and hurt. She ran her hand through her hair and held it pulled straight back from her forehead. "I want you to do it, and I don't want you to do it."

Sheen turned his head just slightly, enough to look at the windows in the corner.

"That's my feeling too," he said.

"I don't think it is, Sheen. I think you're indifferent. You don't care either way — that's not the same thing."

"You're splitting hairs," he said, looking at her.

"No, I'm not." Marty spoke softly, but her voice was tinged with emotion. "You use indifference as a shield. It's the way you hide from yourself what you're feeling. Even now you

200

have trouble admitting that someone, Andrea, could have affected you so deeply, because you're so afraid of that affection — and its loss. That's the wall between us."

A breeze lifted the curtains and parted them slightly, and through the crack Sheen could see an oak tree, a section of late afternoon sunlight on green leaves and rough gray bark.

"I want to do it," he said finally. "I want someone to pay."

"I'm glad," Marty replied honestly. She turned her head to follow his glance, looking at the windows so that he could not see her eyes.

Special Agent William Dryden had turned his chair to face the windows, and he sat with his feet propped on the windowsill, knees bent. With his elbows on the arms of the chair, hands fingertip to fingertip in front of his face, he had sat there through the sunset and watched as the river changed in the changing light. Because the D.E.A. office was fully occupied, he had been given the conference room to use, and just then he wondered how many conference rooms he had used as offices, how many places he had taken over temporarily during brief stops in a peripatetic career. He did not hear the light knock on the door.

When Red entered, he thought the special agent was asleep in the chair, and he said tentatively, "Mr. Dryden?"

Dryden turned his head, not enough to look over his shoulder but enough to show that he was awake, and said, "Pull up a chair, Red." When Red was seated next to him, he added absently, "That's quite a river."

"Three hundred and fifty billion gallons of water pass here daily — two hundred and forty million gallons a minute," Red replied. "I looked it up."

Dryden gave Red an amused look, and said, "You would."

Red smiled briefly. "Vicedomini just called. He's in."

"Good," Dryden replied, pushing his fingertips one against another.

"He wants Avila."

"We anticipated that."

"He also wants a safe contact within the Miami P.D." Red hesitated just slightly, but the pause was distinct enough to make Dryden look at him. "And he wants Profit."

"To work with him?"

Red nodded affirmatively.

"I'll be damned. He's really going to do it." Dryden looked back at the river and brought his palms together. "Okay, let's give him what he wants. Let him make his gumbo. We'll see what happens when he stirs the pot."

15

A DRIVEWAY SURFACED with white shells led through a high chain link fence topped with barbed wire to a long, low tin roof supported by posts. The spacing of the posts, and the flat roof attached to them, gave the appearance of an eighteen-place carport without walls. Exactly fifty-five yards beyond the roof there was a high, steep levee parallel to it. Between the roof and the levee, dirt paths had been worn in the grass by police officers walking back and forth, both to shoot from the various distances required by the course and to retrieve their targets. When Sheen got out of his car near one end of the roof, the pistol range seemed deserted, but the gate was open and he knew that the range instructor, Merlin Coast, was somewhere nearby.

Next to the range shack was a stack of bull's-eye targets, and Sheen took one and walked halfway to the levee. Then he stopped and extended his arm straight out from his side, holding the target beneath his forearm, much like a bullfighter holding a cape.

Six shots came so quickly they made one sound.

Sheen looked at the target curiously. Only one shot had strayed into the ten ring. The X-ring center of the target was gone, pulverized by five squared-off target projectiles that had left a hole the size of a quarter.

Thirty yards away Merlin Coast stood up from the high grass at the edge of the range.

"You're losing your group, Merlin," Sheen shouted over his shoulder. "You better put on your glasses."

"You better *get* glasses if you think that's losing a group," Merlin shouted back, indignant.

Holding the target in front of him and pretending to consider it seriously, Sheen said, "I gave you half the afternoon to aim."

As he walked toward Sheen, Merlin Coast smiled. He was more than sixty years old and weighed well over two hundred very solid pounds. Everything about him was thick — thick neck, thick trunk, thick arms and legs — and when he brought his hands together slowly to cup his Model 66 Smith & Wesson stainless, his whole broad back bunched and the revolver was locked on target as solidly as if it were clamped in a vise. His silver-gray hair was cut so short the scalp gleamed beneath it.

Merlin gave Sheen a hug that lifted him off the ground.

"You shithead. You quit the department, you quit your friends too?"

Sheen stepped away from him, arching and twisting his back, trying to realign it. "I wasn't sure I was welcome," he said.

Merlin's eyes went wide, and he took three steps backward, dropping his hand to his revolver, fingers extended lightly to touch the butt: the perfect parody of a Wild West gunslinger ready to draw.

"You getting stupid on me, Sheen?"

The corners of Sheen's mouth pushed out in a grin. "Probably."

"You want to shoot?"

"Maybe I should," Sheen replied, furrowing his brow thoughtfully. "By now you must need a refresher."

Merlin snorted, "Ha! Me? I taught *you*, remember? When you first came out here, you weren't sure which end to point. At least you learned fast. You still have that raggedy Colt?"

"You bet," Sheen said, "but I also have a problem." He

held up his right hand and wiggled the stumps. "I'm not sure I can handle the factory loads."

Merlin looked at the hand, then at Sheen, his expression losing its playfulness as he stepped forward, brusquely grabbed Sheen's hand, turned it over and back.

"What caliber?" he asked.

"Forty-four," Sheen replied.

Merlin dropped the hand and looked up at Sheen. "You're lucky you have any hand at all. I've heard some strange stories about you, Sheen. I hope they're not true."

Sheen looked down and said, "Will you make a box of light loads for me?"

Merlin put his hand on Sheen's shoulder and squeezed it hard, digging into the muscle until Sheen had to look up. When he did, he saw the concern in Merlin's eyes, and heard him say, "I've got a little money stashed. If you need it, you're welcome to it. Don't do stupid things."

"I'm fine," Sheen said. With his left hand he patted Merlin's hand on his shoulder. "Really. I'm working with the Feds. I may need a few things from the armory."

Merlin gave him a long, appraising look. "Later," he said. "The rookie class will be here in half an hour for part two of their six-month checkup. You're going to put on a demonstration."

"I don't know — " Sheen began.

"*I* do. There's a cocky kid who thinks he's hot on the practical combat. He's been bothering me for months — he needs to be taken down a notch."

"But I'm out of practice," Sheen protested. "My hand — "

Merlin stopped him. "*You* will never lose your touch." He smiled, his eyes bright with a contrived deviousness. "Besides, do you want the light loads or not?"

"You're something, Coast — and you call *me* a shithead?"

In response, Merlin put one thick hand on top of his head and rubbed it back and forth, causing the skin to move and his eyebrows to pull up and down humorously.

Sheen gave a genuine smile and followed Merlin to the range shack. It was arranged just like a kitchen — counters on three sides, work island in the middle — but the appliances were different: on one counter there was a metal lathe; on another there were two bullet presses and a vise. Tools hung on the walls, and there was a rich, pungent smell of Hoppe's gun oil, silicon rags, and fresh metal shavings.

Merlin stood in front of the press counting the gray pellets of smokeless gunpowder that fell into each casing, then sealing the casing with a lead projectile. Sheen stood next to him and enviously watched his surprisingly dexterous fat fingers moving with easy assurance. When Merlin had made exactly sixty light loads, enough for Sheen to shoot the course once, he said, "That's enough for now. Give me your piece."

Sheen took out his pistol, cleared it, and handed it to him, expecting a disparaging remark, but Merlin simply clamped the pistol into a vise and turned back to him. In the same brusque way he had before, Merlin took Sheen's hand in both of his, positioned it, and pressed it palm down into a ball of putty. He then motioned for Sheen to move away, and, using the putty impression as a template, marked and cut a hard rubber block. He tapped the Colt, drilled the block, and attached the rubber piece to the handle, neatly forming an extension that would allow Sheen to rotate his grip and partially compensate for the missing fingers.

Outside, there was the sound of car doors opening and closing.

"In the nick of time," Merlin said, handing Sheen the Colt, butt first. "I'll round the edges later. See how it feels."

Just then the training sergeant stuck his head through the door and said, "They're all yours, Merlin, but they have to be back at the academy by four-thirty."

Merlin nodded and started to follow the sergeant outside. At the door he turned back. "Hey," he said gruffly to Sheen. "No excuses."

Before he left he winked conspiratorially, opening both eyes wide before he closed one in a way that caused his eyebrows to slant ludicrously across his forehead.

Sheen smiled indulgently and turned to watch through the window as Merlin rounded up the rookies. In their ill-fitting dark blue training uniforms and dark blue ball caps, one rookie looked very much like another. They clustered in a group around Merlin, elbowing and shouldering each other good-naturedly, joking and laughing, anticipating the shoot. It seemed to Sheen that they were very young, and for a moment he felt nostalgic, remembering his own recruit class. Then he saw Merlin wave and heard him call his name, and reluctantly Sheen walked outside and stood on the edge of the group.

"This, ladies and gentlemen," Merlin said, pointing at Sheen, "is a civilian — an injured civilian, I might point out. I taught him to shoot. With or without his fingers, if you ever pull a weapon on him, it is guaranteed to be the last thing you will ever do."

Sheen rolled his eyes in embarrassment.

"What's your best?" one of the recruits asked doubtfully.

"It's been over a year since I've shot the course," Sheen replied, trying to attach the voice to a face.

"I shot a three hundred *yesterday,*" the voice said, and Sheen saw him then: a tall, well-built young man with an arrogant cast to his face and challenging eyes. "I'll do it again today."

Sheen put his injured hand in his pants pocket and rolled his shoulder indifferently. "I'll probably just shoot the bull's-eye today," he said.

"I *own* the bull's-eye. I broke the range record four months ago. There's nothing to it. Old men like Merlin shoot the bull's-eye because the target doesn't move. But on the street you haven't got all day to aim. Unless you're just an instructor, you better be hot on the practical combat."

Sheen started to let it go — *Let the street take the edge off him,* he thought; *Let him learn the hard way* — but then he saw Merlin standing quietly in the center of the group, both hands in his pockets, shoulders rounded uncharacteristically, and he said to the rookie, "Talk is cheap, buck. A smart mouth doesn't put holes in the target."

"I got a Smith & Wesson for that, mister. Why don't you and I shoot a little match?"

"Why don't we?" Sheen asked, feeling the quietness and the attention directed at him. "A hundred dollars a point. Fifty dollars an X."

The rookie glared at him, and his Adam's apple rose and fell. "I don't have that kind of money."

"You *will* if you can shoot," Sheen said easily, cocking his head to one side. "I'll take your marker."

"Hell, mister, I'll take your *money.*"

There was an outburst of laughter, and the rookies began to talk excitedly among themselves. Sheen turned and went back into the range shack, and there was a general movement down-range, toward the start of the course. Through the window Sheen watched Merlin gesturing and cajoling, wheeling and dealing with the rookies before he joined him in the shack.

Merlin shut the door and said, "Thanks, Sheen. That little bastard — "

"I haven't won yet," Sheen interrupted, taking off his jacket to adjust the shoulder holster he wore beneath it. "You didn't tell me he was the one who broke my bull's-eye record."

"You never did like the bull's-eye — you told me so yourself."

Sheen pulled his belt tight so that it would anchor the holster to his side. He looked at Merlin and said, "I need some incendiaries with timers and maybe a half pound of plastique."

Merlin replied, "I took even points and gave away five Xs."

"Shit, Merlin, what's his best?"

"Three hundred, eighteen X."

"That's not too sloppy, you know?"

"I've got four hundred dollars out so far. And I bet my revolver against his." Merlin smiled and hitched up his pants, pulling up one side and then the other. "I'll get you five phosphorus grenades and four ounces of plastique — that's the best I can do. Are you *sure* you're working for the Feds?"

Sheen nodded, and said, "Five phosphorus grenades, one concussion grenade, and six ounces of plastique — and the timers."

"The timers go for ten Xs over. I'll get three to five."

Sheen laughed out loud, a good laugh that came from his chest, and ran his hand over his face.

"You old fart. I'll consider it as we go, but the kid gets to keep his revolver."

Merlin smiled broadly. "Of course he does, Sheen, but *I* get to give it back to him."

Sheen laughed again and picked up his pistol. For the first time in what seemed a very long time, he felt relaxed. The new grip felt solid. The light loads were easy to handle, and it took Sheen only forty-five minutes to win the explosives he carried in his suitcase to Miami.

Viewed from various directions, the building seemed to change. The east end was rounded like the bow of a ship. The west end was square. The north and south facades were like giant billboards sandwiched together back to back, and through the middle a huge cube seemed to have been punched out. The cube, having moved ninety feet, lay on the ground beside the tennis courts and had been handily converted to squash courts and an exercise room. The twenty-story condominium building combined elements of Art Deco and Hollywood in a way that made it typical of Miami. Its mirror glass reflected white clouds slowly floating past in a blue sky.

On a balcony on the eighth floor Sheen was leaning against the red metal railing, elbows on top of one round metal tube, one foot raised onto the tube beneath, watching a sailboat motor across Biscayne Bay. Behind him Profit lay stretched out on a lounge chair. Profit was shiny with suntan oil, and every so often he turned himself over to tan evenly. Between them on a low iron table was the chess set they had abandoned when it had become apparent that Sheen's plodding thoughtfulness was no match for Profit's lightning quick changes in strategy. The sun was so bright the light itself seemed thick and heavy.

Sheen had arrived the day before, Profit early that morning, and they were waiting; but they were both accustomed to waiting, both felt easy about it, and there had been a long silence that had been very smooth.

Sheen turned around and leaned back against the railing, propping his arms on top of it and extending his legs straight out in front of himself. He looked at Profit on the lounge chair, slick in his striped nylon bathing suit, slick with oil, and it occurred to him that Profit fit the building as well as the gaudy building fit Miami.

He said, "I don't understand why you were so greedy, why you weren't satisfied with what you were making legitimately." Sheen heard himself say "legitimately," and he realized his references had changed.

"I got used to the money," Profit replied. "The more I made, the more I needed." Arcing his hand lazily over the arm of the lounge chair, he reached for his drink. "And every time I put together a decent amount, something happened, and I lost it. I was ready to score big once and split."

The wet napkin under the drink stuck to the table, and when Profit moved the glass to his lips, cold sweat dripped onto his stomach. "Damn," he said, turning onto one side so that the sweat on the glass would drip onto the tiles rather than onto him.

"What did you do with it?" Sheen asked, amused by the way the drops of water beaded up on Profit's oiled skin like raindrops on the hood of a recently waxed car. "Do you gamble?"

"Sure I gamble — you do too. But that's not how I lost the money. One time I was out-finessed. That didn't happen but once. Another time I was taken off big, with guns, probably by Moses. Just before we began the pyramid, Elaine came to me with a story so outrageous I was sure it was true."

210

Sheen reached into the pocket of his baggy cotton shorts for a stick of lip balm.

"Had she by chance come across some bales of marijuana floating in the Gulf?"

"How do you know that?" Profit asked, then, making the connection, he smiled. "Not you, too? Man, you'd think they'd come up with something new, but I guess there wasn't any reason to. It worked once, and who would ever have guessed we'd be swapping stories?" Profit's smile changed to a good-natured, hopeful grin, without malice. "Did they get you?"

Holding the canister by one end Sheen smeared the waxy lip balm across his lower lip and pressed his lips together.

"No," he replied. "I went to see you instead."

Profit said, "You lead a charmed life. I wonder what Moses was planning for *you?*"

"What do you mean?"

"I mean, he wouldn't do it without something in mind."

Sheen started to say, "If it *was* Moses, and if it *was* a plan to rob me," but he thought better of it, and said simply, "The something might have been seventy-five thousand dollars."

Profit shook his head, denying the possibility. "The money is the small part of it. Moses would hardly walk across the street for seventy-five grand. The *lack* of money is the thing. He hooks you by letting you earn a lot, then he reels you in by taking away what you manage to accumulate. That's basic strategy. I've done it myself, and I *know* it works — from both sides. Elaine is just naturally mercenary. She's short, anyway. She lost a bundle in the pyramid, dollars as high as telephone numbers. Millions. Moses was planning something for you, just like he had me in mind for the pyramid."

Sheen saw himself reflected in Profit's sunglasses, his image distorted by the curve of the lenses. Behind him he heard a powerful, deep-throated roar, and he looked over his shoulder at a sleek white motorboat passing at high speed, water foaming in its wake.

"Who is this Avila guy?" Profit asked.

"N.O.P.D. Narcotics," Sheen replied, watching the boat even after it had passed because he was uncertain how much to tell Profit about Tony Avila. "He's driving down. He's supposed to be our connection back to New Orleans, but I suspect they want someone to keep an eye on us. He speaks Spanish, too."

Profit looked to one side of the lounge chair, then the other, saw the brown plastic bottle of suntan lotion, picked it up, and unscrewed the orange plastic top.

"Who would ever have thought I'd be working for the Feds?"

"You're *not* working for the Feds," Sheen said pointedly. "You're working for *me.*"

"Yeah?" Profit asked. He turned the lotion bottle over quickly and squeezed it; the yellow cream made an obscene splattering sound as it squirted out. He grinned sourly at Sheen, dropped the bottle on the deck, and began to rub more oil on himself.

"Dryden is one cold son of a bitch," he said matter-of-factly, his attention on his shoulders.

Sheen imagined the interview that had taken place between Dryden and Profit, Profit being nailed down by someone who was as quick as he but more powerful.

"He can be persuasive," Sheen agreed.

"Persuasive? He scared the shit out of me. I didn't know they let people like that loose with a badge. Scratch that. I didn't know they let people like that loose *at all.* If he were Cuban, he'd be a Marielita." Profit rolled over onto his stomach and stretched out, his cheek on the back of his hands. "But I can't complain about the accommodations he's given us — it's nice to see how my money would've been spent if I'd been paying taxes. When do we start to earn it? Not that I'm pushing, you understand."

"We're supposed to wait for Avila, but whether he gets here or not, Moses's party is tomorrow night."

Profit gave a contented sigh. "Have you ever been to one of his parties?"

Sheen shook his head and said "No," assuming that Profit's eyes were closed behind his sunglasses.

"Go late," Profit advised. "The first hour or two is all business, more a staff meeting than a party, all men and lots of cigars. But once business is out of the way, the women arrive. They just appear, like magic, and they are *unbelievable* — they're enough to make you learn to speak spic."

"Do other distributors go?"

Profit moved one oiled shoulder. "Maybe one or two will be there. They overlap meetings in other parts of the country. Moses is senior — word comes down from him."

"Where do you think Moses gets *his* orders?"

Profit extended one arm and moved his hand cautiously, blindly feeling for his drink. When he wasn't able to find it by touch, he pushed himself up on one elbow, opened his eyes, saw the drink on the table, and took it.

"*That,*" he said, "is the best-kept secret around." He took a long swallow from his drink then pressed the cold glass against his cheek. "Moses's orders may come directly from Cuba, but I doubt it because that could be pretty awkward: it's not too easy to get people in regularly, and they can't use the radio — too easy to monitor. I don't know." He shrugged and replaced the glass on the table. "He's *your* buddy. Why don't you ask him?"

Profit collapsed down onto the lounge chair lazily. "I do know this," he continued. "Three-quarters of the people at Moses's parties — both men and women — are security. Watch yourself."

"You'll be there," Sheen said. "You can watch out for me."

Profit sat up, twisting until he was straddling the lounge chair.

"You're out of your mind," he said, his voice a mix of protest and disbelief. "If Moses sees us together, we're dead meat."

"The idea is to agitate him and hope he'll make mistakes."

"Agitate him? You may be suicidal, Sheen. I'm not. If Moses sees us together, he *has* to kill us — and he's got a whole army. The Marielitas are deadly. You do *not* agitate their boss."

"As I recall, last time you said Moses had a navy."

"He's got that too."

"We'll divert his attention later. He'll forget all about us."

"You'll never divert him that much, Sheen." Profit leaned forward and put his elbows on his knees. His expression was convincingly earnest, and his tone was explanatory. "Don't you see? Once he learns we're together, he's got to protect himself. We're a link back to his plan to swindle his own organization. He can't trust us to keep our mouths shut, so he'll kill us, as in kill us *dead.*"

Sheen did not reply, and Profit studied his face, seeing there that his explanation had done nothing to change Sheen's mind.

"No way," Profit said, changing tack and getting to his feet. "There's no way I'm going in there with you. You and Dryden can both take a walk. I'd rather be in federal prison. At least it's safe — safer."

Sheen pushed his shoulders forward, pushing himself away from the railing.

"I have Dryden's phone number in my briefcase."

"Come on, Sheen. This is crazy. You go to the party and tell Moses you've seen me — that's agitation enough."

"But think of the entrance we'll make."

"Man, it's the *exit* that's the problem." Profit put his hands on his hips and moved his head back and forth adamantly. "No way. Get me Dryden's number. No way."

Sheen raised one shoulder and dropped it in a gesture of reluctant concession, moved around Profit, and slid open the glass door, which moved with a squeak. Inside, the air-conditioned air was frigid, and because the heavy curtains were drawn, it was dark. Sheen went to his bedroom, sat on the bed, put his briefcase on his lap. After his eyes had adjusted he took out his address book and decoded the phone number Agent Dryden had given him. Even though the code was his own, it took him two tries to unscramble the numerical jumble.

Number in hand, he left the bedroom. In the living room,

he saw Profit slouched down low in an overstuffed leather chair. The heel of his hand was against his forehead, propping up his head, and his expression was so premeditatedly gloomy that Sheen almost laughed out loud.

He said, "You're getting suntan oil all over that chair."

Profit mopingly looked at him.

"Man, you put me between Dryden and federal prison and the Marielitas and Moses. Maybe I should just jump off the balcony and save all those bullets. I don't deserve this, really I don't. What did I ever do to you?"

Sheen smiled a slow, easy smile, diverted by the thought that Profit had looped around so far he didn't recognize his own trail.

"Do you want the number," he asked, holding the address book shoulder high, "or do you want to hear the plan?"

Profit lifted his head enough to move his hand to his cheek.

"Let me hear the plan, then I'll decide if I need the number."

"It's one or the other, Profit. You can't go both ways."

"The shit," Profit said, his voice forlorn. "Here we are, aren't we?"

16

S HEEN HAD directed Profit to park more than a quarter mile from Moses's house, on a corner from which, using binoculars, they could see the entrance to Moses's driveway. For more than an hour they had watched one expensive car after another stop at the gate, wait for it to open, accelerate through. The evening was warm, the air thick and tropically soft, sensuous, tinged with the smell of the ocean, but Profit had insisted on air-conditioning the car so that the creases in his slacks would remain crisp, and the refrigerated air blew cold through the vents, whistling steadily, displacing the soft night. The engine labored at idle as the compressor kicked on and off. The engine speed varied, changing the low background hum. Between arrivals, Profit watched the red needle on the temperature gauge slowly rise and fall.

Sheen dropped the binoculars to his leg and said to Profit, "I was sitting just as you are now, my right hand on top of the steering wheel." He waited for Profit to look at him. "The first bullet passed under my arm and went through the dashboard. The second bullet nipped off my fingers."

Profit did not respond immediately. He waited for Sheen again to lift the binoculars to his eyes before he shifted his position on the seat and removed his hand from the steering wheel. Out of the corner of his eye Sheen saw the movement and smiled to himself. Through the binoculars he saw another car stop at Moses's gate.

"Mercedes-Benz seems to be the vehicle of choice," he said.

"And BMWs," Profit added. "Cars are important to these people. What happened then? After the second bullet?"

"I ran like hell," Sheen said.

Profit pursed his lips thoughtfully, then said, "If we had pulled this stunt when *I* wanted to, we'd be thinking retirement. How much will we get?"

"Let's take one step at a time — we have to get through the party first. Give the cigarettes about ten minutes." Sheen twisted his wrist to look at the small gold watch on his arm, angling it slightly to catch the light from the streetlamp on the corner. "Are you sure you don't want a piece?"

"I'm sure," Profit replied. "I'd probably shoot myself in the foot. I'm so nervous I'll be lucky to get the cigarettes lit — they're not going to be very loud."

"I know," Sheen said, nodding agreement and remembering his protest to William Dryden: "Exploding cigarettes? You must be kidding." Agent Dryden had replied, "There will be innocent people in the house, Sheen." "Yes, there will," Sheen had agreed, "like Profit and me. Loaded cigarettes are a pretty feeble way to create a diversion, and we have to get *out* of the house." Agent Dryden had looked directly at him, and in his eyes there had been a trace of humor. "You and Profit aren't so innocent," he had said.

Sheen now said to Profit, "Let's hope that with the lights out, the cigarettes will *seem* loud. Avila delivers the message exactly at ten o'clock. Watch for it. And see that distributor."

"Eduardo."

"Eduardo," Sheen repeated. "Tell him anything, but get an appointment."

"If he's there, that's easy." Profit pressed the heel of his hand to his eye and rubbed gently. "I was the golden boy around here, salesman of the month. Eduardo wanted me to work for him."

Profit dropped his hand from his face and put it back on the steering wheel. "What's the message Avila is going to deliver?"

"Dryden came up with it: an old Omega watch and the number seven."

"I don't get it."

Sheen put down the binoculars and turned to lean against the car door.

"According to Dryden, Omega 7 is the most militant of the anti-Castro groups — I guess he should know. He says that Omega 7 will bomb anything related to communist Cuba or to Castro. Their last target was the Cuban ambassador to the United Nations, but they missed. The car hit a bump and the bomb fell off. They've been quiet since then, and they're due. If Dryden is right, Moses will understand."

"If Dryden is right," Profit said, his voice as sour as his expression, "we're about to start a war."

"That's the idea. It takes a general to run a war."

Sheen stared out of the windshield for several seconds, then turned his glance to Profit. "Stay away from the pool. The concussion grenade will damn near empty it."

"You don't have to tell me *that* twice. What does a phosphorus grenade do?"

"It burns," Sheen replied, smiling vaguely at his understatement. "All but two are in place. If any phosphorus hits you, *do not* put water on it. Water will make it burn hotter. Pack it with dirt."

Profit glanced at Sheen with eyes that were wary and frightened.

Sheen forced a lightness into his tone, and added, "It should be a show worth seeing."

"What a combination," Profit said, more to himself than to Sheen, "exploding cigarettes and hand grenades."

He picked up the binoculars from the seat as Sheen shrugged doubtfully. Profit looked briefly through the binoculars, held them away from his eyes, adjusted the focus, looked again.

"The meeting is over," he said reluctantly, "or it's about to be. That's the first carload of women."

Sheen glanced over his shoulder, down the street behind them. In a dark blue Ford fifty yards back and across the street, Tony Avila's cigarette glowed, an orange pinpoint of light.

"Good," Sheen said, looking back at Profit. "Shall we make our entrance?"

Profit put the binoculars beneath the seat and his hand on the gearshift. Before he put the car in gear, he asked, "Do I have a choice?"

Sheen leaned forward and patted him on the shoulder. "We'll be all right," he said, his voice tinged with the overstressed optimism of uncertain self-assurance. "It's *our* surprise."

Profit moved the gearshift so deliberately that it caught in reverse, and the car lurched backward before he moved it again and they jerked forward. Sheen smiled thinly.

At the entrance to the driveway the gate opened slowly, and they accelerated through.

The house was lit brilliantly. There were floodlights in the palm trees, aimed upward through the fronds, and there were floodlights beside the walkways, on the walls, on freestanding poles. Profit parked far down the driveway, at the edge of the light, and, walking slowly, they followed the row of candles in hurricane glasses that delineated the stepping stones across the wide lawn. Behind the house a low stone fence formed the boundary between the lawn and the beach, and along the fence were more floodlights. On a raised stone square a twenty-piece orchestra was playing Baroque music over the sound of the waves. Huge banquet tables adorned with intricate ice sculptures were attended by footmen in formal dress. Guests stood clustered in small groups around the swimming pool, talking quietly. Sheen noted the position of the tables and the spacing of the candles, as if he were making a map.

On the terrace just outside the open doors to the living room, they stopped momentarily. The interior light was soft,

219

reflected indirectly from the ornate hand-carved ceiling panels; in the soft light the red shag carpet did not seem quite so red. Near them, a newcomer was being introduced to a group of four. There were obligatory shallow smiles and awkward handshakes. Two men, both holding drinks, stood so close together their drinks almost touched; looking between them, Sheen caught a glimpse of Moses. He was standing in the far corner of the living room, on the edge of the crowd, near the steps that led to the gallery. He wore a cream-colored silk suit and a red silk shirt open at the collar. His expression was one of aloof superiority; whether he was a reluctant host or a self-conscious one, it was impossible to tell. In an amiable manner Sheen took Profit's elbow and steered him inside.

Moses's attention was focused on two long-legged young women who stood near him, and he did not see either Profit or Sheen until they were very close. Sheen's grip on Profit's elbow was tight, and he felt Profit tense when Moses did see them. The champagne in Moses's hand stopped moving in the arc that would bring glass to lips; his eyes narrowed slightly. The young women felt the shift in his attention and turned poised, unformed looks toward Profit and Sheen, looks that would change quickly according to Moses's reaction.

Moses completed the movement of glass to lips, sipped the champagne, and held the nearly empty glass out to the woman on his right, who accepted it automatically. He smiled a tight, carnivorous smile, and said, "How very good to see you both — and together — a very nice surprise."

Sheen released his grip on Profit's elbow and replied with feigned casualness, "We've mended our fences. A woman, especially a dead woman, should not separate friends, don't you agree? There's money to be made, new pyramids for us all."

Sheen's words brought a hot glint into Moses's eyes. "Tonight you are my guests," he said. The edges of his teeth were set together, and the words hissed between them. "Enjoy the party. Enjoy your little joke. We will meet very soon."

Moses stared first at Profit, then at Sheen, holding their gaze long enough for both of them to see the promise in his level, dark eyes; then, abruptly, he walked between them, toward the center of the room.

The young women followed him, their expressions vexed.

"You had to say *that?*" Profit whispered furiously.

Sheen rotated slightly so that he could glance at Moses as he pretended to look at his watch. He saw the thinning hair on the crown of Moses's head, the hair combed across the thin spot to conceal it, and said softly to Profit, "Get going with the cigarettes."

Profit's hands jumped so quickly to his pockets that Sheen realized that he had forgotten all about the cigarettes.

"And find Eduardo," Sheen pressed. "We're on a schedule."

Profit fumbled in his coat pocket, brought out a lighter, tried to light it, failed, tried again; then he realized that he had forgotten to put a cigarette in his mouth.

"I haven't seen him," he said, his voice urgent and nervous.

"*Find* him. Circulate outside." Sheen took the cigarette pack out of Profit's hand, removed a cigarette, returned the pack to Profit. "Keep the candles in sight. When the lights go, stay wide of the path but follow it back to the car. I'll meet you there."

Sheen jerked his chin forward, indicating that he needed a light. As Profit cupped one hand over the other and flicked the lighter, Sheen noticed that his eyes were moving quickly back and forth, scanning the crowd. They were shiny and wild, the eyes of a very frightened animal, and Sheen realized the depth of Profit's fear. He reached out and pinched Profit's arm hard.

"Go, my friend. We have less than ten minutes."

Profit did not seem to notice the pinch but moved his head up and down, more in a twitch than a nod.

Sheen gave him one final look before he moved away deliberately, controlling the urge to move quickly, taking the three steps to the gallery one at a time. At the top of the steps he stumbled on the uneven stone floor, caught himself, leaned back against the wall, and surveyed the crowd. Moses had left the room. Profit had not moved at all. The bathroom door opened. A woman smiled briefly, apologetically, and moved past him.

Sheen stepped calmly into the bathroom, pulled the door closed, and locked it before he dropped to his knees, took out a small wrench, and worked furiously to loosen the four bolts that held the toilet to the floor. One bolt was rusted and seemed to strip as it turned. He flushed the toilet, turned off the water, tried it again. The bolt bit and loosened. He lifted the toilet just enough to force a phosphorus grenade into the soil pipe. Water spilled onto the floor and made a small puddle. He retightened the bolts and stood up to wash his hands. In the mirror over the sink, Sheen saw that his own eyes were wild and frightened. He counted slowly to ten, breathing deeply, then dried his hands and adjusted the grenades on his belt and his suit coat over them. When he heard an impatient knock at the door, he realized that he had forgotten to turn on the water to the toilet. He gave the valve two quick turns and opened the door, only then noticing the round wet spots on the knees of his pants. He moved quickly past the man at the door and down the gallery, suddenly wondering whether he had remembered to start the timer on the grenade.

Again Sheen forced himself to slow down, and at the top of the stairs he took out his pack of cigarettes and lit one, holding it between his fingertips in a way that showed he was not a practiced smoker. He saw Moses across the living room, leaning back against the red leather couch, talking quietly, dividing his attention between a middle-aged man and a young woman who were standing in front of him. He held a champagne glass casually in one hand, and when a waiter passed, he took a canapé in the other. Sheen dropped the loaded cigarette into an ashtray and started to descend the stairs. As he moved forward, he saw a heavyset man shouldering his way through the crowd, moving in a straight, urgent line to Moses and tapping him on the shoulder. Sheen stopped, standing very still and holding his breath.

Moses responded to the interruption with an annoyed look and put down his glass before he accepted the message that was offered to him. His face became drawn and pale, his eyes wide.

Sheen descended the stairs and worked his way across the crowded room, hoping to catch a glimpse of Profit. He did not see him. From the threshold of the open doors Sheen surveyed the living room a second time before he moved outside, littering the loaded cigarettes as quickly as he could light them, forcing himself to search the patio, the pool area, the groups of guests near the banquet tables and the orchestra. He did not see Profit.

Two blocks away, a soft white glow, a hazy dome of white light that seemed to flicker, showed above the treeline: the first phosphorus grenade had ignited, high up an electric pole, on top of the area transformer. In the distance there was a muffled explosion. The lights went out suddenly, creating a vacant blackness after the brilliance of the moment before.

Inside, there was a nervous, shrill laugh in the darkness and strained, expectant voices murmured. A cigarette popped, and silence followed.

Sheen waited, removing the grenades from his belt, anticipating a blaze of emergency lights. He waited through five deep breaths. No lights came on.

A woman screamed when another cigarette popped.

The grenades splashed quietly as they dropped into the swimming pool.

Sheen moved quickly then, allowing himself to run as he had wanted to for fifteen minutes. He followed the candles across the wide lawn toward the driveway. Behind him the water in the pool erupted with a huge concussing force, then the phosphorus ignited and the water itself seemed to catch fire. Simultaneously there was a quaking rumble beneath the house as the phosphorus in the soil pipe ignited the sewer gas, and both burned. From the roof white phosphorus sprayed, sizzling. A fire began. There were screams. More cigarettes popped. A heavy magnum shot replied.

Sheen kept the line of candles on his left and circled wide. Knowing he had a lead and not wanting to be the first to appear in the driveway, he stopped near a palm tree and squatted down at its base, breathing heavily, feeling the sweat rolling down his back. He wiped the stumps of his fingers across the thin, oily film of sweat on his forehead.

He heard shouts, popping cigarettes, the distinctive *crack-crack-crack* of an AK-47 automatic rifle, the burping chatter of an Uzi returning fire in a long burst. *Too long,* Sheen thought, surprised by how calmly he seemed to be thinking. *The shooter is untrained, undisciplined.* And then he knew that bodyguards were firing at unfamiliar security men, and the security men were firing back.

The burning phosphorus made an eery, pulsing white light that stopped as suddenly as it had begun, leaving only the dim yellow light from the fire on the roof. Sheen caught an acrid smell like burning matches, and the smell of burning wood. A tracer round skipped on the terrace; the whining ricochet bounced once and angled its glowing green trail straight up into the black sky then faded as quickly as a shooting star behind the smoke that was thinning on the breeze.

A man and a woman came running across the lawn. The man held the woman by the wrist and pulled her along as she hopped clumsily, reaching down, trying to get her high-heeled shoe loose from her foot. Behind them three more guests came running. A panicked man stumbled on a stepping stone, fell, slid on his knees, and got up in one motion, his legs never stopping their running steps. Sheen joined the third group to appear, deliberately holding back, trying to see in the flickering yellow firelight.

In the driveway chauffeurs with drawn weapons were crouched behind expensive automobiles, waiting for sight of their employers. Sheen kept his hands well away from his body and slowed to a fast walk, moving down the line of cars. In the distance there were sirens. Near the rental car he heard a thrashing sound in the bushes, and he too crouched down, his hand on the butt of the Colt, ready but reluctant to show the weapon.

A shadow moved in the bushes, disappeared, appeared again.

"Profit?" Sheen asked tentatively.

Sheen heard, "Holy shit," and the shadow disappeared again. "Holy shit."

He moved quickly to the curb and saw Profit bending over, scooping up handfuls of the loose soil beneath the bushes. There was a pungent smell of burned flesh.

"Are you hit?" Sheen asked.

Profit straightened up, smearing the dirt on his forearm and tamping it, squeezing the arm. "Some of that shit got on me. I'm packing it with dirt, like you said. Man, it burns. It burns." Profit's voice was strained and brittle, edged with panic.

Sheen stepped close to him and grabbed his arm, pulling it toward him, trying to see the wound; but it was too dark to see anything other than the dark smudge of dirt.

"I'm all right. I'm all right," Profit said too quickly, too adamantly, and pulled his arm back and cradled it across his chest. With his right hand he tried to reach into his left pants pocket.

Sheen heard the keys jingle and understood what he was trying to do. He grabbed Profit's belt, pulled him close, and dug his hand into the pocket, taking the keys and saying firmly, "It's okay. I'll drive."

Profit did not seem to understand, and Sheen turned away quickly, unlocked the passenger door, dove through to the driver's seat. Profit got in behind him and sat down numbly.

"We're doing great," Sheen said, and started the car. "We're almost home."

Profit said, his voice very faraway, "It reminded me of *my* house. There was so much fire. Everything was on fire."

Sheen waited for a Mercedes limousine to pass and pulled out behind it, following it at a distance without turning on the headlights. Going in the opposite direction, toward the house, two cars passed at high speed.

"The troops have arrived," Sheen noted, but Profit did not seem to hear.

The gate to the driveway was open and unattended, the

225

guards recalled to the house. Sheen turned onto the street, then turned again, driving slowly, looking at Profit and wondering how to calm him. A battered Plymouth followed them.

"Where were you?" Sheen asked. "I couldn't find you anywhere."

"I was with Eduardo," Profit replied, his voice distant and mechanical. "Upstairs. When the fire started, I jumped out of the window. That's when the shit got on my arm. It got in my hair, too."

"Do you have an appointment?" Sheen asked, wanting to keep Profit talking. "When are you going to see him?"

"I'm supposed to call."

Just then, in the rearview mirror, Sheen saw the Plymouth. He grabbed Profit by the shoulder, shaking him. "Listen to me," he said, his voice urgent.

Profit turned his head slowly to look at him.

"We've got company. Someone is following us. Get on the floor and ball up."

Profit looked behind them, then turned dull, vacant eyes on Sheen. "No more," he said, his voice plaintive.

"Get on the floor," Sheen replied harshly. "Now!"

Very slowly, Profit leaned forward and to one side, bent his legs, and slid to the floor, balling up and cradling his head between his arms.

The Plymouth was only five car lengths back when its headlights flashed on bright, and Sheen saw that it was accelerating, pulling out to pass. He accelerated also, but the Plymouth was more powerful, its speed greater. When it was nearly alongside them, Sheen stomped on the brake pedal and threw himself down on the seat. The sudden, skidding deceleration rolled him forward, tossed him over Profit, and cracked his ear against the dashboard as all the glass in the car suddenly exploded. The back window, the side windows, then the windshield were pulverized in one long explosion that showered dust and glass fragments over them.

For what seemed a very long time they lay still, breathing

226

shallowly, Profit's shoulder beneath Sheen's chest. The cool air whistled steadily through the vents. The compressor kicked on and off. Finally Profit said, "You're breaking my neck," and Sheen pushed against the dashboard, sliding himself onto the seat.

Profit sat up and opened the passenger door. "Are we still alive?" he asked, his eyes no longer either dull or vacant but very bright and glowing.

Sheen ran his hand back and forth through his hair, brushing out glass fragments. "We're in much better shape than this car."

"Speak for yourself," Profit said, extending his legs through the open door, deftly pushing himself out of the car. "I told you not to fuck with Moses. He's got a whole army, Sheen."

"It wasn't Moses," Sheen said, grabbing the steering wheel and pulling himself upright. "Moses didn't have the time to set this up — it was too quick."

Glass crunched beneath Profit's feet as he walked around the car and said to Sheen through the hole where the back window had been, "Look at this mess." He picked up three oblong pebbles of safety glass from the trunk lid and shook them in his hand, making a noise like a rattle. "If it wasn't Moses, who was it?"

Sheen did not reply but got out of the car to inspect the damage. On the driver's side, from the trunk to the front fender, the rental car was peppered with hundreds of small, deep dents. The left front tire was flat. Sheen put his fingertips into the dents, feeling smooth, bare metal in some, jagged splits in others, where the pellets had almost penetrated.

Two blocks away, a siren wailed.

Before Profit could ask more questions, Sheen said to him, "Let's change the tire and get out of here." He opened the trunk, inspected the spare, removed the jack.

Sheen knew both from the pellet marks and from the number of them that the weapon turned on the car had been an automatic twelve-gauge shotgun; and he knew that only the military and the police had access to such tightly controlled weapons.

Working together, Profit and Sheen changed the flat tire very quickly.

Although the neighborhood to which Profit and Sheen drove was only forty blocks away, it was separated by more than distance from the mansions that fronted the beach. The houses were close together on small lots, and children's toys were strewn on sinking, cracking sidewalks. Old automobiles and rusted trailers awaited repair in side yards where grass grew up around them. The neighborhood was not unlike the one in which Sheen had found Profit in California, and Profit was uncharacteristically glum as he looked about, observing the houses. Naked porch lights harshly illuminated peeling paint, splotches of weeds, settling driveways. Behind open windows and torn screen doors, other naked bulbs showed the bleak interiors from which emanated a grating cacophony of blaring televisions, crying babies, and radios tuned to Latin music. Sheen parked with the driver's side of the rental car next to the curb, confident that the broken glass and the undersized, temporary spare tire made the car less conspicuous, another derelict in need of repair.

"Is this the house?" he asked.

"This is the one I always came to," Profit replied. "I wonder why they haven't changed the location."

"They've never needed to, I guess — I was pretty surprised when Moses sent me directly here to pick up coke." He looked from Profit to the house. "When you think about it, these guys have had an easy time of it." Sheen smiled easily. "But they'll tighten up some after tonight. There aren't any cars. The troops are still at the house. Do you want to sit it out?"

"Are you kidding? I've dreamed of this for years."

"You don't get to keep it."

"I know," Profit said lightly, the corners of his mouth turning up in a grin Sheen could not read. "I just like the smell."

Sheen started to say something, thought better of it, and

said instead, "We'll only take what we can carry in one trip — two trips are too risky. I'll pack the door in case they won't open to a knock."

"They'll open," Profit said confidently. "They like me."

Profit opened the glovebox and took out the two black Lone Ranger masks he had bought the day before.

Sheen said, "Moses will know we did it. We could wear gorilla outfits, and he'd still know."

"So indulge me. I like the effect."

Profit separated the masks and handed one to Sheen, smiling curiously as he did so. He put on his own mask and adjusted it carefully, pinching the nose to a tight fit. "How do I look?" he asked.

"How do you think you look?" Sheen replied, slipping the elastic band over his head and putting his mask across his forehead. "I'll slip it down before we knock," he explained.

Profit nodded an agreeable okay, opened his door, got out of the car. Side by side they walked quietly across the street to the small house.

Sheen packed plastique around the doorknob and up the door frame as Profit watched impatiently, his hands on his hips. When the detonator was inserted and crimped on the cord, Sheen stood up straight and nodded to Profit that he was ready. Profit motioned for him to pull down his mask and waited until he had done so before he knocked on the door three times, slapping it with an open palm.

"Abran! Ya volimus; era falsa alarma," he said loudly. He gave a self-satisfied, good-humored wink, and whispered to Sheen, "Didn't know that I knew that, did you?"

The door opened a crack, and Profit pushed against it with his shoulder, shoving it wide. A boy no more than sixteen stepped away from the swinging door. At the sight of strange men wearing masks, the boy's eyes went wide, without fear but sullen, realizing the mistake he had made opening the door.

Sheen pointed with the Colt to a chair, and the boy sat.

229

The room was furnished with only a card table, five metal chairs, and a large television set on a stand. The cards strewn on the table showed a game hastily abandoned. The single ashtray was filled to overflowing with the stubs of cigars and cigarettes. Using electrical ties he had brought for the purpose, Sheen tied the boy to the chair and turned the television so that the boy could watch it as he waited to be released; then he followed Profit down the corridor to the back bedroom.

"Look at it," Profit said, waving his hand wildly to indicate the bedroom. "Just look at it."

On the floor there were at least two dozen thirty-gallon plastic trash cans arranged in neat rows, rim to rim. Each can was lined with a black plastic bag, and each was filled to overflowing with uncut yellow-white cocaine. Three dehumidifiers on the floor and two window air conditioning units hummed, filtering and drying the air, but still the medicinal smell was so pungent it was difficult to breathe.

"There must be a thousand pounds here," Profit said, his voice excited and reverential. "Twenty-five million dollars easy, without a cut. Look at it," he said again, "just look at it."

Sheen said, "We'll take one can each. Grab a lid, too — our windows are open."

"I can carry two cans."

Sheen put his hand on Profit's shoulder and held it there until Profit looked at him. "Don't be greedy. Two cans should be close to a hundred pounds."

Profit moved out from under Sheen's hand, squatted down, hugged a trash can to his chest. "You're right," he said, standing up again and speaking to Sheen across two feet of coarse yellow-white powder. "This baby alone must weigh sixty pounds. Let's get out of here."

Profit leaned his head forward and took a deep breath, looking at Sheen playfully and making a sound as if he were snorting. "Just to give me strength," he said.

Sheen smiled and picked up a black plastic lid from the floor. He put the lid on the trash can Profit was holding and pushed down until it fit.

230

"You go first. Get the car in gear. I want to get the plastique off the door."

Profit nodded his head excitedly and turned away quickly. Sheen grabbed a second trash can by its handle and dragged it down the corridor and across the living room, stopping just inside the front door. Tucking one end and rolling the plastique much like a baker rolling croissant dough, he peeled it from the door frame, top to bottom. Squatting to complete the roll, Sheen felt the thin plywood beneath the vinyl floor covering bend. He shifted his weight slightly, enough to feel the plywood spring back to its old position, and as he did so he glanced up, in time to see Profit drive past the house and down the street, his Lone Ranger mask still in place, a thin, determined frown fixed below it.

Sheen watched the right rear taillight, the working one, fade as the car moved away, and he felt his heart sink. A sigh escaped his lips.

Near him, the boy tied to the chair watched curiously, his eyes dark and serious. He said something in Spanish that Sheen could not understand.

Sheen put his elbows on his knees, his hands dangling limply. He did not know what to do or what to think. He moved his head slowly side to side, allowing himself to look up and down the now empty street; he was hopeful, but he knew the hope was false. As he surveyed the street he was reminded again of how similar the neighborhood was to the one in which he had found Profit in Rayton, and he chided himself for allowing Profit to go to the car first.

His glance shifted to the trash can of cocaine that was within his reach. *The cocaine is all he has,* Sheen thought sadly, *all that separates him from this neighborhood — or one just like it.* His glance shifted again, to the boy in the chair, and though he thought the boy was unlikely to understand, he said to him, "It's all you have, too, isn't it? Cocaine is your ticket out of here."

Sheen moved his hands to his knees and pushed himself up heavily. *Who can blame either one of them?* he thought, but he blamed himself for the lapse, for trusting when he should have remained doubtful, for refusing to see what Profit had never tried to conceal.

The troops will return soon, he thought, and he stared blankly at the trash can filled with cocaine, trying to decide whether or not to take it with him, whether it was possible to carry it a few blocks until he could find a car or a phone. He stepped near it, turning his feet out and pressing his knees against the flexible side of it. He tugged at the handles, testing the weight and feeling the white powder shift as if it were a living thing.

Outside, tires squealed on the pavement, and Sheen moved with the quickness of sudden fear, crouching and turning, reaching for the Colt. Then he saw the windowless rental car, Profit behind the wheel, waving him on and saying, "Hurry, hurry!"

Sheen checked the lid, picked up the trash can, winked at the boy, half ran across the yard. Profit opened the passenger door, and Sheen leaned in and set the trash can upright on the back seat before he jumped in and slammed the door. Profit accelerated hard, and before Sheen could remove his mask, he had turned the corner.

They drove three blocks before Sheen said, "Maybe you should take off your mask."

"Maybe I should," Profit agreed, pulling it off by snapping the elastic band. "We don't want to be conspicuous — I mean, since there's no glass in the car, someone might see in."

Sheen gave Profit a sour look and leaned forward to turn off the air conditioning.

"That's right, too," Profit said, the pace of his words quickening ludicrously. "Turn off the air conditioning so you can tell the rental-car people, there may be six thousand dents in it and there may be a perforated tire in the trunk and all the windows may be broken, but honey, that air conditioning is" — his speech slowed for emphasis, and he looked at Sheen out of the corners of his eyes — *"brand new."*

Sheen gave a short, indulgent laugh as Profit continued.

"And besides, we are *too cool* to need air conditioning: we got a car that's a rolling disaster, and sixty gallons of cocaine." He laughed and slapped the steering wheel. His eyes were shiny bright and excited, intoxicated.

"We should take the lids off the trash cans and spray the area like a cropduster. Can't you just see it? We'd make a ninety-percent-pure vapor trail — the *trees* would be numb."

Sheen shrugged agreeably. "That's all right with me," he replied, and feigned reaching into the back seat.

"Not on your life," Profit snapped, and grabbed his wrist. Then he saw the wide-eyed, comic look on Sheen's face.

Sheen started to laugh, and his laugh was infectious. Profit laughed too. They both laughed so hard tears rolled down their cheeks.

17

THE PHONE booth was far up the beach, well past the tide line, but still it was surrounded by sand, and it showed the corrosive effects of the abrading grains: windblown sand had scratched the clear plastic windows and pitted the aluminum mullions; sand under bare feet, feet in sandals, and feet in flip-flops had worn right through the stainless steel floor and made a small hole in its middle. Although it was only midmorning, the sun was hot, and inside the phone booth the metal was hot to the touch. The air was thick and heavy as greenhouse air, and smelled of suntan oil. Sheen left the folding door open, stacked quarters on the coin ledge, dialed William Dryden's number, turned his back to the phone, and leaned against it. Before Agent Dryden answered, a wave broke, curling white.

"Where are you?" Dryden asked Sheen.

"I'm in the Miami area," Sheen replied. "That's as much as I'll tell you on the phone."

A short distance down the beach, a woman in a white two-piece bathing suit unrolled a towel and sat down on it.

"Last night, just after we left Moses's party, we were hit. The car made one pass. We took twenty double-aught rounds from a twelve-gauge shotgun firing full automatic."

William Dryden did not reply for a moment, and Sheen watched the woman take out a bottle of suntan lotion, cup some in her palms, and apply it to her legs with long, narcissistic strokes.

"I don't understand the weapon," William Dryden said. "Whoever was using it must have known that buckshot won't penetrate a car — it's as if they weren't really after you."

"I find it hard to reach that same conclusion," Sheen said dryly, enunciating each word angrily. "Have you ever been in a car when all the glass explodes at once? Go to the back parking lot of the Ramada Inn Northwest, by the dumpsters. Look at the car. Sit in it. *Then* tell me they weren't after us. I've read about those shotguns, but I've never even seen one: they're too tightly controlled."

"What's your point, Sheen?" Dryden asked, his tone mollifying but firm.

"My question is this: other than the Marines, who has that kind of weapon? My list includes the Miami police, the New Orleans police, and the D.E.A."

"And any arms dealer up on his ordnance."

"Why don't you call Alcohol, Tobacco, and Firearms and see how many are missing, Bill? Then call and see how many are legitimately in circulation."

"All right," Dryden agreed, "I will. But whoever made the hit didn't know your plans, not if they were on the Marielitas' string."

"How do you figure that?"

"Because it was *after* the party. Now tell me what happened."

The phone receiver was greasy, and Sheen shifted it to his other hand, pulling the phone cord against his neck. Down the beach, the woman had finished stroking lotion on her arms and legs, and she stretched out face down on the towel. She twisted one arm behind her back, undid the snap on her top, and allowed the thin straps to slide off her back and coil near her ribs.

Sheen said, "It went well. We were lucky. Moses was angry when he saw us, angry enough to make me believe it *was* his pyramid. The Omega 7 gag really threw him."

235

"Do you think he connected you with the message?"

"I don't know. Maybe he's sorted it out by now, but last night he didn't have time to make any connections. He *had* to take it at face value. Anyway, after we were hit, we still got to the storage depot. They'll move it now — I'd keep an eye on it."

"How much did you get?"

"We took two trash cans out of the two dozen or so that were there. Profit is still trying to figure out how to weigh it." Sheen smiled at the memory of Profit walking around and around the trash cans, excitedly multiplying weights and dollars. "It's about a hundred pounds, I guess."

"You left Profit alone with a hundred pounds of cocaine?"

"He could have left *me* last night, Bill, when I was way out on a limb."

The woman on the towel did not seem to be able to get settled comfortably. She pushed against the towel to rearrange the sand beneath it, arching her back and momentarily revealing her breasts. Just then she saw Sheen watching her. She gave him a sour look and again lay flat, turning her face away from him.

Sheen heard William Dryden ask, his voice very sharp, "Who had the phosphorus grenades?"

"That's a good question," Sheen replied quickly, ready with an answer, "but, whoever it was — "

"How long has it been," Dryden asked forcefully, his words spaced apart and distinct, "since you were out at the range? What's that instructor's name, the one who taught you to shoot? Merlin Coast? He may be in serious trouble, Sheen. Items are missing from his armory."

When Sheen pictured Dryden's face, the image seemed to form around the man's eyes, clear blue and very cold. Sheen wiped his hand on his shorts and said, "You really expected me to go in there with only loaded cigarettes?"

"Yes, I did," Dryden snapped. Then his voice softened just a bit, and he said, "Look, Sheen, I'm willing to let Omega 7 take the blame — or the credit — for last night, but remember that you're playing *my* game and you'll play by *my* rules. If anyone had been killed, *we* would be to blame, not the Marielitas. There will be no more surprises. Am I clear?"

Sheen looked at the woman on the towel, but she had not moved. "What about Merlin?"

"In the future," Dryden replied, "Merlin is going to keep a tighter grip on his inventory."

Sheen smiled to himself, and thought, *I don't have to worry about the Marielitas. Merlin is going to shoot me.* He asked, "Am I still going to meet with Omega 7?"

"Yes. It's set for tonight. They're going to run you from phone to phone. Keep a map handy."

"I'll call back at five. Have your phone checked." Sheen started to hang up, then added, "Has there been any traffic through the communications center?"

"It's picking up," Dryden replied indefinitely, the optimism of his tone revealing a lack of specific information. "It should get better if tonight is successful."

"I want to see the transcripts."

"I'm having a copy made for you, but it takes time to break the codes — they're very complex, progressive algorithms. Be careful at the meeting. I'm not sure how much Omega 7 liked reading about itself in this morning's papers. Do *not* take a weapon."

"Okay," Sheen said, nodding into the phone. "By the way, where is Avila?"

"He's on standby at the condominium. You have the number."

"Okay," Sheen repeated, turning to face the phone. "I'll talk to you at five."

Sheen hung up the phone and stepped out of the booth before he remembered his quarters on the coin ledge. He stepped back, retrieved them, and decided to take a walk down the beach. The on-shore breeze was brisk, and near the water the sand was firm — easy walking. With both hands in

237

his pockets he strolled along, allowing the waves to wash over his feet. Once he stopped and bent to examine an unusual seashell.

Behind him, out of hearing, the pay phone rang twice in unnaturally rapid succession. The woman on the towel held her bathing suit top in place with her forearm as she got up to answer it.

After they had hidden the rental car behind the dumpsters at the Ramada Inn, Profit and Sheen had searched the parking lot until they had found a car with the keys left in the ignition. From the Ramada Inn they had driven to Old Miami Beach and checked into a "motor court," an old one-story motel built in the shape of a horseshoe; then Sheen had insisted upon returning the car.

"You do not return a stolen car," Profit had objected.

"But you do return one you've borrowed," Sheen had countered.

"And what will we use for transportation?"

"Tomorrow we'll rent another car — this one we'll put in *your* name."

Profit had stood with his hands on his hips and his feet spread. "Will you please explain to me," he had asked, "why it *is* okay to steal a hundred pounds of cocaine and why it is *not* okay to steal a four-year-old car?"

"That's a tough one," Sheen had conceded. Then he had gone off to return the car.

After his walk on the beach, Sheen returned to the motor court, driving the car they had rented in Profit's name. The room smelled of mildew and medicine. The old bed creaked each time Profit scooped a Tupperware bowlful of cocaine from the trash can set in its middle.

"It's obscene," he said, smiling as Sheen closed the door and locked it. "My scooper" — Profit held up the opaque plastic bowl — "holds about a pound, give or take fifteen grams. *Fifteen grams.* With a good cut, the 'give or take' is worth three thousand dollars."

238

Profit wiped his brow by rubbing his forearm across it. "I put fifty scoops in each of the two big bags, ten scoops in the shoe bag, and two scoops in the Baggie. This is left over." He flicked his fingernail against the trash can on the bed. "In a bearish market, we have in this room two million five hundred thousand dollars worth of cocaine. I'm getting loaded just putting my *hand* in it."

"If that's your story," Sheen said as he crossed to the bed, "you should wipe your nose."

Profit rubbed the back of his hand across his nose, snuffling as he did so.

"Wrap the little bag for Overnight Delivery. Double-wrap the shoe bag. The big bags go in the suitcases — do the big ones first. When do you meet Eduardo?"

"I don't meet him. I call him. Are you going to help me with this?"

"I will after I take a shower. Don't call Eduardo from here. Find a pay phone."

Profit gave Sheen a sullen, how-dumb-do-you-think-I-am look and again began to fill the plastic bowl. Sheen dawdled in the bathroom, and by the time he had shaved and showered, Profit had the bags packed, double-wrapped, and laid out neatly along the wall, largest to smallest.

Sheen lay down to take a nap as Profit paced back and forth in front of the louvered windows, nervously looking out through the thin cracks between the frosted glass slats.

Sheen delivered the smallest package to Overnight Delivery, then he drove by the condominium before he called William Dryden at exactly five o'clock to receive the number that would connect him to Omega 7. The number was answered by a heavily accented male voice. The man spoke slowly, in a monotone of painstaking formality that was inflected only when he raised his voice to be heard over the traffic noise in the background. The voice directed Sheen north on the beach access road to a phone booth in Delray Beach; once he was there, it directed him south to the courtesy phone in a piano bar in Bal Harbour. Sheen followed the directions carefully, driving deliberately, and he found himself enjoying the search for the phones, anticipating the pregnant pause before each phone rang. He knew he was being watched, and he speculated about the cars that passed and about the people who came near. But he never saw the van.

In front of the Pompano Beach Inn, awaiting the third call, he stood in a phone booth, his back to the highway. The phone booth smelled of urine and stale beer, and he stood far enough away from the phone to catch some breeze but close enough to block the door to the booth. Through the windows he could see the beach and the late sunbathers packing up their things. He heard a vehicle stop behind him, but before he could turn his head he was grabbed by the belt and the collar, swung in an arc, and flattened face down against thick carpet. A metal door slammed. He was bound hand and foot and blindfolded by two men working quickly. A needle pricked his arm. He was searched thoroughly, rolled over and back. His pockets were emptied. Headphones were placed over his ears, and he listened to a slow Latin rhythm as the mild tranquilizer took effect.

The carpet was rough against his cheek. Saliva drooled from the corner of his mouth and made a wet spot beneath his chin. Sheen felt the van moving, turning, stopping and starting. The motion was lulling, and he slept a light, dreamless sleep that seemed to last only a moment.

The tape ended with a loud, metallic click. The metal door slammed open and closed. A hand cupped his chin and lifted his head.

"Breathe deeply," a brusque voice ordered, "through your nose."

An ammonia smell burned its way into his sinuses and brought tears to his eyes. The headphones were removed from his ears, and his hands and feet were untied. Sheen rolled onto one shoulder and sat up slowly, shaking his head to clear it. He started to remove the blindfold but thought better of it.

240

An oddly nasal voice asked, "For whom do you work?"

Because he was blindfolded, Sheen's other senses were acute, and he heard the words reverberate from the bare metal walls of the van and he smelled cigar smoke on the breath of the speaker.

"I work for myself," he replied, stopping because his mouth was very dry. He licked his lips and swallowed before he continued. "But I work with a man named Dryden. Dryden is an agent for the D.E.A. He directed me to you. I'm looking for a killer."

The van started up without warning, and Sheen put one arm out to brace himself.

"Who was killed?" the voice asked. It was a sharp, incisive voice, without accent.

"Someone about whom I cared."

The van bumped over two sets of railroad tracks, slowed, bumped again.

"Why was *she* killed?"

Sheen replied, re-placing the emphasis, "Does it matter *why?*"

A long silence followed his reply, then suddenly the blindfold was removed with a jerk. Sheen pressed the heels of his hands into his eyes and rubbed them, reminding himself of Profit.

"I am called Omar," the voice said. "I speak for Omega 7. What do you want?"

Sheen dropped his hands from his eyes and blinked, trying to see in the dim light. Opposite him, a man sat on the wheel well, his hands on his knees. Sheen blinked again and ran his hand over his face, taking the opportunity to study the man who called himself Omar.

His hair was black and cut short, parted on one side and combed across. He had a black mustache, neatly trimmed. His body was thick and heavy, like a wrestler's, and although he appeared relaxed, moving easily as the van swayed and bumped, there was about him a determination, a set cast to his face that indicated a wary, resilient toughness. A fighter's mashed nose accounted for the oddly nasal sound of his voice.

241

Around both of his eyes were white flecks of scar tissue. *He is the sort of fighter,* Sheen thought, *who wears down his opponents by going after them and after them, taking the blows and pursuing relentlessly.* His ears did not match: one was not as long as the other, torn off raggedly across the top.

To Omar's left, a second man sat on the motor cover, a heavy revolver laid across his thigh.

Sheen said, "I want Omega 7 to take credit for the attack last night."

Omar studied him without pretense. Then he said, "We have already been credited with the attack."

Sheen held Omar's gaze. "The credit was given to you; you didn't take it."

Omar acknowledged the distinction with a barely perceptible movement of his head, a slight movement to one side.

"And there is more than the newspapers reported," Sheen continued. "I also want you to take one hundred pounds of the Marielitas' cocaine. I want one thousand dollars per pound for my expenses — one hundred thousand dollars. The cocaine is more than ninety percent pure. Depending upon how it is cut, it is worth between two and three million dollars. You have the keys to my car. There are two bags in the trunk."

Omar's eyes narrowed thoughtfully. "Why should I pay for what I can simply take?"

"The money is only a convenience, a way to help me continue," Sheen replied, his voice as level as his gaze. "If it were more important, I would sell the cocaine myself. Whether you take it or buy it, word will get back to the Ministry of the Interior in Cuba. Such things are verifiable — the result is the same."

Omar lifted one hand to his face, pinched his lower lip, released it, and rubbed his fingers together. "One hundred pounds is such an even amount. Perhaps there is more."

"There *is* more, about ten pounds, but I have another use for it. There were only two of us. We took only as much as we could carry."

"There were only two of you?" Omar said, the faintest gleam

242

of amusement showing in his eyes. "You have more boldness than good sense."

He reached into the pocket of his pale green knit sport shirt and took out two thin cigars. He handed one to Sheen, along with a worn Zippo lighter. On one side of the lighter a faded crest read BRIGADE 2506. Sheen looked at the crest curiously, holding the lighter close to his face to see it more clearly; then he flicked the lighter open and ignited it. Looking past the flame that flared as he puffed on the cigar, he saw Omar watching him very closely, and he realized that he was being given some sort of test. Sheen closed the lighter and handed it back, wondering if he had passed the test or failed it.

"To do what you ask would mean a war," Omar said, holding the lighter upright on one knee.

"I'm trying to find an animal," Sheen said, holding the cigar between his teeth. "I want to set fire to the brush."

Omar licked his cigar before he lit it, cupping one hand completely around the flame. He allowed his eyes to close slightly as he inhaled, and his head rolled back as he savored the smooth taste of the smoke. He exhaled out of the corner of his mouth, puffing his cheek and sending a plume of smoke toward the rear of the van.

"I do not like to deal in drugs," he said. "I do not like my men around them. I do not like the people drugs attract."

"Then there are other organizations."

"Yes. There are other organizations."

Omar took the cigar out of his mouth and rolled it between thumb and first finger, holding it so that the gray ash was in front of his face. Idly he studied the evenness of the burn. He looked to his left and said, "Anda ve a sucarro y revisa la valojera. Avisame por el radio."

The man sitting on the motor cover holstered his revolver, turned around, climbed into the front seat. The van stopped. He got out.

Sheen assumed that a car was following them and, possibly, that a second car was leading the way.

"I am wary of you," Omar said, slowly returning his gaze to Sheen. "Timeo Danaos et dona ferentis."

The van started forward with a jolt, rocking them both.

"The Latin is in your file — the D.E.A. is very thorough. I was myself raised by the Catholics."

Sheen knew that a reply in Latin was expected, and he said, "Nonne ulla putatis dona carere dolis?"

"Do I think any gifts lack treachery? Yes — but only when they come from my mother." His thin smile was without humor. "Have you asked your Agent Dryden why he has such close contact with Omega 7, a terrorist group?"

Sheen shook his head. "No, and it doesn't concern me."

"Of course it concerns you," Omar snapped, the sharpness of his retort surprising Sheen and making him draw back. "All things are interrelated," Omar continued, more to himself than to Sheen. It sounded like a phrase he used often, a personal creed.

He took a deep pull on his cigar, his eyes narrowing slightly, his scarred eyebrows knitting together.

"The C.I.A. trained me," he said, exhaling. "For the Bay of Pigs, the C.I.A. trained an anti-Castro Cuban army of gunmen, explosives technicians, and men skilled in secret landings and guerrilla warfare. But you never heard of us — most Americans never heard of us." He waved the Zippo lighter at Sheen. "We were called Brigade 2506." For a long moment he looked at the lighter, then he dropped it into his shirt pocket.

"After the fiasco," he continued, his voice even, "after we were left stranded, without the support we had been promised — after most of us had been killed — it was apparent that there would never be another direct assault on Cuba, so the C.I.A. trained still more men, men to liberate Cuba covertly. But recruiting and training take time. The Vietnam war escalated. The C.I.A. money stopped, shifted to another area."

Omar raised his shoulders and spread his hands, palms up and fingers wide. "But Castro did not shift to another area," he said, dropping his shoulders and bringing his hands together.

244

"Rather, he formed the D.G.I. — Cuban Intelligence — and directed his spies to infiltrate our groups. We eliminated these spies whenever we found them, but it was often too late: whole organizations were wiped out. Before the Bay of Pigs, the newspapers had called us heroes, 'free men fighting for a free homeland.' But then U.S. policy shifted. There was to be 'normalization' of relations with Castro's Cuba. The trade embargo was lifted. Our fight continued just as it had, but in your press we were no longer heroes but terrorists, no longer eliminating spies but murdering innocent citizens."

Omar rubbed his forearm absently, and Sheen noticed a dark green smear, a tattoo. The Cuban seemed not to hear his own words, to be thinking of something else.

"Several years ago, I was approached by your D.E.A. The Mariel boatlift had brought 125,000 Cuban refugees to this country. The D.E.A. was concerned that many of those refugees had been sent here to deal dope — and of course they were right. Would I, the D.E.A. asked, again become a hero? Would I infiltrate the Marielitas, just as the D.G.I. had infiltrated our groups? Nicaragua was then daily on the front page. U.S. policy was shifting away from 'normalization.' I did not feel I could trust the policy not to shift again, and I told the D.E.A. I knew nothing of the Marielitas."

Omar momentarily turned his gaze to the front of the van, and Sheen saw that his interest lay there, not in the story he was telling.

"Last year," he started again, looking back at Sheen, "I was approached a second time about the Marielitas, this time by a man who had been with my brigade, Brigade 2506. This man said he was working for a large international company doing business in Central America — that was his way of implying that he was still with the C.I.A. This man said to me that the D.E.A.'s vision is limited by dope, that the D.E.A. does not have the whole picture. He said that if I harmed this new organization, I did Cuba, a free Cuba, a grave disservice: Castro, he claimed, is only the broker for the new organization; he is not the true beneficiary. The man said that his company had financed and trained the Marielitas' organization. He said that Castro receives a percentage of the profit for allowing the organization to exist, but that the other profits are channeled through his company back to the Cuban Nationalist Movement. Whether or not it is true, it is a clever idea. Castro's nose is very big. Much could be hidden under it." Omar's eyes showed a vague amusement. "But I could neither prove nor disprove his claims, and I told this man too that I knew nothing of the Marielitas.

"Your Agent Dryden wants to destroy this organization, but it may in fact be a C.I.A. exercise, a means of financing a covert operation — such things are not unheard of. If the Marielita dope dealers *are* the bank for the Cuban Nationalists, to take credit for the theft would place me between pro-Castro and anti-Castro camps. It would, of course, mean my end. On the other hand, all may be as it seems — an effort to eliminate Castro's drug network. Or the D.E.A. may have intentions unknown to me. *You* may have other intentions. You are dark enough to be Cuban."

Omar sat forward and put his elbows on his knees. His eyes showed a confident self-sufficiency, and he studied Sheen's face.

"So, you come to me with a three-million-dollar gift, and you say it does not concern you why the D.E.A. approached me, why they sent you to me. If you are telling the truth, you do not even know for whom you are working or what your work accomplishes."

In the front of the van, a radio squawked softly. The driver responded in a low voice, then turned his head enough to say to Omar, "Las valijas estan en el auto."

"And, of course," Omar said to Sheen, relaxing noticeably, "the gift is real, not a bluff — the cocaine is in the trunk of your car, as you said."

Omar stubbed out his cigar, and Sheen noticed two things: that his knuckles were as scarred as his eyebrows, and that he stripped the butt and put it in his pocket, a gesture Sheen liked because it showed that Omar, like himself, had spent time in the field, carefully covering his tracks. He knew that Omar had been talking idly, giving himself time to think; and he read in the Cuban's eyes that he had already made his decision.

"Last night," Sheen said, "before the theft, someone shot at me. Do you know of an organization that uses fully automatic shotguns?"

A slow smile crossed Omar's face. "You are not easily put off of your track," he said. His voice became matter-of-fact. "The Miami police favor automatic shotguns. The firepower is excellent, but the range and penetration are limited. Both bystanders and civil suits are avoided." He raised his scarred eyebrows. "The police can be very mean when their payoffs are threatened." Omar saw the questioning look on Sheen's face, and added, "You would do well to remember what I said: all things are interrelated."

He pushed himself up to a crouch, moved to the motor cover, and spoke to the driver, pointing through the windshield at something Sheen could not see. The van stopped, and he turned back.

"Up the street you may call a taxi. Your car is not far from here. The keys are under the sun visor." Omar reached over and threw open the sliding steel door.

Sheen stepped stiffly out onto the street. When he turned back to the van, Omar squatted down on his heels in the open door, his thick arms crossed over his knees. Their faces were very close.

Omar said, "This general you seek — if he exists, he is not in Miami. I would know of him."

For a long moment their eyes locked, and in that moment an understanding passed between them.

Omar gave Sheen a curt nod then reached across to slam shut the steel door. The van pulled away.

Sheen found himself in a residential area of low houses concealed behind dark shrubbery. He repeated out loud, as if to reassure himself that he had heard correctly, "He is not in Miami."

A dog barked, and he started walking.

Sheen knew then that Omar had taken the cocaine.

18

THE OLD bed in the motor court was too soft, and it sank under him, bowing his back uncomfortably. The air conditioner vibrated loudly. By throwing his arms toward his feet, Sheen sat up, twisted his legs off the bed, and put his bare feet flat on the floor. The carpet was thin and damp, and as he stood up to turn off the air conditioner, he noticed that the wall too was damp. In the quiet, he heard a steady *drip, drip, drip.* Sheen turned the crank that opened the frosted glass slats and lay down on Profit's bed, slapping the thick, hard pillow to make a place for his head. The coarse cotton bedsheets chafed.

Sheen felt very tired and very much alone: both Profit and the remaining cocaine were gone. When he crossed his ankles, the bed creaked just as it had when Profit had filled his scoop from the trash can set in its middle. Sheen turned on the bedside light, then turned it back off, choosing darkness. He put his hands behind his head and stared blankly at the ceiling.

Just then Sheen preferred not to think about Profit, so he occupied his thoughts with past events and the prospect of events to come. In the morning he would call Marty. He pictured her as he had first met her, her hair swept back and up, her shoulders made to look square by the blouse she wore. He knew he had to call Bill Dryden. Suddenly he remembered a book he had once read, and it took him a moment to understand why the memory had come to him. He remembered the book distinctly, though he could recall neither its title nor what it had been about.

When he had been in school, Sheen had bought used books whenever possible because they were less expensive than new ones. Often the books had been in poor condition, and the one he remembered now was no exception. As he had read it, he had found yellow-brown flakes of tobacco between some pages and heavy pencil marks on others. Many pages had been turned down, dog-eared, and near the middle of the book he had found a claim check taped to a page, rudely obscuring the left margin. But as his reading had continued, Sheen had developed from these small clues a sense of the previous owner, an eerie feeling of the owner's presence, a certain knowledge of where he had been and what he had thought at a particular time. And Sheen realized that he had recalled the book at that moment because he had a similar sense of Profit's presence, a certain knowledge of his thoughts and actions from the small clues he had left behind: the fear smell on the pillow; the dirty shirt thrown hastily over the back of a chair; the open book face down on the bedside table.

I asked too much of him, Sheen thought sadly, *expected more than he had to give.* Anger seeped into his thoughts, but it was diluted by sorrow. *Profit never hid his intentions,* he thought. *I looked right at them and refused to see them — even after he left me at the house.*

Sheen moved one shoulder, adjusting his back to the curve of the mattress, and the bed creaked.

I hope there was enough left for his retirement.

Outside, in the horseshoe-shaped driveway, car doors opened and big American engines ran at fast idle. *Too many doors,* he thought suddenly, and jumped up from the bed. *Too many engines.*

Brilliant white light flooded the room, shining through the cracks between the window louvers and making striped shadows on the wall. The frosted glass slats seemed to glow.

"Damn, damn." He pounded a fist against an open hand and moved quickly to stand between the door frame and the windowsill, inclining his head forward just enough to look out. He saw four sets of headlights turned on bright and three spotlights. Behind the lights there were silhouettes crouched down low in the awkward posture men assume when they are aiming weapons.

An amplified, machinelike voice said, "Sheen Vicedomini." There was a high-pitched squeal as the microphone passed too near metal. "Sheen Vicedomini," the voice repeated, "this is the police. You are under arrest. Come out with your hands clasped behind your head. You have sixty seconds." There was another pause, another hollow squeal. "This is your only warning."

Sheen drew back his head and closed his eyes tightly, seeing behind his lids a brilliant white glow and feeling a rush of fear that held him motionless, his arms rigid at his sides, his jaws clenched. Sheen did not know whether he faced arrest or execution; but he did know he had no choice. He was trapped.

He shouted, "I'm coming out. I'm unarmed." His voice broke. "I am *un*armed."

He turned and leaned back against the wall, his knees weak. He forced himself to open his eyes. The striped shadows changed angles from one wall to the next, like something in a dream.

He put his palm flat against the doorknob, then closed his fingers around it, squeezing it tightly, hesitating before he twisted the knob and threw open the door. He pulled his arm back and waited, giving the men behind the lights time to prepare, without surprises or quick movements.

"I'm unarmed," he shouted again. "I'm coming out. I'm unarmed."

Sheen clasped his hands behind his neck, interlacing his fingers and noticing more than he ever had before how his hands did not fit together, how two fingers did not match up to four. He faced the wall before he sidestepped into the open doorway, head down, eyes closed, feeling the intense white light on his skin.

The amplified voice commanded, "Walk forward," and as he did so, his legs unsteady, he heard the unmistakable sound of a pump shotgun chambering a round. The car engines idled high, a steady, rushing drone.

"Stop," the voice ordered. "Drop to your knees."

Sheen rocked forward, shifting his weight onto the balls of his feet and squatting down before he put one knee, then the other against the concrete.

"Fall forward," the voice commanded, no longer using the loudspeaker but yelling directly at him. "Put your face on the deck, arms and legs spread."

Deck. Sheen repeated to himself the navy term, knowing that few sailors went on to become policemen. *He is an ex-Marine, taking orders just as I took orders, because that is what we were trained to do.* And he wondered what the orders were and who had issued them.

Very slowly, keeping his hands clasped behind his head, Sheen leaned forward, rotating his torso enough to allow him to put down one elbow; then he pushed his legs back and spread them, unclasped his hands, and extended his arms straight out from his sides. He felt the concrete against his chest and face, the hard pressure against his pelvis and knees. He heard footsteps, leather soles running on pavement.

His arms were yanked brutally behind his back and held there. He heard the clicking ratchet of handcuffs and felt a painful bite as they were clamped too tightly around his wrists.

A man knelt on his back, leaned close to his ear, and said, "Gotcha, motherfucker," enunciating each syllable clearly, with hatred.

In the curve of the horseshoe-shaped driveway, Sheen saw open doors to other rooms, and he thought, *Witnesses,* but the man who had knelt on his back lifted him by the handcuffs and the hair and dragged him to a car before he could be sure.

"Get in the car," the voice shouted.

The man held Sheen's handcuffed wrists up high behind his back, forcing him to bend at the waist, head forward. The rear door of the police car was open, and he took a step toward it. He was shoved hard, slammed against the fender.

"The door, stupid, go in the door."

The man grabbed his hair, yanking back his head, and again he was shoved. His face cracked against the door post. "Not that way!" the man screamed, pulling him back as he bounced. "This way!" And he threw him at the open door, bouncing his shins off the doorsill and sliding him across the seat until his head hit the opposite side.

Sheen felt blood on his face and in his mouth. He lay still. He heard a moaning sound.

From the door, the voice said, "I'll ride in back with him. You drive."

Sheen's feet were thrown off the seat. The door slammed shut. A hand grabbed his ear and pulled him to a sitting position.

"Where is the rest of it," the voice whispered viciously, "the other hundred and thirty pounds?"

Sheen tried to speak, but his tongue was thick. A heavy wooden nightstick cracked across his kneecap. Sheen's breath expelled in a groan.

"I'll cripple you, you bastard."

The nightstick cracked across his mouth.

"Baby food, motherfucker, you'll eat baby food." The voice was frenzied, savage.

Shards of Sheen's own teeth choked him.

The nightstick cracked again.

"The rest of it. The rest of it. I want the rest of it."

Gray acoustic tiles covered the walls and the ceiling of the windowless interrogation room, making it soundproof. The room was small and square, not much larger than a closet. A worn gray carpet covered the floor. Overhead, two bare fluorescent tubes hummed quietly, but the hum was absorbed by the acoustic tiles so that there was no reverberation, no echo whatsoever, just a flat, dull, timeless hum. Because there were no vents or windows, the air did not circulate, and the room was musty.

Sheen's wrists were bound behind him, one over and one under the back of a folding metal chair. His head was slumped forward, his chin on his chest. Blood dripped steadily from his face and his mouth onto the thighs of his trousers.

The door opened, and a familiar voice said angrily, "Get the goddamn handcuffs off of him."

A man replied, "He refused to get in the car, sir. He fought us all the way here." The man's voice moved behind him. "There were two pounds of cocaine in the motel room. He must be loaded."

Sheen shook his head from side to side.

William Dryden knelt down by the chair. "I know that's not true," he said to Sheen. "I know. Relax. I know."

"Dentist," Sheen mumbled thickly. "Get a dentist."

The handcuffs came loose, and Sheen slumped further forward, falling. William Dryden caught him and gently laid him on the floor.

Sheen grabbed his hand and held it tightly.

Sheen saw his face reflected in the dentist's eyeglasses. Distorted by the curve of the lenses, his eye seemed grotesquely swollen, his mouth stretched impossibly wide. The dentist had been working for what seemed a very long time. Sheen's knee hurt, and his right arm and his ribs hurt, but after the pain in his mouth those were minor pains; and his mouth was very numb. In an odd way the pain was reassuring, because it confirmed his injuries, and the injuries gave him an excuse, a reprieve, an end to his obligation, an end to his duty.

Duty is a wonderful thing, he thought. He did not know what he would have done without duty in the months since Andrea had been killed, since he had decided what it was he had to do, what was his duty, and had set out to do it, one distracting step after another.

254

I could have gone back to school, he thought. *Or I could have done something useful.*

Maybe.

Maybe duty is all I know.

But now he had an excuse, a reprieve — if he chose to take it.

There was a pressure against his numb jaw. The dentist's drill whined, and he felt a light spray like dew settling on his eyes. He relaxed in the chair and tried not to think at all.

After a while Sheen felt himself lifted and moved, but he was too tired to protest or to ask where he was being taken. When he awoke, he found himself lying on a long leather couch, his head propped on the arm. With his fingers he tentatively probed his mouth, trying to assess the damage.

"Can you talk?" William Dryden asked. He was sitting near the couch, slouched down so that his head rested wearily against the back of his chair.

Sheen dropped his hand away from his mouth and replied, "As long as the Novocain holds." His speech was a slurred monotone, midrange sounds caused by a swollen tongue and a very sore jaw. "How many teeth?"

"You didn't lose any, if that's what you mean. Four were broken off; one was cracked. The dentist is very good. You'll have to see him again in a couple of weeks — those are temporary caps."

Again Sheen touched his mouth. "I hate to lose my teeth."

Dryden waited for Sheen to look at him, and when he did, he said, "I'm sorry, Sheen."

"Not your fault," Sheen said. With two fingers he tapped his own chest. "My fault. I shouldn't have gone back to the same motel."

"All the officers involved have been suspended. The two who were in the car with you will be fired, I guarantee it. I'm pushing for criminal charges — "

"Doesn't matter," Sheen interrupted, waving his hand from

255

the wrist as if he were fanning away annoying smoke. "It happens."

"No, it doesn't happen," William Dryden said, his voice sharp, "not to people who work for *me.*"

Sheen shrugged. "It did, and it's done."

Dryden took off his glasses and tiredly rubbed the red spots on the bridge of his nose. Without the shiny lenses in front of them, his eyes seemed naked and much less hard.

"I'm bringing in Profit, too. He won't see daylight for twenty years."

"No," Sheen said too quickly, opening his mouth too far and immediately regretting it. "It wasn't Profit."

"From the time you two left the storage house, Profit intended to steal what he could, Sheen. You let him weigh the cocaine, and he hid some for himself, knowing you couldn't feel the difference in weight — or maybe he cut it. When he knew you were back at the motel, he called the police. Your arrest gave him the time he needed to disappear, which he has."

"No," Sheen said again, thinking, *He could have had it all,* but saying, "I *know* it wasn't Profit."

"To legitimate your arrest," Dryden continued, "he stashed two pounds of cocaine in your motel room. He could have called the Marielitas instead of the police, but they're after him, too, and he's afraid of them — or maybe he didn't think you deserved to die."

Sheen tried to sit up, but a wave of nausea overcame him.

Dryden sat forward and patted him on the arm. "You rest. I'll find Profit, and we'll talk to him."

Sheen badly wanted to reply, but he knew that if he opened his mouth, he would be sick.

He heard Dryden say, "We broke the communications center code. The transcript of the transmissions is on the coffee table. I'll look in after a while and see how you're doing."

Sheen nodded just enough to show that he had heard. It took a minute for the nausea to pass, and when he was able to open his eyes and sit up, Dryden was gone.

Punctuated intermittently by the rude spitting sound of a high-speed printer, a rapid keyboard clicking came through the closed door. The lamps at both ends of the couch were on, and the dim bulbs cast a pleasant yellow light through sharply pleated lampshades. Across the room, behind the large wood desk, tan curtains swayed slightly in the cool air that flowed soundlessly through the vents.

Sheen put both feet flat on the floor and wrapped his left arm across his middle as he leaned forward to pick up the transcript from the low table in front of the couch. Beside the transcript, in a heavy glass ashtray, was a clump of black, grainy ashes where Dryden had emptied his pipe. Sheen sat back and rested a moment, allowing the transcript to lie across his thighs. Behind the door, the keyboard clicking stopped. Responding to the quiet, he dropped his chin onto his chest and looked at the top page of the transcript.

The poor quality of the dot matrix printer made the pale gray words difficult to read. Between the words there was little punctuation, and in the places where the code had not been broken completely, symbols took the place of letters; even when a transmission had been completely decoded, the message was usually obscure. Because he did not then have the patience for puzzles, Sheen noted primarily the transmission times and durations, skipping quickly over whole pages. After a few minutes he fell into an exhausted, dreamless sleep. When he heard a voice nearby, he opened his eyes quickly, surprised to see the curtains open and bright sunlight outside the windows.

Dryden was standing over him, a concerned look on his face, a cup of coffee in one hand.

"I hope you feel better than you look," he said, smiling thinly.

Sheen blinked in an exaggerated, unfocused manner, closing his eyes tightly, then opening them wide. Dryden extended the coffee cup toward him, and he accepted it, holding it uncertainly, as if he did not know what to do with it.

"I have something that might make you feel a little better."

Sheen blinked again and rubbed his eyes. "I guess you do: your evidence room must look like a pharmacy."

Dryden patted the side pocket of his rumpled suit coat. Not feeling his pipe, he patted the other pocket, but his pipe was not there either. An annoyed frown crossed his face, a frown Sheen misread as disapproval.

"That was a joke," he said.

"The dentist left a prescription for you," Dryden replied, distracted, looking on the coffee table for his pipe. When he did not see it there, he gave a little shrug and returned his attention to Sheen, continuing, "but what I have for you is non-narcotic: Profit called. He wouldn't talk to me, but he's going to call back to talk to you."

Sheen put down the coffee without tasting it.

"Help me to the desk," he said. He tried to stand, but his knee was so stiff he could not straighten it properly and he fell back. "Help me," he said again.

"Sit still, Sheen. We'll use the speaker phone. You can hear it where you are."

"I want to sit at the desk," Sheen said, spacing his words so that the determination behind them was apparent.

William Dryden pursed his lips, and his brow furrowed in vexation. Reluctantly but firmly he took Sheen's arm and helped him across the room. Sheen dropped so heavily into the desk chair that it rolled backward until one caster slipped off the plastic floor protector and snagged on the carpet, tilting the chair slightly.

When the phone rang, Dryden turned on both the speaker phone and a cassette tape recorder before he handed the receiver to Sheen. Sheen gave Dryden a sour look he did not see, then said hello.

"Who is this?" Profit asked, speaking rapidly, a tense edge on his voice. "And speak up — I can't hear you."

"This is Sheen," Sheen said, disconcerted by the simultaneous sound of the little voice from the receiver in one ear and the big voice from the speaker phone in the other. "Sheen," he repeated. "Are you okay?"

258

"I don't know what to do," Profit replied, the fear evident in his tone. "I didn't know how to reach you."

William Dryden leaned forward, listening intently, and Sheen said to him as much as to Profit, "Don't stay on the phone over two minutes: the call can be traced." He turned the chair away from the desk, away from Dryden and the amplified sound of the speaker phone. "Start from the meeting with Eduardo. What happened?"

"He wouldn't meet me — I told you that. We talked by phone. Wait." There was a brief pause before Profit came back on the line, and from the speaker phone there was a low roar — the sound of the ocean or a surging line current, it was impossible to tell which. "I set my stopwatch. Ninety seconds and I hang up."

"Good," Sheen said, nodding into the phone and picturing the small digital stopwatch Profit always carried. He remembered how he had kidded Profit because he was never on time, although he carried a device that measured time in hundredths of a second. "It doesn't give the time of day," Profit had countered, belaboring what was, to him, readily apparent. "It tells how *long* the day is."

"I laid out the whole pyramid," Profit said, "just like it happened. Eduardo ate it up. He wants the Miami area franchise badly — it's the most lucrative — and any dirt he can get on Moses, so much the better. Just like a real capitalist. I think he's tired of New Jersey, too, not that you can fault him for that."

"Why wouldn't he meet with you?"

"He said that we were poison, that the general himself had ordered our arrest, either by the Marielitas or by the police. The general wasn't convinced by the Omega 7 gag — Omega 7 doesn't usually fool with drugs. But the distributors *were* convinced. They are *shook*. So the police are looking for us, too. Tell *that* to Dryden."

Sheen looked at Dryden, but his expression was difficult to read. His cool blue eyes were fixed skeptically on the speaker phone, his pale lips pressed together in a thin, tight line.

259

"Why did the general bring in the police?"

"He wants to find us fast, Sheen, and we're not part of the Cuban community. He *had* to bring in the cops — he knows he can get to us in jail, anyway. But he doesn't want us killed before someone has a chance to talk to us. I wanted to warn you that we had to keep moving, but you were out with Omega 7 and there was no way to reach you. I cleaned out the room and kept driving around, passing by the motel, but when I saw the cops, I split. I have no desire to have a talk with either the Marielitas or the police — particularly not the police. Tell that to Dryden, too."

Profit paused, and again there was a low, surging roar. "Did they find my stash?"

"Two pounds, they said."

"It was more like a kilo. I was in such a hurry to grab the leftovers, I forgot about it, and by the time I did remember, I wasn't going near that room. I have the leftovers, about twenty pounds. I can't believe I *forgot* a kilo."

"What was it for, Profit? Why did you split up the leftovers?"

"Come on, Sheen. The kilo was for me. I figured I'd earned it."

Sheen wanted to smile, but he knew better than to try. "Get to another phone and call again."

"Give me fifteen minutes. Is Dryden taking care of you?"

"Like a mother hen," Sheen said. "We're all right, really."

Profit did not reply, and Sheen momentarily felt, just as he had in the motel, that he knew Profit's thoughts and feelings as certainly as if they were his own.

"Really," he repeated.

There was a long delay before the line went dead, a questioning silence behind the low, surging roar; then there was a click and the dial tone hummed loudly before Dryden snapped off the speaker phone.

"He's too good to be true," Dryden said. "He's buying time."

Sheen said, his voice low but certain, "You're wrong." He turned the desk chair to face Dryden. "Stashing a kilo for himself is exactly what he'd do; and the leftovers held his attention. It fits."

"No one else knew your location, Sheen — you didn't even tell *me.*"

Sheen picked up a pencil from the desk and held it with both hands, wrapping his fingers around it and flexing it slightly. "Avila knew. I went by the condominium yesterday. I didn't see him, but he must have seen me." He put the pencil back on the desk, knowing he would break it if he continued to play with it. "I hid cocaine in his car."

Neither Dryden's posture nor his expression changed in any way.

"I could tell you I thought it was a good hiding place," Sheen continued, "but you know why I did it: I wanted to set him up. I wanted him to know what it feels like. He's done it to me twice. I knew it would never get to court, and I knew it was wrong — even as I did it, I knew it. I just wanted him to know."

For a long moment Dryden looked at Sheen coolly, evenly, without surprise or anger but with a clinical sort of detachment that made Sheen feel very small. "I expected better from you, Sheen," he said, his voice as detached as his gaze.

Sheen met his gaze but could not hold it. He looked away, but still he felt Dryden's eyes on him.

He heard him say, "Work backwards, then, assuming it was Avila."

Before he began the explanation, Sheen glanced up quickly, almost furtively, but Dryden had shifted his gaze to look past him, over his head. His pale blue eyes were disturbingly vacant.

"Avila must have seen me fooling with his car," Sheen began. "He checked it out, found the coke, and followed me — that part was easy because I expected to be followed by Omega 7, and I was obvious. And Avila is thinking. By working with you, I'm already a double threat. You give me leverage, but you also protect him: he knows you can't get at him without

261

dumping on me. But if I get on your shit list, I may still have leverage, but he definitely loses his protection. He knew you hadn't sent me to set him up — you have other ammunition — so that meant I was out on my own. If the setup worked, he was in one trick; if you found out, I went on your shit list, and he was in another trick. He has two options: he can throw away the coke and forget it happened — but then I'm likely to do something else, and he doesn't know what — or he can have me killed and keep the coke. Avila flipped for the second option because he thought it would get you off his back, *and* he would make a small fortune. All he had to do was follow me back to the motel and call the police."

William Dryden moved one hand to the back of his neck and massaged the muscles there, the point of his elbow moving in circles as he rubbed. "So much for entrapment," he said.

"If you're placing blame, I already accepted it."

"And you paid the price," Dryden replied, his tone very flat. He gave Sheen a withering look that effectively communicated his unwillingness to discuss the subject further. "You're on your own with that one," the look said. "You lived through it; now you have to live with it."

He moved his chin upward, flexing his neck. "We're working backwards, Sheen, not against each other." He dropped his hand from his neck. "If Avila wanted you killed, why didn't he go to the Marielitas?"

Sheen delayed for a moment before he replied, looking at Dryden pointedly, showing that he had understood the message but did not like it.

"Avila hasn't been around long enough to have a direct line to the Marielitas, and he had to move quickly. What if I reported the stash in his car? He knew the Marielitas have too much money not to have bought some police, and he knew the Marielitas are after Profit and me because of the party. What he didn't know was that we had hit the storage depot — and that's what saved my ass. The Marielitas want us alive long enough to recover their cocaine."

262

Sheen put one fingertip on the edge of the desk and moved it back and forth thoughtfully. "Anyway, he must already have had a line to the police — someone got him that automatic shotgun. He just didn't know that his buddies had been ordered to keep me alive. They'd have kept me alive anyway. They wanted the cocaine."

"You think Avila was the one with the shotgun?"

"I do now. I'm a major nuisance to Avila, but at that point he couldn't kill me because he would have been suspect number one. So he dropped a hint. You were right about the shotgun. He knew it wouldn't penetrate the car. He wasn't really after me. He just wanted to frighten me enough to make me leave or hurt me enough to get me out of commission. When I put coke in his car, I gave him the opportunity to do more than hint. But there's an easy way to check it out."

Sheen paused, waiting for Dryden to look at him. But Dryden did not look away from the window when he asked, "How is that?"

The tone of the question was too polite, almost disinterested, and Sheen asked, "Do you have something on your mind, Bill?"

Dryden did look at him then, with a quick glance out of the corners of his eyes, a glance that showed a troubled, wary skepticism. "Only how to check out Avila," he said, though it was obvious that checking out Tony Avila was not what was troubling him.

Sheen felt a rising anger he controlled only with effort. "Search his car," he said coldly. "If the coke is still under the back seat, I'm wrong."

William Dryden put both hands in his pants pockets as he turned away from the window. "What if Avila found it and threw it away before he called his friends?"

Sheen shook his head. "He wouldn't do that. If he found it, he kept it. And he'll be trying to sell it. Why don't you see if he'll sell it to one of your people? The only thing is, to make it work, you'll have to report me dead."

263

William Dryden pursed his lips, pulling the skin taut over his jaw. On the file cabinet near the desk was an open briefcase, and he reached into it, picked up a file folder, dropped it in front of Sheen. When he started to speak, his lips moved with a soft, wet, smacking sound. He licked his lips and said, "Officially, you died at three-thirty this morning. The cause of your death was multiple head injuries."

Sheen opened the folder curiously, reading over the medical examiner's neatly typed form.

"I'll make some calls," Dryden said, "and find out if the cocaine is still in Avila's car."

Sheen nodded without looking up.

"You know, Sheen," Dryden added, his tone reflective, "the report of your death could just as easily be true" — he waved his hand at the folder Sheen held — "and I wonder who, you included, would give a good goddamn?"

Sheen allowed his anger to show in his expression; but Dryden turned away, closed his briefcase, picked it up, and without again looking at him, left the room. Behind the open door a chair scraped and a keyboard began to click, hesitantly at first, then rapidly.

Sheen closed the folder and put it on the desk. With a great deal of effort he pushed himself out of the chair, took the few steps to the table in front of the couch, retrieved the transcript, and returned to the desk. When the phone rang, he made certain the speaker phone was off before he picked up the receiver.

"You there?" Profit asked.

"I'm here," Sheen replied, thumbing one corner of the transcript, fanning the thin pages like playing cards. "But why are *you* still around?"

"Shit if I know, Sheen. I should be in New York getting my passport." Profit paused, then added, "I'm afraid."

Sheen looked at the folder that held the report of his death. "Me too," he said. He opened the transcript and glanced at the transmissions from the day following Moses's party. "When was our arrest ordered?" he asked.

264

"I don't know," Profit said, "but it had to be before I talked to Eduardo — before you went to meet Omega 7."

Sheen flipped forward through the transcript, then backward, looking for the transmission that had ordered their arrest, knowing it had to be within the few pages that covered the time between Moses's party and his meeting with Omega 7.

"I can't find it," he said out loud.

"Can't find what?" Profit asked.

Sheen reread the pages, becoming convinced that the transmission was not recorded in the transcript; then, irritated, he flipped further forward.

"Can't find what?" Profit asked again.

Sheen did not reply because finally he saw the order for their arrest; but the sequence was incorrect — the transcript made it appear that the order had been received by the distributors before the general had transmitted it to the communications center — and he checked to see which pages were misplaced.

"Are you still there?" Profit asked.

But the pages were numbered, and they were not out of order.

"Wait a second," Sheen said, puzzled, and he again checked the transmission times. *If the order was received* before *the general transmitted it,* he asked himself, *what does that mean?*

And suddenly he knew what it meant, knew that the content of the radio messages was not nearly as revealing as the timing of the messages. "This general you seek," Omar had told him, "he is not in Miami"; and Sheen knew what that meant, too.

The unknown general was a blind. The orders were not issued *through* the communications center but *from* the communications center. *It's that simple,* Sheen thought.

"I need a day," he said out loud, "maybe two."

"For what?" Profit asked.

"I need to check out a few things. Call again tomorrow."

"Yeah, I'll call," Profit replied, peeved that he was being dismissed, "but it may be long distance — like from Rome."

Sheen looked up to see William Dryden standing in the doorway.

"Ciao," he said absently, and hung up the phone, moving his other hand to his face and gently rubbing the swelling around his eye. He looked at Dryden and wondered whether or not to tell him.

19

AGAINST A sky dark purple with the first coming of light, its whiteness intensified by the dark background, a solitary snowy egret flew past, coming from the right. The large bird flew so low its long wings made an audible *whoosh-snap,* a startling intrusion in the quiet. After it passed the swamp was so quiet that even the sound of the water lapping against the side of the canoe was distinct, reverberating dully against the aluminum shell.

"I wish I were as sure about this as you seem to be," Profit said. Although they were out in the open where he was certain not to be overheard, he whispered.

"I'm dead sure," Sheen replied. He put his hand in the tepid water, then remembered that there were snakes and withdrew it, rubbing his thumb over his fingers and wondering if the oily feel was caused by algae. He marveled at the lushness, the abundance of life. Plants grew in odd shapes and endless variations. Ripples in the water, strange sounds, small splashes evidenced a thriving animal community. *It is better to talk,* he thought, *better to talk than to worry alone.*

He said, "He was so clever he foxed himself." Sheen held the top of his paddle with his right hand and the shaft with his left, choosing to strain his weak arm rather than his weak hand as he began to paddle again.

"The communications center uses two separate systems, radio and telephone. The distributors radio their reports to the communications center; then, apparently, the reports are relayed to the general. The general has several ways to respond: he can either radio or telephone his orders through the communications center, or he can call the distributors directly. Most of the traffic goes back through the center, so direct calls are special occasions."

Profit thought about that for a moment, then said, "So the distributors never see the general — they don't even know who he is. They radio their reports to the communications center, and most of the time their orders come back by radio."

"Right — and of course it's all in code."

"But every once in a while, out of nowhere, they get a call from the man himself." Profit put his paddle across his knee. "That's night-sweat material."

"You bet. That's the whole point. The general seems to be both everywhere and nowhere — spirit and substance, so to speak." Sheen smiled, though he knew the general's elusiveness was calculated to give just that effect. "And Dryden told me he uses a voice synthesizer. On the phone, the general sounds like a machine."

The channel narrowed, and an entangled fabric of water lilies completely covered the surface of the water, weaving what seemed to be a solid field. *It's that smell,* Sheen thought, *musky decay, the smell of growing things.*

"An airboat would skip right over this mess," Profit said.

They paddled near the bank, and they both got out of the canoe to carry it past the obstruction created by the water lilies. Profit misjudged a step and slipped chest deep into the water. Sheen took out his pistol, watching for snakes.

"This is for the birds," Profit said, grabbing a clump of grass and pulling himself out of the water. "Maybe *they* can find their way around this swamp."

"I remember this part," Sheen said. He plucked one of the thick, rubbery water lily blooms and looked closely at the flower's parallel veins and odd opaque color. With his thumbnail he split the stalk and turned it back, disappointed to see that the sap was clear rather than red. "Between the two of us, we'll find it."

The canoe rocked as they got back into it.

Profit wrung out his shirt, twisting the front into a knot, and asked, "Why didn't Dryden just trace the phone calls?"

"He did," Sheen replied, adjusting the pad beneath his knees, "but the general makes his direct-line calls from pay phones in a half-dozen states — he *is* everywhere and nowhere."

Sheen saw a ripple in the water near the bank, and when he looked closely, he saw a small, furry head peering at them cautiously; he remembered the beaver Willie had pointed out to him as they had toured the island, remembered that the beaver had slipped smoothly into the water and disappeared neatly beneath the surface, without a trace.

"Dryden recruited us," he continued, "to create a disturbance big enough to cause the phone traffic to increase. He hoped that maybe the general would slip up somehow, use the same phone twice, make an appointment — something."

"The disturbance part worked. The distributors were seeing car bombs in their sleep."

"The general didn't buy it, but still he had to reassure his troops. And he had to do it before someone started a war with Omega 7, something he definitely did not want to happen. That's when he screwed up. He got in too much of a hurry. The order for our arrest came *out* of the communications center before the transmission from the general had been received *at* the communications center."

"But if there is no general, who gives the orders?"

"There *is* a general, Profit, but he's not at some unknown location. He's in the communications center. All the broadcasts to and from the roving general are a cover — it's very hard to find someone who doesn't exist."

A breeze moved through the cattails and waved the slender stalks like wheat in a field.

"I can't believe that Willie — " Profit began, but he stopped because the breeze had moved the cattails just enough for them to see it in the distance: the house on the rise, the low island in the swamp, the communications center. "I can't believe that Willie is the general," Profit said, completing his sentence.

With the coming light, the color of the water changed from black to dark gray, and they paddled quietly. The bayou they were following curved, and they lost sight of the island until they were very near, in the channel that flowed around it. Profit spotted the pier in the high weeds and dragged his paddle until the canoe turned, drifting toward the low wooden walkway. Sheen brought his paddle inboard and shifted his weight from his knees to his feet, ready to step out when his end of the canoe swung around. The canoe bumped lightly, and Profit stood up, leaning forward to take hold of the pier, just as an automatic rifle erupted, cracking through the razor grass in a long burst. Profit's head jerked toward the sound, and Sheen saw the fear and surprise on his face as he grabbed to pull him back; but Profit's shoulder spun violently under his hand, his whole body twisting. Sheen dove to his right, pushing against the wobbly bottom of the canoe, rolling, grabbing his pistol and bringing his right hand up beneath his left arm, firing two quick shots at the muzzle flash, knowing that Profit had been hit and hit solidly.

Sheen struck the shallow water shoulder first, and before his legs were wet, his arm was mired in the muddy bottom. The dive rolled him onto his back, and he squirmed, twisting and kicking, to free himself. Under water, he set his knees firmly on the bottom and extended his arms in front of him so that his head and hands could break the surface simultaneously; then he straightened up just enough to see.

A cordite haze billowed lazily over the water in a thin, transparent cloud. Through the haze Sheen saw that the canoe had drifted away to his left; and he saw Profit on his back on the pier, unmoving, his legs sprawled one over the other, his right arm flopped across his chest. Halfway down the pier, at the edge of the water, Bear pushed through the tall grass, waving a rifle back and forth, using the barrel to clear his way. Bear moved cautiously but clumsily, his massive shoulders hunched forward as if he were about to drop down on all fours. He looked at Profit with evident satisfaction as he advanced toward him; then he cleared the grass enough to see Sheen watching him from the water, and, surprised in his dull way, he squinted his eyes in his bad-ass look and swung the rifle toward Sheen. In that moment Sheen squeezed the trigger on the Colt.

The single shot echoed, the sound rolling away past the house in the shadows. Sheen pushed toward the tall grass, moving deliberately, listening and watching. Not rising higher than a crouch, he stepped up onto the pier, glancing at Bear only long enough to see that the bullet had struck him squarely on the cheek. He did not want to see any more. Then very quickly he moved near Profit and squatted down on his heels.

In the hollow of his left shoulder, beneath the collarbone, Profit's shirt was stained with bright red blood. His eyes were uncomprehending and sadly questioning. "It hurts," he said in a small voice.

"I know," Sheen replied, looking at him for a long moment and feeling a great sadness well up.

Taking hold of the knot in Profit's shirt, Sheen pulled him upright, struggling to get his shoulder beneath Profit's belly and to lift, standing up and draping him across his shoulders. The walkway creaked, wobbling unsteadily. Sheen felt a sticky wetness on his back. When he was certain he was over solid land he stepped off the pier and into the high weeds, moving as quickly as he could, away from the house.

Near the tip of the island there was an oak tree, and behind it Sheen dropped to his knees, tucking his chin into his chest and rolling Profit forward over his shoulder. Thinking he was falling, Profit grabbed Sheen's shirt, pulling him down. Sheen's mouth bumped against the ground, hard enough to loosen the temporary cap on his front tooth.

From the house, there was the distinctive sound of the screen door slamming shut.

271

Sheen took off his shirt, folded it into a pad, pressed it against Profit's shoulder. "Hold it there," he said, but Profit did not seem to hear.

Sheen took Profit's right arm and draped it across his chest, elevated his feet, and left him. He walked back the way they had come, back toward the pier. It was not difficult to retrace his steps. The tall grass was mashed and bent, and there was Profit's blood in big drops, still red. Before he reached the pier, carefully, leaving no signs, he left the trail.

He knew he had to think clearly. The problem was what Willie would do. Where was he? He must have heard the exchange of shots, and he would come to investigate.

Sheen considered as carefully as he could, surprised by the orderliness of his thoughts. The pier, and the jutting finger of land around it, formed a small peninsula. Willie would go out on the pier, find Bear, and see the trail. He would parallel the trail, or he would go back to the house to radio for help. *He will see that the trail was left by one man,* Sheen thought, *and he will follow it. The general would not radio for help to track one man.*

Unaware that he was doing so, Sheen wiggled the loose cap on his tooth with his tongue. *I will wait,* he thought. *I will find a place where I can see both the pier and the trail, and I will wait.* And moving very quietly, he did just that.

As the sun rose higher the heat became palpable, a thick presence. The air was very still, and the whole swamp was hushed, without expectation. The sky was unusually clear, and the few clouds were far apart and too high to give hope of shade or rain. In the tall grass that completely enclosed him, Sheen sat unmoving, his arms wrapped around his knees, right hand holding left wrist. His whole body was wet. Sweat rolled in rivulets down his back, across his ribs, down his chest. Sweat rolled into his eyes and burned. His breathing was very shallow.

Twice a bird had flown up, and Sheen knew that the general was moving very cautiously and very slowly toward the pier. He tried to think as Willie would think, but he knew he was thinking only mirror images of his own thoughts, not Willie's.

A fly buzzed in loops and lit intermittently on his face.

The stillness was as thick as the heat.

Sheen thought of how he had come to be sitting in the tall grass, waiting, of how he had decided to tell Bill Dryden about the general and of how Bill Dryden had protested before agreeing to let Profit and him come in first, succumbing to the ineluctable possibility of a leak.

"Avila had to have a conduit to the Miami police on the take, Bill," he had argued, "and he hasn't had time to meet many policemen — he's spent all of his time with your people. The leak is in your office."

"Police meet each other easily, Sheen. You know that."

"Not when something is foul; then they're tight-lipped — I know that, too. And if there is a leak, as soon as you mobilize, as soon as you make two phone calls back to back, the general will know, and he'll relocate."

And Profit, Sheen thought, *the one person I would* never *have trusted, was the only person I could* trust.

We should not have come in so close in the canoe, he thought. *We should have come in swimming. And Bear would have waited for our heads to poke up like turtles' heads above the water, and he would have taken time to aim.*

Profit will be okay, he reassured himself, but the reassurance was hollow.

With his tongue Sheen wiggled the loose cap on his tooth. *I was too quick to use the canoe,* he thought.

The canoe.

That was a good day, he remembered, allowing his thoughts to wander.

The canoe was a fine way to travel. It moved quietly and slowly, and there was a stroke Andrea made that kept them in a straight line, without alternating sides to paddle. The canoe responded to her touch like a living thing — her strokes were not strokes as much as they were tickles and cajolings and teases. And he remembered the first morning on the small river — a stream, really; there had been a low fog, a mist that rose two feet from the surface, an eerie, steaming cloudbank that made it seem they were in a glider, not a canoe, he watching the muscles work in her back, gliding in their own very private world, the red and white ice chest between them, the gray blanket folded beside it. *The gray blanket,* he thought.

Sheen knew he would never get over Andrea, not completely, but he allowed himself to recall the good things. He liked to think of her as she ran, her wrists limp, her stride overlong and too high — an oddly comical prance; and as she read, her brow furrowed, the corners of her mouth drawn down; as she licked her finger before she turned a page.

And suddenly he thought of Marty, whom he had never really given a chance.

To his left another bird flew up, settled in a tree, whistled shrilly. The sound made him recall . . . what? It took him a moment to remember.

When his tour in Vietnam had ended, on his way home his plane — his "freedom bird" — had stopped in Tokyo for six hours. Wandering through the airport, he realized he was not ready to go home, not ready simply to pick up where he had left off, among too many people, so he had taken a bus into the city, and from there he had taken a train. The train had traveled out through the countryside and stopped in a small village, the name of which he had never learned because it had not occurred to him to ask and he had not been able to read the signs. For a week he had stayed in a guest house. Unable to sleep, he had stood by the window at night, looking out at the black ocean; and he remembered that every morning, just before sunrise, he had heard a shrill whistle just like that bird's. But the sound had come from a man pushing a cart, not from a bird, and Sheen had learned that it was the noodle man delivering fresh noodles, whistling just loudly enough to alert those who were expecting him but not so loudly that he disturbed those asleep. And something about that sound had reassured him and given him peace, quelled his sadness enough for him to rest as he thought of the sleeping households, the daily routines beginning, the simple courtesy of a man who whistled softly rather than shouted.

Behind him, less than twenty feet away, a rifle cracked three times.

Sheen moved extraordinarily fast, jumping to his feet and springing with long strides through the tall grass. Listening, moving, listening, he circled wide in short, quick bursts, then from the flank knifed straight back toward the sound. He heard movement, the thrashing sound of someone rushing through the weeds, and he dropped down in a tense crouch, ready to spring.

Willie passed by him, so close that he could see clearly the taut cords in the general's neck, his black eyes over his pitted cheeks, the automatic rifle in his strong tan hands. Quietly, Sheen moved behind him. When Willie stopped, Sheen stopped too, and thumbed off the safety on his pistol.

Willie heard the click and stood still, poised. He turned his head slightly, cocking his ear toward the sound. "I had you," he said over his shoulder. "I knew exactly where you were."

"Put down the rifle," Sheen said evenly.

"You were waiting for me where you could see both the pier and Profit's trail," Willie said. "It wasn't hard to figure. Bodies make good bait."

Willie was wearing a faded green fatigue shirt without sleeves and ragged cutoffs. The short barrel of the rifle pointed to his left.

"Put it down," Sheen repeated.

"I was right behind you, on my belly. I was so close I could smell you, Sheen." Willie laughed a self-satisfied, tense laugh. "I was moving the grass one blade at a time, moving maybe ten feet an hour. I put my head over a log, just my head and one hand. It was a little log, and not a foot from my face, all coiled up, sunning itself, was a water moccasin, a big black son of a bitch — as big as the one I gave Freddie for the freezer."

Willie laughed again, and he pivoted more quickly than

Sheen thought possible, the rifle tucked in close to his body. The rifle snagged on the heavy grass, and Sheen aimed and fired once. The bullet smashed into the forearm stock near Willie's fingers, and the rifle ripped out of his hands, spinning away and falling to his right, the barrel pointed at his feet.

Willie looked at the rifle, then shifted his gaze to Sheen. He shrugged indifferently. "For about ten minutes," he continued as if nothing had happened, "we looked each other right in the eye. Have you ever looked a snake right in the eye? They don't blink, not at all. I had the rifle in my other hand, and I was moving it up slowly. I must have done something to frighten the snake, or maybe it knew what I was up to. It struck at my face, but the head bounced off my cheek — it felt like a little kiss. It hit my shoulder."

Willie pulled open his shirt and moved his head to the opposite side. Sheen saw two thin trickles of blood from a double puncture in the taut muscle high on his shoulder.

"Maybe it liked me, and it *was* a kiss," Willie said nonchalantly, closing his shirt. "That's when I jumped. You were lucky twice." He jerked his chin at the tip of the island, at the oak tree under which Profit lay. "I could make you a very wealthy man, Sheen."

Sheen shook his head, his eyes guarded.

"I didn't think so," Willie said, raising his eyebrows in a gesture that added, "but I had to try." His left arm twitched spastically, and he looked at it with annoyance. "How did you figure it out?" he asked.

Sheen looked at him warily, wondering whether the twitch was a calculated ploy or the effect of the poison. *How long does it take?* he wondered. *How long has it been?*

"Your timing was off," he replied. "You radioed the order for our arrest before you transmitted the cover."

Willie gave him an oddly puzzled look, then his lips pulled tight in a sneer. "They are pitiful little sheep. They had to be calmed. They had to know it was not Omega 7."

"*You* made the mistake, Willie."

Willie waved his hand in a negligent gesture. "What I meant

276

was, how did you figure out that I was the one who killed your little sweetheart?"

A muscle jumped in Sheen's jaw, but he said nothing.

"You *didn't* figure it out, did you? You didn't know."

Very slowly, as though something very heavy was pressing down on him, Willie collapsed to his knees.

"I drove the car myself," he said, his voice mocking, his eyes feverish. "The bicycle flipped way up in the air, higher than you would believe, but — what was her name, Andrea? — she bounced on the hood and nearly came through the windshield." Willie's nostrils flared challengingly. "You were perfect, Sheen. You set Moses and Profit against each other. Their pyramid collapsed. I could keep Moses and let you replace Profit. You were perfect — I just had to keep you interested."

The cords stood out on his neck as Willie struggled to stay upright. As if he had been hit with an electric jolt, a tremor passed through him. He looked directly at Sheen with eyes that were too hot and glassy, and said, "Your face looks terrible." Then he fell forward, sprawling on the ground, his hands by his sides.

Sheen circled him, pulled his arms behind his back, handcuffed him, and rolled him over. Willie's eyes were open but unseeing, moving feverishly from side to side. Sheen dropped to one knee, watching the spasms rack him and seeing the pain in his face.

"I *was* perfect," Sheen said with disgust.

On Willie's belt was a folding knife, and Sheen lifted him just enough to take the knife from the scabbard. Willie began to speak unintelligibly, a mumbled combination of Spanish and English. Sheen could understand only one sentence: "I will not go back." And Sheen believed then that Willie had killed Andrea, and had taunted him so that he would kill him or allow him to die.

I can shoot him, Sheen thought deliberately. *I can put the barrel of the .45 in his mouth, and it would make such a mess of him that the flies and the ants would feast. Or I can sit here and watch him die from the poison, watch the convulsions and the cramps rack him — and no one would ever know.*

Sheen opened the knife, then closed it.

He deserves to die and he wants to die and he is less than an animal.

Sweat poured from Willie's face, and he continued to mumble.

He would kill me, Sheen thought, *but he would not waste a bullet. He would walk to the house, and he would eat lunch and in an hour or two he would come back to be certain I was dead.*

Gently Sheen rubbed the swelling around his eye, knowing that his thoughts were idle because there was no conviction behind them.

He is less than an animal, Sheen thought again, *but I do not want to watch him die and I do not want to kill him.*

Sheen opened the knife and tested the blade with his thumb.

I have wanted the distraction, but I have never wanted the killing, any of it.

With his left hand he pinched Willie's shoulder, bunching the big muscle and squeezing so that the punctures bled. He laid the sharp blade of the knife directly over one of the small holes.

It is time to end the distractions, he thought, and he pressed down on the knife and cut deeply.

Sheen cut an X over both punctures and put his mouth over them to suck out what poison he could. When he spit out Willie's blood, he did so with such force that he inadvertently spit out the loose cap on his tooth. A sharp pain seemed to run behind his nose and into his eye, but Sheen did not bother to look for the cap, because he wanted to radio for help as quickly as possible.

20

BEHIND MARTY'S apartment, enclosed by a high wooden fence, there was a small rectangle of grass. The grass was thick and neatly trimmed, and over one corner of it, in the shade of a willow tree, Marty had spread a red-and-white checked tablecloth. Sheen lay full length on the tablecloth, his head propped on his shoulder, and watched as she took fresh fruit, cheese, and crackers from a large wicker basket.

"Where's the pâté?" he asked lazily.

"It's coming," Marty said, feigning impatience. "Your convalescence is about to kill me." She leaned over to hand Sheen a glass of wine, and her breasts swelled, barely held in by the top of her bathing suit. "So, as I was saying, it was *very* odd."

"What did he look like?" Sheen asked coyly. Through his lashes he could see the fine golden hairs on her thigh and the shaved stubble of coarser hairs at the line of her bathing suit.

"He had short blond hair, and he smoked a pipe," Marty replied. "He was rather unremarkable, actually, until he took off his sunglasses. He had the bluest eyes I've ever seen, electric blue — like electrified glass."

"Glass isn't a conductor," he said.

"You know what I mean." Marty threw a wadded-up paper

napkin at him. It landed within easy reach, and Sheen threw it back.

"He selected three dresses," she continued, picking up a pear and a knife to slice it, "all very expensive. He said he wanted to take one home to his wife but that he was tired from traveling and couldn't make up his mind; so Elaine invited him back to her office — her standard procedure. A few minutes later he came out and told us all to go home. The store was closed."

She handed him an oval-shaped slice of pear, moist with juice.

"I don't think I can chew that," he said.

"Oh, try it. What do you think happened?"

Sheen put the slice of pear in his mouth, and said around it, "Why ask me?"

Marty looked at him with amused eyes, knowing he was playing a game and enjoying it. "No reason," she replied. "It does strike me as a little curious that when I got home, you were here with a picnic basket and a cooler — but that's no reason."

"Coincidence," he said.

"And that silly grin."

"That's swelling."

"The swelling is gone," she said matter-of-factly. She opened the pâté and allowed it to slide onto the plate with the slices of pears.

There was a knock on the wooden gate, and Marty jumped up, alarmed. Sheen started to tell her not to worry, but when she quickly threw on his shirt, he realized that she was alarmed only by the possibility that someone would see her — a lot of her — in her bathing suit. He pushed himself up slowly, heard the friendly clank of the gate latch, heard Marty say, "I'm *not* surprised."

Still dressed in the gray three-piece suit he had worn at the boutique, William Dryden came through the gate, looked around uncertainly, saw Sheen, and walked over to him.

"I hear you've been shopping," Sheen said, smiling. "Have a seat."

"No, thank you," Dryden replied, his tone indicating that he was there only for business.

Sheen was mildly surprised by the tone but was in a good enough humor to overlook it. "How did it go?" he asked.

"It was not enjoyable, Sheen," Dryden replied. "Elaine told the truth: Overnight Delivery had delivered two pounds of cocaine to her."

"It was a kilo," Sheen interjected.

Dryden gave him a cross look, his forehead furrowing with irritation. "She didn't know who had sent the cocaine to her, though she mentioned you as a possibility. I told her there wasn't a court in the country that would believe her, and I flushed the cocaine down the toilet. I also told her I would send undercover agents around periodically to make sure she stays clean."

"What did she say to that?"

"She didn't say anything, Sheen. She was frightened."

Marty moved an aluminum yard chair near Dryden before she sat down on the corner of the tablecloth, near Sheen. She said, "I don't get it."

Sheen waited a moment to see if Dryden would explain. When he did not say anything, Sheen said to Marty, "*I* sent the cocaine to Elaine, then I told the D.E.A." — he waved his hand carelessly at Dryden — "him, that I knew someone who had a quantity of cocaine. Since I was technically working for the D.E.A., I was considered a reliable source."

William Dryden, whose eyes were fixed absently on the pale green bottle of wine in the red and white cooler, added, "And I was in a position where I couldn't let it go." He shifted his gaze to Sheen, his eyes focusing in a hard, distasteful look. "The result was a very sleazy entrapment."

"Oh, come on, Bill," Sheen protested.

"While we're on the subject of entrapment," Dryden continued, "Tony Avila went up before a disciplinary review board and was fired."

Sheen smiled, genuinely pleased, and looked down. He saw the bunch of grapes near his feet and leaned forward to pluck one before he said, "So when do you round up the Marielitas?"

"We already have, or I wouldn't be here."

Sheen popped the grape into his mouth. "I didn't see anything in the newspaper."

Dryden reached into an inside coat pocket, and momentarily Sheen had the disconcerting thought that he was taking out a gun; but he pulled out an envelope which he held with both hands.

"The arrests were kept confidential," Dryden said. "The State Department prefers to keep the whole thing quiet. There's nothing to be gained by allowing a few criminals to create animosity toward a whole group. Most of the people from that boatlift are law-abiding."

Sheen plucked another grape and looked at it speculatively. "Or maybe *you* prefer to keep it quiet," he said, looking from the grape to Dryden, his tone skeptical but his expression amused. "Maybe you never made any busts. Maybe Omar was one of your men, and this whole operation was a scam that netted you a hundred pounds of cocaine."

William Dryden tapped one end of the envelope against the back of his hand.

"That was a joke, Bill," Sheen added. "Did Omar pay up?"

"Both you and Profit were employed by the D.E.A.," he said, ignoring Sheen's question. "Not technically, *officially*. The payroll was backdated, and your check includes the standard reward; Profit got the other half." He held the envelope out to Sheen. "After taxes, you made about enough to cover the cost of two semesters at Tulane. I hope you *do* use the money for school."

"I have to pay taxes?" Sheen asked.

"Yes," Dryden said. "You have to pay taxes — so does Profit." He waited for Sheen to take the envelope, nodded curtly, then turned away to leave.

Sheen started to call out to him, but before he could, Dryden turned back and extended his hand. Sheen stood up to take it.

Marty watched curiously as they shook hands, trying to read the emotion that passed between them. She saw Dryden's cool blue eyes scan Sheen's face before they fixed on his eyes, and she saw the muscle pulse in Sheen's jaw as he returned the gaze, his own eyes dark and serious. Then Dryden again nodded curtly, dropped his hand, turned away, and without looking back, crossed the yard and left.

Sheen looked after him until the gate closed and there was nothing more to see. He crossed his arms on his chest and said, "It's going to kill Profit to have to pay taxes."

Marty did not reply. Sheen looked at her, then dropped down and stretched out next to her. Absently he picked up a slice of pear and bit off a piece.

"See, you *can* chew it," Marty said.

Sheen studied the tooth marks left by his bite. "I don't understand *that* at all," he said, gesturing at the gate. "He's always been cool toward me, but that was the first time he's been rude. He knew I was kidding. The idea that he ran a scam is ridiculous. And that was nonsense about entrapment — no one was arrested." Sheen shook his head and reached for a knife with which to open the envelope Dryden had given him. "He wasn't making sense."

In one quick motion Marty slipped Sheen's shirt over her head and tossed it aside. "Yes, he was," she said. She stretched luxuriously, yawning, and arched her back as she lay down next to Sheen. "He was showing that he cares for you, you dummy."

Sheen slipped the knife under the flap of the envelope and cut halfway across it, but he stopped for a moment to think about that before he completed the cut.